About th[e]

Jo Freeman divides [...] Estrella near Pavones in s[...] Rica and Wythall, the village on the outskirts of Birmingham where she grew up. She lives with her husband, Crispin, and their three children, Estrella, Arturo and Ruby.

When in England she can often be found behind the bar at the Coach and Horses pulling pints of real ale and chatting to locals about her and Crispin's crazy jungle adventures.

'A Friend Laughs' is Jo's first book and tells of their first 18 months in Costa Rica. The follow-up will be out in 2009.

www.southerncostaricaland.com has photos, video and more information about land for sale and rental houses at Finca Estrella.

For my sister; we are miles apart but always together.

Acknowledgements

There are lots of thank yous to be made and I apologise if I've forgotten anybody.

To Crispin, for reading this a hundred times and not laughing <u>too</u> much when I told him I was going to write a successful book about our crazy life in Costa Rica.

Our friends and family all over the world, who visited us; emailed us; sent us goodies and lived our adventure with us through letters, phone calls and emails. Also the friends, family and the complete stranger (sorry I didn't get the sloth story in Paul; I'll put it in the next one) who gave me feedback, particularly Lizzie for going through it with a fine toothcomb and Clare Foss at Headline Books who assured me it should be published.

Our friends in Costa Rica as, without them, this book would have been very dull; I've changed some names to avoid confusion, embarrassment or being pursued by lawyers!

Mike Sneath for taking the beautiful cover photograph of our house, Casa Amarilla. See end for other photo credits.

Crispin's parents for (still) bank-rolling our projects and almost last but not least, my parents for giving me wings.

Thanks also to www.youwriteon.com for encouraging new authors to get published. You wouldn't be reading this if it wasn't for them.

A Friend Laughs

by

Jo Freeman

Prologue – December 2005

Estrella was asleep, exhausted from her disturbed night. I was pretty tired too; three bats had been swooping in and out of our room all night and each time they made a pass I had jumped out of my skin.

I noticed a huge brown toad sitting by the flapping bug screen that hung in our doorway, where the door should be. It must have hopped in during the night. I intended to swat it out with a broom but needed both arms so I bent down to put Arturo on his play-mat.

It was one of those fancy play-mat 'gyms' that had toys dangling off its arches: a monkey, a parrot, a frog and an elephant; and mirrors and flashing lights and it played Mozart and nursery rhymes; everything you needed to make your baby more intelligent. It had been left out the previous evening and instinct told me to check underneath it.

There, in a tangle, lay a long thin brown and cream snake. I swore quietly and covered it with the play-mat again, thinking how appropriate its jungle theme was.

Great, now what was I going to do?

1 The Beginning - January 2005

Crispin arrived home at 5.20pm, disappointed that he had missed saying goodnight to Estrella. I was amazed to see him so early. Usually when he tells me he is going to the bank he is gone for hours as he finds lots of other things to do that he's neglected to tell me about. Or the car breaks down. Or the ferry gets stuck. Or there is a fallen tree across the road (he joins the locals; attacking it with machetes whilst they wait for the local police to arrive with a chain-saw). Or someone he vaguely recognises greets him like a long lost brother and when Crispin says 'Adiós' to them half an hour later, he is none the wiser as to whom he has just been chatting.

Although it is unlikely that he will have any cell phone signal I call once, sometimes twice. I leave messages, trying to sound casual and not in the slightest bit annoyed that the lemon risotto I've spent an hour making is rapidly becoming lemon sticky goo. The third time I call I can't hide my anger and my message usually includes a couple of choice swear words. If he arrives home now, then I yell. A lot.

By 7pm my mood has changed from one of anger to one of worry and within half an hour I have worked myself into a frenzy, certain that he is dead in a ditch somewhere. If he walks in at this stage I fling my arms around him a sobbing wreck, grateful that he is alive. My husband never ceases to be surprised that I am upset or angry with him and is completely oblivious to the fact that my tears are his doing and feels I am crying because I am pregnant and that is what pregnant women do best. How dare he suggest such a thing?!

By 8pm I have passed into my favourite stage. My favourite because I am a born organiser and because I am no longer angry or worried about him and not because it is something I actually want to go through you understand. The calm, sensible 'funeral planning stage'. This consists of thoughts such as: how would I fly his body home? Do I just phone BA or should I notify the British Embassy first? (I'm sure their phone number is in the 'Lonely Planet'). Maybe he would want to be sprinkled on the *finca*, mmm, there's a thought. What would Estrella and I do? Would we stay here or would we go back to the UK? Another good question. At least I would be able to read my magazines before he settled himself in a hammock with them. Hey, maybe I could start dating Ruben!! My sister would love to see us; I wonder how much flights to Canada are? And so I continued until I was actually ever so slightly disappointed when he walked through the door.

The fact is that he could quite easily have been dead in a ditch somewhere as the one and a half hour round trip to the bank is on potholed roads. Some of the holes are big enough to lose your car in! Half of the road is unpaved, with bridges that look like they are about to collapse, and sometimes do, there's maybe a handful of street lights and three severe bends that Crispin always misjudges when it's dark (and it gets dark early here) and, of course, lots of ditches.

It doesn't sound like your average London suburb does it?

We live in Costa Rica. In fact we own 165 acres of Costa Rica and no, that's not a coast in Spain near Costa Brava. Nor is it an island in the Caribbean, that's Puerto Rico, a mistake some of our friends still make, and where I thought Costa Rica was when Crispin and I decided to get married on a beach there. It's the very skinny bit in Central America by the way, in case you haven't managed to locate your atlas yet. Panama is below, Nicaragua above and

Costa Rica, nestled between the two, is smaller than Scotland.

Getting married on a beach in Central America is a bit of a strange thing to agree to do, you might think, but then everything about our lives together has been a bit strange including how we met: It was September 1999 and I had taken some time off work to go travelling. I was staying with a friend of mine in Vancouver and we had drunk a lot of wine.

"I think we should have been sisters," my friend slurred. Yes, THAT much wine.

I dipped a pizza flavoured Pringle in some delicious roasted red pepper dip and nodded enthusiastically. "Is your brother single?" I slurred back, sisters-in-law would do.

She shook her head sighing sadly. Suddenly her eyes lit up and I knew she had just had a fantastic idea. "Crispin's single!" she said excitedly as she stood up. She wobbled a bit then dashed upstairs, there was a thud as she missed a step and caught it with her knee.

Crispin?! Admittedly, I had been out with somebody called Johnny Pratt but I couldn't marry anyone called Crispin.

My friend appeared again, rubbing her knee, and thrust a photo of her husband's brother into my hand. Crispin had his head tilted down slightly as if he was watching his step; you could see the beginnings of a bald patch. He was returning from the beach, a day out with the family in Dorset and was carrying a cooler or picnic hamper. He looked rather nice.

"He's a lawyer," my friend informed me, "and he's got an MG sports car!"

Interesting. I was starting to get over his rather ridiculous name; maybe he would let me call him Cris (or Crisp. Or Pin even). I made a note of his email address, just in case.

I continued with my travels and, although Crispin's email address remained in my address book, other guys arrived on the scene and I didn't think much more about him. In the meantime Crispin went skiing in Whistler and visited his brother and sister-in-law in nearby Vancouver. After a couple of glasses of wine, a photo of me was found and handed over to Crispin who said he stared at it for hours. He knew that he was going to marry me. Much later he would admit to me that he also thought I looked fat. I would then explain to him that the wall behind me was the same colour as the dress I was wearing (my 'fat' was actually the wall). It was an easy mistake to make and I forgave him.

Anyway, a few more months went by and I sent a group email with my latest travel news to friends and family. I wrote about camping on deserted beaches in Hawaii and helicopter rides over glaciers and three-day tramps in New Zealand and, at last minute, I decided to copy Crisp in. This was the start of our email relationship. Ten months after I first saw his photograph and three months after he first saw mine, we met in London. I had accepted a job with a company in Canada and had flown back to England to pack up all of my worldly goods, that were currently taking up space in my parents' loft, and emigrate. Coincidentally, Crispin had emailed me to say he was having a barbeque on the roof terrace of his flat in north London the day I was due to land so why didn't I come along? Why not? I thought.

I dragged one of my best mates along for moral support. "There'll be lots of single guys," I told her.

The following morning there were two fewer single guys. I had been standing on the roof terrace. It was getting dark, there was no longer any heat from the barbeque and the breeze was getting up. I'd shivered a bit. Crispin appeared with my denim jacket and put it around my shoulders. <u>That</u> was the moment that <u>I</u> knew.

Much later that night we had a conversation that changed my life in many ways.

"So, what do I call you then?" The issue obviously needed tackling.

"Crispin," replied Crispin.

"Not Cris?"

He shook his head, "Only the lads call me Cris."

"What about 'Christmas'?"

"Nope, only my best mate calls me that."

"He calls you 'Crisp'n'Dry'!" I'd heard him earlier in the evening, before he'd vanished with my mate.

"He calls me 'Christmas' in December."

"How about 'Crispy Peking Duck'?"

"You would rather say your boyfriend was called 'Crispy Peking Duck' than Crispin?" asked Crispin laughing.

I nodded, my heart desperately trying to get my attention by hammering away at my breastbone. It didn't need to; I had already heard. "Does that mean I'm your girlfriend?" I couldn't resist saying 'girlfriend' in a silly voice.

"I guess so," he said, staring into my eyes. Wow, his eyes were green. I had always been a 'dark brown eyes girl'; my sister was the 'green eyes girl'.

"Where do you want to get married?" he continued. It seemed like the most natural question in the world.

"Y'know, I quite fancy a beach wedding." I had stumbled across one in the middle of nowhere whilst tramping in New Zealand and thought at the time what a fantastic idea it was.

"The most beautiful beaches I've ever seen are in Costa Rica," Crispin said.

"Isn't that an island in the Caribbean?"

15

And that was how it happened.

Christmas 2000 after six difficult months and seven exhausting, not to mention expensive, round-trips to Canada for Crispin, he officially proposed and I moved back to the UK and into the London flat with the roof terrace.

I started organising our Costa Rican beach wedding. We moved out into the country and bought our dream home: a barn conversion with a huge garden complete with a 100 year old wisteria draping over the oak pergola. I found a job and we both started our long daily commutes. Crispin's into Central London, now a busy partner in a law firm, and mine clockwise around a third of the M25 - the slowest and most accident-prone third of the M25 at that – to the head office of a company that ran clinical trials for pharmaceutical giants, although all of my friends if asked will tell you that I was a medical rep and they will smile childishly (they can't help themselves) and say, "Jo sells drugs."

Early mornings, late nights, traffic jams, train delays, too tired to cook, too knackered to talk. Our life together had started.

A year later, during a beautiful February sunset on a beach in Tamarindo in the north of Costa Rica, Crispin and I vowed to be together in sickness and in health and also, as part of the incredibly sensible Costa Rican marriage vows, to share the household chores and share the responsibility of the upbringing of our children. The wedding was perfect in every way, if you forget about the minor hitch a couple of days earlier when I threw my ring back in my fiancé's face determined to never marry him. EVER!

Fortunately his sister worked wonders in diplomacy and I accepted his re-proposal. This meant we could avoid the embarrassing task of telling our 27 family members and friends who had travelled that huge distance that the wedding was off, in essence, because Crispin couldn't tell the time.

We spent a further two weeks travelling around and I fell in love with the country that Crispin had fallen in love with whilst travelling seven years earlier. We hiked near active volcanoes, saw turtles laying eggs in the sand at midnight, feasted on fresh pineapple and mangoes, watched monkeys with tiny babies on their backs jumping in the trees, sat in hot springs and slathered our bodies in volcanic mud. I had an embarrassing moment when I vomited and then fainted on a zip-line whilst dangling over a deep canyon and there was a very funny moment when Crispin was swinging Tarzan-like on a vine over a river and it broke and he landed on his head - I guess I still hadn't properly forgiven him for his pre-wedding drunken arrival at 4am (he thought it was only 1am and I never did reach the calm, sensible 'funeral planning stage' that night).

We decided we were going to move out there and open a jam shop. That was our first idea. Crispin's mum was going to teach us how to make jam and, with all the fantastic fruit around, we would be a huge success. It's okay, our ideas would improve. A bit.

Once back in the UK summer soon arrived and life didn't seem too bad after all. There were parties and barbeques and we spent time making our garden beautiful and enjoyed weekends with friends and family. Even our three hour daily commutes seemed bearable. Then winter hit again. I think it rained for 100 days straight. We got a 'light-box' and signed up for Adult Education courses in the evenings and at weekends; Crispin in photography and car maintenance (wow, do we regret that he was too tired to go to that one); me in wood carving; both of us in picture framing and rock 'n' roll (we were trying to inject a bit of fun into our rather grey life). We had knocked the jam idea on the head and decided we were going to open an art gallery out there instead. We both handed our notices in at work and put the barn up for sale.

We had brilliant reactions from our friends and Crispin's family and almost everybody was very encouraging. Obviously, they thought we were mad but were very encouraging anyway. My parents however, although they had supported many a crazy idea of mine in the past, couldn't support this one. They couldn't understand why we would give up well paid jobs and sell our beautiful barn to go and live in a Third World Country where every house had metal bars on the windows - the metal bars comment would come back to haunt us later. Of course, they had a good point.

Then came a teensy-weensy complication; I found out I was pregnant with my parents' first grandchild. I was 31, my brother four years younger, my sister 15 months older. They had waited a long time for this moment. They had earned the right to a grandchild, to fawn over it, to spoil it, to brag about its first steps, its first wee in the potty and we would be whisking 'it' away and denying them that right.

We slowed our plans down slightly.

The day after the 20 week scan that showed the 'it' was actually a 'she', we flew to Costa Rica. Not permanently, as had been our original plan, but for a ten week 'recce' trip. Both the barn and the London flat were being rented out, they would go back on the market once we returned in December if we were still going to go ahead with our crazy plans - there was no doubt in our minds that we would be. The aim of the trip was to find the perfect area to live in. We weren't planning on buying anywhere we were just going to look. Plus we were going to do some research into how realistic the art gallery idea was so we could put

18

that business plan together that people kept mentioning we should probably write.

We travelled to the Caribbean coast and camped on a beautiful white sand beach for three days. We shared a hammock and read books, our only company a family of noisy howler monkeys. I will never forget how bright the stars were during my frequent trips outside the tent in the middle of the night, the sight made me eternally grateful for the ever decreasing size of my bladder. We then crossed the country and drove almost the whole length of the Pacific Coast. We took Spanish lessons and found out how wet the rainy season really is. We had some great adventures, made some good friends (we would even spend our first Costa Rican New Year with a couple of them), and got stuck in the mud a lot.

During our ten week trip we got the car stuck in the mud FOUR times. I say 'we' although I have to say, Crispin was driving every time. On one occasion I looked with scepticism at the narrow muddy path he intended to drive down. "There is no way we are going to get through there," I said.

Half an hour later we were pulled out by a resourceful young lad with a plank of wood and an old Tico on horseback. (A Tico, by the way, is a Costa Rican, as opposed to a Gringo which is officially an American but Ticos use the term to cover all manner of English-speaking foreigners).

"Don't say it," Crispin said as he reversed the car back onto the main road.

"Say what?" I asked innocently. "What a great driver you are?" He smirked and I gave him an 'I told you so' smile. He was to have the last laugh.

"Is that left or right?" he said pointing to my side of the car. He was referring to several wrong turns and back-tracks that had already occurred on the trip that were down to my inability to give directions. I had to admit, I had no idea!

We went back up to Tamarindo to see the people who ran the tiny hotel where we got married. It happens to be one of the most beautiful beaches in the country and I was hoping we could buy some land there. There was already an established 'ex-pat' community, mainly Americans, so I wouldn't be short of any much-needed friends.

The back road approaching Tamarindo was dire and I bounced up and down on a pillow, which was doing little to cushion the bumps, and held on to the handle for dear life whilst Crispin swerved crazily from one side of the road to the other trying to miss the various potholes. He was failing miserably. People don't drive 'on the left' or 'on the right' the way they do in other countries, they drive on the side of the road with the least potholes. It is completely normal to have someone driving towards you on what you feel certain is your side of the road, as if they want a head-on collision, only to swerve back onto their side of the road as your hand is poised to connect with your horn.

"I think you missed one," I said indicating a pothole on the far side of the road. He stopped the car, reversed, aimed it at the hole in question, bumped through it, swerved back again and we continued on our way.

"Happy?" he asked.

I nodded. "I just didn't want it to feel left out." This was kind of my fault; I had found the road on the map and it had looked like a short-cut.

We eventually made it to Tamarindo, without breaking an axle or my waters, and were shown some land by a real estate agent. $86k for an eighth of an acre and if you stood on tiptoe you could just about see the sea. Although ridiculously expensive at the time, we seriously thought about buying it. It would have been a huge mistake.

Whilst we were discussing the pros and cons of our potentially huge mistake, we popped into the hotel where we were married for a drink.

"Where's your latest venture then?" Crispin asked the owner on a whim. He and his wife already had several very successful hotels dotted around this part of the world so he was as good a person to ask as any. He bent his head over the map we had spread out on the bar and followed the road south with his finger until he reached a 'dot' with 'El Higo' written next to it. The sea next to it said 'Bahía Pavon' (Pavon Bay).

"Here," he said enthusiastically tapping the dot with his forefinger. "You want to head down south to Pavones. The area is amazing. No mosquitoes, fantastic breezes and land is the cheapest in the country. It's the end of the road." So, with nothing better to do and three more weeks remaining with which to do it in, we did.

We drove for hours whilst the roads got steadily worse and I, sitting on my pillow, got more and more uncomfortable. They had reduced to little more than muddy farm tracks again. Suddenly the farm track ended at a wide fast-flowing river. We must have taken a wrong turn but there was only one road on the map and we were on it. There were signs of a bridge being built but it looked like it hadn't been worked on for years. Then we saw the ferry on the far bank.

It is a bizarre sight that always gets our visiting mates reaching for their cameras. It takes three cars, maybe four at a squeeze, and sometimes heavily laden trucks. (Just recently a huge truck loaded with freshly cut logs had to dump its entire load in the river to save the ferry. The dumping narrowly prevented it from sinking but the truck still managed to rip the roof off it!) It is powered by a small outboard motor and is held in place by four huge metal chains that stretch across the river and prevent it from floating away with the current. It doesn't always run. Sometimes the sandbanks pile up too high in the rainy season for it to be able to reach the shore. Sometimes you don't think it has reached the shore but are waved aboard anyway and, not wanting to look like a big girl's blouse, you take a deep breath before making the plunge into the river, never too sure if you'll make it onto the ferry or not. I have to say it's great entertainment for a dollar. One story goes that the US army started building the bridge but then stopped because the family who run the ferry complained they would lose their livelihood. Nice of the States to listen like that but I can't imagine the story is true, I'm guessing lack of funds was the main issue.

We finally reached Pavones - our mosquito-free, breezy paradise. If you look at a map, on the Pacific side of Costa Rica are two sticky out bits, the northernmost being the Nicoya Peninsula where Tamarindo is and the southernmost is the Osa Peninsula which would become the view from our terrace. Pavones is a small village really with a few restaurants, a couple of small supermarkets, some (but not too many) Americans and the odd European. It is a beautiful area where the jungle meets the wild rocky black sand beaches. The road is dire, wildlife is abundant, the waves are incredible and every surfer has heard of its world-class left-hand break. Tourists are just starting to discover it and it is literally the end of the road.

We stayed in a B&B called 'Casa Siempre Domingo' (Always Sunday) run by a lovely American family: Greg, Heidi and their three year old son, Jackson. They have the most amazing view of Matapalo, the tip of the Osa Peninsula. We decided that was the view that we wanted. Nothing less would do. Some of those huge scarlet macaws that

22

landed on the terrace and insisted on eating Crispin's sandals would also be good. They were part of a recent release programme and were regularly 'shooed' away back to the trees where they were less likely to be harmed by poachers. As for the cute squirrel monkeys that ate the bananas that had been freshly macheted from a banana tree growing in their garden, throw in some of those too please.

Heidi put us in touch with the local real estate agency run by two very different people Malcolm and Lenny. Malcolm, the older of the two, is very observant and will tell it like it is. Lenny (Fast Lenny or 'Lenny Loco' - Crazy Lenny as he's often called) is the handsome salesman/surf dude, who never finishes a conversation, never gives a straight answer and is unrealistically optimistic with an enthusiasm that is infectious. Both are lovely guys.

The next few days were spent driving around looking at what Malcolm and Lenny had on their books but nothing grabbed us and certainly nothing had a view to match that of Casa Siempre Domingo's. Another day of driving and walking around land that just didn't feel right had left me feeling more that a bit fed up.

Lenny stopped the car in front of a little wooden shack where a lone poster of a bottle of *Fresca* was pinned up.

"What do you guys want to drink?" he asked me and Crispin. An unfriendly face had appeared at the counter, it seemed the shack was a shop. I would never have dreamt of stopping there to buy anything, preferring to pay twice as much at the tiny supermarket in Pavones; the owner just looked too scary. "I like to spread my business around and support the locals," said Lenny smiling and raising his hand in greeting at the unfriendly face. The unfriendly face broke into a stunning smile at which point I vowed to stop at the little wooden shacks that

23

dotted the road more often and also to smile and wave at the locals; particularly the grumpy looking ones.

Lenny came back with a bottle of bright green *Fresca* for Crispin, one swig of the sickly grapefruit flavoured fizz and he was addicted. "The country ran out of fruit the first year *Tropicale* started making those," he said as he handed me a bottle of mixed fruit *Tropicale*.

"Really?" I had no idea whether he was telling the truth or whether it was information that had been made up on the spur of the moment but he said everything so earnestly and enthusiastically that it was hard not to believe every word he said. That was what made him a good salesman.

We sat in the car swigging from our bottles with the air conditioning blasting out cold air.

"Why don't we go off on horseback tomorrow, Crispin?" Lenny asked my husband. "We could ride around and when we find a piece of land that you like we could find the owner and ask if he'll sell." It sounded like a good idea, even though my bump meant I wouldn't be able to go with them.

"Are there any waterfalls around?" I asked Lenny, I suddenly quite fancied one. "Then we could do walking tours to it and guests could have a swim." I could see the art gallery idea being knocked on the head quite soon.

"Well, tomorrow, let's go and ask the locals if they know of any waterfalls then," he was almost bursting with excitement. Crispin and I smiled at each other, Lenny's enthusiasm filled the car and I felt we were nearing the end of our search.

Over the next few days, I spent a lot of time on my own reading; sleeping or watching the howler monkeys and huge green parrots that would sit in the trees around the house and admire the view. Sometimes I would join them and admire the view myself, and other times I would be entertained by little Jackson. He would put on plays for me. They always had lots of monsters and growling in them and involved lots of running about and rolling around the floor. One morning his dad asked him if he could do a play about something other than a monster.

"How about a princess?" his mum suggested winking at me.

"There was a princess who lived in a tower," Jackson started in a lovely quiet voice, "AND THEN A MONSTER CAME AND ATE HER GRRRRRRR," he finished. He was very funny and had an amazing amount of energy. He was already a surfer dude and went out with his dad on his surf-board. Incredible for a three year old!

Crispin would report back on his adventures every night. They had found some beautiful waterfalls and amazing *fincas* (farms or large pieces of land) but no one had wanted to sell or they were out of our price range. The following day Lenny Loco had arranged for them to see the *finca* of an elderly local called Lorenzo. Maybe tomorrow would be our lucky day. Crispin put his hand gently on my ever-increasing belly, trying to calm down the wriggling little girl inside and fell asleep. I lay awake being kicked to glory from the inside.

Crispin left after our usual breakfast of fresh pineapple, banana, watermelon and star fruit – wow the fruit was good here – followed by bacon and eggs. I waved him off and settled back to watch more of Jackson's monster plays.

On their return, Crispin had some really good news. "Lorenzo wants to sell his *finca*," said Crispin happily. "It's huge; I've never seen so much land!"

"Is there a waterfall?" I asked him.

"No, but the views are amazing!"

25

"As good as here?" I asked sweeping my arm across the expanse of blue and green.

"Better!" said Lenny.

Crispin agreed with him, "You can see more of the peninsula and the gulf. You'll love it," he said.

"Can I go and see it?" I asked hopefully, I needed a break from Jackson's plays; three year olds were tiring I'd decided.

"It's too far off the main road for you to walk, you can't ride and there isn't a road. We'll have to put one in," said Crispin.

"Build a road?" I said amazed. How on earth do you go about building a road?

"It will only cost about three thousand dollars to get a bulldozer up there and put some material down," said Lenny in an 'easy peasy lemon squeezy' voice. "You can use my lawyer, Artoodle, for the closing too," suggested Lenny. "He speaks English."

"Who?" I asked, not hearing the name properly.

"Artoodle," he repeated. "He's in San José and you have to fly out from there next week anyway so I can arrange a meeting and he can draw up the paperwork. I'll drive Lorenzo up to make sure he gets there." We all shook hands and then, as that hadn't felt right, I put my arms out and we had a group hug.

Our search was finally over.

Lorenzo had one of his sons with him for the closing. Neither of them spoke a word of English and neither one had a bank account. Lorenzo either couldn't see well enough to read or couldn't actually read but, either way, he had to have the contract that Artoodle had drawn up, read to him. Crispin and I signed it. Lorenzo put an 'X' for his signature and, handing over one million colones (about $2k), we bought an option on Lorenzo's 80 acre *finca*. We had to come up with the balance within a year or we would lose our deposit and Lorenzo would be free to sell to somebody else.

26

On the 10th December we headed back to England with changed plans. We were no longer going to open an art gallery but were going to build some little rental houses (called *cabinas*) instead. Whilst we waited for the life we wanted for ourselves to start we had the flu, the real flu that is and not 'man-flu', immersed ourselves in National Childbirth Trust classes to prepare ourselves for parenthood and saw lots of friends and family. We put the flat and barn up for sale again and then we became parents to a beautiful healthy baby girl.

Estrella Rose Freeman was born on Friday 13th February 2004. We had flown out to Costa Rica for our wedding two years earlier on the same date so we knew it wasn't unlucky for us. We gave her a Spanish name to make her life easier in Costa Rica. Estrella means star and is pronounced Estraya. My hopes of a water birth were somewhat stuffed when we found out she was breech; I had a caesarean section.

When Estrella was five weeks old Crispin's parents lent us the money to pay Lorenzo the balance for his *finca* so Crispin and his dad flew back to Costa Rica to pay him. His dad was also very interested in what we were doing and wanted to see our dream for himself.

"Lorenzo had opened a bank account but I still had to hand over the money in used bank notes as he wouldn't accept a bank transfer!" Crispin told me, once we were officially the new owners. We both laughed

"Well, have a safe trip back hon and I'll see you in a couple of days," I said. I had missed him.

Oh, there was a scorpion crawling up the leg of dad's bed last night," Crispin said as I was about to hang up.

"A scorpion?!" I was horrified. "They have scorpions over there?"

"Of course they do. And snakes. It is the jungle."

"Oh," I said in a small voice. "I hadn't thought of that."

"They are more scared of you than you are of them," he assured me.

Want a bet?

Malcolm, Lenny Loco's business partner, had been managing the task of putting in the road so the *finca*, previously only accessible on foot or on horseback, could now be driven to. Talking of horses, when Crispin arrived back home I found out we were the proud owner of two. A very tall Tico (which is almost unheard of) came to the *finca* to see Crispin during that week. He had sold his *finca*, bought a car and had no further use for his horses. He offered a grey mare and her foal to Crispin for $200. Now that's something I never ever imagined us owning. He emailed friends to get some ideas for names and Gilly, a friend of his from work, emailed back saying 'name the mare after me'. So Gilly she was. The name of her foal took a little longer to come up with but we eventually decided on Lucero, meaning 'bright star' in Spanish. George joined them not long after.

Our barn conversion and the London flat seemed to take forever to sell but Estrella kept us busy (and sleep-deprived) and finally, on 1st September 2004, ten months after arriving back in the UK we were on a plane again and on our way to our new life; the three of us.

For the guys reading this thinking 'but what happened to the MG?'; that had been the first thing to go. Crispin still had tears in his eyes when he thought about selling it.

Also, in case you were wondering, we still hadn't got around to writing that business plan.

2 Arrival at Lenny's

We had been in San José for three weeks and were desperate to leave. Our hunt for a car had dragged on for much longer than we'd anticipated. We had been staying at Jack's girlfriend's house and their turbulent relationship and our six month old baby meant it hadn't been easy at times. Sofia was a beautiful model and aspiring actress who was working at the local internet betting office to support her two young children from previous relationships and wanted to find Mr Right. She spoke excellent English and her insecurities from her previous relationships showed. Jack did nothing to put them to rest, bless him. He was a mate of my brother's from school and had a heart of gold but could be an insensitive chap at times and really didn't understand how a woman's mind worked. Mind you, haven't I just described most men?

Jack also worked at the internet betting office, was a well-respected manager and was enjoying all the excesses that a city like San José could offer a young, single bloke. They were both fantastic people but seemed to bring out the worst in each other and we really weren't too sure if they were destined to be together or destined to kill each other. Either way, our presence wasn't helping and we needed to leave. The car we eventually settled on was a black 1996 Nissan Pathfinder. It didn't meet either of our two criterion; 'diesel' and 'not black' (we felt a diesel car would be cheaper to run and that the interior of a black car would get hotter in the sun) but there wasn't an awful lot of choice and $12k seemed like a reasonable price for a car that can drive vertically up mountains, or was that a Land Rover advert?!

Crispin left Sofia's house at 8am to go to the local INS office, to get some ridiculously expensive car insurance. INS was government run with zero

30

competition; Costa Rica was big on monopolies. I continued to pack our things. It was the rainy season and it was chucking it down. An hour and a half later Crispin was back.

"Sorted?" I asked hopefully. The annoyed look on his face said otherwise.

"No, I need our company document that we registered the car in, the 'cedula hoody' or something, have you seen it?"

"I don't remember it," I said looking around at the piles of our stuff that lay everywhere. We started rummaging around randomly then I remembered a Spanish document that Estrella had been chewing. It had looked important so I'd shoved it into my handbag for safe-keeping. I pulled it out and it said *'Cedula Juridica'* at the top of it. It was missing the corner and was a bit damp but I handed it over and Crispin breathed a sigh of relief.

"Now I've got to go and find somewhere that does photocopying," he said sighing.

"Do they not have a photocopier in the office?" I asked in surprise.

"No, that would be considered making your life easier and that would never do." With that he left. It was our first brush with the Costa Rican obsession with documents and umpteen copies of them. It was an important lesson in things to come.

"Good luck," I called as the door banged shut.

By 10.30am the rain was nearing 'driving rain' definition. I had finished packing and was sitting with Estrella on my knee playing her favourite game. "Round and round the garden like a teddy bear, one step, two step, tickly under there." Estrella collapsed in a heap of giggles as I tickled her armpit. I had started off on her hand, moved to her foot and was now on her tummy. Teddy was running out of body parts to go round. Even Estrella was beginning to find it a tad dull when, thankfully, the doorbell rang.

31

"Got them," announced an out-of-breath, slightly annoyed, but nevertheless triumphant Crispin. "I had to go back and photocopy things three times as they kept asking for different documents but I think we are covered for every eventuality. Cost an absolute fortune though: a thousand dollars and it's only for six months!" He was brandishing the car insurance documents and I half expected them to be gold plated. "Right, let's go!" With that Crispin picked up a suitcase, carried it out through the door and hoisted it into the boot. What wouldn't fit inside the car, he strapped to the roof. Finally, he squeezed Estrella and her car seat into the tiny space he'd left for them and off we went. Or at least that was what was supposed to happen but the car wouldn't start.

The car had this ridiculous immobilizer system on it and you had to press a button in the door and another one hidden by the handbrake and then crank the engine. Nothing. He tried again; press, press, crank. Still nothing.

"Are you sure you are doing it in the right order?" I asked helpfully. He tried the buttons the other way around just to humour me. He then turned the key again, still nothing. We got out of the car, extracted Estrella and went back inside the house. Crispin phoned the garage where we'd bought the car and got the non-English speaking owner, luckily his English speaking son was there too.

"He's on his way," said Crispin as he hung up the phone.

"Y'know, I think I'm going to have to feed Estrella," I said half apologetically knowing that Crispin wouldn't be very happy about a further delay. I had been hoping we could get on the road and then she would sleep for a while and we could feed her later but it was getting past her lunchtime and the last thing we needed was a fractious baby in the car. Whilst I cooked some pasta, Crispin waited impatiently outside. Ten minutes later I heard a car pull up.

"I went press, press, crank but the engine didn't turn over," I heard Crispin explain. Less than a minute later I heard the engine roar into life. The car drove off again. A rather sheepish Crispin appeared in the doorway.

"What happened?" I asked him.

"He did exactly the same as I did and it started first time," Crispin said in a hurt voice.

"That's embarrassing," I said as I handed a rather tomatoey Estrella to him to strap into place once more before setting off in the rainy half-light towards 'Cerro de La Muerte'.

That we were going to be driving through a mountain range where 'Death Peak' was the highest point of the road didn't fill me with much optimism for our journey ahead. The name apparently came from the olden days when people died of hypothermia whilst doing the crossing. We were about to find out that the name was just as apt today.

An hour outside of San José the road started to climb and the car wound its way up into the mountains. The now driving rain hadn't eased at all, a thick fog had descended and we were crawling along. A huge articulated truck overtook us on a blind bend, I held my breath thinking he was never going to make it past us but he did and then another one casually followed him. What were these guys on? Even without the fog and the rain they couldn't possibly see around that bend!

It wasn't long before Crispin started to get a bit cocky and tried to overtake an unusually slow bus on a hairpin bend. It was a bend that I certainly couldn't see around but I guessed that Superman was using his x-ray vision. I once again held my breath as he slammed the brakes on and tucked the car back in behind the bus whilst another huge truck appeared from around the bend and shot past in the opposite direction. The driver had his hand on his horn.

"I think we'll stay where we are," Crispin said lightly. I breathed out, removed my hand from my mouth and nodded in agreement. I was however sure that he would morph into a mad truck driver again soon enough. I took Estrella's approach to the situation and shut my eyes figuring the drive would be less stressful if I was asleep.

Suddenly the car swerved dangerously from side to side.

"What on earth was that?!" I asked in alarm, my eyes snapping open.

"The road wasn't there!" said Crispin in horror. I glanced in the wing mirror and could just make out the huge hole where the road should have been. Our entire side of the road had fallen away down the mountainside; a tree branch was stuck upright near the spot to serve as a warning to oncoming traffic. Fog quickly enveloped the scene.

"I can understand why the Lonely Planet says don't drive this road at night!" I said. "Cat's eyes would be nice."

"Some white lines would help," added a still shaken Crispin. He was right; there weren't even any of those.

A short while later a very wet, miserable looking young man appeared in the middle of the road waving a red flag.

"Must be something serious if they are bothering to warn people," I said to Crispin. Crispin stopped the car and put his window down. Without a word the man handed the flag to Crispin, gesturing that we continue on our way. Crispin automatically handed the flag to me as if it was a car park ticket or a toll receipt then carried on driving past a terrifying looking machine that had just loomed out of the fog and resembled a blow-torch on wheels. "What's the flag for?" I asked Crispin.

"No idea," he replied. For a few seconds, flames licked around our wheels and the heat was stifling. There were a couple of traffic cones indicating it was probably road works; patching up potholes. Another young Tico guy with an orange jacket waved as we drove past him. We waved back.

"Friendly chap," I commented. Crispin suddenly slammed the brakes on and reversed. "What are you doing?" I asked.

"I think we should have given him the red flag back," said Crispin laughing.

"Ah, it's instead of traffic lights!" I said as the realisation hit home. "That's how they know who the last car to be let through is." It was a clever system, providing some dozy tourists didn't drive off with the flag that is.

Considering what could have happened, I suppose you could say that we got through the mountains without a hitch. Even the rain seemed to be easing as we stopped to fill up with gas. We needed jump-starting to get going once more. Crispin didn't dare turn the engine off on the ferry for fear of never getting on dry land again.

We arrived at Lenny's house way after the 5.30pm sunset. There were no lights on, nobody was home. Our original plan had been to stay at Greg and Heidi's again but a chat with them the previous day had revealed that a bridge between Lenny's place and theirs had collapsed with a heavily laden truck on it. The road had been in a terrible state, even worse than usual. Delivery trucks and buses had been unable to get through for almost a week so the locals residents had decided to do something about it; they picketed the local government offices. Ironically it was a truck filled with material to fix the road that had collapsed the rotten wooden bridge. The only way around was to drive along the beach at low tide.

After my conversation with Heidi I had then called Lenny and he told us to go straight to his place instead. He and his Costa Rican (Tica) wife Karin had visitors and needed to go to Canoas to pick some things up but he'd assured us that they would be back at 5pm. Paso Canoas, often shortened to Canoas, was the less than charming Costa Rica/Panama border town that I had yet to experience.

For something to do we continued past Lenny's house to the collapsed bridge to take a look. One side of it had snapped completely in two. "Look," said Crispin pointing to several trucks lined up at the side of the road. "They are already waiting for the 10pm low tide so they can drive along the beach."

There was nothing along that stretch of road of any use to us; no restaurants; no hotels, just brightly painted wooden houses scattered here and there amongst the trees. We returned to Lenny's and waited. The rain had slowed to a drizzle but it was still too heavy to sit in the car with the windows open as Estrella was getting wet. It was too hot and steamy with the windows closed and we couldn't sit there with the air-conditioning on as we were about to run out of gas. To top it all, the car had decided not to start again and we hadn't parked with our nose downhill so a jump-start was out of the question.

"Let's wait around the back of the house," I suggested. "Maybe there are some chairs." There was no path so we walked through the grass and found a small terrace which had a solitary stool. Whilst I sat on the stool feeding Estrella, in the pitch black, I couldn't help thinking that it didn't seem like the most promising start to our life here.

By 8pm the rain had finally stopped but we were getting fed up. "I'll try and start the car again," said Crispin.

"Have we got enough gas to join the trucks do you think?" I asked

"What, and drive to Casa Siempre Domingo and stay with Greg and Heidi?"

I shrugged my shoulders, "Just a thought."

"Only one way to find out," he said.

As we walked back to the car I had visions of us running out of gas and getting stuck on the beach. They weren't pleasant thoughts. Where are you Lenny? I thought.

"Look,'" I said pointing to the main road, "car lights." We watched thankfully as the lights turned in, drove up the steep driveway and stopped next to us.

"Hey!" said Lenny's cheerful voice. "Been waiting long?"

"Not really," I said with typical Britishness. Karin climbed out of the car and greeted us all, going completely gaga over Estrella. She was closely followed by their friends.

"I'm Mac and this is my wife Penny," said Mac. We introduced ourselves and shook hands.

"Jump in!" Lenny said with a sense of urgency.

"Where are we going?" I asked him.

"To get Coral. She's at church and she's desperate to meet Estrella." He stopped in front of a little wooden building two minutes away, jumped out of the car leaving the engine running and vanished through the open door. He came out seconds later carrying a gorgeous three year old. She had long wavy blonde hair and was wearing a pink fairy dress. She was the spitting image of her mother. However, she would have to wait until the following day to meet Estrella. Coral was fast asleep in her dad's arms.

Mac and Penny had ordered a couple of sofas in Canoas and they were due to be delivered imminently. I naïvely pictured them arriving in a Debenhams-type delivery van. They had built a one-bedroom house a couple of minutes walk away and were in the process of finishing and furnishing it. They wanted to rent it out. Coincidentally, we needed somewhere to live.

"It's ready to rent," declared Lenny in his best salesman voice. "The only thing we are waiting for is the kitchen countertop."

When the sofas arrived, my image of a Debenhams' delivery van soon disappeared; they were tied to the back of a very old and dirty pick-up truck. Crispin went to the house with Mac and Lenny to take a look at it.

"What did you think?" I asked Crispin on his return.

His reply wasn't very encouraging. "Well, it turns out that 'ready to rent' and 'only missing the kitchen countertop' is 'real estate agent speak' for 'ready to rent if you don't mind living in a place that's not finished' and 'the absolutely only thing in the kitchen is a fridge/freezer'!"

"Oh," I said, rather disappointed. "What about the two-bed place that Lenny also mentioned; the one with no view?" I continued.

The answer was even less encouraging. Even Lenny had admitted that that one wasn't finished yet.

"Not finished how?" I figured I could live without a view and I really, really wanted two bedrooms.

"No roof," came the reply. Okay, that was quite an important feature of a house.

It was getting late so we slept in Lenny's lounge that night. Mac and Penny were in the spare room, so even they didn't want to sleep in their house, eh? Estrella was next to us in her travel cot.

I awoke early the next morning – the sun rises 12 hours after it sets at 5.30am and only ever changes by half an hour at the most – and lay there watching their gorgeous black Labrador, Shadow, sleeping on the back terrace. He'd been bitten by a snake the previous week and one side of his face was still very swollen, he was lucky to be alive.

Something else was watching Shadow. The biggest spider I had ever seen in my entire life was walking towards him. Now, living in a converted barn we had seen some pretty big spiders, especially at harvest time when they were driven out of the surrounding fields and into our lounge. Crispin threw a tea towel over the larger ones before picking them up and relocating them. Once, a tea towel had looked wholly inadequate so Crispin vanished into the bathroom and came back with a bath towel. He stood there looking at this eight-legged monster before stating it was a job for our neighbour. Our neighbour had lived there longer and so was used to them but even he looked a bit shocked and gratefully accepted the bath towel when Crispin offered it to him.

The beast that I was looking at was easily twice the size of that one. Oh my goodness, it suddenly hit me that it was the same back terrace that we'd walked around to in the pitch black the previous night, walked to through the grass in our flip-flops! WE were lucky to be alive!!

I watched as the spider disappeared under one of Shadow's legs. He was bound to get bitten and then die, the spider finishing off what the snake hadn't quite achieved. I watched for a couple more minutes debating whether to wake someone. Shadow suddenly stretched lazily, stood up and wandered off – no doubt wanting to find somewhere quiet to keel over and die. There was no sign of the giant spider. Crispin stirred at that moment and I told him what had happened.

"Don't worry," he said, "I'm sure he's fine. Look at him." He was pointing at Shadow running around happily in the garden. Dogs must be immune to spider venom I thought.

For breakfast Karin cooked us individual omelettes with tomato sauce inside. Not just a pretty face then.

"They are fresh tomatoes," announced Lenny, obviously proud of his wife's cooking abilities. He had reason to be. I could probably make an omelette but wasn't too sure how I would go about making a sauce with fresh tomatoes. In my past life I would've opened a tin of them but I supposed I wouldn't be able to do that any more.

Whilst Karin smeared mashed avocado over that pretty face, put yoghurt in her perfect long blonde wavy hair, finished the look off with a slice of cucumber over each eye and lay outside sun-bathing in the tiniest bikini I had ever seen, the rest of us went down to Mac and Penny's place so I could see the lack of everything for myself. As we lazily drove the three minute walk I couldn't help thinking of my last image of Karin and that maybe I was going wrong somewhere with my £16 pot of Vichy face cream, £11 tube of Vichy eye cream and I won't even start on the money I put into my curly untameable hair. I certainly didn't look good enough to eat.

Lenny turned in through a metal gate and stopped at the top of a steep muddy driveway. The house was at the bottom. "The 4x4's broken so I'll leave the car here," explained Lenny.

"Lenny's going to get some more material on the driveway soon," said Mac. It was good to hear that rock was going to be arriving soon; after all we didn't want to be getting stuck!

It was a nice little house with orange stucco walls and clay tiles on the roof. It was, however, of a slightly odd design in that every place you would have expected to see a window to show off the view; there was a wall, or a solid wooden door. The outside terrace faced the view but there was no respite from the blazing afternoon sun as it ceased to be in the shade after about 11 o'clock.

"I sent a rough idea to an architectural college and got a student to draw up the plans," Mac said.

"So the architect had never been here?" I asked.

"No," confirmed Mac. The design now made sense.

The house had also been built in front of a little hill as opposed to on top of it which surprised me until Lenny admitted this had been his idea. I realised why the first time I walked up the aforementioned hill. The view and breeze up there were amazing and when I turned around I saw the reason: Lenny's house. If Mac and Penny had built up there it would have been smack bang in the middle of Lenny's view. I decided right then and there that, when we built our house, we were going to have a proper architect, he was going to visit our site and we weren't going to be asking Lenny's advice!

Crispin and I, carrying Estrella, followed Lenny, Mac and Penny inside through the front door. It led into an open plan kitchen/dining room/lounge which had the two sofas that had arrived in the night and the aforementioned fridge/freezer but that was it. In fact it was an open plan kitchen/dining room/lounge/bedroom as there were, as yet, no internal doors but at least the bedroom had a bed in it, oh and a battered old chest of drawers. Rather bizarrely, the only air conditioning unit was in the bedroom (Lenny Loco's idea) and it meant that once Estrella had gone to bed she had to freeze just so we could get the lounge vaguely cool.

The house was small; maybe as little as seven metres square but it was nicely decorated and I was sure it would be lovely when it was finished. Due to our lack of other options we were going to be calling it home for a while. A long while as it turned out. We agreed with Mac and Penny a reduced rent until the house was finished – we would never pay full rent. As they were going back to the States shortly, Lenny was going to be our landlord as well as our neighbour and real estate agent.

We moved in later that day and Penny gave us a more detailed tour. She explained the reason for the second shower room right by the back door. "They have red bugs here y'know?" We didn't. "Some people call them chiggers but they're the same thing. So if you've been out walking, you come in, take your clothes off, put them straight in the washer and then shower straightaway. They like your elastic-line so up here and down here," she gestured to her bra and then her knickers, "for women and round the waist for men. Some people say put nail polish on them to kill them and others say use alcohol, others say just diaper rash cream." We had no idea what on earth she was talking about but nodded and smiled and she left us to it.

We unpacked our three suitcases. (Stuff that we couldn't part with was being shipped over by sea freight and most of our furniture was either on loan or had been given away to friends and family. We had been brutal during our packing and a lot of items had ended up in a 'garage sale'. Crispin's baby elephant poo however, collected during a trip to Africa, was in his parents' loft – he could not be persuaded to throw it away and I could not be persuaded to include it in our shipping!).

Estrella sat in one of the suitcases and 'helped' by throwing clothes all over the floor and giggling madly. It was lucky we didn't have much stuff as the majority of our entire belongings had to fit either into or on top of the battered old chest of drawers. You know the type, the drawers collapse off the runners if you pull them out too far or load them over half full.

Our kitchen stuff, which initially consisted of four plastic plates and plastic mugs, two knives and forks, Estrella's two plastic spoons and a tiny gas camping stove, all fitted on a rustic hand-made work bench that the builder's had left outside in the rain. The builders were still around as they were finishing off the building to the side of the house which Penny called the 'bodega'. It was a car port and also had a lockable storage area. Lenny said the builders didn't need the work bench any more so we wiped it down, dried the wood in the sun and dragged it inside. Lenny was wrong; we <u>did</u> have a kitchen countertop.

3 Jackie

We spent quite a bit of time at the *finca*, walking around up there just soaking it all in: the bubbling streams; overgrown pasture that the neighbours' cows grazed on; the maize field; the expanses of rainforest; undulating hills – it really was 80 acres of paradise. The first time I saw it I thought it had the most incredible views I had ever seen, and still do. They were stunning; a million times better than on the video that Crispin had taken during the trip over here with his dad.

"This is where dad and I thought we could build the *cabinas*," Crispin said pointing to a large hillock a short distance from the road, "then the pool down below, a big rancho just here that we could have the restaurant in one day and another *cabina* in front of that mango tree over there, unfortunately the bulldozer cut too many of its roots when it was flattening the site." The mango tree looked incredibly sorry for itself; half of its leaves were curling up and turning brown.

"It won't die will it?" I asked, rather horrified. I didn't want to be killing our trees!

"No, I'm sure it will be fine. Come and see the guest house site," he continued enthusiastically so I followed Crispin up the road to a gorgeous spot surrounded by mango and palm trees, the bulldozer had also been in there and scraped out a large building site.

"Impressed?" he asked me. I was speechless, it was incredible. "Wait until you see this." He led me across to the other side of the road and back down the hill a bit. We then left the road and crossed a pretty little stream. I had to crane my neck to look at the tops of the trees that lined the stream bed; they had obviously been there a very long time.

"I often see the squirrel monkeys here," said my very own Tarzan. I listened and watched the trees closely for signs of movement but couldn't hear or see anything, except birds and Estrella's babbling.

The shaded path was muddy and headed steeply up a slope under an archway of trees before curving around to the left. It wasn't easy walking and I was just about to pause for a breather when I was stopped in my tracks anyway and it was all I could do to stare in amazement. "This is where I thought we could build the family house one day," Crispin announced with a smile on his face, "I think it's the highest point of the *finca*."

I felt my eyes prick with tears – it was beautiful. From left to right there were sweeping views of the Pacific Ocean then the entire Osa Peninsula to the green undulating hills the other side of the Río (River) Coto and finally the mountains.

"That's Volcan Barú" said Crispin pointing to one of the distant mountains. "It's in Panama." Wow, we could see to Panama! "The lot's quite small though," continued Crispin. "This is the edge of the *finca*," he said indicating a line of trees and some rusty barbed wire a couple of metres away.

"Why do they put their *finca* dividing lines right through the middle of hills?" By 'they' I meant the original settlers. It seemed very odd to me.

"Maybe they felt they were the useless bits," offered Crispin, "after all they can't grow crops up there as it's too steep and they would wash away and it's difficult to graze cattle up there so better to split it with your neighbour so you have a useless bit each." It was a believable theory.

"Do you know who owns the other half of the hill?" I asked him; I had an idea.

"No, but I'm sure Lenny will know."

"Can we ask the owner if we can buy the other half of the hill off him?" I said as we walked back down towards the road. Crispin hurriedly dropped me and Estrella back at the house and then drove off in search of Lenny Loco.

45

The owner of the other half of our family house site was called Urbano and he lived in a little town in the mountains. However, he still had lots of family in the area and one of his sons owned one of the local *pulperías* that Lenny Loco liked to frequent.

We found out that Urbano wanted to sell not just half a hill, but the whole *finca*. He wanted double what we had paid for our *finca* the year before. At the time it seemed like a lot of money but it was very sad to think that someone else would buy it and hence own the other half of our family house site. They would then probably divide the land up into lots, sell them off and make heaps of money. With our grand plans of building the guest house, a couple of *cabinas*, a pool, and not to mention the family house, there was no way that we could afford to buy it as well.

In the middle of the night I lay awake trying to soothe Estrella who seemed to be coming down with something and didn't want to go back to sleep again. I was mulling over our problem when suddenly a brilliant idea struck me. I elbowed Crispin.

"I wasn't snoring, I was awake," he said which is his standard answer when he gets elbowed in the middle of the night.

I ignored him. "Why don't <u>we</u> buy Urbano's *finca*, divide some of it into lots, keep the other half of the family house site obviously, but sell the others off? We could get the money back that we'd spent and still finance our plans." My enthusiasm rivalled that of Lenny's. Crispin grunted in approval, rolled onto his back and started snoring.

Lenny sent word to Urbano's various family members that a path needed clearing in the *finca* so we could walk around it and take a proper look.

The following day Lenny picked us up. It was a sunny day and the locals were taking advantage of it and were drying their washing. Every suitable bush, tree or flower had washing draped over it. Even the barbed wire fences had clothes hanging off them. With the dust in the summer and the mud in the winter it would never cease to amaze me how their washing remained clean out there.

As we drove up our road to have that proper look at Urbano's land, Lenny screeched to a halt.

"Look there's a snake," he said as he opened the door to climb out to get a closer look. Was he mad?! 'Loco' yes, of course he was. "It's okay," he added. "it's not a dangerous one." At that second the bright green snake made a lunge for Lenny's leg. He screamed and jumped back into the car slamming the door shut. I have never ever seen anybody move so fast. I craned my neck to see what the snake thought of losing his victim and then saw that he hadn't: he had a frog in its mouth. "It was after the frog," said Lenny with relief, laughing nervously.

The entrance to the *finca* was through a wooden corral, where Urbano used to keep his cows. The thick mud and cow pats made me very grateful that I was wearing wellington boots. Lenny, as always, wore flip-flops. I had learnt my lesson the previous week when some mud got stuck between the sole of my foot and my favourite pair of Fat Face flip-flops. It was incredibly difficult to walk and my foot slipped sidewards suddenly, the movement snapping the bit that sits between your toes. Rather begrudgingly I took Lenny's advice and the flowery pink and grey birthday present were left at the side of the road for a passing resourceful local to fix. Lenny would never learn his lesson.

We hoisted Estrella into the back carrier and off we went. We had a steep climb down, walked along a river bed and then up again to a long ridge covered with guava trees, it was as beautiful as our *finca*. It was difficult to keep our bearings initially but a very tall dead tree that looked like it had been struck by lightning, stuck up skyward like a long bony finger and made it easier. We wandered around for hours, stopping when Estrella needed feeding or we needed water. At one point we paused under a mango tree and gazed across a tree-covered valley - it was difficult to comprehend that we could own it soon. It was stunning and I knew it was going to be difficult for us to sell even an inch of it. Eventually we reached a riverbed and our guide stopped and said he thought it was getting late and we shouldn't walk any further because of snakes - better to get back. I certainly wasn't going to argue with him. Whenever I was out walking I spent my entire time looking for bugs/reptiles/scary creatures - it's amazing I even noticed the views. It took at least a year for me to get over this fear and, having never seen anything that could hurt me, actually start enjoying our walks!

The sun had gone in and it was starting to drizzle as we made our way back to Lenny's car and clambered in. Our car was still being unreliable and that was why Lenny had offered to drive. The road was in reasonable shape but was starting to suffer a bit because of the rains and definitely needed much more rock putting on it. Lenny had parked at the side of the road, in a shallow ditch next to a high bank. As he tried to drive forward his wheels started sliding and the car stopped wedged against the bank. He tried to reverse but I could hear and feel the wheels spinning in the mud.

"The 4x4's still broken," said Lenny almost apologetically but with his ever present smile.

"Do you want us to get out?" I asked helpfully, after all I knew the routine; they would find branches next.

We all got out of the car and Lenny and Crispin started hunting around for branches; shoving them

48

under the wheels to give them something to grip on. I stood in the middle of the road holding Estrella in her car chair. She needed a sleep and I hoped she wasn't about to get antsy.

There must have been half a tree under the car when Lenny got back in and started the engine. He reversed a couple of metres and I felt a wave of relief but then the car slid sideways back against the bank again, now it was well and truly stuck. At least he was wedged against the bank and wasn't 15 metres further down the road where there wasn't a bank, just a steep drop into a deep gully. We needed a plan B before the rain got heavier, the mud muddier and we were stuck here for the night!

Just at that moment I heard a noise from down the hill and turned away from the stuck car and the muddy guys; plan B was coming up the hill on horseback. In fact, plan B had his daughter with him – at least I hoped it was his daughter, it was difficult to tell here sometimes. It also wasn't unusual to see whole families crowded onto a horse, or as they sold off bits of their land and could afford motorbikes, four to a bike was quite common. Dangerous; coming from a world where seat belts, crash helmets and child car seats were law, but common.

Plan B had very dark hair, like most Ticos, and a handsome friendly face. He pulled the horse up a sensible distance behind the car, jumped down and started grabbing branches. The girl remained on the horse but she looked at me and gave me a dazzling smile. I guessed she was about six or seven years old and was incredibly beautiful. She had long dark hair, although not as dark as her dad's and pearly white teeth. She wore shorts and wellies, like her dad - standard dress in the rainy season, shorts and flip-flops in the dry season, all except Lenny that is. He always wore board shorts and flip-flops, sunglasses (even indoors) and, occasionally, a t-shirt.

49

I smiled back at the girl and after a while she slid down from the horse and came over to where Estrella and I were. We were now sitting in the middle of the road, Estrella still in her car chair, fast asleep from the energy she'd expended trying to grab hold of overhead leaves and branches from the back carrier. As the girl came closer I noticed a dark shadow on the right side of her face. She crouched down next to me and stroked Estrella's hand.

"Her name's Estrella," I said in Spanish. "I'm Jo." I pointed to her and looked quizzical having forgotten how to ask somebody their name.

"Jackie," she said, understanding. I was inches away from the dark shadow on her face and it was really difficult not to stare. The shadow was clearly a birthmark but unlike any I had seen before: like thick black animal fur that almost entirely covered her right cheek. The strangest thing was that it didn't detract from her beauty at all and she clearly wasn't in the slightest bit embarrassed by it. We continued to smile at each other.

The rain got heavier so I got an umbrella from the car and Jackie and I huddled under it, Estrella between us. My Spanish was limited and Jackie's English non-existent but by the time Lenny's car was out of the ditch and I watched them wave as they rode off up the road; I felt we had made a friend.

4 Beach Lot Dream

Lenny, Karin and Coral made good neighbours. We ate together frequently and they showed us the local sights: 'La Piña' (The Pineapple) that did great pizza; 'The Cantina' where you could sit and watch the surfers; 'Doña Dora's' which did cheap local food; the Italian place that never had its prices up outside and for good reason as it was quite a shock when the bill arrived; and the fantastic vegetarian restaurant that did the best broccoli quiche and spicy baked potatoes I have ever tasted, their chocolate brownies were pretty amazing too. We were taken to the river in Pavones, shown the rocky tide pools where the bright blue fish darted about and also struggled and skidded down a long, steep slippery path to a beautiful local waterfall.

Lenny Loco and Crispin were becoming great friends and, if they didn't see each other every day then they certainly spoke on the phone. Whenever I heard "Hello you big dummy!" I knew who Crispin was talking to. It was what Lenny called Crispin too. Manly banter. We had asked him to find a small beach lot for us and this was keeping him busy.

A car pulled up outside the house early one morning and skidded to a halt. "I bet it's Lenny," I said without looking up. It was and he was incredibly excited.

"You have gotta see this!" Lenny gushed.

"What?" I asked him. He pressed his lips together and shook his head indicating he wasn't telling us anything else. As we had no choice and were more than a little intrigued, we got in the car.

He headed off in the direction of Pilon, our nearest beach, and stopped outside a Tico house. A middle-aged Tico was waiting on the terrace for us. Lenny chatted away to him in rapid Spanish, translating for us occasionally. They were basically swapping gossip.   The Tico said he'd had a plant sprayer stolen from his terrace the previous night, Lenny was telling him about a surfboard that had gone missing in the town.   We were pretty much ignored.

Half an hour later, with gossip dispensed with Lenny said, "Let's go" and we followed him through the Tico's fields towards the beach. We climbed over barbed wire fences when there wasn't room to go under and after a few minutes we were in what looked like a cemetery.   There were a handful of graves, one looked freshly dug.

"It was an Indian girl," said Lenny. "She had worms," he continued, "and one of them grew so big that it came up her throat and strangled her."   Nice. I hoped he didn't actually <u>mean</u> 'strangled'.   "You should take tablets for worms every six months just to be on the safe side," he added.   We'd be sure to remember that.

"Is this why you brought us here?" I asked.   "To show us what might happen if we don't take our worming tablets!"

He pointed to the piece of land directly in front of the cemetery.   "That is why I brought you here.   It's yours for twenty thousand dollars."

It was beautiful. It bordered a beautiful stream and was right on the beach.   In the centre stood a tree whose trunk was so thick it would have taken all of us holding hands to give it a hug!   The lot was perfect and I could picture a little beach house where Estrella could take a nap and I could make lunch when we were at the beach for the day.

"There would be bits of dead people in your well," Karin pointed out as she gathered some lemons from one of the lemon trees.   "These are the best lemons for making lemonade," she continued without pausing for breath. Bad news and good news then.

"I want to be in on it too," said Lenny.   "There's plenty of room for two houses, you could have the front bit, and we could have the back bit. We could save the very front bit and make a kind of beach club there with a shower and a bar area..." He was getting carried away.

"Lenny, Crispin and I have always said we would never go into business with anybody and we really don't want any close neighbours. We had a very bad experience with some neighbours in England and have learnt our lesson and just don't want to go there again."

We explained to Lenny and Karin what had happened. How we had been good friends and then our neighbours had gone very weird on us, around about the time I got pregnant as it so happened. They had scared our first buyers off telling them out and out lies about our property. Bearing in mind we were desperate to sell up and leave the UK we had found losing our buyers very difficult. It had become all-out war, with Crispin writing 'Jo 4 Crispin' (how old is he?!) in their wet cement and them smashing a hammer into our back door. We didn't want our friendship turning sour the way that had.

"I understand," Lenny said eventually. "But let me go to the *muni* and see what the *plano regulador* says and we can take it from there." I had absolutely no idea what that meant but if it stopped him from dreaming up beach club plans then it was a good idea.

We went down to Pilon beach a few days later. It's a beautiful bay with Pilon at one end and Zancudo the other and seven miles of black sand in between. The Pilon end is quite rocky in places but with sand so fine it sticks in the material of your swimming costume and is impossible to get out, making it look mouldy. The rainforest comes right down to the beach and is lined with palm trees. The blue sea and sky and the vivid green of the jungle still amaze us now and one of the few ways I know to 'de-

53

stress' is to wade out into the water and float, just gazing at the beauty all around. In just a few minutes you forget you are an exhausted mother who rarely finds the time to shave her legs any more, mind you the locals don't either so I don't stand out too much!

We found a wonderfully shady spot with very few rocks and set up camp. I use that term as, although we don't have a tent we are quite a sight at the beach. With cooler for lunch, stroller so Estrella can sleep, bucket and spade to amuse her, mat to sit on, umbrella for shade, the list goes on. You never see a Tico family with any of the above.

Suddenly I recognised the nearby lemon tree; it was the one Karin had raided. "That's 'our' lot!" I said to Crispin. Completely by chance, our perfect shady spot was directly in front of it. If we bought the lot, this would be 'our' bit of beach!

After a paddle in the warm water we went for a walk with Estrella in the stroller to get her off to sleep and also because we wanted to explore our beach a bit more. There was a Tico family a bit further along, amongst the trees by the river; we hadn't noticed them when we'd arrived. They had made a fire and were cooking fish, the smell was wonderful. They gestured we join them, and greeted us warmly offering us fish. We gratefully accepted and as we sat there sharing their lunch a troop of squirrel monkeys appeared in the trees overhead.

"This is where Lenny wanted the beach club," I reminded Crispin.

"I prefer it like this," Crispin said. I couldn't agree more. It was perfect for us and we couldn't wait to hear Lenny's news from the *muni*.

"It's been designated green zone" said Lenny.
"What does that mean?" I asked.
"It can't ever be built on," was the bad news. We were gutted.

"You may be able to overturn it though. The *plano regulador* hasn't been approved yet," Lenny added with his usual enthusiasm.

We saw Malcolm, Lenny Loco's business partner, in the *cantina* (the sign outside the bar/restaurant read 'Esquina del Mar' but everyone calls it 'the *cantina*') a few days later and, over a *banano con leche* (banana smoothie) asked him about the *plano regulador*. He explained that Costa Rica had consulted Japan for help on allocating land usage. Apparently deciding which areas should be for residential or commercial usage, or should have the hospital or airstrip or should never be built on i.e. green zone, was something that the Japanese were very good at. That was what the *plano regulador* was: the zoning plan on land use.

"Danny apparently had one approved years ago but since he's been in jail for 18 years the *muni* have seen fit to do another one," explained Malcolm. "It's in the local government offices, the *municipalidad* or *muni* for short, for public viewing." Okay, so that was what Lenny had consulted to find out about our beach lot. I'd heard the name 'Danny' before. His name was always said in the manner of 'you must know who I'm talking about.' It was about time I asked who he was but before I could, Crispin stepped in.

"Can you recommend any architects, Malcolm? We would really like to start building before Christmas if we can."

"I don't know about 'recommend', but I know of one in Golfito. His name's Ernesto. I've never worked with him so if things go wrong, don't call me!" He laughed as he wrote Ernesto's phone number down and handed it to Crispin.

"Thank you," said Crispin and stood up to leave, Estrella had started squirming. I joined him; my question would have to wait.

55

"Why are you asking about the 'plano regulador' anyway?" asked Malcolm curiously. Crispin and I assumed that Lenny had updated his business partner on our hunt for a beach lot but we now realised that he hadn't. Crispin explained and told him exactly where it was.

"Oh, that's Danny's land," Malcolm said.

"Who's Danny, Malcolm?" The time had come! "I keep hearing his name but have no idea who he is."

"Well, I've just got back from visiting him in the States so I'm as good a person as any to tell you the story. Sit down again and I'll tell you what I know."

We sat eagerly; even Estrella stopped squirming and seemed to listen.

In 1974, Danny Fowlie discovered the now legendary Pavones surf break for himself. A friend, who was probably the only person to have ever ridden the wave, had told him about it so it was no accident, and Danny set up home.

When he arrived in Pavones there were no roads and the only way in was by boat from Golfito. There were very few families down here. Keeping cows and chickens, hunting and growing rice, beans and corn was the way of life and still is for many. Although hunting is now frowned upon it still occurs. We've been to a local's house and eaten *tepesquinte*, a small wild pig, caught during a night's hunting expedition which I was horrified to find in our 'Costa Rica Eco-Travellers Wildlife Guide' when we returned home!

Danny instantly set about buying up about 85% of the beach front, shipped machinery and skilled workers in, and set about building roads, schools, bridges, a new saw mill and the cantina. Most importantly for him, he surfed.

In 1987, when the US government clamped down on drug-smuggling, Danny was arrested in Mexico. He was found guilty of a possible trumped-

56

up marijuana smuggling charge and given a 30 year jail sentence (as part of the zero tolerance drug policy in the States at the time). Some of his trusted right-hand men, who were supposed to be looking after his Pavones land for him, started selling it. Whether it was with falsified title deeds or fake power of attorneys Malcolm didn't know. To make matters worse when United Fruits (the banana company) moved out of nearby Golfito, workers who were left unemployed and homeless needed somewhere to live so they moved south and became squatters living on the vacant land that Danny had left behind when he moved away in 1985. He had other huge properties in California, Mexico and San José. One thing is for sure, no-one in their right mind deals with Danny's land: it is a legal mine-field. Danny was out of jail, wanted his land back, and had a team of lawyers that promised to do just that.

"I told him about the bridge collapsing, that one side had snapped in two," said Malcolm. "Danny was surprised because he'd built it using good strong wood. I had to remind him it was 30 years ago and he couldn't believe that much time had gone by. He asked if the other side had been replaced too, or just the broken one. When I said 'just the broken one' he laughed. 'The other side came from the same tree!' he said."

We all laughed and guessed it wouldn't be long until the bridge collapsed again.

5 British Citizen

Although Lenny wasn't the best landlord in the world things slowly started to get finished, often in spite of him.

I was washing up one day when his face appeared squashed against the glass, on the side without the bug screen. His arms were spread-eagled and he had a shocked look on his face. He slid down the window and out of sight.

"Another pigeon's hit the window!" I yelled to Crispin, laughing (sadly, several hummingbirds had also gone the same way). Crispin was in the bathroom showering with Estrella and didn't hear me.

Lenny reappeared grinning and then stood outside looking thoughtfully at the bug screen. We had mentioned to him the previous week that we were missing a couple. Mind you, the ones that we did have didn't fit very well and let loads of bugs in, especially in the evening when it was dark outside and we had the lights on. A myriad of tiny biting black bugs had descended on us at the last full moon. We sat there all evening just slapping ourselves desperately trying to kill the little blighters!

He slid his hand behind it and gave it a tug; it came off in his hand.

"What are you doing?!" I was no longer smiling: badly fitting bug screens were better than none at all!

"It came off in my hand," Lenny said still grinning. He moved around to the lounge window.

"What we need is ones with Velcro on then you could just rip them off," another tug and off came another one, "and put them in the washer." It was a good idea, but one that would never materialise. Five minutes later, our bug screens lay in a twisted pile in the garden. Three months later, Crispin would rescue the ones that weren't too badly damaged and prop them up against the windows with branches.

"I've got you a phone, big dummy!" Lenny said to Crispin who had just appeared from the bathroom with a towel wrapped round him. He was carrying Estrella.

"Great!" said Crispin.

"One of Toli's sons wants to sell his line to you." I suddenly noticed a short, thin man with a Hitler moustache standing behind Lenny on the terrace, presumably Toli's son. He was holding a tape measure and looked very uncomfortable.

"Who's Toli?" I asked Lenny, smiling at the man. I got a worried little smile back off him.

"My builder. He is one of the few Ticos I would have sitting at my kitchen table with me. He finished off this place, and mine. He's doing the bodega outside. Very trustworthy."

"Why can't we just go and buy a new line?" I asked.

"There aren't any cell phone lines."

"What do you mean?" How could there not be any cell phone lines?

"The country has run out of them and won't be releasing any more until November." We didn't want to be incommunicado until November! I was hoping we would get a land-line soon as the telephone exchange in Pavones had recently been completed but there had been no news as to when they would be arriving. I found it amazing that Pavones only got electricity eight years ago!

The short, thin man took advantage of the break in the conversation to say "con permiso?" to Crispin.

"Pase," replied Lenny and the man lowered his head humbly and entered the house. He started jabbering away to Lenny in rapid Spanish. I didn't understand a word he was saying. He turned to Crispin, said something, held up his measuring tape and gestured to the bedroom. Lenny answered him and the man went into the bedroom, smiling at

59

Estrella as he passed her. She was now in her walker.

Lenny was looking down at the phone he had just taken out of his shirt pocket and was walking around the room slowly.

"You get signal here," he said, holding it above the kitchen windowsill.

"What's going on? Why is Toli's son in our bedroom?" Why did Lenny never introduce anybody properly?

"It's not Toli's son, he's my carpenter and he's measuring up for the built-in closet. He's amazing. He's making me some coffee tables at the moment. Toli's worked with him before, that's how I found him." He continued walking slowly back out onto the terrace. "You get signal out here too. It's good that you are up here as there isn't any signal in Pavones."

"Any news on getting the air-conditioning fixed?" I asked. It had been mentioned to him several times, it only worked randomly which wasn't a huge problem at the moment as it was the coolest month of the year but it was going to start getting hot again soon.

"Yes! Have you seen the new *pulpería* just down the road?" Lenny asked me. I smiled, knowing this was going to be good. No, we hadn't seen it.

"With their high power fridges they must be draining all of the power from your transformer, that's why your a/c won't work properly."

Later that day we drove past a tiny little wooden hut. It hadn't been there a few days earlier.

"Is that what Lenny was talking about?! The new *pulpería*?!" I asked Crispin in amazement. "That man is sooooo full of 'ca ca'," I said. Crispin gave me a confused look. "It's a word I heard Coral use when she needed to go to the toilet yesterday," I explained. "It seems an apt word to use when talking about her father!"

60

Ernesto, the architect that Malcolm had suggested, had visited us and the house site a couple of times. When the house plans were ready we approached three local builders for quotes and we decided to go with Toli, Lenny's builder, as we couldn't afford the other two. The house we were going to build first would be a practice house (the guest house). We would live in this whilst we built the *cabinas* and then we would build the family house and the pool. We would then rent out the guest house. We wanted to get started on it straightaway as Mac's place was very small and Estrella really needed her own room, or rather Crispin and I really wanted our own room.

We told Ernesto that we wanted an open plan kitchen, dining room and lounge, two large bedrooms with walk-in closets and en-suite shower rooms. He suggested that we put the hand basins outside the shower rooms, apparently this is standard in Tico houses but it sounded like a daft idea to us.

He asked whether we wanted wood or tile floors – they cost about the same he said so we decided on wood for the bedrooms, hall and lounge and tile for the others. We also wanted a huge terrace that stuck out between two of the mango trees and he told us about *cara de tigre* a tree trunk called 'tiger face' because the pattern in it supposedly looked a bit like one. They are often used as supporting columns and Ernesto thought it would be a good idea to use them around the terrace. I wanted to use the thickest concrete block to build the house with as I felt it would be cooler inside. He thought it would cost roughly $80k and would take about six months to build. He seemed like a nice guy; competent too and in the early days he said he would visit the building site every week to check that everything was going to plan. It was very exciting designing our own house and fantastic that we would be living in it by the following May, a mere seven months away!

Ernesto had suggested various stores in San José that we should visit to look at tiles, lights, sinks, granite and everything else you need to choose when you are building a house. We were busy getting ready for the trip and were planning on spending at least a week away. We were almost ready to leave. It was no mean feat travelling with a baby, having to ensure that we had the cot; high-chair; cold weather clothes for the mountains; toys; change bag; snacks; water and that was just for Estrella. It took a couple of hours to get ourselves organised. Crispin was just walking out of the door to put Estrella in the car when he groaned.

"She hasn't?" I said, knowing that he had just smelt something horrible in her nappy.

"She has." He put her on the bed to change her whilst I finished washing up. Less than two minutes later Estrella screamed. It was the most awful noise I had ever heard. I spun around and saw our eight month old angel lying face down on the hard tile floor next to the bed. Crispin was nowhere in sight. He appeared a split second later from the bathroom.

"I only left her for a few seconds whilst I went to wash my hands," he said defensively as he scooped her up.

"Don't ever, ever..." I started to say in an icy voice and then stopped: it wasn't necessary. I was quite sure that Crispin wouldn't be leaving her unattended on the bed again. I took her off him and hugged her tightly, trying to soothe her, but she kept screaming.

"Can you grab the paracetamol?" I asked him. I somehow managed to get a spoonful of it into her mouth and she started to calm down.

"Is she okay?" Crispin asked.

"I don't know. She looks pretty dozy but I don't know if it's because she's tired, it's the shock or something more serious. Did you see if she banged her head on the tiles?" He hadn't. "I think we need to get her to a doctor. If we started driving to San José and something happened we would feel terrible."

Lenny and Karin were sympathetic and told us to find a friend of Karin's who lived next to the clinic in nearby Conte saying that she would help us get to see a doctor. Lenny said he would sort out a *cuidador* for us, someone to sleep in the house whilst we were away. Javier, his *cuidador*, wouldn't be able to, he said, as he and Karin were also going away for a couple of days and would need him to sleep at theirs. "Don't worry, I'll find somebody trustworthy!" Lenny yelled as we drove off.

Conte Clinic was a miserable place, boiling hot and full of sick people (obviously). It was my first time in there and I hoped it would be my last. Karin's friend got us in to speak to a doctor but he said Estrella needed a head x-ray and we should go to Neily hospital. We had heard that Golfito was probably the better hospital but there was no guarantee that the ferry would be running due to the build up of sandbanks and we could waste a lot of time trying to get there if it wasn't.

We broke our own safety rules and I held Estrella in my lap whilst Crispin drove to Neily an hour and a half away. She fell asleep almost instantly. It was really unusual for her to sleep at that time of the day and I kept watching her chest to make sure she was still breathing. I checked her head for the umpteenth time but it didn't seem to have any bruising.

We found the emergency department and sat whilst a woman plinked away on an incredibly old typewriter filling in our admissions form. It took a long time as we simply couldn't understand each other. Crispin eventually just handed over Estrella's passport and left the admissions clerk to find what information she needed herself.

We were sent to sit outside on two equally old and rickety chairs before being called into a room by a young male doctor. Between us, Crispin and I muddled through in Spanish what had happened to Estrella and explained how dozy and tired she had been afterwards. Estrella by this time had woken up and was looking pretty alert.

"Can she walk now?" the doctor asked. Oh, thank goodness he could speak a bit of English.

"No," I replied. He looked concerned and started to feel her legs. Estrella started giggling. "But she couldn't walk before either," I added quickly. "She's only eight months' old." He looked relieved and stopped feeling her legs. Next he shone a light in her eyes. As he bent over towards her, quick as a flash, Estrella took his pen out of his top pocket. Nothing wrong with her reflexes then either!

He continued to fill in his form, asking questions in Spanglish, us answering in Spanglish. "Do you give her tit?" he asked.

"I'm breastfeeding her, yes," was my curt reply.

Eventually he said, "She seems okay but she needs an x-ray to be sure." We went to find the x-ray department.

As I entered the x-ray room with Estrella my eyes lingered on the Spanish equivalent of a 'TELL THE TECHNICIAN IF YOU THINK YOU MIGHT BE PREGNANT' sign on the door.

I held Estrella still whilst the probe was held against her head. She didn't know what was happening to her and was crying and struggling frantically. It made me cry too.

Once outside we were sent to another room to wait for the results and Estrella, having forgotten her recent trauma, was now on top form. She was gurgling at everybody and waving and loving all of the "Qué bonita!" (she's beautiful) cries she was getting.

Another young doctor came in and called out a name. A woman seated near to us stood up and followed him. Five minutes later he came in again

"British Citizen," he called. How odd? Then I saw the form he was holding: it was Estrella's. Next to 'Name' it said 'British Citizen'. The admissions clerk must have copied it from her passport presuming it was her name. We'd given her a Spanish name to make her life here easier!

As we entered the room he already had her head x-ray on the light box. You could see a big crack running along her cheekbone. Oh my goodness, it looked awful.

"She's fine," he said.

"What's that then?" I said pointing to the crack. How could he not see it?

"That's just a vein," he said. "Everyone has that."

Phew! That was a huge relief. Crispin and I smiled at each other and cuddled Estrella.

"Oh, by the way," Crispin asked the doctor as we stood up to leave, "where do we pay?"

"I don't know," the doctor admitted. "Try going back to Admissions."

The admissions clerk shrugged her shoulders. "I'm not sure you have to," she said. Well, we think she said that! We thanked her and left, emotionally drained but very relieved.

6 Car Trouble

That night was spent in a nearby hotel and we continued to San José the following day. It was an exhausting few days, trying to find everything for the house that we needed, and shopping with an eight month old was challenging to say the least. Thank goodness for the phones on the electronic door entry systems in Abonos Agro. I'm amazed we didn't get thrown out of the store with all of the 'buzzing in' Estrella was doing with the display models.

We also spent a bit of time with our lawyer Artoodle getting various documents sorted out with regards to Urbano's 70 acre *finca* that we had recently become the new owners of. It was approaching lunch-time when we left his office to drive over to the other side of San José to look at yet more things for the house. We were on the main road out of San José, the one that heads up to the airport. All of a sudden, approaching the exit we needed, the car started to lose power; it started up the exit ramp and then simply ground to a halt. This came as a bit of a surprise as it had been running well since Don had fixed it.

A couple of days after we'd arrived at Lenny's he had taken us to see a Gringo mechanic called Don. He was a skinny, somewhat surprisingly for down here, non-surfer who was house-sitting for a friend in La Hierba (Grass), an area that is rumoured got its name from Danny's crop but nothing I have read seems to suggest he grew any of it down here, if he grew it at all of course.

Don gave the car a quick once over. "It's the solenoid," he announced. "You are going to have to go to the *frontera* to get a new one." The *frontera* was another name for the border town, Paso Canoas. "Okay," he said, "first rule: when you go to the *frontera* to buy car parts always take the original part

66

with you otherwise you will come back with the wrong thing, that goes for pretty much anything that you want to buy." What he didn't add was that quite often you were still given the wrong thing, but it certainly increased your chances of coming home with the right thing. "In the meantime, do this." He lay under the car and showed Crispin where to bash it with a spanner. "Try it now," Don said to me. I went press, press, crank and hey presto – it started! The car was to get many spanner bashings over the next few days, until Crispin had the time to take the broken part to Canoas to get a replacement.

The following day my window refused to go up. Maybe the car was rebelling over its frequent spanner bashings! A plastic bag and some tape temporarily fixed that problem.

Lenny gave us a ride to Paso Canoas with the damaged solenoid. It was the first time I had been there. It was a very bizarre place, as you drove along the Costa Rican road you could look to your right and see the Panamanian road not ten metres away. The official border crossing was at the far end of town and as the roads ran parallel for a mile or so you could cross back and forth easily enough just by driving over the central reservation. The road on the Costa Rican side was full of holes; the road on the Panamanian side was being redone with fresh smooth tarmac. Wow, I hadn't seen smooth tarmac for a long time. If you looked closer you couldn't help thinking that the road they were fixing was better than the road we were driving on.

Lenny swung the car over the thin strip of land that divided the two very different roads and parked in front of a shop that seemed to sell everything you could possibly want for your car.

"We're in Panama now," he said. "Illegally," he added. I felt quite daring but also a teensy bit scared. We went into the shop and waited to get served.

Estrella got loads of attention as usual with her blue eyes and blonde hair, which had finally started to appear so I could stop worrying she was going to be bald for life.

It was a strange system that took forever. There was a long counter that all of the salesmen stood behind. When you eventually caught the eye of one of them they would vanish into the back of the shop to see if they had what you were looking for. When you, and they, had found all of your purchases you were sent to the *caja* (till) to pay for everything. The *caja* was usually a girl sitting behind a piece of reinforced plastic with a calculator and an old style till. Then you were sent to the packing area where any electrical purchases were checked in front of you to make sure they worked. Then you picked up your purchases and could leave. Sometimes there was even a security guard at the exit to check off your purchases against your receipt. This system was the same in almost every store except the supermarkets and although incredibly slow for the customer at least there was no shortage of jobs for the locals!

Lenny did the talking, Crispin stood behind him waiting. Estrella and I wandered off to admire the fluffy steering wheel covers and brightly coloured tree-shaped air-fresheners.

"What's happening?" I asked Crispin, Estrella was getting bored and wanted to chew the air-fresheners.

"They don't have a replacement but have something similar so they are cutting bits off that and welding them back onto our solenoid."

"Sounds dodgy," I said warily, remembering Don's warnings.

"I know, but what's the alternative?" He was right, there wasn't one. Estrella and I wandered off again to count how many types of engine oil there were.

The fudged piece had worked perfectly and the car had continued to start for three whole weeks without any problems, until now. We got out of the car, stood on the grass at the side of the busy exit ramp and wondered what on earth we were going to do. I didn't expect the AA or RAC to arrive any time soon.

"Do our really expensive car insurance documents have any useful phone numbers on them?" I asked Crispin.

He reached across to the glove compartment, pulled out a wad of papers in a plastic wallet and leafed through them, "No, nothing useful at all."

"It's a shame we haven't got the phone number of the guy that we bought the car off," I said.

"There's a thought," said Crispin extracting the water bottle from its holder by the handbrake, then the loose change it had been sitting on; underneath was a business card.

"Where are we exactly?" Crispin asked his navigator. He had the phone to his ear.

"On highway one heading towards the airport, at the La Uruca exit," I said with certainty.

Crispin repeated what I'd said into the phone. "Yes, I'm sure it won't start. I've tried it four times now," he said just a teensy bit sulkily. You couldn't really blame the guy for asking after what had happened the last time he'd come out to rescue us. "He's sending a mechanic," he said hanging up. We were lucky; they weren't obliged to do anything.

We waited. I hoped I'd been right about our location, suddenly I thought maybe there were two La Uruca exits.

A car stopped and the driver put a tree branch in the road short distance behind us; that almost invisible warning to oncoming traffic. Then I remembered we had warning triangles somewhere in the car and set about trying to find them.

"Have you run out of gas?" the man with the branch asked.

No, we were quite sure that wasn't the problem. "Are you the mechanic?"

He said he wasn't and then drove off.

The warning triangles were set out and then we sat on the grass and waited some more. The shade we were sitting in was rapidly vanishing as the sun climbed higher in the sky. We were breathing in lots of carbon monoxide from the passing traffic and were also about to run out of water. Estrella had just drained the water bottle when the mechanic arrived. Hurrah!

He spent ages fiddling around with the engine before admitting defeat. "I'll call a tow truck," he said.

Our Spanish was still pretty awful so we had no idea where we were being towed to. We were eventually deposited outside a tiny dirty garage in a really horrible part of town. Thankfully they had a water dispenser and Crispin went to fill our water bottle up whilst a couple of grubby guys looked at the engine. I was sure we were going to be robbed and murdered.

"Are you getting out?" Crispin asked me handing me the full bottle. I declined thinking it would be safer inside the car. When the inside of the car became unbearably hot I ventured outside with Estrella and sat on her change-mat to avoid sitting on the filthy floor. We ate some snacks and waited. A huge mangy looking dog came over. Great we were going to get mauled now too. I tried to shoo it away but it was too interested in the crumbs that we had dropped. Now the heat outside was becoming unbearable too; sweat ran down between my shoulder blades.

It wasn't long before Estrella had fallen asleep on my knee. The mangy dog had eaten what he could and had left. Crispin was talking to the grubby guys. He had his little fingernail resting between his two top front teeth and he was nodding a lot. The look on his face said 'I have no idea what you are saying to me so I'll just nod a lot'. He used that look frequently.

All of a sudden he looked over at me, "We can go."

"They've fixed it?" I asked in amazement. He nodded, amazed himself.

"What was wrong with it?"

"I've no idea," admitted Crispin. "I didn't understand a word!" We were charged a tiny sum, weren't robbed or murdered and best of all, the car started first time. We drove off. Unfortunately, in our hurry to leave, I left Estrella's change-mat on the ground.

Whatever the problem had been it seemed to have been sorted out as we made it back to Pavones without any more delays. It was dark by the time we arrived home. There were no lights on in the house. Crispin opened the door and turned on the lounge light and I was surprised to see a strange little man asleep on our sofa. He had a Hitler moustache, looked vaguely familiar and it took a while to rouse him. If we had been burglars we would have had a field day!

When the little man eventually opened his eyes, he looked very shocked to see us and made to leave instantly. We tried to ask him where he was going to go as it was pitch black, we lived in the middle of nowhere and what's more, he was on foot. He blabbered away in rapid Spanish and then left.

"I hope he finds his brother's house okay," I said. "Who is he anyway?"

71

"I don't know," said Crispin, "I thought he said he would go and walk somewhere. I don't think he mentioned a brother. He does look familiar though doesn't he?"

"I know who he is." It had suddenly come to me. "The carpenter who came with Lenny that day to measure up for the built-in closet. The guy I originally thought was Toli's son." Where on earth was he going to sleep?

There was no sign of him the following day as we made our way to the beach in Pavones. It was the day of the surf contest that Lenny Loco had organised and we were going to show our support. I had made banoffee pies for the cake stall and hence started the Pavones addiction to them. It was a recipe I'd learned from an old house-mate (thank you 'H'). It was difficult to get double or whipping cream for the topping over here so I'd improvised and used *natilla* which is kind of like our sour cream. The flavours of the *natilla*, bananas, digestives and boiled condensed milk blended amazingly well and the new recipe was a huge hit. I'd also managed to work out how to make posters on the laptop so I helped out by doing the advertising for the event. It was a lovely day which brought the community together. Crispin took his camera as he wanted to try to get some good shots of the surfing and I spent a blissful couple of hours playing in the river with Estrella, Karin and Coral.

It inspired me to start thinking about organising something too. Something for the local kids. Perhaps a sandcastle building contest? I would bounce the idea off Heidi the next time I saw her. I'd have to make sure I got the tide right though, as it's no good trying to build sandcastles if there's no beach. Getting the tide right was something we hadn't been very good at recently. A few times now we had spent ages getting ourselves ready for a beach trip only to find when we arrived that we had the tide completely wrong and there was no beach. Probability says we should get it right about 80% of the time so we were pretty unlucky. The idea needed a lot of work anyway, and probably a tide timetable, which we knew they sold in the local surf shop but we hadn't managed to be in Pavones when that was open either! Our planning sucked.

More lack of planning would mean that the only things I would be organising in the near future were doctor's appointments.

7 Settling In

We had been trying to decide on a name for the *finca* for weeks now and it hadn't been easy. We had originally wanted a name that made sense in English and Spanish and would appeal to tourists e.g. the word 'toucan' sounds very similar in both languages but eventually we settled on 'Finca Estrella'.

It wasn't just because of our daughter but was also to do with the trillions of stars you can see from up there due to the complete absence of light pollution. I knew we were going to get some odd pronunciations and spellings, after all Estrella gets called 'Australia' by some people and even her own grandmother pronounces the 'll' in her name as an 'l' instead of a 'y' at times, but the name seemed to fit so 'Finca Estrella' it was.

So the 150 acre Finca Estrella which now incorporated both Lorenzo's and Urbano's *fincas*, needed a lot of work doing to her. The undergrowth needed cutting back, trees needed planting to re-forest certain areas, paths needed cutting, fences mending, the internal road needing putting in and the location of the lots thought about; Crispin really didn't know where to start. We desperately needed some *peones* (workers). We had previously been using Malcolm's guys. They consisted of the unusually tall Tico who we had bought our first two horses off, some of Lorenzo's boys and a quiet hard-working guy called Enrique, whose father incidentally had been one of only four original landowners in the area who hadn't sold his *finca* to the infamous Danny Fowlie. We wanted our own full-time workforce and Crispin figured that two guys would be enough. Malcolm agreed to let us keep Enrique but we still needed somebody else.

Crispin came home from the *finca* one day a happy man.

"I met a neighbour of ours today, Amado. He asked if I would employ his son. He said he was a hard worker and that if he ever gave me any trouble I was to let him know and he would flog him!"

"Reassuring," I said rather surprised. "I hope he was joking."

"He also suggested that his son could be our *cuidador* once we were actually living up there."

"We'll only need someone to sleep over occasionally when we are away won't we?" I said, thinking about the time that we had found Lenny's carpenter on our sofa.

"Look at Lenny and Karin," Crispin said. "They have Javier or his wife Cata in their house whenever they are out." He was right, Lenny was always saying 'my house is never left alone' plus Javier and Cata's four children were a near permanent fixture on the comfortable leather sofas, their eyes glued to the huge television which had hundreds of satellite channels, something they certainly didn't have in their little wooden house. I couldn't imagine having people in my house all the time, I was sure it would drive me insane.

"Surely it's not necessary and it's just Lenny being Lenny," I said.

"It's what all the Gringos do apparently. It's a poor area. Why tempt fate and get our stuff stolen?"

"But we don't have anything," I said.

"We have more than a lot of people here. Anyway, he'll be a 'handyman' too."

I could see I was going to have to admit defeat.

Amado's son appeared at the house the following morning to start work. His name was Freddy. I recognised him immediately although he looked much shorter than I remembered. It was the man on the horse who had helped with Lenny's car: Jackie's dad.

Freddy pointed to Estrella and said her name. "Jackie told me," he said in Spanish.

I understood and smiled. I drew my finger down my right cheek. "What happened to Jackie's face?" I asked in Spanish with a quizzical look on my face.

"It's a lunar," he said rolling his 'r' – something I was very bad at doing. I shook my head indicating I didn't know what he meant.

He continued talking and I grabbed the dictionary and tried my best to follow. I found his last word and looked up in astonishment, "Jackie's mother looked at a lunar eclipse when she was pregnant?" I repeated in Spanish. Freddy nodded and I laughed. He was joking right?
Freddy was smiling but it was a serious smile. "If it was a solar eclipse it would have been a red birthmark, a solar," he said earnestly.

Wow, he wasn't joking. Poor Jackie's mum, being blamed for that. He pointed to my leg. The left side of my left knee has a round dark brown birthmark.

"Your mum looked at a lunar eclipse too didn't she?"

"We don't believe things like that," I said.

"Really?" he said looking surprised. "What causes them then?" It was a good question and one to which I had no answer. I would have struggled explaining in English never mind Spanish.

"We are going to take her to see a doctor at the Children's Hospital in San José soon. She will be starting school next year and we're worried that she'll be teased. Kids can be cruel."

So Jackie wasn't at school yet. "How old will she be when she starts school?" I asked.

"Almost seven," he said.

Wow! I had started school at the tender age of three. It was a little private school around the corner from our house. We had recently moved to the outskirts of Birmingham, Worcestershire really, and the local primary school didn't have room for my older sister until the following year so she was going and I apparently wanted to go with her. I had hated it. The teacher was a dragon. I have vivid memories of her making me sit on the floor in the corner of the classroom with my back to the class. I honestly had not been able to see the vacant chair that she was pointing at, gesturing frantically for me to sit on it. She eventually got fed up with my disobedience and put me in the corner. Patrick Swayze wasn't to hand to get me out, it was a while before his "nobody puts Baby in a corner" line, so I was left there feeling very embarrassed. At break-time when the milk monitors came in with the milk crate and walked past me acting as if I didn't exist I could have died. Fifteen years later the dragon played a round of golf with my dad and wouldn't remember me. I certainly hadn't shed a tear when I heard years later that the school was being demolished to make way for more houses.

Maybe six going on seven was a better age to start school....

Freddy left with Crispin and the carpenter reappeared to install the built-in closet. He looked a bit sheepish, maybe he was embarrassed that he hadn't woken up when we arrived home the night he was supposed to be looking after the house.

"Where did you sleep that night?" I asked him. He fired something incomprehensible at me. "Más lento," (slower) I said.

After several failed attempts I found out that his name was Juan Carlos and began to understand his rapid Spanish a little better.

"I found one of Lenny's surfboard bags up there and slept in that." He looked very embarrassed and pointed in the direction of Lenny's house.

"Outside?!" I was mortified.

He nodded. "I lay awake all night terrified that a snake was going to cuddle up to me for warmth. I can't stand snakes." He was laughing now. I couldn't apologise enough but he brushed them away with his hand and continued with his work.

Toli's men were still working on the garage/bodega outside and they had just started cutting metal for the roof with an electric circular saw. The screeching noise cut right through my head and vibrated in my teeth. Juan Carlos then started banging with a hammer. I had put up with varying degrees of noise for weeks now but screeching and hammering were two things that I couldn't cope with. By the time Estrella started crying I thought my head was going to explode. Thankfully, at that moment the door swung open and Crispin walked in. "I forgot the tape measure," he said.

"Good timing, get us out of here!" I yelled above the din and we drove up to the *finca* for some peace and quiet. Crispin wanted to measure the house site. Ernesto's preliminary house plans had arrived and at 24m long for the kitchen/diner/lounge he was sure the house was too big for the site. We needed to check the measurements and then would phone Ernesto to get him to reduce the entire length of the house. Plus we wanted to feed the horses.

We were trying to get Gilly, George and Lucero used to us by shaking a bucket of horse feed and waiting for curiosity to bring them to us. It was working and now they came running. George, our newest addition was a bit of a bully and always tried to eat all of the feed before Gilly and Lucero arrived. Consequently he was getting fat. Gilly was also getting fat but for other reasons. She was pregnant and we were expecting a new foal the following year.

We popped in to see Lenny and Karin on the way. Javier was cutting a tree down with a chain-saw to improve the view from the terrace. Lenny wasn't one for getting his hands dirty. It took a while and the tree didn't exactly fall where it was supposed to but no one got hurt and the already stunning view did look marginally better. Crispin thought it was a great idea.

"Can I borrow that tomorrow so I can improve our view?" he asked Lenny.

"Yeah!" came the reply.

"Have you ever used a chain-saw?" I asked him.

"Sure, I borrowed my dad's when we were at the barn to cut branches off that big tree in the back, remember?" I really didn't. I was convinced it was utter madness and he was going to end up losing an arm. I didn't think my mother's sewing skills had been passed down to me, my sister inherited those, and we were a hell of a long way from the nearest hospital. Mind you, before law and order arrived here ('arrived' in the loosest sense of the word) in the mid-1990's, arguments were settled with machetes so there are quite a number of older *campesinos* (literally 'country folk') walking around with only one arm. Crispin wouldn't look too out of place.

"But have you ever cut a whole tree down?" I continued.

"No," he admitted.

We changed the subject and talked instead about birthdays. It was Crispin's the day after tomorrow and Karin's the day after Crispin's, on Bonfire Night. We told them what people did in England for 5th November: bonfire parties with lots of fireworks and friends and huge bonfires with a 'Guy' sitting on the top and I felt a bit sad that we wouldn't be doing any of that here. They invited us over for dinner to celebrate Crispin's birthday which cheered me up.

The next day I readied the video camera and Estrella and I waited on the terrace whilst the chainsaw whirred down below. Crispin had vanished into the undergrowth twenty minutes earlier. There were two trees that were obscuring our view of the surf at Zancudo Bay and he'd gone to cut them down. Suddenly there was a loud cracking noise and the tree to the right of the two that needed felling started to fall. It landed with a crash. I caught it on video.

"You okay?" I yelled.

"Yeah, how does it look?" he yelled back.

"Wrong tree!" I informed him. Silence. The chain-saw started up again. Fifteen minutes later we heard another crack and the tree to the right of the wrong tree also fell over. Crispin appeared a few minutes later looking hot and sweaty. I couldn't tell him that he had done it again because I was laughing too much. He slowly trudged up to the terrace to join me and Estrella so that he could see for himself.

"It's really difficult when you are down there," he said when he arrived. He had a hurt look on his face. "It's kind of in a dip and you can't tell which tree you need." I gave him a sympathetic look and handed him a welcome glass of iced water. He'd picked a hot day to do manual work.

He eventually got the right trees and it did make a big difference to the view. He then spent a bit of time posing for photographs with Estrella and the two cows that had wandered into the garden. We often had monkeys and toucans and even chickens but never cows before. Estrella was chuckling away and kept 'mooing' at them. A horse had also started wandering in recently. Rather bizarrely it was managing to close the gate after itself too. Lenny Loco hated its presence. The garden had recently been landscaped with hibiscus and nice grass and the horse just ate everything. Lenny was forever chasing it out, swearing at it and he even aimed his car at it once – just to try to scare it away. It turned out that she was pregnant and a local was putting her in the garden because there was lots of food for her. Once the foal arrived Lenny gave up the chase and left them in peace.

The morning of Crispin's birthday we had a cleaner called Bilkez start work with us. She was a pretty local girl and at 22 she was the eldest of six, soon to be seven, children. Her mum, who was about my age, was pregnant with her last child.

Bilkez had visited us a couple of times wanting to know if we needed her services. I had said no initially as I was perfectly capable of cleaning the house but her family lived nearby and they were obviously very poor and we wanted to help them out so I changed my mind. She had previously cleaned for Lenny and Karin, and came with their recommendation. We decided that, for the few dollars a week it was going to cost us, it would be worth having her for a couple of hours each weekday morning. Estrella would be on the move soon and the number of insects and amount of dust that accumulated on the floor was unbelievable; it needed sweeping thoroughly every day. Estrella loved Bilkez and although cleaning would never be her strongest point, she was brilliant with Estrella and I'm sure Bilkez significantly reduced the number of bugs that Estrella would otherwise have consumed.

Lenny and Karin hadn't let us know what time they wanted us for dinner. They were off to Paso Canoas and just said that they would let us know later. By 4 o'clock we still hadn't heard from them so Crispin called Lenny's cell phone.

"Come over when we are back," Lenny said.

"How are we going to know when you're back? Will you call us?" asked Crispin.

"Oh, you'll know," said Lenny mysteriously.

At 6pm we were just debating whether to give up waiting and put Estrella to bed when there was a loud bang outside followed by another one. Fireworks? We went outside and looked in the direction of Lenny's house as another rocket squealed its way into the heavens. BANG. It exploded in a shower of silver and gold sparkles.

"I guess they're home," I said to Crispin smiling.

Lenny was grinning inanely when we walked in. "Happy Birthday you big dummy!" he said to Crispin and handed him some huge rockets. "Got them in Canoas! You can find anything there."

Unfortunately it started raining so we weren't able to set them off but with Estrella asleep in Lenny and Karin's bedroom it was probably just as well. We would save them for another day. We gave Karin a copy of a 'chill-out' CD of ours and a black and white birthday card of a sexy man lying bare-chested on a car bonnet; it was something that I knew she would appreciate even if Lenny didn't.

"Come and look at these," Lenny said excitedly and we followed him into next-door. He lived in what Americans called a duplex and we call a semi-detached: two houses adjoining one another. Next door was owned by another partner in Lenny and Malcolm's real estate business, Dee. Dee and her husband spent most of their time in the States. It was the first time I had been into Dee's side. Lying on the kitchen countertop were a dead tarantula and two dead scorpions. Yuck. "I found them on the walls outside when we got back tonight," he said proudly. My mind once again went back to the day we arrived when we sat on his back terrace in the pitch black waiting for him to show up; a shiver ran down my spine.

During dinner I turned to Karin. "Have you ever been stung by a scorpion, Karin?" I wanted to know what to expect.

"Right here," she said lifting her shirt up and pointing to a spot just below her belly button on her perfectly flat belly. "It was hiding in my jeans."

"Did it hurt?" I asked curiously.

"Not too much," she said, "it was a bit like a bee sting but my tongue went numb too." I shivered a bit, not liking the thought of it. "I found one inside Coral's pillowcase one night," Karin continued. I was horrified. I was going to have to start checking inside the pillowcases now too!? I already folded our bedding up in such a manner that it had to be completely shaken out before you could straighten it and get into bed. It drove Crispin crazy but I knew if I didn't he would just climb into bed without checking for nasties. So far I'd only found a cockroach, a little lizard and some funny flat oval things that seemed to have a mouth at either end of their bodies which a long thin tongue moved in and out of. The tongue, if that is what it was, also served as a foot so they could pull themselves along the bathroom floor, fascinating to watch and better than any book whilst you were sitting on the loo. I had no idea what they were but made a mental note to invite David Attenborough over one day so he could film them and make a documentary about the new animal that we had discovered.

The conversation moved on from scorpions. "Why don't you buy a quad bike?" said Lenny randomly. "You could go up to the *finca* on it, Crispin, and it will use less gas than your car and it would mean Jo could still use the car." I was pretty much house-bound listening to the noisy builders when Crispin wasn't around. It was happening more and more recently and it was starting to drive me insane so a quad seemed like a good idea.

"There's a garage in Paso Canoas called 'Hayco' that usually has second-hand ones," Lenny continued. "I could give you a lesson," he said to

Crispin with a grin. So this was what it was really about: a new toy for the boys!

I waited in the car with Estrella for what seemed like an age. Crispin eventually came out of Hayco with a middle-aged woman and climbed into a car with her. She had on a very short skirt and her large boobs were barely covered by her skimpy top. I was a bit annoyed. He gestured for me to follow them so I clambered into the driver's seat and set off in hot pursuit. They only went a short distance and stopped outside what looked like a scrap metal yard, '*Hayco vehiculos usados*' was painted on the wall in Spanish. When Crispin appeared again he had a smile on his face which I was relieved to discover had nothing to do with the length of the woman's skirt, or the size of her boobs: he had found a quad bike.

It was delivered that night on the back of a trailer and Lenny appeared at the crack of dawn the following morning to give Crispin his first lesson. They were like giggling school kids as Crispin gingerly started the engine and then zoomed off up the driveway with Lenny hanging on for dear life. I caught the moment on video.

8 At one with Nature

Estrella was awake. I opened my eyes to find the room spinning. I quickly shut them again. I felt terrible, very dizzy and all I wanted to do was lie here and go back to sleep. Unfortunately there was a nine month old to see to.

"Could you grab Estrella, hon?" I asked Crispin in a weak voice, "I don't feel very well. I'm really dizzy."

He groaned.

Great, I could only imagine what his reaction was going to be when I asked him to stay in the house and amuse her for a few hours.

"Sure," he said, surprising me. He sat up and lifted Estrella out of her cot. "I'll get you some paracetamol. Do you want a cup of tea?"

Wow, the body-snatchers had replaced my husband in the night!

It was Saturday and I could hear Toli's team had already started work outside. I debated closing the windows but that would have meant moving and I really couldn't. I dozed off.

I awoke a bit later to Estrella's snufflings. Crispin must have put her in her cot for her nap whilst I was asleep. It was against the wall under the window and I pulled the curtain back to let some light in before leaning over her cot to pick her up. I suddenly saw something strange out of the corner of my eye and straightened up again. The top of the window frame was covered in wasps! There were thousands of them and my pulling the curtain back had disturbed them and started them swarming. I grabbed Estrella and ran out of the room yelling "Crispin!" at the top of my voice. If we'd had a door at that point I'd have shut it but I guess it was still on Juan Carlos' list of 'things to do'.

"What is it?" asked Crispin. He was sitting on the sofa reading one of my 'Now' magazines that my parents had sent over. An 'Independent' and a 'Heat' were lying next to him on the floor. I suddenly realised why he hadn't been desperate to leave the house this morning.

"Wasps," I said. "Millions of them!"

Crispin went to take a look whilst I stayed in the lounge still cradling Estrella in my arms. He came back looking shocked.

"What do we do?" I asked him. Never having had wasps nesting in his bedroom, Crispin wasn't too sure. "Aren't the builders outside?" I asked him. He went off to consult one and returned with one of Toli's sons, Einar.

"Fuego," Einar said. *Fuego*, what was *fuego*? Crispin didn't know either. I deposited Estrella on the sofa, grabbed the dictionary and started flicking through it.

"Fire!" I yelled. "He's going to burn them!!" I dragged the curtain back before that went up in flames whilst Einar got some newspaper and fashioned it into a torch. He lit the end and walked towards the constantly moving mass. After saving the curtain I ran to the far end of the lounge with Estrella, which was probably only six metres away but I hoped it would be far enough away for us to not get stung. The instant that Einar touched the flame to the nest the wasps went crazy; those that didn't drop dead instantly that is. It was amazing to watch. Thousands of them just dropped to the floor. Einar ran back into the lounge, brushing wasps off his arms and head and miraculously escaped with just two stings. The wall was slightly worse off with a big scorch mark.

We later learned that there are different types of wasps, and nests. The wasps that make the flat nests are considered lucky, although not for Einar

86

unfortunately, and are usually left alone. They are small and black and rarely sting unless provoked and I suppose you could say that having their house torched is kind of provoking them. The round nests however are nasty wasps and need getting rid of. Yellow and white wasps *pican muy dura*, which loosely translates as 'sting like hell'. The black ones the size of your index finger should also be avoided at all costs. Obviously, any inside the bedroom of your house need to go whatever shape or size!

It's funny actually because in England I am terrified of wasps and I'd even go as far as saying I have a phobia about them. I do actually go cold and start sweating when I see them; then I run like hell. My dad had always said, "Just sit still and they won't sting you" but I think it makes much more sense to run away and then they can't sting you and I stand by this philosophy. I am 34 years old and have never been stung by a wasp, or a bee for that matter. In fact I might have been once in Spain, posing for a photo with friends under an orange tree. My friend taking the photo told us all to jump pretending we were picking the fruit and something hurt my finger in the process. Anyway, except for that (and I have no proof it was a wasp) my run away technique seems to work. However, the wasps over here don't bother you the way they do in England. If you are sitting in a pub garden in the summer with a pint of cider they hover around you and land on you and try to get in your pint. Here they mind their own business so I don't mind them so much.

The following day we went for a walk up past the mango and palm trees where we were shortly going to be building the guest house. There was a beautiful garden on the other side of the road and Crispin had met the owner a few days before: a chatty Tico nicknamed Peter. He had insisted we went for a tour and it sounded like a lovely and different thing to go and do.

We entered through a rickety barbed wire gate which led into a cool shady area with some beautiful trees in which Freddy later told us you were almost guaranteed to see a troop of squirrel monkeys at 5pm. We then turned right and walked up the gentle grassy slope, I'm even tempted to use the word 'lawn' here, which led to a rancho at the top of the garden. Bordering the 'lawn' were many different varieties of brightly coloured flowers, and trees with bizarre shaped seeds hanging from them, some I recognised as house plants my mum had!

Peter walked down to greet us. He spoke Spanish slowly and clearly and was reasonably easy to understand. He was a born 'tour guide' and was obviously very proud of this little corner of his *finca*. He showed us different varieties of ginger and garlic and a fruit that after biting it, made a lemon taste sweet! As an aside, down here, everything you learn in life about citrus fruits and colours goes out of the window. You know the 'oranges are orange', 'lemons are yellow', 'lemon yellow' for that matter. Well the 'fruit and colour naming committee' definitely didn't do its research here in Costa Rica. Let me explain:

Limones (lemons) can be green with green flesh, green with orange flesh and as they ripen become orange with orange flesh. There is also the *limon dulce*, (sweet lemon), which isn't actually sweet at all but pretty tasteless and is the size of an orange but is yellow in colour and looks more like a small grapefruit. Oranges are green or orange. You would expect the green ones to not be ripe but they are incredibly sweet and nicer than any orange orange I've bought from a UK supermarket.

There were some green coconuts stacked by his rancho that Peter had knocked down prior to our arrival. They are called *pipas* when they are young, the coconut inside is still a creamy texture and *cocos* when they are old when the coconut is hard and used to make Bountys with I suppose. Peter neatly hacked the top off one with his machete and passed it around that so we could drink out of it. It was like sweet water and Estrella loved it. Apparently green coconuts are sweeter than orange ones. Yes, coconuts come in rainbow colours too!

Peter spent the rest of the morning pointing out the bird of paradise flowers, bougainvillea, hibiscus and a myriad of others that I instantly forgot the names of. He had some wild coriander the leaves of which were long and slightly prickly, completely different to the common variety but the smell was identical. He then pointed out a large thin curved fruit hanging from one of his trees. When they were ripe you could split open the tough green outer shell by twisting it with both hands. You could then suck off the sweet white flesh that coated the smooth brown seeds. The first time I tried it I thought it tasted like ice-cream and then discovered that the English name for the tree is ice-cream bean tree. "They are called *guava*," Peter said.

Now that was something else incredibly confusing. I imagined the first explorers pointing to the round speckled aromatic yellow fruit with the pink seeds, (more vitamins that any other fruit my sister told me recently) and asking a local, "What's that called?" The local, thinking he was pointing to the green curved things that grew on the tree next to it, says, "G*uava*" and the name gets noted in the botanist's notebook and the English-speaking world has a new (albeit mis-named) fruit. The yellow fruit that we know as a guava, in Spanish is actually a *guayaba*. To further complicate matters there is also the large green prickly fruit which tastes revolting and is called a *guayabana*. It's good for *frescos* apparently. A *fresco* is a watery sugary drink with a bit of fruit and a teeth-rotting amount of sugar in it. Whisk it all up in a blender and you have something drinkable, usually. If anyone says about a fruit "it's good for *frescos*" then you know that it's pretty inedible and don't try it. I learnt my lesson with a revolting little orange ball called a *nance*. The taste is indescribable, kind of sharp and fatty (there I tried) something that even a whole kilo of sugar couldn't improve, in my opinion.

It was a lovely, albeit confusing morning and I pictured us including something similar 'a *finca* walk' in our 'activities to do' when we had our *cabinas* built. I started to feel a bit sick on the way home but put it down to the variety of things I'd tried that morning or maybe too much coconut water.

9 The Run

Karin had been nagging me to go running with her for ages and it was something I would have wanted to do if it hadn't been for the following reasons:

1 It was hot,

2 It was hilly,

3 I wasn't used to being without Estrella and I thought I would worry about her,

4 Karin had told me that recently every time she went running she had seen a snake as it was now snake mating season,

5 I knew she would look gorgeous in her running gear and I really wouldn't.

Luckily, my trainers were in with our shipping and that hadn't arrived yet so, until recently, I had had a good excuse not to go. Unfortunately when we went to look for a quad in Canoas, Lenny had also suggested I buy some trainers (well, he had said 'running shoes')and being unable to think of a good reason as to why that was a bad idea, I had. Today was the day and I was feeling a bit apprehensive as I squeezed my post-baby body into my Lycra running gear. It still fitted so that was promising and the Lycra was holding any wobbly bits in.

I looked out of the window and was more than a little relieved to see it was chucking it down as I was sure Karin wouldn't want to go in the rain. She appeared at the door at 7am in her running gear. I guess I was wrong! She was soaked and looked amazing. Someone once described Karin to me as a 'goddess' - they were pretty much spot on. I've seen her with avocado smeared over her face and seen her prancing goat-like up near vertical hills in 25°C torrential rain – still a goddess.

"Are you ready Jo?" she asked me as she nimbly jogged on the spot outside our back-door, stopping occasionally to stretch her hamstrings. I kissed Crispin, then Estrella and nodded slightly reluctantly.

"Vamos!" (Let's go!) she said enthusiastically. As Karin sprinted and I ambled up the driveway Crispin caught the moment on video, probably focusing it on Karin's backside.

It was actually nice and cool running in the rain but it wasn't long before I got a terrible stitch. I walked for a while and then started running again. Several cars with surf-boards strapped to their roofs passed us and tooted their horns, tanned guys hanging out the windows waving madly. I was under no illusion that the display of testosterone had anything to do with me. As far as I know, no one has ever called me a goddess. My nickname in the university swim team had been 'Glow Jo' due to the bright red colour my face turns under exercise. It doesn't return to its normal colour for several hours. True to form I could feel it burning away brightly whilst Karin, chattering away, hadn't even begun to get short of breath.

"How on earth can you talk and run at the same time?" I managed to pant.

She laughed, "Oh, Jo, we've only just started!"

Eventually, Karin headed off the main road and up a steep driveway. You could see from the road that there was an abandoned rancho at the top.

"I'll wait down here for you," I said, glad of the rest. I didn't think I could run up any more hills!

"Come on, the view's great. Then we can turn around and go back."

"Okay," I said and stumbled up the hill after her.

By the time I jogged back down our driveway I reckon we had done about 3km and I was feeling really really good. I had actually done something for myself, and by myself (Karin didn't count), for the first time in ages. It felt like I had achieved something and I literally buzzed for the remainder of the day.

The good feeling lasted less than 24 hours. The next day I crawled out of bed, unable to walk. In fact, I could barely move; absolutely everything hurt. The phone rang.

"Karin for you," said Crispin as he handed the phone over to me.

"No! Tell her I'm out," I hissed, desperately wafting the phone away with my hand. Ow, even that action hurt.

"Out where?" he asked incredulously. He was right, where else would I be?

"Are you ready, Jo?" Karin's voice said in my ear. I could hear her doing little warm-up prances around the room.

"I can't walk, Karin! Don't make me go again! I don't think I can bend over to put my trainers on never mind find the energy to tie my laces!"

"No pain, no gain remember, Jo!" she teased. "It will do you good," she insisted but no gain was worth this. Thank goodness we were getting ready for a trip to Panama so I had a valid excuse not to go and could recover the use of my legs over the next few days.

10 Panama

As well as going over the border to explore, Ernesto, our architect, had told us that building materials were cheaper in Panama so we were going to check out prices. Lenny Loco advised us it was easier to get a taxi to Panama than it was to drive over yourself and besides, you needed permission to take your car out of the country and this we didn't have and weren't sure how to go about getting. We would try and find out for next time. Lenny suggested a garage where we could leave our car; it needed a couple of things fixing on it so they could work on it whilst we were away.

The border crossing at Paso Canoas is confusing and really really horrible; rather like Canoas itself. The town is aptly named as *canoas* is the word for the gutters on a house and it really is a gutter. The town has only two types of weather; boiling hot sunshine which sends up a revolting stench from the litter that piles up everywhere you look or torrential rain when the streets turn into open sewers, black rivers carrying the aforementioned litter, and fortunately the stench, away.

As you park the car, lots of young boys run up to you and start nagging you to let them look after it for the equivalent of 20p. They put cardboard on the dashboard so the inside only reaches 'ridiculously hot' as opposed to 'burning hot' and assure you they will guard the contents, although what a six year old boy is going to do against an armed robber I don't know

The long main street is 'one-way' indicated by the smallest sign in the world which is barely visible; almost totally obscured by a corrugated metal roof. Stalls line the street selling pirate DVDs and video games; knock-off designer clothing and; rather bizarrely, grapes, apples, giant-sized tins of mixed fruit in sickly heavy syrup and bars of every flavour of

Cadbury's chocolate. But be warned, it is made in Panama and, in my opinion is nowhere near as nice as the stuff made in Bournville down the road from where I grew up. I used to train in their company swimming pool and the energy used to heat the water came from the chocolate factory; I used to imagine myself swimming in a huge vat of chocolate. Mmmmmmmm.

If you manage to find a gap in the stalls and push your way through you reach department stores, (Wong Chang's is the good one I got my trainers from) and duty-free shops selling alcohol, aftershave and electrical appliances.

There was a huge queue of people at Costa Rican Immigration and we thought we were going to have to wait for ages. As we approached the chains that guided travellers to the Immigration window, the people in the line looked at Estrella in Crispin's arms and moved aside, gesturing for us to go to the front of the queue. It was incredible and we had no idea why. We filled out forms, our exit visas, and handed them back to the official sitting behind the barred window. He stamped our passports and waved us on. We walked back out into the busy road again and started walking towards Panama, not really knowing what to do next.

Articulated trucks lined the road and hundreds of red taxis inched passed us tooting their horns. A grubby guy with long dark curly greasy hair approached us on foot. I cringed and hoped we weren't about to be mugged. "Where are you going?" he asked in English. An American mugger! We ignored him.

"Are you going to David?" he persisted. Crispin gave me a sidelong glance and I could tell he was wavering. I stuck my nose in the air and tried to look like I knew exactly what I was doing and where I was going.

95

"I'll take you to Immigration," he said. I caved in and we walked alongside him hoping he wasn't going to rob us. He led us about half a mile to a guy tucked away at the side of the road sitting at an old table. To the right of him was a little barred window with lots of notices in Spanish around it. We had no idea what anything said. This was Panama Immigration?!

The grubby guy's name turned out to be Ken, like my dad but that was where the similarities ended.

"Give him three dollars, one for each of you and he'll put a stamp in your passports," Ken said pointing to the guy sitting at the table. "You can then go to the Immigration office." Ken pointed to the little barred window. He had to be joking. Surely table guy was a friend of Ken's and this was a scam so they could buy beer. Table guy couldn't actually be a Panamanian Civil Servant?!

Not knowing what else to do, Crispin reluctantly handed our passports over to table guy with three dollar bills. Table guy stuck a yellow stamp in each one then gestured us to go to the barred window. The guy behind the window gave us more forms to fill in. Crispin and I scribbled away busily. Once completed he took them off us, stamped our passports and, hey presto, we were free to go. Ken flagged down a taxi for us, we gave him a couple of dollars for his trouble and we were on our way to David, the nearest town in Panama which apparently had a shopping mall and a PriceSmart (an American bulk buy place that sells everything you could ever need and lots of things that you don't need but think you do!)

The roads were incredible, smooth as a baby's bottom. Surprisingly I was feeling a bit travel sick. It was something I used to suffer from an awful lot when I was younger but not so much now. I presumed it was because I was in the back of the car, travel sickness was worse then wasn't it?

There was a police check-point almost immediately but our passports must have been in order as we were waved through. I was feeling pretty queasy by the time we reached our hotel, again something that Lenny Loco had also recommended, and it was only when I collapsed on the bed that I thought I had better work out when my last period had been. I dug my diary out of my handbag. 48 days ago. Ah.

It wasn't conclusive proof as I'd only had one period and was still breastfeeding Estrella so my periods were bound to be irregular surely? I thought I'd better get some folic acid tablets, just in case. I mentioned it to Crispin in passing but assured him that it was probably something else as I didn't want to scare the life out of him if I wasn't sure. I felt quite excited as we went outside to find a *farmacia*. My sister and I were 15 months apart and were great friends. If I was pregnant then Estrella and the new baby would have about the same age gap. It would be wonderful that they would have each other to play with, I thought.

We spent the next few days enjoying civilisation. We did lots of Christmas shopping, bought half of PriceSmart and found a brilliant toy shop. Crispin collected prices for concrete block and sacks of cement and we took a day trip to a little town in the mountains called Boquete. We had some friends that lived there, people we had met when we were taking Spanish lessons during our previous ten week trip and they had recently left Costa Rica to go and live in Panama. We didn't have an address for them but, ever optimistic, thought we may bump into them if we wandered around for long enough. We hailed a taxi outside the hotel.

"Boquete," Crispin said to the driver. He zoomed off in the wrong direction and stopped outside a bar. He yelled at a woman and motioned her to come over and then borrowed her cell phone and called somebody. He turned and smiled at us and gibbered away in Spanish. I had no idea what he was saying so just smiled back at him. He drove off again, still driving away from Boquete. Were we being kidnapped? How long did we leave it before we said something? I looked at Crispin and he just shrugged his shoulders. "Maybe he knows a shortcut," he said.

After a few minutes we stopped outside a house. A woman came out. She was middle-aged and wore stilettos and a short tight skirt (wrong, wrong and wrong) and hastily thrown together make-up, she was still applying her bright red lipstick as she tottered up the path. She climbed in the front seat and we drove off again. "Es mi esposa," the driver said to us. Finally we understood. He had decided to take his wife out on our day trip!

They dropped us at the park in Boquete and we had a lovely day. The temperature was nice at that altitude, almost cold even. We didn't find our friends but did stumble across a new development called the Hidden Valley which had a bar that sold really good hot chocolate. We also found a second-hand book shop and spent a fortune in there; it was difficult finding books in English in Costa Rica so we really stocked up. The owner gave Estrella a blue teddy bear whilst we were browsing to keep her amused and to ensure we weren't distracted hence maximizing the money we spent. Very clever man.

When we got back to Canoas we, rather embarrassingly, couldn't remember where we had left the car. Our taxi driver spent almost half an hour driving up and down identical back-streets in the pouring rain and the pitch black trying to find the garage. He was a Panamanian taxi driver, it was a new car, and he wasn't used to driving on Costa Rican roads. Bang. He drove into another axle-breaking hole. We all cringed and I could almost see tears in the driver's eyes!

There is a weekly English newspaper here called 'The Tico Times' and the first issue I read had a letter from an American guy on the fascinating but often depressing 'Letters' page. He said that he loved Costa Rica but felt the country had two problems: litter and giant potholes in the roads. He continued by saying he felt one was the answer to the other. He suggested putting the litter in the holes. Ta-da. Only thing was, he suggested first standing at the edge of the hole and yelling just to make sure there wasn't some poor soul stuck down there in his car.

"Try this next right," said Crispin beginning to panic. It looked vaguely familiar but that could have been because we had already driven down it four times. Suddenly we saw the garage up ahead; our car was parked on the forecourt. Crispin handed the taxi driver a large tip and he smiled for the first time, his car axles briefly forgotten.

11 Birthday Cake

Back in Pavones we had our first party to go to. It was Bilkez's sister's 15th which is the equivalent of our 18th. At the tender age of fifteen Costa Rican girls are considered to be women! Seems crazy to me. She would be pregnant within the year but that's another story.

We had forgotten to buy a present and wrapping paper seemed impossible to buy around here so I wrapped up a giant Toblerone (courtesy of PriceSmart) in white printer paper that Estrella had decorated with crayons. I was very sad to see it go. Nice chocolate is very hard to come by!

Most of the families living around us were poor but Bilkez's family was one of the poorest. The only family members with paid jobs were Bilkez and her older brother. They lived in a tiny wooden house at the corner of the road that led up to our *finca* and the party was to be in the garden. Rosie, the birthday girl, was very quiet and shy and although I had met her several times with Bilkez I had never heard her speak. It was rumoured she was seeing one of Lorenzo's nephews who was at the party but I never saw them speak to each other. I immediately spotted Freddy and Jackie and steered Crispin over to them.

"Margarita and Yailin," said Freddy introducing his wife and younger daughter. Margarita had Jackie's stunning smile and long dark hair. Yailin was also beautiful and had a head full of ringlets. She was a year older than Estrella but Estrella was already a lot bigger than her. I knew where Estrella's old clothes would be going.

One of Bilkez's younger siblings appeared with a drink for me. It was thick and purple. I looked at Freddy for guidance. "It's good," he assured me. I took a sip, more of a slurp really due to its consistency. It resembled the glue we used to make out of flour and water when we were kids.

100

"What is it?" I asked Freddy. Turned out that there was a reason why it resembled flour and water: it was a special kind of purple corn that they ground to a flour and mixed with sugar and water. It was incredibly popular over here and I later noticed all kinds of flavoured cornflour in the supermarket for just that purpose.

Another of Bilkez's siblings appeared with a plate of *arroz con pollo* (rice with chicken i.e. lots of rice with tiny bits of chicken and vegetables, coloured with annatto which is a natural red dye and is reeeeaaally difficult to wash out of party clothes!) and crisps. They were standard fare at birthdays and weddings. It was tasty and I gratefully accepted seconds. Freddy took Estrella off me so that I could eat unhindered.

It was something I was going to have to get used to: people, often strangers, taking my baby away from me and walking off out of my sight. It freaked me out (and Estrella when she wasn't in the mood) for a long time but Ticos love babies and they love cuddling babies but they also, I think, really do it as a kind gesture to give you a break so you can eat in peace or just to give your arm a rest. I eventually got so used to it that when we did take trips back to England I found it strange that the English didn't do it. The downside to this is that Estrella was often handed back to me clutching a lollipop or a handful of boiled sweets. As for Ticos wanting children to have constant sugar rushes and rotten teeth, I don't understand that side of it at all. Lack of education is my only suggestion, and I am constantly confiscating Estrella's 'stash'.

The garden went quiet and a man with a cowboy hat that we didn't know started singing in Spanish. He had an amazing voice and was fantastic to listen to. I pictured him serenading our diners if we ever got around to having a restaurant.

Estrella was still sitting on Freddy's knee when the cake was brought around. Tico cake tends to be quite dry and almost always has *dulce leche* (boiled condensed milk) spread in the centre and over the top. This had the *dulce leche* but was surprisingly nice and moist. I finished my piece and glanced over at Estrella. I was horrified! Freddy was feeding her a huge piece of cake! She was nine months old! She was supposed to be eating fruit, vegetables, lean meat or chicken and unrefined carbohydrates - I had read all about it in Annabel Karmel's baby recipe book. Tico cake didn't fall into any of these categories. Not knowing what was politically correct in these situations – was it rude to take her back? - I nudged Crispin and nodded towards the horror that was unfolding before my eyes. Estrella had finished off her first piece and had now started on Freddy's. Crispin also looked horrified and went to rescue Estrella's teeth before Freddy could give her the coca-cola that he was reaching for and later admitted was intending on giving her!

The next day was Sunday and we set off to find the swimming hole that Lenny Loco had told us about. We drove past the road which led to the *finca* and took the next right. The road looked pretty bad even by Costa Rican standards so we left the car at the top of the hill and walked down to the river past some beautiful rainforest. We paddled through the blissfully cool river and continued up the hill a bit until we reached the spot that Lenny had described. There was a bend in the river and it had carved out a deep pool, deep enough to swim in. The water was clear and you could see hundreds of little fish darting about. A tree had fallen over and had conveniently stretched itself across the pool. It was at the perfect height for Estrella to jump off into Crispin's arms. She loved it and was very happy floating about with her armbands and floaty vest on as long as she could hold on to one of us.

We hadn't been there long when we heard voices and presently Bilkez arrived with the majority of her brothers and sisters. Her grandmother, Emilse, lived at the top of the hill and they were on their way to visit her. We had met her at the party the previous day, a lovely little lady with gold teeth, a stunning smile and beautifully smooth skin. She was an amazing woman and lived on her own *finca* in a little house without electricity. She had invited us up there and we promised we would go and visit her when we could. I'm ashamed to say that almost a year would go by before we would keep our promise.

As Bilkez and her entourage waved goodbye, one of the youngest gave me a smile that would have been beautiful except for two things; the rotten brown front teeth.

12 Fatima

Summer officially started on 15th November, a week ago (the day we went to Panama) and today was a typical summer's day – hot and humid. Crispin had left the house early to walk around the *finca* and probably to let the news sink in; he still looked a bit dazed. We'd bought a pregnancy test in Neily the previous day. As well as feeling sick, for a while now I've had a stuffy nose and then there was that strange smell when I went to the loo which I don't think any pregnancy book or leaflet has ever mentioned as a sign but was a dead giveaway where my pregnancies were concerned.

Anyway, by the time we'd got back from Neily and unpacked all the shopping and got Estrella to bed and then waited for my bladder to fill sufficiently it was 11pm. We sat on the sofa holding hands, watching my hormone-loaded urine moving across the little white window, waiting for that little red line to appear.

My sister had had an ectopic pregnancy in May and she said that her line had been really faint which can indicate problems. There was a slight possibility that I was already pregnant when Estrella had her head x-rayed and I couldn't get the 'tell the technician if you might be pregnant' sign out of my head. What were the consequences I wondered if I had been pregnant at the time of the x-ray; would we have a deformed baby?

The line appeared, my hormones had done their stuff. It was strong too so that was a good sign. I looked at Crispin, I was smiling. Crispin just looked shell-shocked.

"Are you pleased?" I asked him, I was worried now.

"Pleased," he said, "but shell-shocked. Estrella's only nine months old!"

"I'm a bit worried about Estrella's x-ray," I said and I told him why. I slept badly that night thinking about it. I was also concerned about how my sister was going to take the news. I was sure she would be upset. She was older than I was, had only one functioning fallopian tube and desperately wanted a baby. I would have to tell her soon but wasn't looking forward to the phone call.

I was desperate to get out of the house and tell someone our news. After our day in hot, sweaty Neily, which is quite a pleasant place if you compare it to Paso Canoas, Estrella and I both needed some fresh air so I put her in the pushchair and headed towards Lenny and Karin's house. By the time I reached the top of our driveway I was already breathing heavily. I couldn't believe the run I had done with Karin the previous week! I kept remembering something a friend had told me a couple of years ago: if you are out of breath then the baby isn't getting enough oxygen, I stopped to rest. The next bit towards the gate was flat but then once on the road it was all uphill. I took it steadily and kept stopping to adjust the parasols to keep the sun off Estrella, who had dozed off. It still amazed me how she could sleep whilst being bumped up and down and lurched crazily from side to side but kids are strange creatures aren't they? I made it to Lenny's driveway and then stood at the bottom looking up, blimey it was hot. They had recently put material on it, big lumps of rock that would have been great had I been driving but were going to make the steep driveway almost impossible to manoeuvre the pushchair up. It would have made sense to leave it at the bottom and just carry Estrella up but I didn't want to risk waking her so I laboured on. It took a while, the front wheels kept hitting large rocks and refused to budge without extra effort. Halfway up I glanced up at the house and noticed that Lenny's car wasn't there. Maybe he'd gone out and Karin was in. I continued on up. I reached the top red in the face and out of breath. The lengths you have to go to to visit your nearest neighbour eh? I banged on the door. No answer. Damn. I looked through the windows in case they were just pretending to be out. But, unless they were hiding under the beds or were flat against the wall behind the bathroom door (I would still have been able to hear Coral yelling anyway) they weren't in.

I adjusted the parasols once again and started back off down the hill, it was going to be much easier going back, downhill all the way. I reached the road and saw Cata with a pretty young woman whose long dark hair fell in spirals. It was really unusual to see hair like that on a Tica. She had two young children with her: a boy a few years older than Estrella and a girl maybe as little as six months older. They stopped to chat. "This is Fatima," said Cata. "She's married to my brother, German."

Fatima went completely gaga over Estrella, as was the norm. "Look at her blonde hair, white skin and blue eyes," said Fatima, "como un gato!" I was always being told that Estrella had eyes like a cat.

"Hola Estrellita," said Cata. Estrella was now wide awake.

"Que gordita Estrellita," (little Estrella, what a little fatty) continued Fatima. I managed to force a smile. If 'ita' is added to the end of a word it means 'little' e.g. 'Estrellita' means 'little Estrella'. The 'fat', so *gorda* or *gordita*, comment is used an awful lot in Costa Rica and is considered to be a term of endearment. Ticos say it to their wives a lot. Having grown up in a very different society, I hate the expression and find it quite insulting.

To change the subject I pointed to my belly and said, "She'll have a brother or sister soon."

"Pregnant?" Fatima said in English. Ah, she spoke a bit of English, that was very unusual. I nodded and said my name was Jo.

"Joy," she smiled. I was a bit confused and then realised it was an attempt at my name.

"No, Jo," I repeated.

"Joy," she said again. I forced another smile and let it go. It was a problem that several of the locals had. It frustrated me – it was only two letters for goodness sake! Mind you, I find it impossible to pronounce *pero* (but) and *perro* (dog) any differently and often confuse *ordenar* (to tidy) and *ordeñar* (to milk – as in 'a cow'); Bilkez would sometimes give me strange looks when asked to tidy our chest of drawers, at least that was what I thought I was asking her to do!

Fatima and her family were moving down from San José. German had been a long distance lorry driver but was now tired of it and was looking for different work.

Over the next couple of weeks they built a little house from concrete blocks and plasterboard opposite our gate and strung an electric cable from Cata and Javier's electric meter. German seemed like a really nice guy, quiet and unassuming, not unlike Cata. She was Lenny and Karin's cleaner, Javier their *cuidador* and they were a lovely family. He was also the local vicar, an odd religion that banned dancing, music and alcohol but, each to their own and I wasn't going to hold that against him.

Fatima came round to see me one day. She caught me at a bad time as I'd been on the phone to mum and was feeling very emotional and hormonal. I was missing her a lot and had had a bit of a cry; more of a lot of a cry really. I'd also called my sister to let her know I was pregnant and she had reacted how I had expected her to react. I tried to play my pregnancy down and told her that we were trying not to get too excited about it because of what the x-rays may have done to the foetus but she was silent and I knew she was trying to hold back her tears. When she started talking again she said that she had to go and quickly put the phone down. It wasn't fair and I knew it. It made me very sad and I wished more than anything in the world that I could give her a hug.

I tried to explain to Fatima that I missed my family and friends, Crispin was out a lot and wasn't much of a talker even at the best of times. I was a 'people person' and I felt pretty lonely. It was nice to have someone to talk to although I'm not sure how much she understood through my tears, occasional heaving sobs, and with my appalling Spanish.

She said she was from Nicaragua (so she wasn't a 'Tica' she was a 'Nica') and had met German when he was doing one of his long distance lorry journeys, she also missed her family. She seemed nice and I naïvely felt that I may have found a friend.

After Fatima left, the phone rang again. "Hi Jo," said my sister's voice. She had managed to get her feelings under control again.

"Are you okay?" I asked.

"I'm sorry. I'm sorry I couldn't talk to you or congratulate you. I just feel it's my turn now."

"You don't have you explain. I understand completely. It is your turn and it is unfair. You'll be pregnant again soon though," I assured her.

"My chances have halved now though haven't they?"

"How long had you been trying when you got pregnant last time?

"A month."

"Well this time it will take two months then won't it?" I had maths A' level.

She laughed and it was a wonderful sound. "I've done some research on the effect of x-rays and you would have miscarried instantly and you didn't so you'll be okay." She had her scientist head on now.

"But it still might be ectopic," I said, trying to make her feel like she still might be able to have a baby before me.

"You'd be in agony if it was. Absolute agony," she said. She was welling up again.

"I wanted to get on a plane that day y'know. I desperately wanted to give you a hug but Crispin wouldn't let me!" I was being a bit unfair to Crispin as we also didn't have the money for flights to Oz and there was also three month old Estrella to consider but he wasn't around to defend himself and he had said at the time that it was a daft idea.

"That would have been amazing," she said, "the kind of crazy thing you would do." I could hear the smile in her voice.

Her ectopic pregnancy was something my sister and I hadn't talked about very much after the event, after all she was living in Australia at the time and I was a sleep-deprived new mum so I'm ashamed to say that there hadn't been much opportunity to chat. I had never had the chance to tell her that I had felt some of what she had been going through.

"It was the left side wasn't it?" I asked her. She didn't answer and I could feel her confusion; that she didn't know where the conversation was going. "Your left fallopian tube," I clarified. One Saturday morning, I felt a sharp stabbing pain in my left-hand side where I assume my left ovary is. It was severe enough for me to grab my side, double over from the pain and comment on it to Crispin. It didn't stop until we were halfway to my parents' house in Birmingham after the horrible phone call from my dad telling me that my sister was in hospital in Sydney undergoing emergency surgery.

I tried not to cry whilst I told her what had happened.

"I was wheeled into surgery at 11pm local time, that would have been 2pm UK time," she said through her tears. "And yes, it was the left fallopian tube," she managed. It meant that my pain had stopped a little while after they wheeled her into surgery. I'm guessing it was the exact moment they relieved the pressure caused by the growing foetus that had lodged itself in her fallopian tube and her pain stopped too. We both sat there, on different continents, bawling our eyes out and desperately wanting to be together.

A couple of days later it was Fatima's turn to arrive crying. She spoke quickly and the only bit I understood was that they were without electricity and she was worried that scorpions would sting her little girl. Our power was always going out and we certainly weren't short of our fair share of scorpions but even in my hormonal state I didn't cry about that. I must have missed something important. I asked her to slow down and explain again. She did.

"Cata and Javier have cut our electricity off. We had a line from their meter. Their bill this month was 12,0000 colones (about $24) higher than usual. We couldn't pay so they cut us off. But it couldn't be our fault, we don't use much electricity." Tears were still pouring down her face.

It was a fair assumption for Cata and Javier to make, it was a sizeable jump in their electricity bill and they had attributed the excess to the additional cable that had been strung from their meter to German and Fatima's house. Javier, the vicar, with the season of goodwill fast approaching, had cut the cable leaving German's family without electricity.

"We don't have the money to pay them, German doesn't have a job," Fatima wailed.

I was suddenly on my guard when I realised that it wasn't a shoulder to cry on that she wanted, it was money. We sympathised and then Crispin and I conferred.

"We could give her the money," Crispin said.

"I want to help them too but if we give them the money then the same thing is going to happen next month isn't it?" I argued.

"You're right. I could see if Toli can use German on the house but they aren't due to start building for another couple of weeks," said Crispin.

"Can you use him on the *finca*?"

"Maybe, I'll speak to Freddy and Enrique and see if there's enough work. At least he'll be earning some money until he can find something more permanent."

"We'll see what we can do," Crispin told Fatima as she left.

The whole family returned later that night. They were all crying! German was bravely trying to hold back the tears but they were certainly welling up in his eyes. Fatima spoke for him, she always did the talking.

"Cata's been throwing rocks at the house," she said angrily. "One made a hole this big in the plasterboard wall and almost hit my little girl." She placed her perfectly manicured fingertips together and made an 'O' with her fingers. I couldn't believe it. It seemed pretty odd behaviour for a vicar's wife; my mother-in-law was one and I couldn't see her doing it.

"Why on earth would she do that?" I asked.

"I don't know," she said. "She's crazy!" The whole episode seemed very odd and out-of-character for Cata.

Crispin offered German a temporary job on the *finca* which he accepted, and a beer, which he also accepted and some wages in advance which he also pocketed. Fatima then asked if she could charge up her cell phone. I thought it strange she could afford

111

to run a cell phone when they couldn't afford to pay a $24 electricity bill.

"I need it so my mum can call me every Sunday," she said, reading my mind. They left what seemed like ages later with a fully charged phone and all of our torches and spare batteries, oh, and all of the ice from our freezer.

Our power went out that night and we were left sitting there in the pitch black, regretting we'd been so generous with the torches.

After that the visits came almost daily. Sometimes Brian, the little boy, came alone; sometimes Fatima came with Brian and Lis, his little sister. Sometimes they wanted ice, sometimes the phone needed charging. Once it was because Brian's birthday was coming up and she wanted to make pizza. She needed to borrow an oven. I didn't have one so she left empty-handed for a change. She returned later looking very sad. She couldn't afford to make pizza she said. I was getting sick of hearing the phrase "No tengo plata" (I don't have money) and dreaded their visits. I had complained about being lonely, I needed to be careful what I wished for. Fatima now wanted a cake recipe instead. I found a couple and translated them for her as best I could then sent her away with my kitchen scales and a cake tin. She returned them the next day, turned out that she couldn't afford to make a cake either. I was determined not to give her any money for a cake as I was sure that was what she wanted. I was beginning to see her as conniving and manipulative and I certainly regretted ever crying in front of her.

We were due to go to San José the day before Brian's birthday. I had my first pregnancy scan booked and we needed to continue to look for tiles and toilets and other stuff for the house. My iron resolve wavered the night before we were due to leave.

It wasn't fair that Brian wouldn't have a birthday cake just because his mother was the way she was. The following day, as we drove out of our gates, Brian was walking in, phone and charger in his hand. He held it up, gesturing and Crispin nodded and asked him to plug it in in the bodega, there were electrical sockets there. Brian spotted the pineapple and star fruit cheesecake on my lap.

"What's that?" he asked me.

"Never you mind," I replied smiling. His eyes lit up and he broke into a smile and I knew that I'd made the right decision.

13 For the want of a phone line

We had just packed away the rest of our shipping in the still unfinished bodega. It went back into the cracked plastic boxes it had arrived in. It had turned up that morning in the back of a dirty pick-up truck fresh from the customs men. It was wonderful to see everything again; our books and clothes and pans even the beautiful Purbeck stone chess set from a quarry in Dorset that we had received as a wedding present. It was like Christmas had come early. Amazingly, only two things were broken; one of the stone chess pieces and our electric bug swatter that was shaped like a tennis racket.

Estrella was in seventh heaven as she peered into boxes and 'helped' by yanking the bubble-wrap off things and throwing books all over the floor. There still wasn't an awful lot of room to put anything so most of it got packed up again. As we now had a closet in the bedroom, the rickety old chest of drawers had been moved into the lounge and functioned as a book shelf.

With the unpacking dispensed with, I sat on the floor in my dungaree shorts which were the only shorts from my normal clothes (as opposed to my maternity ones) that I could comfortably wear. I was staring at all of the Christmas presents that I had to wrap from our Panama trip. It was December in a couple of days' time and I really had to find the motivation to do them so they could be posted off. If only I could stop throwing up. At least my cold felt better now. I'd had a couple of days tucked up in bed with Estrella. We had both felt pretty rotten. The first day of our colds Crispin went off to the *finca* and left us to cope on our own. I was annoyed as the last thing I wanted to do in my state was look after a sick baby and the last thing Estrella wanted was to put up with a sick mother. I just wanted to curl up in a ball and sleep all day and she just wanted lots of attention so I was in a foul mood when Crispin eventually came home. Luckily, for him, he got the message and made up for it the following day: he stayed at home and looked after both of us.

Crispin hated being stuck in the house and I was to find myself left there with Estrella more and more as my pregnancy progressed. He was usually either at the *finca* or off somewhere with Lenny Loco. As we were dividing Urbano's *finca* into lots to sell he spent a lot of time walking around it trying to work out where the building sites were going to be, which was the best route for the road to take, how was he going to get electricity up there, etc. Lenny, from what I could work out, just introduced him to different people or showed him new pieces of land or they simply hung out together. Lenny was also our local newspaper and always knew what was going on: who was arriving, who was leaving, who was buying, building or selling. Sometimes things got exaggerated I am sure but he was certainly an entertaining guy to have as a friend.

Our human newspaper arrived one day with two bits of news. One was that we had new neighbours. There was a new couple in town: a Gringo (Les) with a Tica wife (Carolina). They were building a nice hotel in town and would be managing it. She was from San José had experience in hotel management and spoke English flawlessly; Les was a surfer and he arranged trips for clients to Costa Rica.

They were renting the unfinished two-bedroom house nearby that was roofless when we'd first looked at Mac's place. It had been our 'other option' that wasn't really an option. The house now had a roof but had no bug screens and huge gaps all around the windows. The place was crawling with bugs and a cockroach had crawled into Carolina's ear in the night. They'd driven the hour and a half to Neily hospital to have it taken out. My skin crawled just thinking about it but it was nice to know that we had new neighbours and vowed to look out for them.

(They would never have much luck with bugs. The first time I met them, halfway through our conversation, there was a loud buzzing noise and we were suddenly surrounded by a swarm of bees. Les yelled, "RUUUUUN!" and I didn't need telling twice. I had no idea whether they were the aggressive African killer bees or not and I had no intention of finding out. I grabbed Estrella and ran as fast as I could back to the house closely followed by Les whilst Carolina, rather sensibly, ran in the opposite direction and jumped in their truck which was a darn sight closer than our house).

Lenny's second bit of news was even more exciting. "ICE are releasing a whole load of new phone lines tomorrow." We really wanted another one because, as Crispin was out so much he had our phone with him so I never knew when he was coming back, or if he really was dead in one of those ditches, and he could never phone me to let me know he was going to be late.

"Where will I have to go?" asked Crispin. Lenny didn't answer him; he was standing in front of the fridge rearranging the fridge magnets.

"Lenny?" Crispin asked again.

"I love these things," Lenny said deep in concentration. "Oh, Neily, at the main office."

"I've got to pick something up from Artoodle," Crispin said, "so I was thinking of going in to Neily tomorrow anyway. I'll just go in earlier." I was confused.

"But Artoodle isn't in Neily is he?"

"No, but he needs me to sign something so he's sending it down on the bus."

"How?" I was still confused.

"He bought it a ticket." I had visions of this big envelope sitting comfortably on a bus in a reclining

116

chair, with headphones on. "He gave me the ticket number and I have to go to the bus station with my passport and ta-da," he finished. So the bus company, Tracopa, also served as Royal Mail, or Consignia, or Royal Mail or whatever they are calling themselves nowadays. Clever. You know, they text you your phone bill here too. How clever is that? And you can pay your electricity bill at the *pulpería*, the little food shack that sells batteries, toilet paper and tomato purée and other useful stuff - the bills get left there at the beginning of the month. I don't yet know how the bills get to the *pulpería* but I'm picturing a toucan with them in his bill (ha ha) or more likely a little man on a motorbike. And another thing, the best thing ever actually: pregnant women (and people with babes in arms – hence why we queue-jumped at Costa Rica Immigration on our Panama trip) automatically get ushered to the front of queues, without anybody glaring at them. How cool is that?! I can assure you THAT doesn't happen in Tesco's. Unfortunately we didn't know that little bit of trivia the day Crispin went to get our new phone line.

I looked at the fridge after Lenny had left. I scanned the mass of words searching for Lenny's new sentence 'eat green vegetables', 'miss your vast magic smile', no, those were already there. Ah, there it was: 'the long hard hot naked summer of love' it read. I rolled my eyes and smiled.

Crispin left the house at 4.30am the following morning without waking us. Estrella was having trouble shaking off her cold and was very grumpy. I felt very nauseous but managed to force some breakfast down me. It reappeared twenty minutes later.

Whilst Estrella was having her morning nap one of Lorenzo's nephews, the guy from Rosie's party who was now her ex-boyfriend, came to see me. His family were regular visitors and normally we enjoyed seeing them although their visits were a bit strange as they usually arrived at sunset, Estrella's bedtime, and normally with a baby in tow (wearing a woolly hat oddly enough!) We didn't want to invite them in; partially out of embarrassment as with a baby and nowhere to put anything, our place usually looked like a bomb had hit it five minutes after Bilkez had finished cleaning it; but also because, although it was the size of a shoebox and wasn't yet finished, the house was a million times better than the rustic wooden shack where they lived; finally we were wary about having people in the house as we had so much and they had nothing in comparison. This resulted in us sitting outside in the ever increasing darkness with the mosquitoes; yes, they had finally discovered Pavones.

Anyway, I was in no mood for seeing anyone that day. We sat on the terrace, me with my head in a bucket and Rosie's ex trying to make polite conversation. After I had vomited for the seventh time he made his excuses and left. I didn't blame him and was glad to see him go; I was surprised he'd stuck around for seven.

I then spent the afternoon the way I spent most of my mornings and afternoons; amusing Estrella. I made 'dancing dollies' - chains of boys or girls cut out of a fan of paper. She loved waving them around - making them 'dance' - whilst I sang 'dancing dollies la la la' over and over again. I had seen a photo in a book of a heavily pregnant woman lying on a bed with a young child; a book open between them. The article talked about what you could do to 'rest' whilst you were still spending quality time with your child. So, I had perfected the art of making dancing dollies whilst lying on the floor with Estrella surrounded by pillows for when I inadvertently dozed off and she fell backwards. Every now and then I would 'come to' with a jerk and extract the paper from her mouth and start mumbling 'dancing dollies la la la' again.

When she tired of this we would move onto 'folding the washing' which consisted of me emptying the contents of the dryer over her. She would pull everything off her head and appear grinning, if I did manage to fold anything she would grab it off the sofa and throw it on the floor. When she tired of this I would open the bottom kitchen drawer, we now had them, and lie there whilst Estrella took out its contents and put it all over me. I hope Estrella remembers it as quality time.

Lenny Loco arrived later in the afternoon to find me lying on the floor covered in plastic food storage boxes, lids, plastic pastry cutters and ice cube trays; Estrella was sitting on my tummy. He looked at me without an ounce of surprise, as if this was completely normal behaviour. "I saw Crispin in a line of people outside the ICE office this morning," he said. "There were like a hundred people in front of him. I took him something to eat."

"A hundred people!" I got to my feet and starting throwing things back into the drawer. Estrella was protesting, not yet tired of the game. She grabbed a lid out of the drawer and threw it on the floor.

"There were more than that behind him. He's going to be a while yet. Why don't you come up to the house with me and Karin can fix you something to eat?"

"I would love to, thanks." I had started to feel a bit better and was now glad of the news, the company and the thought of someone else cooking my dinner.

"Where are you going to have the baby?" Karin asked me. It was something that Crispin and I had discussed and didn't agree on.

"Crispin wants me to go to the local hospital in Golfito," I said miserably. Malcolm had told us that his children had been born there. His son was the first baby to use their brand new kerosene-powered incubator. Call me stuck up but I didn't want to give birth in a place without air conditioning, where they may not have up-to-date equipment to deal with a medical emergency and where I had to eat rice and beans three times a day. Karin wrinkled her perfect nose.

"Golfito? You don't want to do that. I had Coral in CIMA. It was nice."

"It's like a hotel," Lenny chipped in.

"What's CIMA?"

"It's a new private hospital in Escazú, San José."

"Did you have a c. section?" I asked. She nodded.

"I had a mirror placed above me so I could watch the whole procedure." Yuck! I was definitely going to give the mirror a miss. "He's gorgeous," she said as I wrote down her doctor's phone number.

I heard the car pull into the garage at 11pm. I threw my arms around Crispin's neck as soon as he walked through the door.

"Not crying?" he asked surprised.

"Lenny warned me that you would be late but I was just beginning to think you were dead in a ditch."

"I was so pleased to see him, he was amazing. He brought me some lunch over. I was starving but didn't want to lose my place in the queue so couldn't go and get anything."

"You've burnt your face and neck, you wally." Normally it was nothing unusual, he could never be bothered to put sun cream on, but he had taken an umbrella with him for shade knowing he could have a long wait.

"There aren't any trees outside the ICE offices and it was boiling hot so I lent the umbrella to a woman with a young child, I figured they needed it more that I did. How are you feeling by the way?"

"A record 11 times today. Seven of those were when Lorenzo's nephew was here." He gave me a big hug. "How did it go anyway?"

"Well, I got there at 6am and there were already at least a hundred people in front of me, the queue stretched right around the building."

"What time did the offices open?"

"Not until 7.30am. At about 9am I started talking to a Tico standing next to me. He said that I needed a phone and the receipt or they wouldn't give me a line."

"You're joking! Why do they do that?"

"So that only those who really need them buy them and people don't buy them in bulk and sell them on at a higher price. So I had to go and buy a phone. All of the cheap ones had gone unfortunately. He also said I needed various photocopies so I got those done and went back to ICE."

"You didn't have to go to the back of the queue again did you?"

"No, fortunately the same guy saw me and let me in again."

"How many people did ICE have issuing the lines?"

"Three. I got to one of them at 7pm after queuing for 13 hours! I was sure I would be missing a document and kept expecting the clerk to say something but he didn't, he just stamped everything to say it was all okay."

I listened in amazement; things were never this simple in Costa Rica. Just the previous week we had decided to drive to Panama for the day. Juan Carlos, the carpenter, said we needed to go to Neily to get permission to take the car out of the country. When we got to Neily we were told that he was wrong and we had to drive for five hours in the direction of San José – San José is completely the opposite direction to Panama by the way. Of course, we arrived at the office we needed five minutes after it had closed so had to find a hotel for the night. <u>Nothing</u> is easy over here.

"That's brilliant!" I said but Crispin held his hand up.

"Hold on, I've not finished yet. He went away, to get the next available number, came back and said 'we've run out of lines, you'll have to come back tomorrow at 5.30am'," Crispin was laughing. The heat must have got to him.

"No!!!! All that time and you didn't get one?" He was still laughing, shaking his head. "Can you go to the front of the queue tomorrow?"

"No, he said I had to queue again with everyone else." He wasn't laughing any more.

"There'll be a hundred less people," I said, trying to be positive.

The following morning I had to nudge Crispin awake. The beeping alarm was getting louder and louder and he was so exhausted he hadn't heard it. I made him a coffee whilst he showered. Estrella, still not well, was in the land of nod. She normally slept through the night now and religiously had two cat-naps a day of a miserly twenty minutes. We tended to nap on the bed together, along with her cuddly caterpillar and her dummy, and I used to dread the twenty minutes being up. Some days I would worry about it so much that I couldn't actually go to sleep and would lie there listening to the noisy builders, frantically willing sleep to come. In no time at all I would feel Estrella move and the bell inside her cuddly caterpillar would tinkle and I would know that she was awake and that precious opportunity to nap had gone. I was incredibly jealous of the mothers who said their child slept for two hours during the day, something that Yailin did regularly even now and she was approaching two years old! Maybe we would be that lucky with the next one.

Crispin arrived home at lunchtime triumphant. After queuing for half an hour, the kind Tico from the previous day had spotted him. He was right at the front of the queue and gestured for Crispin to join him. After that it was plain sailing. I would never complain about British Telecom's service ever again.

14 Hospital Visits

"Would you make me some flyers for my house?" Lenny asked me one morning. "I want to sell it." Although I knew he had bought a small piece of land near the beach over by Greg and Heidi's I was surprised and also a bit sad at the thought of losing him and Karin as neighbours.

"Is that the same house that you said you were going to stay in forever and not sell?" teased Crispin.

"I want to pay the bank back so I don't have a choice," he said seriously, not realising that Crispin was teasing him. I hadn't realised that he'd built it using a bank loan.

"How does Karin feel about it?" I knew that she loved the house.

"She's okay about it," he said shrugging his shoulders. "All I need to do now is find a builder seeing as you guys stole mine."

"It was you who suggested we use him!" said Crispin. I kept quiet; Lenny didn't yet know that we had stolen his prized carpenter too. Juan Carlos had just agreed to work on our new house; he would rather work for us he said.

"Sure, I can do you some flyers," I said, wanting to change the subject. He handed me a sheet of paper with his writing on and a CD with photos on it.

"I'll come and get them after lunch," he said.

"I won't have time to do them by then!" I said indignantly.

"Why not, what else do you do all day?" he said grinning cheekily. I threw a tea towel at him.

"Why don't you come work for me in the office? You could do a flyer for each of the properties on our books too."

"Are you offering me a job?" I asked amazed and also flattered.

"Sure," he said.

"What am I supposed to do with Estrella?"

"Bring her with you."

I pictured the small office near the beach; I could feel the intense heat, the computer cables perfect for chewing on and yanking and see the open doorway with the steep steps. I shuddered. I also hated the thought of someone else looking after Estrella. What was the point of having her if I wasn't going to be with her? Then I thought of having Lenny as a boss...

"Lenny, I couldn't," I said eventually. "You would drive me insane!" He laughed, gave me a crushing bear-hug and left.

"I've got to go and show clients round a *finca*," he yelled as he reversed up the driveway.

A couple of days later Crispin arrived back from the *finca* mid-afternoon with some disturbing news about him. Dee, Lenny and Malcolm's business partner and the woman who owned the unfinished half of Lenny's duplex (where he kept his dead arachnid collection), had stopped Crispin in the road. She said that Lenny was very ill and was in hospital in Neily having various tests done. They didn't know if it was a mosquito-borne illness i.e. dengue (you do hear of cases down here occasionally) or malaria (which you don't) or something he had caught whilst he was out surfing. The bulk of the surfing down here is done at the mouth of the Rio Claro (Clear River). Pavones is the name used by tourists and guide books but you will never hear a local Tico calling it that. Pavones takes its real name 'Rio Claro de Pavón' from the river and the bay that it empties into, Pavón being the name of the bay 'Bahía de Pavón'. Incidentally we live in 'Cuervito de Pavón'.

Anyway the Rio Claro wasn't always a very aptly named river; notably when the trucks working on the road drove into it to wash themselves off creating small slicks of oil, diesel and all the dirt that they had accumulated. There wasn't a garbage collection so locals threw their rubbish into the rivers and the odd pig almost certainly paddled in there too. So, although it was *claro* compared to a lot of other rivers in the world, it did have its problems. One theory was Lenny might have inadvertently swallowed some pig poo. Dee said she would let us know more when she heard.

The following day Lenny and Karin hadn't returned and we had a very important 'house meeting' in Golfito with our architect, Ernesto, our builder, Toli, and our carpenter, Juan Carlos.

The meeting was to agree on a labour price with Toli and talk about Juan Carlos' scope of work and agree a price with him too. We also wanted to change the house design a bit. As I was pregnant and we had spent quite a bit of our money on Urbano's *finca* we figured we would have to live in the guest house for longer than we had originally planned so we wanted to modify it slightly. We were keeping the two bedrooms and the two walk-in closets but were changing one of the en-suite shower rooms and making it into a third bedroom. The remaining en-suite shower room would no longer be en-suite but would be a family bathroom big enough to house a large shower and a corner bath (I had spent a lot of time in the bath when I was pregnant with Estrella and, towards the end of my pregnancy, it was the only place I felt slightly comfortable so I desperately wanted one). Finally we were adding a small bathroom that would just have a toilet and hand basin in. We were going to have an outdoor shower too so thought that this and the indoor one would be sufficient for when we had visitors.

"Don't trust your builder to order your construction materials," Ernesto said to us in English, "they are all paid a commission by the builder's merchants," he explained. "I will do it instead." I glanced across at Toli, feeling very uncomfortable that Ernesto was talking about him in this manner but Toli showed no signs of understanding and was busy scribbling in a notebook. I guess we should have been pleased that Ernesto had our best interests at heart but it didn't feel like that. Ernesto had been talking to Toli and Juan Carlos like they were beneath him and I was going off him rapidly.

"I'll get a new set of plans incorporating all of your changes to you and Toli by next week," Ernesto said efficiently.

"Great, that fits in with when Toli wants to start building," said Crispin.

Taking Ernesto's advice we agreed a 'labour only' price with Toli.

"I know people who've got suitable wood for sale and I'll continue to ask around for more," said Juan Carlos. "We are going to need a lot of wood." He had just confirmed that he would do our roof structure, beams, floors for the lounge, hallway and bedrooms, terrace, doors and windows.

"I'll speak to Artoodle and get contracts drawn up for you both to sign," said Crispin. I suddenly caught a whiff of Estrella's nappy.

"I'll go and change Estrella's bum," I said.

On our way back from the meeting we drove up to Lenny's house to see how the patient was doing. Karin opened the door. Lenny was curled up on one of their leather sofas clutching his stomach; he looked terrible. Karin looked tired too.

"I can't believe they let you out," I said.

"They didn't," Lenny replied in a weak voice. "I refused to stay in. We stayed in a hotel last night. After we got the results this morning we got a taxi back here. I've got really bad cramps in my gut and I'm so cold all the time." I could see he was shivering, for once the air conditioning wasn't running.

"Do they know what it is yet?" I asked him.

"No, they've ruled out dengue and malaria and they're doing more tests."

"Dee said you might have got it from surfing."

"I don't think so. I was walking round a *finca* with clients after I left you and I sank knee deep in all this mud and cow shit in the corral. That's where I think it came from."

"Why don't you get yourself some wellies, you idiot?" I said to him.

"Wellies? What are wellies?" he said with an English accent. At least he hadn't lost his sense of humour.

The next day Lenny looked even worse and Karin, Crispin and I debated what we should do with him. One of Karin's nieces was staying with them and was supposed to be returning home to Neily that day so we offered to drive her and also take Lenny back to Neily hospital. The niece said she had a cousin who was a doctor at the hospital and called him once we were on our way. We left him in what we hoped were reasonably good hands and promised to visit the following day. We left one of our cell phones with him so he could call us and Karin if he needed anything.

The following day I waited in reception in Neily hospital with Estrella whilst Crispin checked on him. I didn't want Estrella to catch anything and, being pregnant, I didn't want to catch anything either. Crispin was a big boy and could look out for himself.

"It's lep... something or other," Crispin said when he came back.

"Leprosy?" I said, smirking at his inability to remember anything after more than two minutes had elapsed.

"No, something else."

"Leptospirosis?"

"That's it."

128

It was one of the options I'd come up with after trawling through my 'Merck Manual', looking for a diagnosis. Weil's Disease is a severe form of it and it is caught from an infected animal's urine or contaminated water or soil. It can enter through broken skin. Cut feet are pretty usual for surfers around here because of the rocks, but the majority of them then don't walk through animal corrals with flip-flops on. At least they now knew what it was and could treat it with antibiotics.

Crispin said that Lenny was starting to look a little better but he wanted desperately to leave. It was an eight bed ward and he had just had a terrible night. The guy in the bed next door was a crack addict and had screamed all night, someone else had been admitted with a gunshot wound, another guy had dengue and the guy in the bed opposite him had died. Lenny had had very little sleep, looked knackered and wasn't totally convinced he was going to make it out of there alive. Crispin reassured him as best he could (considering he was a bloke and blokes are crap at that sort of thing) and said his goodbyes, not because he too was secretly expecting the worse but because we were off to San José for my first meeting with Karin's handsome Gynaecologist.

15 First Scan, First Visitors

I loved going to San José. It meant eating in restaurants and not having to cook. TGI Friday's was a favourite; it was like being back in Covent Garden in London. It meant lots of lovely shopping. There was another PriceSmart that sold exactly the same stuff as the one in Panama, still stuff that we didn't need but bought anyway. It meant Estrella and I got to see Crispin all day, even though Estrella amazingly spent most of the time asleep. Crispin couldn't escape from us; he had no *finca* to hide in. He hated it.

Unfortunately, it also meant being stuck in the car for hours in horrendous traffic. We were trying to get from one side of San José, where Jack and Sofia lived (they had split up – twice - and were now back together again) to the other, where the hospital and most of the tile and light shops were. It was fine driving from west to east, from the hospital to Jack's, as you could just drive straight through the middle of the city but the crazy one-way system didn't allow you to drive from east to west without me getting us horrendously lost. I was trying to find a better route and had the 'Lonely Planet' guide book open at the maps' page.

"I don't understand why we can't get on it," I mumbled.

"On what?" asked Crispin.

I sighed. "There's a thick line around the bottom of the city, look." I shoved the book under his nose.

He pushed it away frowning, "I'm driving!"

"I'm sure it's a ring road but I can't find it." I was getting frustrated.

"Oh, so there is actually a plan then? I thought we were just driving randomly," he snapped at me. I glared at him. How dare he suggest there wasn't a method to my directions.

"Go that way," I said to him, pointing.

"Left or right."

"I don't know, THAT way," I said sticking my arm across his face.

"Why have you got the 'Lonely Planet' upside down?" he asked turning right. He was gunning for an argument, so was I.

"I'm a woman," I snapped, "and that's what women do. Our brains are wired differently to yours. Better," I finished. We had stopped at traffic lights. There were millions of them and they were always on red when you arrived and stayed red for at least five minutes. During rush hour the traffic police arrived too to make sure the traffic lights were obeyed or ignored depending on what kind of mood they were in and whether they wanted to delay you more. I suddenly noticed that all of the traffic in the street opposite was pointing in our direction.

"Damn!" I said out loud. It was happening a lot. The traffic either side of us would suddenly veer off to the right without warning. Somehow everybody else knows that the road in front is 'one way'. I snapped the 'Lonely Planet' shut and dropped it dramatically in the foot-well. We were once again stuck in San José's crazy one-way system.

We spent the next two hours inching along narrow streets squished between buses and hundreds of local merchants, their carts piled high with unrecognisable fruits and mobile phone accessories. It was a nightmare but I think what made it worse for Crispin was the radio. I had discovered Evan Luck at 99.5 Radio Dos. Although he was no Chris Moyles, whom I missed with a passion, he was an American DJ who told us daily that it was 'another beautiful day in paradise' and played 'the best music from the 70s, 80s, 90s and today' all morning. We picked up the signal as we were coming down out of the mountains about an hour from San José and from then on it was

Bananarama, Duran Duran, Wham, Howard Jones...
I was in heaven and it drove Crispin insane. Evan
Luck also read the commercials and his voice had
this rare quality about it that made everything he
said entirely believable. He made me want to try the
'all-day brunch at Café de Artistas' and buy the 'office
building that was up for sale in Zapote'. The man
would be dangerous if he ever got in a position of
power!

On prior visits we had stayed in the middle of
San José at a casino hotel that Jack had
recommended as it was managed by a friend of his.
Jack and Crispin would hit the casino in the
evenings; Crispin even managed to pay for our stay
once with his winnings. There were huge mirrored
wardrobes in the rooms that I could sit Estrella in
front of and she would amuse herself for ages, almost
long enough for me to eat my room service dinner.
She could also run up and down the long hallways in
the walker that Jack and Sofia had bought her. The
hotel did the most amazing breakfast buffet and we
would start with juice and fresh fruit and move on to
eggs and bacon and rice and beans followed by
Danish pastries and muffins. It was $100 a night
though and although ideal in lots of ways it was a
long way away from the hospital. This time we were
staying at a small hotel that Lenny and Karin had
recommended. It was right over the other side of San
José, much closer to the hospital, had a swimming
pool, lots of colourful bougainvillea that reminded me
of my childhood holidays in Portugal and was almost
half the price of the casino hotel.

The hospital was a mere five minutes away,
brand new and very impressive. The hour long wait
wasn't quite so impressive.

"Let's find the stairs," I said to Crispin
eventually. I sincerely hoped my doctor would be

quicker than the lift; Estrella got bored with books and toys very quickly nowadays.

"It's your turn," I said to Crispin. He took Estrella's hands from mine and left the waiting room to continue walking her up and down the corridor. I very gingerly straightened my back and then eased myself into a seat – wow that was hard on the back! I picked up a magazine and leafed through it. A tall man with a nice smile came out of the next door office occasionally to escort a presumably pregnant woman out and another presumably pregnant woman in.

Crispin only lasted five miserly minutes. When he came back in, he was almost bent double.

"Your turn again. My back's killing me," he complained. I sighed, took Estrella's hands in mine once again and set off down the corridor. I noticed some potted plants at the far end; maybe we could go and check those out. I wondered if they would let us bring her walker with us the next time.

Eventually it was our turn to be escorted into the office. Dr Smile had trained in Germany and his English had a slight German accent to it. He remembered Karin (who wouldn't I thought) and entered notes into his computer whilst I gave him my medical history.

"A previous caesarean doesn't necessarily mean a second one but the scar tissue is in danger of tearing, especially with it being a relatively recent caesarean," Dr Smile said.

Tearing, ummmm, I didn't like the sound of that. "If we do go for the natural delivery option," 'the tearing option' I thought, "how long before my due date will we have to come up to San José to stay?"

"A month." Wow, I liked San José but not that much. "You've got plenty of time to think about it," he said. "Let me take your blood pressure." He put the cuff on my arm and I was just about to mention the 'please tell the technician if you think you may be pregnant' sign after Estrella's bed rolling incident when she started to squirm on my lap. Crispin took her outside and my 'baby brain' forgot what I had intended to ask and I was left with that familiar 'wasn't I about to say something really important?' feeling.

After another long wait, a different doctor performed the ultrasound scan. Estrella sat on my tummy and rubbed her fingers in the cold gel. A little wriggly thing appeared on the computer screen and I reached out for Crispin's hand. He took it. Suddenly the sound of a heartbeat filled the room. I looked at Crispin and he smiled at me with tears in his eyes. It was suddenly very real.

"You are going to have your hands full in July," the doctor said watching Estrella trying to grab the computer cable. "Everything is absolutely fine," he added. "The head is big but still normal." From the dates he calculated from the measurements he had taken I realised that I couldn't possibly have been pregnant at the time of Estrella's head x-ray. It was a huge relief.

There was lots of good news when we got back home. Lenny was out of hospital and on the mend. He had lost an awful lot of weight and needed Karin's home cooking and one of my banoffee pies to put some meat back on his bones. The other news was that Toli had started building our house on December 13th. It was so exciting going up to the site and seeing the string pegged out showing the house outline. The side that we were converting from an en-suite bedroom into two bedrooms and the small bathroom wasn't pegged out yet as Toli hadn't received the revised plans from Ernesto. Ernesto had assured us he would be attending the site every week in the early stages and had also said he wanted to see the outline pegged out to make sure the house was in the right place. Surely he would arrive soon.

Unfortunately Toli's team were unable to wait and had already started digging out the trenches for the foundations for the side of the house that we weren't changing and the through lounge/diner/kitchen at the back of the house.

I told Toli about the baby's due date and he now said they would have the house finished in June. I also thought he said something about having attended his daughter's wedding the previous weekend. He must have more than one daughter, I thought, as I had met a daughter called Angie but she was just a child, certainly not old enough to get married.

The good news continued: Fatima and German were no longer around and had gone to live in Laurel near the bank. German had found work there which was great for them and fantastic for me and worth the fact I would never again see the Pyrex dish that I had made Brian's birthday cheesecake in, even though it had been shipped over from England and I was very fond of it.

Finally, and the best news for me; Lizzie and Steve were arriving imminently. I was so excited! I was exhausted from our trip, nauseous and bad-tempered but more than anything I was excited. They were good friends from England who had been travelling in South America for a year and were on the final leg of their journey. They were currently in Panama, catching a bus to Canoas and Crispin was going to pick them up. Their bus was due in at lunch-time so I hoped, taking into account the queues at Immigration that they would be here before it got dark. They would be our first set of visitors. Our second and third sets would closely follow as Matt and Sharon were arriving from Canada on the 26th December bringing a double 'go anywhere' three-wheeler pushchair with them as ours was proving to be pretty impossible to manoeuvre on these roads and Kathryn and Kevin, friends we had met whilst travelling around when I was pregnant with Estrella, would be with us in time for New Year's Eve. The four of them were renting Dee's side of Lenny Loco's duplex. Lenny had considerately moved his gruesome arachnid collection!

Lizzie and I had tears in our eyes when we finally hugged. Not too unusual for me admittedly, I was crying a lot these days. We had often been mistaken for sisters but now her long red curly hair was almost blonde, bleached from their year-long adventure in the sun, and maybe a bit of bottle. She was a bit on the skinny side too, courtesy of a very long bout of diarrhoea and had seen the inside of a hospital in most South American countries. They had enjoyed their trip but were glad to be seeing familiar friendly faces and to be staying in the same place for a couple of weeks; even though it meant sleeping on an inflatable mattress in the lounge, which was never quite as inflated the following morning, and having a ten month old climbing all over them at 5am, thrusting books and toys in their faces.

We decided we would take it in turns to cook and wash-up at meal-times and Lizzie and Steve dug out my cookery books and hungrily looked through the recipes. After months of managing on a tight budget and eating rice and beans, not to mention Lizzie being unable to eat properly for a long time, they wanted 'real' food.

"Baked potato and salad." Lizzie's eyes had a faraway look in them.

"Fish finger butties and baked beans on toast with cheese on top," I added and my mouth watered in spite of my nausea. Maybe I was finally moving on to the cravings stage of pregnancy. I found myself wondering if Heinz would ship their baked beans out here (I later found a company on the internet that would ship me a tin from the UK for $50!!).

"Oh, you've got the 'Food for Thought' recipe book," Steve said with interest picking it up and leafing through it. It was from a vegetarian restaurant in Covent Garden near Crispin's office where he had bought his lunch from daily. Crispin had now lost the weight he'd accumulated eating their desserts. (To be fair, it was probably the bacon and egg croissants he had consumed at Guildford station every morning that had caused his triple chin). I had never used the book. I had opened it when Crispin brought it home one day but it didn't have any photos in it and I couldn't see the point of a cookery book without photos so I'd closed it again.

"I used to go there for lunch every day," Steve said.

"So did I," said Crispin. Wow, that was a coincidence.

"It's got their 'scrunch' recipe in it!" Steve added excitedly.

"Really?" said Crispin, "I used to have that every day for dessert."

"So did I," said Steve smiling. Lizzie and I smiled too: the boys, neither of them particularly sociable, were bonding.

I joined in the hunt through the cookery books. My Chinese one was well thumbed but the others had barely been opened. It was certainly about time they were put to good use. We ate well over the next couple of weeks and I discovered a skill that I never knew I had: cooking. Breakfast was always fresh fruit but for lunch and dinner we had lemon chicken with egg-fried rice, meatballs with mushrooms and cheese, spinach and ricotta cannelloni, French peasant soup, fresh pineapple cheesecake and, of course, scrunch.

It was so nice and normal to have a girlfriend to sit and chat to for hours, in English. Better even than going to a Debenhams' sale. We walked around the *finca* together, went to the beach for sunset and showed them the house site where the walls were already starting to go up as Toli had got fed up waiting for Ernesto; our architect had vanished off the face of the planet. They loved everything they saw and Steve couldn't grab his camera quickly enough when 'our' toucan, perched in the tree outside the house, started his daily noisy ritual. ('Mournful cry' a friend would suggest when asked how best to describe the noise a toucan made). We all joined Steve by the garage and stood there watching the toucan throwing his head back, listening to his friends answering him. I was usually busy getting Estrella ready for bed at that hour and barely had the time to register hearing his 'mournful cry' never mind glance at him through the window. He was stunningly beautiful: black with a yellow and red 'bib' and a green flash across both eyes, I was really glad that I had paused in the middle of changing Estrella's nappy to see him.

One day we were invited to Enrique's parents' house to eat deep-fried pork and pig skin on the front terrace. They are delicacies called *chicharrones* and are very popular at this time of year. At Christmas everyone slaughters the pet pig that they have been fattening up for the previous 12 months. Locals actually have pig slaughtering parties but we have always purposefully arrived late to them, thankfully missing the gory bit.

I was struggling a bit through my plate of *chicharrones*. One of the rinds still had quite a lot of pig hair sticking out of it and I think I would have felt queasy even if I hadn't still been suffering a little with morning sickness. I glanced up to see how the others were doing. Crispin was on his second plate of them, pork scratchings had been a favourite of his in England and Steve seemed to be doing okay. Lizzie was studying one of her rinds closely.

"You okay?" I said to her, thinking of her poor guts, although they had been okay since she had arrived.

She nodded then leaned over and whispered in my ear, "Steve was a vegetarian for nine years." I was horrified and a bit confused as, although we had eaten a lot of vegetables since their arrival I was sure he had eaten the Chinese lemon chicken (made from the lemons we had growing in the garden) I had made the previous night. Lizzie was giggling. "He relapsed whilst we were travelling because he found it very difficult to be a vegetarian as we visited countries that eat an awful lot of meat." She was right; it would be very difficult to order a meal in a Costa Rican restaurant without some meat or meat product in it somewhere. "Also his original decision to stop eating meat was to do with the poor conditions that the animals are kept in and what they have injected into them. Here the pigs have a happy life snuffling round the yard and being petted by the local children so it's very different." I agreed with her. I glanced across at Steve; he was certainly enjoying those *chicharrones*.

Other bits of the pig are made into popular Christmas delicacies called 'tamales'. They are a mixture of pork and vegetables surrounded by a soggy cornflour 'pastry', the whole thing is then wrapped in a banana leaf, tied with string and boiled. Freddy said his mum made a whopping 350 of them this year. They are taken to people as presents; we already had a fridge full of them provided by Bilkez's mum, her gran, and lots of other local women that I didn't know the names of but knew they were all related to each other in some distant manner. They are also handed out as snacks when visitors arrive;

equivalent to our mince pies I suppose but a bit more substantial and not quite so 'moreish'.

Estrella loved having Lizzie and Steve around. They read to her incessantly and chased her round our tiny house in her walker, Estrella squealing with delight and dressed only in her nappy as the air conditioning, that had only ever worked occasionally had now given up the ghost. Steve, the rather handy electrical engineer, took a look at it but couldn't see what the problem was. Fortunately, as it gave Estrella more room to manoeuvre, we still didn't have a table or chairs in the 'dining room' part of the room. Now that Juan Carlos the carpenter was working for us and not Lenny Loco we weren't likely to either so we ate our meals on the sofa with our plates on our laps or on fold-up camping chairs on the terrace. The inflatable mattress was carried out to the finally finished garage every morning and carried back in every night.

The house was like an oven. The unused bug nets that had been weighing down Lizzie and Steve's backpacks for the last 12 months were now put to good use. They were draped over the front and back doorways and held in place with drawing pins and a broom laid on the floor which stopped Estrella from going outside and tumbling off the terrace in her walker to probable severe injury. We would shortly invest in proper safety gates. The bug nets meant we had far fewer bugs in the house and the through-breeze at night was heaven. Estrella chewing the permethrin-laced netting was however a bit of a worry and she had to be watched closely. We were finding out that saying 'no' to a ten-month old meant absolutely nothing.

We explained 'the rules' to Lizzie and Steve, trying not to scare them. "Shake out towels and clothes before using them, don't sit under a palm tree with coconuts on it as they can kill you if they fall on you, stay out of long grass because of snakes, check your bed before climbing into it, leave nothing on the floor for anything to hide under and bang out boots before putting them on." Crispin picked up Lizzie's boot to demonstrate how you bang the back of the boot on the floor first, knocking down anything that might be in the toe, then bang out at the 'neck', out fell a scorpion.

"That's why we do it," he finished crushing it with the sole. It had the air of a 'here's one I prepared earlier Blue Peter-ishness' about it. Steve and Lizzie looked at each other, eyebrows raised, Lizzie giggling nervously.

16 Christmas

The day before Christmas Eve we did a practice run for Christmas dinner. It had started out simple enough. We had offered to cook a typical British Christmas dinner for Lenny, Karin and Coral - we would eat at their house as they had a table and we didn't. Over the weeks, as is typical when things involve Lenny Loco, it had gotten a lot more complicated.

His mum and her boyfriend were visiting so that was two more around the table. Dee was now invited: she was pretty essential as she was the only person we knew who owned a proper full-size oven, although it was almost an hour's drive away where she was renting a house on the other side of Pavones. Our friends would soon be staying in her half of the duplex.

Some Italians, good friends of Karin's who had a restaurant in Pavones, had also been invited. It was the place with the good food but where the bill was an unpleasant surprise. They seemed nice enough, although his eye-brows needed something doing to them as they made him look rather evil – think Jack Nicholson in 'The Shining'. They had a daughter about the same age as Estrella and were bringing another couple with them.

Last but not least were Kevin Bacon and his wife Kyra Sedgwick. He had been a hero of mine when I was a teenager. Who could forget that gorgeous sweaty body from the days of 'Footloose'? Crispin and Steve didn't know what I was talking about; Lizzie did.

I couldn't put a face to Kevin Bacon's wife's name until, during a phone call to finalise their visit, I'd mentioned her to Kathryn.

"I'll google her," she said. She phoned back and named a few films that Kyra had been in. When she said 'Premonition' I could place her; we'd seen it

142

back in the UK. Kevin and Kyra were staying just past Dee's place, towards Punta Banco at the Jungle Lodge. They had been having lunch in Pavones a few days earlier and, knowing how I felt about him but also just wanting to be sociable and just maybe a teensy bit of him hoped he could sell him some land; Lenny had invited Kevin and his wife for Christmas dinner. My heart was pounding when Lenny told me.

"You should wear your pink and purple dress," said Karin, "you look gorgeous in it and he'll love you."

I could even try and find my make-up bag; I'd not used it since we'd arrived. Where had I put it? I hoped the humidity hadn't made my eye-shadows go mouldy like the pair of Crispin's smart trousers I'd pulled out of the drawer that morning. Something else was bothering me too. I stood up and turned sideways. "Can you see my bump yet?" I asked her.

"Breathe in."

"I am!"

"Yes, a bit," Karin had to admit.

"It's going to put him off isn't it?" I asked her anxiously.

"No, pregnant women are sexy," Lenny helpfully chipped in.

Crispin rolled his eyes, "Hello, your husband is sitting right here!" I ignored him. Why I didn't feel that the fact I had a husband and he had a wife may have put him off, well, that's an illogical pregnant woman's thinking for you.

We had just left the house when we passed Cata with her brother German walking slowly along the road. German looked very sorry for himself. It was strange to see them together as I had felt, once German and Fatima had left the area that it would be a long time before German would be friends with his 'rock-launching' sister again. I pulled up beside them and put the window down.

"*La Bruja* has left him for an old man with money." Cata used the term 'the witch' to describe her sister-in-law – it was kind of apt.

"Poor German," I said but I couldn't help thinking maybe it was a blessing.

"She took the kids too. He's missing them terribly," Cata said. It seemed that German had permanently lost the ability to speak for himself. He had tears in his eyes.

"If you need work German I'm sure Crispin could use you on the *finca* again if you get desperate." He smiled in thanks and I waved goodbye.

As we drove to where Dee was staying I told the 'Fatima' story to Lizzie and Steve. We had Estrella with us whilst Crispin drove over on the quad. Lizzie and I were going to check what equipment Dee had there and we were going to make Yorkshire puddings to test out the oven. Crispin was going to time himself driving back to Lenny's house as fast as he could on the quad. On Christmas Day Lizzie and I would prepare the potatoes and the Yorkshire puddings and put them in the oven at Dee's and drive the 45 minutes back to our house to cook the vegetables. Dee would be in charge of cooking the turkey. Once everything was ready Crispin could zip it over to Lenny's on the quad coinciding with our arrival with the vegetables and hopefully everything would still be hot and edible. The trial Yorkshire's were pretty good and Crispin managed the trial quad-dash back to Lenny's in 35 minutes. The plan was coming together.

The next day Crispin and Steve went horse-riding whilst Lizzie and I – helped and hindered by Estrella - wrapped Christmas presents, prepared the vegetables for the following day and somehow still found new stuff to chat about. In the evening we all sat huddled around the lap-top and watched 'Love Actually', a glass of Chilean bubbly in everyone's hands except mine. Lizzie and I had a good cry, she was a bit homesick and I was pregnant and maybe a bit homesick too. (I was however reaching a milestone in the pregnancy as it was the first day I hadn't thrown up in six weeks!). We put the presents Lizzie and I had wrapped earlier in the day, along with those that Crispin had picked up from our PO Box in Neily the day he'd also gone to Canoas, underneath our Christmas tree which seemed to be lasting better than its predecessor. That one had been losing its needles when Crispin arrived with it and had lost them all two days later. This one he had bought in Canoas when he went to pick up Steve and Lizzie so it was on its fourth day and doing well. We turned the fairy lights off and went to bed.

Estrella was stirring in her cot when I snuck out of bed, turned the Christmas tree fairy lights on and yelled, "He's been!" A tradition that my parents started when I was little had now become ours. Estrella quickly got the hang of the pulling the paper off the presents lark and loved everything that she saw. It was our first Christmas together as a family and seeing her face light up made it really special. There were phone calls to make to family and friends and then Lizzie, Estrella and I headed off to put the plan into action.

At 7pm that evening Estrella was sound asleep in her cot and the four of us were sitting on our sofas eating Crispin's mum's Christmas pudding with home-made brandy butter, courtesy of Crispin, and lots of cream. Crispin's mum makes her Christmas puddings months in advance and had posted one over to us. The envelope arrived full of sugar ants but they hadn't managed to breach the zip-lock bag it was in. We hadn't wanted to share it with the crowd next-door. We were utterly knackered and although the cooking and quad-bike part of the plan worked okay, it hadn't been the British Christmas dinner that I had intended it to be.

"It's odd that Americans eat fruit salad with their turkey isn't it?" said Lizzie. Someone had arrived with a huge bowl of fruit salad and when I had gestured for them to put it where the desserts were, presuming it was for dessert, I had been told it was to go with the turkey main course. In fact, everyone who arrived was laden down with food offerings; someone even brought half a pig with them. I kept wanting to say "But it's supposed to be a typical British Christmas dinner" but it would have sounded really ungrateful. I had let my 'British Christmas dinner' comment slip out to Lenny's mum. "But we're Americans darling," she had said. I started to explain to her how this had originally started out with her son accepting our offer of cooking his family a typical British Christmas dinner but I was too tired and what purpose would it have served? Obviously that hadn't been how the invitation had been passed on. I blamed Lenny.

"I can't believe I ate my Christmas dinner off a paper plate," I said sadly. I thought longingly of my parents Christmas table decorated with a Christmas table cloth and Christmas crackers to pull and party poppers and a fancy table decoration with a candle and their best crockery. "Or worse, that Kevin Bacon didn't turn up." They were travelling back up to San José that day and had obviously decided they couldn't fit it into their schedule, or more likely, had assumed that Lenny was the local nutter and had had no intention of coming in the first place. "Coral was funny though." We all smiled remembering the very funny moment when three year old Coral came running in from outside shouting "Daddy, the fucking horse is in the garden again!" Lenny had looked incredibly sheepish until everyone had burst out laughing.

146

"At least we've got the Christmas pudding," said Crispin through a mouthful of it. I scraped some Christmas pud, brandy butter and cream onto my spoon and put it in my mouth. Wow, absolute heaven.

17 Friends...

Matt and Sharon arrived the following day and Kathryn and Kevin joined us a few days later. I decided to be brave and drove with Sharon to pick Kathryn and Kevin up in Golfito; they were arriving by water taxi from Puerto Jimenez on the Osa Peninsula.

I usually drove for a couple of hours on the way to and from San José whilst Crispin had a snooze and I drove locally, like to Dee's at Christmas, but I had never done the one and a half hour drive to Golfito before and had certainly never driven onto or off the ferry. When I was a teenager I had managed to get water in the engine of my mum's car whilst driving through a deep ford. I hadn't had to wait very long to be rescued but it meant that driving through deep water always worried me. Plus our car wasn't very reliable and I was scared of it breaking down and leaving me stranded and I doubted that my Spanish was good enough to get me out of a situation like that. In addition, because the roads were so bad I was worried about having an accident, driving off the side of one of the bridges (few had safety barriers) or breaking an axle in a pothole.

It turned out, as is usually the case when you worry about something, that I had worried unnecessarily: the drive was completely uneventful. Even the ferry was close enough to the shore for me to not have to drive into the river at all. We passed the time chatting.

"How do you know Kathryn and Kevin?" Sharon asked me. Now that's a good story....

One night, during our ten week 'recce' trip, we were driving to Montezuma, a pretty coastal town on the Nicoya Peninsula. We usually avoided driving at night, it was hazardous enough during the day, but we'd had to catch a ferry and it hadn't docked until late so we'd been left with little choice. It was 7.30pm, pitch black, bucketing it down and the going was treacherous.

A sign to the left ahead said 'Montezuma' and Crispin started indicating but the turning wasn't where I remembered it to be.

"I don't think this is it, hon," I said to him. "The turning is in the middle of a town. I'm sure of it." We had been there on our honeymoon two years before and we were still in the middle of nowhere.

"What do you want me to do?"

I stared at the sign. It said Montezuma so it must go to Montezuma, surely? "Oh take it," I said at last minute.

It turned out to be a 'dry season only' track to Montezuma – but of course, the sign didn't mention this and it didn't say 'take in the rainy season, at your own peril' either. The road was narrow, the mud was deep and we were sliding around all over the place. Crispin found it impossible to keep the car moving in a straight-line. It was so dark and the rain was still thumping down on the roof of the car. He put the wind-screen wipers up to triple speed but it didn't help. "Bugger," he said, "I still can't see anything." I was getting scared. Suddenly up ahead I saw some car lights. Thank goodness someone else was using the road, maybe we would get through okay.

As we got closer I realised that the lights were at a very strange angle. Crispin noticed it too. "Someone's rolled their car!" he exclaimed. There was a couple standing next to the vehicle. He was wearing shorts and a t-shirt and she had shorts on and a cagoule. They looked very pleased to see us and were very very very wet.

"Hold on, I'm just going to get past you," Crispin yelled at them. The guy, who we later found out was called Kevin, yelled, "Be careful!" I gave the girl (Kathryn) a little sympathetic wave and she waved

149

back. I held my breath as Crispin drove up the bank slightly to avoid them. Our car started sliding back down towards theirs but somehow Crispin managed to keep it moving forward and we cleared it safely. My heart was still pounding as the car stopped and Crispin got out to see what he could do to help. I, now six months pregnant, waited in the car.

I saw more headlights in our rear-view mirror, there was a car following us and they too stopped to help. Kathryn joined me in our car. We watched as the guys huddled together, discussing what they should do.

"What are they doing?" I asked Kathryn when they walked around to the wheels and started pushing the car over onto its roof.

"I have no idea." We watched as the car ended up on its roof, the windscreen smashed on its way over.

Crispin came back to our car.

"Oops, whose idea was that?" I asked, not impressed.

"Mine," he admitted, rather sheepishly. "I thought we could try to get some momentum up by pushing it onto its roof first but it didn't work."

"It didn't did it. What's plan B?" I asked him.

"We go for help."

Crispin stopped outside a house and jumped out. He was back very quickly.

"Oh my God! A man just brandished a shotgun at me!" he said driving off as fast as he could.

"What did you say to him?" asked Kathryn.

"A girl came to the door first and I asked if I could borrow a rope and tried to explain why; then she went off and her dad came back with a shotgun. I said the same thing to him but he didn't look very happy so I ran off."

I instantly realised his mistake. "You said 'ropa' for rope didn't you?"

150

"Is that not rope?"

"'Ropa' means clothing! You asked the man's daughter if you could have her clothes!" We all laughed.

"What's rope then?"

"I have no idea," I admitted. That was the moment we decided we needed Spanish lessons.

We continued to a police station and found the local police glued to a football game on the television. Costa Ricans are football mad and interrupting a football game is sacrilege, however we were kind of desperate.

"Wrong police," said the short one sitting nearest to the door after Crispin had explained, with lots of miming, what had happened. He hadn't taken his eyes off the television. None of them had.

"What do you mean 'wrong police'?" asked Crispin

"We are the local police. You need the traffic police," said short guy.

"So where are they then?"

"In the next town but the station is closed until tomorrow." Great.

Crispin pleaded with them and eventually with great reluctance they tore themselves away from the match. Once they had made their minds up to help they were brilliant and with a rope and a pick-up truck they righted the car in minutes. Not surprisingly, it wasn't in any way drivable so Kathryn and Kevin and their luggage piled into our car. We continued on to Montezuma, checked into a hotel and laughed about the incident over beer and pizzas later than evening. A year later they were still in discussions with their credit card company as to who was going to pay the four thousand dollars that the rental company was demanding for repairs.

"So that's why you call them the 'car-rolling couple'," concluded Sharon as I finished my tale.

It was great for the nine of us to be together. We bought a huge fish from the local fisherman, the scales were like fingernails and we've got some great photos of Matt kissing it, he's a bit mad like that. He and Sharon made a huge scrumptious fish pie that night. We also hiked around the *finca* together and got ourselves lost a couple of times. Sharon had recently had a knee operation and I was now coming up to 11 weeks pregnant so it probably wasn't the most sensible thing for the two of us to be doing but we had a great time. We'd been walking for a long time when we stopped under the mango tree (the one with the amazing view on Urbano's part of the *finca*) to take a break, it was an incredibly hot day. As we all stared down into the fantastic valley covered in rainforest, not a house in sight, I still couldn't quite believe it was ours and I don't think our friends could either.

Crispin cut down some coconuts with his machete and expertly sliced a hole in them to drink the sweet liquid out of, he was becoming quite the Tico and I was as impressed as our friends were. The guys were amazed by everything they saw and heard and it was so nice to tell someone our ideas and show them what we wanted to do.

We watched terrible quality movies from Paso Canoas on our laptop, ate pizza at 'La Piña' (our favourite restaurant at the time), sunbathed at the beach and swam in the river. One night we had everyone around at our house and planned to watch Michael Moore's 9/11.

"I fancy pizza," said Kathryn.

"Pizza and movie is a brilliant idea," I agreed.

"From where?" asked Crispin. "We're not in London now." It was true, we lived in the middle of the jungle but maybe takeaway pizza wasn't entirely out of the question.

152

"Lenny had some pizza pans in his house from getting a takeaway pizza from somewhere," I suddenly remembered. "Maybe La Piña would do a one for us?"

"I'll drive," said Kevin. We all laughed at him. He took the laughter well. "I'm not going to roll the car," he said with smile.

"I'll go," said Crispin, "I know the roads, so I'll be quicker and I'll take the quad. I'll take the cooler to keep the pizza hot." Steve offered to go with him. 'La Piña' was the other side of Pavones and there was no phone.

They were gone for ages. Two hours after they had left we heard the 'putt putt putt' of the quad and the skidding stones as they came down the driveway.

"They didn't have any pizza as they'd run out of cheese," announced Steve as he came through the doorway carrying the cooler.

"Oh no," chorused six very hungry people. I couldn't believe I was going to have to cook.

"Who wants chicken with their rice and who wants shrimp?" he asked as he took the lid off the cooler. Hurrah, it was full of *arroz con pollo* and *arroz con camarones*. Who needs Pizza Hut?!

We had a lot of fun together and for Crispin and me it was like being on holiday. The boys had surf lessons and the girls lay on the beach admiring the real surfer's muscles and had girlie conversations about whether Lenny Loco was good-looking or not and whether Karin's boobs were real or plastic. Estrella loved being the centre of attention and I loved having people around and realised that I had been really lonely before. It was hard work too however. Whenever we went to the beach I had to think like a mother of eight as I knew that five minutes after we had set up camp down there Estrella was going to be hungry. I often found myself throwing baguettes, cheese, tomatoes, mango chutney, bananas, apples and chocolate into the cooler along with plates and

153

knives and making sure there was enough for everyone; knowing that I couldn't just take it for us.

"We're going to cook for you on New Year's Eve," Kevin told us a couple of days before 2004 was due to come to a close.

"Each couple is going to cook a course whilst you and Crispin sit and relax," said Kathryn. "We'll eat up here so you don't have any mess to clear up either," she added.

"That's lovely," I said, "thank you."

"No, it's our way of saying thank YOU for everything. You've both been amazing."

"And we are going to get fireworks," said Matt walking over to the CD player with a glint in his eye. The Prodigy's 'Firestarter' blasted out; Matt's manic singing followed.

I put Estrella to bed in her cot in one of the bedrooms then sat and watched Kevin make tortilla chips by cutting soft round tortillas into triangles and frying them.

"I have lived here for four months and I had no idea that that was how tortilla chips were made," I told him in amazement. In the UK we had always just opened a bag of them. I saved it in my memory bank of recipes for future use. The soft round tortillas were standard food down here. The local Ticos ground corn, mixed the resulting flour with water, flattened them with their hands then lightly fried them. It was a lot of hassle to go to for a tortilla. I dipped one of the triangles into Kathryn's dip – it was very good.

There was an amazing smell coming from a pan on the stove next to me. Matt was adding seasoning to it. "Beef bourguignon, darling," he said in a mock haughty chef's voice. He tasted it with a spoon. "It's missing something," he said. He picked up a bottle of red wine and poured most of it in, stirred it, and then tasted it again. "Much better," he declared. Sharon was busily chopping vegetables.

I went to join Lizzie, Steve and Crispin on the sofas. Crispin held his arm out so I could snuggle into his armpit.

"What's for dessert?" I asked Steve and Lizzie.

"Well," said Lizzie. "It's supposed to be watermelon and lemon granita but I think it's going to be more like watermelon and lemon slush-puppie as it looks like it needs another three days in the freezer!"

Estrella didn't make a squeak all evening. At 10.30pm I went to join her, all that sitting down, eating and relaxing had obviously exhausted me. I woke up to Crispin shaking my shoulder gently.

"It's ten to twelve," he whispered in my ear so as not to wake Estrella. I was so tired that I debated ignoring him and turning over again but I somehow forced my eyes open.

I went out through the door on to the terrace and could just make out the boys running around in the pitch black setting up the fireworks in the garden. They were pretty drunk and it was very funny to stand and watch. Immediately there were bangs and flashes and we could see fireworks going off all around the bay; at Pavones to our left, Zancudo and Golfito to our right and even the other side of the gulf on the Osa Peninsula. We all stood there 'ooooh'ing and 'aaaaaaah'ing at the brightly coloured spectacle. It was a clear night and the stars were incredible. After the usual 'Happy New Year' kisses and hugs (Crispin had whispered, "This is going to be a great one for the four of us," in my ear), someone handed me a sparkler and I wrote 'Jo' in the warm night air followed by 'loves Crispin, Estrella and'. I was just thinking about baby names when it fizzled out.

The boys were now debating whether to ignore 'the firework code' and go back to a lit firework that hadn't performed its duty. "I'll go and light it," said Matt. "I am the 'Firestarter'," he quipped, beginning an amusing repeat of the other night. As Kevin took a step backwards to move out of his way he tripped over an outdoor tap. It snapped off at the pipe and a fountain of water shot up into the air. We all stood there for a few seconds, fireworks forgotten, staring at the geyser whilst the water tank started to empty.

"Bugger, that's our water too!" said Crispin suddenly remembering that the system also served our house and ran around to the front of the house with Steve to look for the stop-cock to turn the water off. There was distant swearing as one of them connected with a spiky lemon tree. In the meantime Kevin and Matt tried unsuccessfully to plug the deluge with a champagne cork, nearly drowning themselves in the process. It was the funniest thing I had seen in a long time, they were both absolutely drenched and I was reminded of the night I had first seen Kevin standing by the over-turned car. It was certainly a New Year's Eve to remember!

Lenny and Karin came back from their night out in Pavones to find they had no water and were faced with the tough task of finding somewhere to buy plumbing supplies on New Year's Day.

Then, all too soon, the holiday was over. Kathryn and Kevin spent their last couple of nights at the Jungle Lodge whilst Matt and Sharon and Lizzie and Steve moved to Greg and Heidi's for a few days for a change of scenery (and water!). On Kathryn and Kevin's last night, Heidi babysat the sleeping Estrella at Casa Siempre Domingo whilst we all went to the Jungle Lodge for a meal out. It was a great evening and we have a wonderful photo of the eight of us all leaning on the bar together. Kathryn and Kevin later had the photo framed and sent it to us from their home in Chicago as a reminder of our fantastic time together. It arrived a couple of months later; on the bus!

They were also going to have a reminder of their time here. We received a phone call from Kathryn about the same time the photo arrived.

"Guess what?" she said.

"What?" I am a terrible guesser.

"I'm pregnant!"

"Congratulations!" I squealed. "That's brilliant news."

"I feel like absolute crap though," she said. "I can hardly get out of bed." I knew the feeling well. "How did you run round after us all feeling like this?" she asked. "Plus you had a toddler to look after! I feel terrible about it." She then apologised a hundred times whilst I laughed at her.

"I thought you said you were going to wait a while," I said, referring to a comment both her and Kevin had made during their stay about not wanting children just yet.

"Y'know, we were but then seeing you guys together with Estrella made us decide to just go for it. Lots of other friends of ours, well, their lives have stopped and yours hasn't." I thought about how Crispin had lugged Estrella in the back-carrier around the *finca* during our walks and how we took her to the beach and to restaurants, had even set her travel-cot up at Dee's for New Year and then again at Heidi's. I was really touched that we were an inspiration to them.

Matt and Sharon were the next to leave and then finally Lizzie and I had a tearful goodbye. They needed to find jobs, plan their wedding and settle down in the 'real world' again. It was awful saying goodbye even though they promised to come back again. I said I would try and make it to her and Steve's wedding but they were talking about having it in July and I had other plans then didn't I?

157

18....& Enemies

Crispin reverted to going to the *finca* alone most days. He had spent a lot of time walking around the new *finca* getting to know it inside out and back-to-front and had decided to cut about 15 hectares of the new *finca* into ten lots, some with amazing gulf views, some with small gulf views and one huge one with a tiny gulf view but amazing rainforest views. Some were a couple of hectares, one only an acre, some on 'our' road and some inside the *finca*, some with waterfalls (Crispin had found two on his wanderings), all with a source of water; there was something for everyone. Lenny Loco was incredibly enthusiastic and said he would sell them all in two weeks.

Crispin arranged for a bulldozer to come to put the internal road into the *finca* so all of the lots could be easily accessed. He discussed with the driver the best route for the road. He arranged for each lot to have a flat area cut that would serve as a building site. He was a busy man and he loved it. He loved being outside in the sunshine, he loved being with nature; he was starting a tree nursery so come the rainy season in May the reforestation would start. He would come home with a smile on his face telling me about the different animals he had seen; the monkeys; a small black cat; an armadillo; a coyote; he loved using his machete like the Ticos and, somewhat surprisingly for a partner in a law firm, he seemed to be a natural at developing a piece of overgrown pasture/jungle land. This was what he had been born to do; his lawyer days were far behind him.

So, Estrella and I were left alone again and I felt miserable, an inspiration to no one. Unfortunately for him, Ernesto, our absent architect, chose my miserable patch to finally drag his sorry backside to the house site. Toli had been working on the house for almost a month. He had been having difficultly trying to get hold of Ernesto to get him to order building materials, as per Ernesto's request. Crispin eventually had given Toli permission to order them himself. We had tried to call Ernesto several times but he never ever answered his phone and when we got through to his voicemail we always got a message saying that his mailbox was full so we couldn't leave a message. He had phoned us once, just before Christmas to say that he had been ill and was in San José for the Christmas period. He said he would visit us within the week.

Two weeks later Ernesto arrived. He gave no apologies and proceeded to walk round the house asking Toli to knock walls down here and build more over there because he decided we needed to have a larger master bedroom. It was a good idea but that wasn't the point. If he'd turned up when he had originally said he would, Toli's team wouldn't have to knock walls down and rebuild them as he could have seen the house layout on the ground and changed his mind without it costing us more money in both materials and labour.

"Have we got the building permit yet?" Crispin asked Ernesto.

"No, I am still waiting to hear," Ernesto replied.

"Did you submit the old plans or the new plans?" I asked him.

"The old ones." I was surprised.

"Have you done the new plans yet?" I asked him. He ignored me. I asked him again.

"It's not a problem," he murmured.

"Do you remember at the meeting in Golfito we said we wanted changes making?" I persisted.

He avoided my question and then tried to finish the conversation by saying, "So this is the walk-in closet..." We were standing in the bathroom.

"It's the bathroom," I said. Crispin took a step backwards. It was habit; he recognised my tone and knew what was coming. "You haven't been here for four weeks," I continued calmly. I guessed Ernesto wasn't used to having a woman confront him, never mind a miserable pregnant English one.

He decided his best course of action was to continue ignoring me. He was soooo wrong. I let rip. "Not only have you not been for four weeks, you haven't phoned us, you haven't done the new plans that you said you would do, you don't even remember us talking about the changes we want to the house design, and you don't know the layout of a house that YOU designed. On top of that Toli has needed materials and hasn't been able to get hold of you to order them." Although tears were now pouring down my cheeks, I spoke clearly and enunciated every word so he would understand everything perfectly.

"What can I do?" he said haughtily without looking at me, "I am here now so let's continue."

"You could apologise," I said to him. I would come to learn that Ticos don't apologise, or say 'thank you' for that matter (maybe I am generalising ever so slightly) and Tico men never apologise, certainly not to a mere woman. A woman should be in the kitchen and not prancing around a building site pretending that she had an ounce of intelligence or an opinion of her own. It was a very macho society and, certainly out here in the countryside, women were second class citizens and were supposed to do as they were told.

"I've been away. What can I do?" he finished.

"You could apologise," I said again.

"Let's discuss the changes you want..."

"APOLOGISE!!!"

"I'm sorry." It was clearly killing him.

"Thank you." I took a deep breath and walked away to compose myself again.

It was the last we were to see of him. He sent our building permission through a couple of weeks

160

later but we never did see the new set of house plans. Crispin and I got together with Toli and worked out the new house design ourselves. We had a signed contract with Ernesto and he was in breach of it. Toli recommended another architect, someone he had worked with in the past. The new architect helped us to write and submit a complaint to the governing body of architects, builders and engineers but we never heard anything. We were glad to be rid of him.

"Who's going to buy our building materials now then?" I asked Crispin. "Can you do it yourself or do we ask Toli?"

"He doesn't want to and I can't," said Crispin, "my Spanish just isn't good enough and I don't know enough about the industry. Marco has said that he'll do it for us." Marco was the manager at *Ferretería Pachicha*, the local builder's merchant.

"But he works at Pachicha."

"He wants to leave and set up his own business, we would be his first customers. He said he'll get us the best prices he can and I've agreed we'll pay him an eight per cent commission."

I met him the following day; Crispin brought him down to the house in the afternoon. I heard them way before I saw them: Marco had a very old motorbike with a very large hole in the exhaust pipe. He also had a humble manner and beautiful black eyes, I liked him immediately.

Now that our friends had left and Estrella and I were alone again, we were pretty much left in the house most of the time with me fighting tiredness and waiting for that 'glowing' stage of my pregnancy to start and Estrella a huge ball of energy that exhausted my already exhausted self. Bilkez was still coming to clean for a couple of hours in the morning during the week and she would play with Estrella for a little while and I relished this time and used it to collapse in a heap. I wasn't involved in any decisions regarding building materials or where to get them from, or what wood to buy or when who got paid what. I didn't expect to be involved as my brain was reducing in size daily and my Spanish was terrible and I knew nothing about any of these things, but I did hear snippets here and there which I instantly forgot about and I trusted Crispin and the people who were working for us to sort everything out. Instead of getting involved, I started throwing up again.

Although I was still feeling nauseous at times I hadn't thrown up for three weeks; since Christmas Eve. So I was surprised when I found myself with my head down the toilet again one morning. I sat on the floor trying to find the energy to stand up, watching the bizarre oval things using their tongues to zip around – wow, they were fast. After two more days of this I was left with no energy whatsoever, I couldn't get out of bed. Suddenly I realised I had to. Great, now I had diarrhoea too. I eventually crawled back into bed. It was a Saturday, Bilkez wasn't coming. Crispin had snuck out of the bedroom with Estrella once she had woken and closed the doors (thank goodness we now had those) to give me a bit of peace. After a while he brought Estrella back in, she was ready for her morning nap, he laid her on the bed next to me, where she instantly rolled onto her side, cuddled her caterpillar, sucked her dummy and fell asleep. "I left my phone at Lenny Loco's yesterday," he said. "I'm just going to pop up and get it." He had brought a bowl in with him and put it down by the side of the bed.

"Please don't be long," I begged him. I knew that Estrella would only sleep for 20 minutes and also knew I was in no fit state to be looking after a toddler.

"I'll be really quick. I promise," he assured me.

An hour later I was on the phone to Karin screaming and crying and swearing like a mad

162

woman. I'd thrown up twice in the toilet, with Estrella sitting on the bathroom floor next to me, trying to pick up and eat the oval tongue things. I then changed ends and sitting on the toilet I grabbed the bowl and threw up again. Estrella was now crying. She wanted me to pick her up. I hoped she hadn't managed to catch one of those things and put it in her mouth. Actually, I didn't care. I was completely empty of everything when I eventually picked her up and just about managed to make it to the bed without dropping her. I had no energy whatsoever. I reached for my phone and dialled.

"Is Crispin there?" I asked Karin in a weak voice. I wasn't in the mood for small talk.

"No, he got in the car with Lenny and they left about an hour ago. I don't know where they were going." I was suddenly hysterical. They always did this. Crispin would pop up and see him for five minutes and then they would end up going off somewhere on some mini adventure that would last for hours; Lenny had found a waterfall that he wanted to show him or a new piece of land or he wanted to see what Crispin had done in the *finca* or wanted to see how our house was coming along or he had a meeting with a new client and he just wanted Crispin along for the ride. They would end up having a nice lunch out and I would never get so much as a phone call, as there was no phone signal in these exciting places they visited. Now was really not the time. I starting yelling and sobbing and calling her husband every horrible name I could think of. Karin agreed with all of them. I decided I would kill him if I ever saw him again.

"I know Jo, they do this all the time, it drives me insane too but you have to calm down, this isn't good for the baby." I knew she was right but I couldn't stop myself. Suddenly I heard a car.

"He's here," I said to Karin and put the phone down. Crispin came through the door as I heard Lenny wheel-spin back up the driveway.

"I am SOOOOOOOOOOO sorry, I got up there and he said get in the car, so I did...," he started saying.

"WHY COULDN'T YOU JUST SAY NO?" I screamed at him. "THAT YOUR PREGNANT WIFE WAS PUKING HER GUTS UP AND NEEDED YOU." He picked the phone up and started dialling. Now who the fuck was he going to talk to? Lenny? Was he going to get me sectioned? He calmly explained to the phone that his wife, Joanne Freeman, had had severe vomiting for several days now and also had diarrhoea and then after a pause he handed the phone over to me. I recognised my doctor's voice. I fought to calm myself down, desperately trying to control my shuddering sobs. I listened to him telling me to taken an anti-emetic for my vomiting and another medication for my diarrhoea. I knew we had both drugs in the medicine bag, he had prescribed me the anti-emetic at my first visit but I had been reluctant to take it.

My mum was convinced that an anti-emetic she had taken during a pregnancy had given my brother a heart problem and that had affected my decision. In the UK you are advised to take only paracetamol during pregnancy, it was very different over here; you took what you needed to feel normal again. I dutifully did what my doctor ordered and then fell asleep for a couple of hours, I dreamt Crispin came in and kissed my forehead.

19 The Quad

I was starting to feel better after my stomach bug and we decided to have a day at the beach. We hadn't been to the beach since our friends had deserted me and it felt like a crime living so close to it but not going. I wasn't really in the mood to get all of our usual 'garb' together; cooler; funky new double stroller; beach brolly etc. Then Crispin had a crazy idea. In a moment of madness I broke out of my sensible mould and agreed to the crazy idea. I drove the car to the beach whilst he rode the quad bike.

There's a beautiful house at Pilon with an immaculate garden and somewhat surprisingly, a three-hole golf course. It looks really out of place amongst the crappy fishermen's huts that line the road, little more than a muddy track really, which leads to it. We had never met the owners but Lenny Loco had given us a tour of their house during our first visit to the area whilst they were in the States to give us an idea of the kind of work the local builders were capable of. It was as stunning inside as it was outside; all wooden beams and gorgeous tiles. I had wished it was my house.

Today we left the car parked in a grassy area next to the out-of-place beautiful house that never would be mine and I (and my belly) then climbed behind Crispin on the quad bike and sandwiched Estrella between us. I pulled her hat down tightly on her head and put my arms around Crispin's waist.

"Ready?" asked Crispin.

"Ready," I said and he started the engine and we bumped over the driftwood and coconuts down onto the beach.

"Okay, let's go!" and he zoomed off in the direction of Zancudo. I squealed.

"Are you okay?" Crispin yelled.

"My face hurts from laughing," I yelled back. It was wonderful; zipping along with the rainforest on one side and the crashing waves and outline of the Osa Peninsula on the other, feeling the wind whipping through my hair...."Ahhh, STOP!" I yelled to Crispin. "My hat's blown off." He did a U-turn so that I could retrieve it.

We had decided to go to the Century 21 real estate office in Zancudo and it was much quicker going along the beach on the quad than driving along the road in the car. It cut a good 20 minutes off the journey. Lenny Loco had said he would sell our ten lots in two weeks and already two months had gone by with very few clients materialising so we had decided to advertise them through other agents, after all it was our prerogative to do so. I told Crispin this a hundred times to try to relieve him of the guilt he felt at what he saw as 'going behind his best friend's back'.

We just managed to get back to the car before the tide washed the beach clean again. The owner of Century 21 hadn't been there and we were told that he would come and see us – he never did.

As we approached the car a man walked through the picture perfect garden towards us. We waved.

"You must be Steve," I said and we introduced ourselves.

"Come up to the house and meet my wife Judy," he insisted so we followed him through this beautiful little corner of paradise. They were a lovely couple and Judy made the most fantastic banana bread. I went on about it so much that she sent me home with some just to keep me quiet. We also left with an invitation to her 50th birthday barbeque that Saturday. It was something I was really excited about – a party!

Bloody typical: the car wouldn't start. We couldn't jump-start it because it was parked in the garage at the bottom of our steep driveway. Lenny Loco wasn't answering his phone so there was no help to be had there and as Toli and his team were now hard at work up at the house site we had no stray builders down here to help in such emergencies as a car that wouldn't start (or wasps that needed burning!), I had to admit though, I wasn't missing their noise!

"We really need to leave," I said to Crispin. "The party started half an hour ago. What are we going to do?"

"We could take the quad," said Crispin. I desperately wanted to go to this party but doing something so daft and dangerous on a deserted beach was one thing but doing it on the road was another altogether. The locals wouldn't have thought twice. You often saw four people on a horse or a motorbike, ten people crammed into the back of a pick-up truck or 30 people squished in the back of a cattle lorry. We were the only people who ever bothered with child car seats or seatbelts; I only have to think of Princess Diana's car wreck to click mine in. Although I had noticed that Crispin was 'going Tico' and at times I had to remind him to put his on.

The Costa Rican government has a brilliant campaign that, as soon as I have a minute, I fully intend to write to our Prime Minister about. Every time someone is killed in an car accident, a huge yellow heart with a halo above it is painted on the road. There are lots of them on the road to San José and it always makes me think about driving carefully. Unfortunately, the government hadn't bothered doing the same campaign in the south of Costa Rica, called the *Zona Sur* (Southern Zone). The government tended to forget about the *Zona Sur* quite frequently and the region was obviously considerably poorer that the northern regions of the country. Mind you, I guessed it would be difficult to paint a heart on a muddy dirt road.   Anyway, as I said; I really really really wanted to go to this party. "Okay, let's go."

It was more difficult on the road than it had been on the beach because of all the potholes, I had to hold on to Estrella more tightly and she was wriggling about all over the place and because of the angle I was sitting at I was getting terrible backache but we made it in once piece and didn't pass any other traffic whatsoever.

There were some lovely people there, and some slightly weird ones including a guy who I was sure would make a great cult leader, if he wasn't already one, with his intense stare and his calm hypnotising voice.

"You're crazy," Crispin said when I mentioned it to him. "He was a lovely man." I looked at him closely. Had he fallen under his spell already? I was going to have to watch out for weird behaviour for a while.

The absolutely best thing about the party had to be the ribs. They were, hands down, the best barbequed ribs I had ever tasted in my entire life and I'm sure I ate 20 of them. As you may have noticed, I was really starting to enjoy my food again. I just wanted to eat constantly. Bizarrely, I even found myself fantasising about, amongst other things, *chicharrones*.

I was talking to Amy, the local yoga teacher, and Candy, an artist who ran the gift shop in Pavones, when Crispin sidled over to me. He had managed to drag himself away from a conversation with his new best friend again; cult guy. "We need to go," he said and pointed to the sky. A huge black cloud was heading in our direction, a storm was approaching. The last thing we wanted was to be caught on the quad in a downpour. We said our thank yous and goodbyes and Steve and Judy promised to have us over for dinner when my parents arrived in a couple of weeks. Unfortunately we felt we couldn't return the favour living in our tiny matchbox-sized house but said we would have them up for dinner as soon as our house was ready in six months' time.

As we zipped back home again Estrella, still squished between us, fell asleep. It had been a lovely afternoon. Thank goodness we had the quad.

The next time I went on it, my parents were here. They'd arrived with a suitcase full of baked beans, HP Fruity Sauce, Shreddies, NOW and Heat magazines, Independents and even Strongbow! We suddenly had something we had never had before - babysitters. Okay, I'm ignoring the fact Heidi had babysat when we went out with everyone to the Jungle Lodge after New Year but that now seemed like a lifetime ago.

During one of Estrella's catnaps, Crispin and I wished my parents luck with our now toddler - Estrella had started walking the day after her first birthday and all grandad wanted to do was video and photograph her every move (and I mean <u>every</u> move) and all gran wanted to do was cuddle her and sing her every nursery rhyme ever written (and I mean <u>every</u> nursery rhyme) and make up for the five months of her life they had missed out on because her nasty parents (yep, us) had kidnapped their favourite (and still only) grandchild and taken her to a godforsaken third world country (hey ho) - and we snuck quietly out of the house. Crispin had left the quad parked at the top of the driveway so Estrella wouldn't hear us make our getaway. We were giggling like young lovers as he started the engine and we vanished through the gates and flew up the road that led to the *finca*. I had escaped.

Crispin wanted to impress me with what he had done in the new *finca* and I, for a while anyway, was suitably impressed; my husband was a genius and was visibly proud of what he had achieved. But the task force who sat making up such sayings as 'too many cockroaches spoil the broth', or whatever it was, didn't think up 'pride comes before a fall' for no reason.

The brand new internal road to the *finca* started opposite the entrance to Amado's house 1.5 kilometres up 'our' road and a kilometre before you reached the house site. The road was flat initially, led past the old dead tree where the bats roosted and then curved around sharply to the right over a pretty stream.

Everything looked very different to when I had been hiking round there, 'pre-road', with our friends not two months earlier. On the left there were some beautiful tall trees one of which had a stunning bright red passion flower snaking up its trunk. On the right were bananas and plantains (a type of banana that was fried or boiled and eaten as a vegetable) and an area of fluffy sugar cane where Amado kept his *trapichi;* his sugar cane crusher. It used a horse to extract the *agua dulce* (sweet water) from the sugar cane. The horse was hitched to a long wooden arm and then walked round and round turning a huge screw which crushed the stems and extracted the liquid that gave you an instant sugar high and kept you buzzing for hours. It was land that we'd only recently acquired from Amado. After buying the second *finca* from Urbano Crispin had found, as usual, that the dividing line between Urbano's *finca* and his neighbour's cut right through the centre of two hillocks, i.e. potential lots, so he had set about acquiring the adjacent halves. The land had originally belonged to German (nothing to do with Fatima's husband) but he had sold a small piece to Amado a few years earlier. This was the piece Amado was growing and extracting his sugar cane on. He agreed to sell that piece to us providing he could keep his sugar cane and his extractor. We agreed – tourists would love it we thought.

Crispin had also been trying to negotiate with German to buy the piece of land behind the bit that he had previously sold to Amado.

"I won't sell you the whole piece," German said, "as it's the highest point of the *finca* and it's got the best view."

"But you'll sell a bit of it?" asked Crispin hopefully.

"I'll swap some of it for some cows." Cows? We didn't have any cows. We had the three horses and were considering chickens and dogs but no cows as yet.

"I'll buy you some cows if you like?" Crispin offered.

"I don't want any old cows," said German, shaking his head. "Amado's got some nice cows. I want Amado's cows." So Crispin went to see Amado and, after much negotiation, Amado gave German some cows and acquired the land and we then bought the land off Amado at the cost of more than a few cows. For an ageing Tico farmer who had come to the area 40 years previously, chopping down the rainforest, planting rice and beans and populating his now *finca* with cows and chickens, Amado was turning out to be quite the shrewd business man. He did well out of the deal. He did even better six months later when we sold the lot that we had imaginatively called 'Amado' and took him an envelope with ten thousand dollars in it. It was half of the profit we had made in the sale, something Crispin and I had agreed between ourselves we would do when or if we ever managed to sell it. It was a 'thank you for helping us out' and we felt it was a neighbourly thing to do and the right thing to do, even though it happened to be Crispin's dad's money!

171

Immediately after this mini-oasis the road turned back to the left and started rising steeply. I clung around Crispin's waist and leaned forward so I wouldn't fall off the back. At the top of the hill the various lots started branching off to the right and left. They were his babies and he had given them all names. In fact, that wasn't true. Some of them had named themselves.

Initially Crispin had asked Freddy and Enrique if they could cut the undergrowth on the lot with the palm trees. Then one day they just started calling it 'Las Palmas'. There was 'Culantro', where wild coriander grew; 'Las Espinas' that had lots of thorny lemon trees; 'Armadillo', where he had spotted one; 'El Corral', opposite Freddy's corral on 'our' road; 'Barú' that had a view of Volcan Barú in Panama; and the two beauties, 'El Señor' and his daughter 'La Hija'.

He was very excited the day he discovered 'La Hija' during his wanderings with a machete. She was beautiful and sat to the left of 'El Señor' which can actually mean 'God' but also 'gentleman' or 'Sir' and this was what he intended it to mean. He was a handsome chap. At almost three hectares or seven acres it was a big piece of land and the view from the lot was even better than where we were building our house. We actually decided that we didn't really want to sell it so we put what we thought was a high price on it, almost double that of any of the other lots.

Crispin gave me the grand tour and finished off by showing me 'Amado', it was the first time I had seen the lot since we had bought it and the fence line had been moved; I was really really pleased with the purchase. It was such a pretty lot and it had a lovely view of Zancudo and the rest of German's *finca* that bordered it.

"I'm just going to go and explore a bit on the quad," Crispin said. It sounded like he wanted me to get off.

"Do you want me to get off?" I asked, surprised.

"Yeah, wait here. I won't be long." I climbed off and he headed away from the internal road and down a slope that looked, to me, to be pretty steep.

"Isn't that a bit steep?" I yelled after him.

"No problem," he yelled back, "I won't be a minute." And with that he vanished into the undergrowth. A few minutes later I thought I heard a bang.

"Crispin!" I yelled. No reply. "Crispin!" Silence. I waited five minutes and then yelled again, still nothing.

"Great, my husband has managed to kill himself on the quad and I am stuck at the far side of the *finca* with the nearest help a good kilometre walk away," I said in a sulky voice to no one in particular. I had thought, in hindsight rather naïvely, we wouldn't be very long so hadn't given any instructions to mum about what to feed Estrella for her lunch. To top it all off, I had no water, was five months pregnant and the poor baby was probably now father-less. "At least there's no danger of his father teaching him to ride a quad," I muttered.

Another five minutes passed by. Maybe it was time I did something. Something other than cry I mean. Maybe he really was dead and I was going to have to follow him down that steep bank through that thick undergrowth that was bound to be crawling with snakes, scorpions and deadly spiders to see for myself.

It was at that moment I heard a swishing through the undergrowth and my husband appeared back from the dead. He was on foot.

"You're an idiot," I greeted him. He grinned at me sheepishly.

"I'm going to go and get help," he said.

"And the quad?" I asked him

"In a ravine."

"Uh huh."

173

"It was a bit steep and I lost control," he said admitting I had been right

"Uh huh."

"It hit a tree but luckily I'd already jumped off."

"Luckily, eh?" I stood there with my arms folded shaking my head in disbelief. I really was married to an idiot. As he walked off I remembered 'cult leader guy' from Judy's barbeque. Did this qualify as weird behaviour? In fact, no; this was pretty normal behaviour for Crispin I decided. I sat down under a tree and waited for Crispin to return; hopefully with some hunky builders, but not Ruben, before something ate me.

The 1st photo Crispin saw of me

7:00 pm Community Worship

Mum and me in Tamarindo for the wedding

175

Our barn in Sussex

Estrella arrives
Friday 13th

Feb 2002

View from the finca

The ferry

Gilly & Estrella

'Our' beach lot at Pilon

Ice cream beans

Paso Canoas Border town

Starting to build

Steve, Lizzie, Kathryn, Kevin, Jo, Crispin, Sharon & Matt
Our last night together at the Jungle Lodge

Crispin surfs at Pavones

The veg man

Pluma de angel (angel feather)

Juan Carlos brings Estrella's bed

House takes shape

Ruben

Freddy & Margarita's house

Giving a buyer a tour of the finca

Gilly & BoBo

Stephen & Jo at the Great South Run

Estrella & Arturo meet

Blue jeans poison dart frog

Our terrace

A FRIEND LAUGHS

Small bathroom

Approaching storm

Arturo huge at 4m
Yailin (centre) tiny at 2yrs

Catkin's waterfall

Juan Carlos' workshop
looking towards the rancho
site where Gilly died

Crispin & Toli at Crispin's party

Arturo's jungle play mat

Grace, Yeudin & Enrique

The bathroom door

Christmas day at the river

Kirsty

Alex

John

Margarita, Jackie, Freddy and Yailin

Me & Kirsty singing "I Will Survive" at the wedding

20 El Viejito

Something else had been happening to me recently; something quite disturbing. I certainly hadn't reached the 'glowing' stage of my pregnancy yet, I was to wait in vain for that, but I didn't feel quite so crap. Maybe it goes without saying that I wanted to eat everything in sight; particularly red meat, anything sweet, fish fingers and baked beans.

I mentioned my fish finger cravings to my sister and she immediately went out and bought a packet from her conveniently placed supermarket (that actually had a frozen foods section, unlike ours). You can do that when you live in the civilised world I vaguely remembered. She actually phoned me when she was eating a fish finger butty to tell me how good it was. Her morning sickness hadn't started yet. Don't worry; it would. Ha ha! No, that's really cruel of me; whether or not she had taunted me with two fat pieces of bread, dripping with butter (those low fat spreads just wouldn't do) and stuffed full of bread-crumbed coated fish, or something that might have once resembled a fish anyway, morning sickness is no joke. By the way, she was pregnant and this time the line on the pregnancy test wasn't faint at all and she knew it was going to be okay and so did I.

Anyway, as well as having fantasies about food. I was, rather embarrassingly, having fantasies about our builders. Well, one in particular. I remembered a friend telling me about one of those 'leave the country and go somewhere sunny' programmes on the telly. A couple had apparently gone to live on an island off the coast of Costa Rica and the wife had ended up leaving her husband and running off with one of the builders. When I heard this I pictured your stereotypical British builder and couldn't fathom out why she had done such a thing. Now I understood; maybe her builders looked like some of ours.

Now Toli's team consisted of his two brothers; Jesús and Juan – both older than Crispin and thank goodness my hormones hadn't gone sufficiently haywire for me to be fantasising about rolling round the jungle undergrowth with either of them, nor Toli I'll quickly add. They were what I expected builders to look like, although not quite your stereotypical British builder with his bum cleavage; these guys wore belts around their shorts to keep that hidden. Then there were their sons.

Firstly, Einar who had his dad's (Toli's) build and presumably was bullied at school for being rather on the large side, although his 'wasp nest torching' trick must have made him popular in the classroom. Douglas was his younger brother and the complete opposite i.e. as skinny as a rake. He used to practice his English on me. "I love you" he would say; "a beer please"; "will you sleep with me?" and other useful phrases when you're 16 years of age.

He would memorise English song lyrics and ask me if I could translate them for him. I was pretty good at recognising his hummings and mispronunciations and putting names to the songs and giving him the vague Spanish meaning. He did catch me out once mind you and, to this day, I have no idea what he spent weeks desperately trying to make me understand, humming and lalalaing for all he was worth. It wasn't unlike 'Walking on the Moon' but he insisted that that wasn't it. It will come to me one day, I'm sure.

Little Toli was their annoying younger brother and you could tell from the spare tyres around his nine year old waistline that he was going to have to cut down on his rice and beans soon or he would head the same way as his older brother and his dad. He hung around the building site during the school holidays and Saturdays. On a Saturday morning, when the team left at 11am, he was often spotted driving his dad's pick-up. Now that was scary to

184

watch. The roads were dangerous enough without having to contend with kids who can't see over the steering wheel or reach that all-important brake.

I'll talk about their cousins in a moment. First I'll just mention the four guys on the team who joined up after the house had been started. Alfredo was Bilkez's dad. We wanted to employ as many of Bilkez's family as possible, anything we could do to get money into that incredibly poor family without actually giving them cash for no reason. We absolutely knew that Alfredo wouldn't accept charity so we asked Toli if he could give him a job instead. Alfredo was softly spoken with the same stunning smile that Bilkez had, he was also incredibly trustworthy and hard-working.

Then there was David who spent most of his time at Bilkez's house. We were sure there would be an engagement announcement soon. She hadn't had a boyfriend for a while and at 22 was shockingly considered to be 'on the shelf'!

Next was happy smiling Walter who lit up every grey day with his shiny white, almost American looking, teeth and his England football shirt that said 'Beckham' on the back (that probably endeared him to me too). Oh, and I nearly forgot about Cristian who was Toli's right hand man and his electrician who, we later discovered when we had to get the house entirely re-wired before it burned to the ground, that he had never actually trained as an electrician.

One day another new guy appeared. He said his name was Gustavo and that he was Toli's *yerno*. It wasn't a word Crispin and I were familiar with. Then suddenly something I remembered Toli mentioning about a month or so earlier flashed into my mind. He had said he had been to his daughter's wedding.

"He's Toli's son-in-law," I said to Crispin as realisation smacked me in the face. "You're married to Toli's daughter aren't you?" I said to Gustavo.

He nodded. "Angie," he said. I stared open-mouthed.

"No, his older daughter," I argued. The one that wasn't just a child I wanted to say. Which was a bit of a silly thing to say, I mean, he should know who he married, right?

At that point Angie came over to us to say 'Hi' kissing us both on the cheeks and taking Estrella off me. Then she put her free arm around her husband and smiled at us.

"How old are you?" I asked Gustavo in a high pitched voice.

"Eighteen," he said smiling.

"Angie?"

"I'm 16 now," she replied, also smiling; as if it was all a big joke.

"We think she's pregnant too," Gustavo whispered to me. I was shocked!!

"When did you meet? How long have you been going out?" I was sounding like a concerned parent and I knew it was none of my business but, coming from a country where the average age of people getting married was rapidly approaching 30, it seemed ridiculous. But what else was there for young people to do down here? University? Travel the world? They weren't options and I couldn't think of anything else other than 'stay at home and help mum look after her other six children' or 'help dad plant rice and beans and milk the cows on the *finca*'. I knew with absolute certainty that I didn't want Estrella to be a child bride; she would have other options.

Okay, now for the cousins. There was Jesús' boy, Roberto. A charming angelic looking lad (probably 17) who wore a bandana tied around his head. Unfortunately he almost cut his thumb off

186

with a saw one day and sadly left, bandana wrapped around it, to have it sewn back together again. He had been replaced by Bilkez's dad Alfredo.

Then there were Juan's lads. Didier, whose nickname for a reason I never found out was Pato (duck). He had the air of a young man (he was probably in his mid 20s) who had broken a lot of girl's hearts and was probably still breaking them. He could incidentally carry three bags of cement at once. Crispin could just about manage one.

Finally, there was Didier's brother, Ruben, who was maybe the older of the two and my problem. Now there was something about watching Ruben's rippling biceps pushing a wheelbarrow laden with bags of cement that I found incredibly attractive (I didn't mind that he needed to use a wheelbarrow).

The first time I noticed that there might be something amiss was when I greeted him one day. Toli, his brothers, Alfredo, Freddy and Enrique and any women around – so any of their wives or Angie - got a peck on the cheek from me. The rest of the team just got a wave. I have no idea how my 'greetings routine' had evolved into this 'peck or wave' thing but now it had it was difficult to change so I now wasn't able to kiss Ruben on the cheek and it was, I decided, a good thing. After all I was a happily married woman. Wasn't I?

So one day I waved my usual wave in Ruben's direction and he smiled his cute smile and I suddenly remembered that I had dreamt about him the previous night. I had been rolling around in the jungle undergrowth with someone. I had woken up in the middle of the night feeling rather like I wanted a bit of company, not remembering why, and had reached over for Crispin who had been incredibly happy to be woken up, once he realised I wasn't poking him because he was snoring. He hadn't been getting much in recent months as all of that jiggling

187

about had made me feel queasy, plus we had had a lot of visitors sleeping inches away from us in the lounge.

Anyway, as Ruben's dreamy dark brown eyes connected with mine, I realised, that my jungle buddy had been him and, what's more, I was sure from the way he looked at me that he knew exactly what I had been dreaming about. I was incredibly embarrassed and almost fell over his wheelbarrow in my haste to get away.

From then on every time I was up at the house site looking at the plaster the guys had put on the walls or watching a group of them mixing concrete by hand, whenever I did sneak a glance at him, a square piece of polystyrene in his hand trying to make the already smooth plaster even more glass-like or standing hunched over a pile of sand and cement, spade in hand catching his breath, he always knew and his eyes would catch mine again and he would give me a cute smile and I would walk away quickly, trying to avoid any stray wheelbarrows, and pretend to be incredibly interested in the hairy caterpillar that Estrella had just found on the floor.

I spent the rest of my pregnancy pretending that Ruben didn't exist, ignoring him whenever I was anywhere near him, like a schoolgirl who had a crush on a boy in her class – well, that was what I had done to Glyn Evans when I was 13 anyway.

I didn't understand the reason for this at all. Something similar had happened to me when I had been pregnant with Estrella. I had spent a good part of that pregnancy dreaming and fantasising about ex-boyfriends.

Chemicals are something I am incredibly interested in as chemistry (along with a bit of biochemistry, physiology and microbiology – although I have to admit the microbiology lectures were 4pm to 6pm on a Friday afternoon on a different campus which was a 15 minute cycle ride away so I didn't

188

attend an awful lot of those) is what I spent my university years studying, (that, the opposite sex, and the odd pint of cider obviously). Chemicals are responsible for everything that happens in your body so I figured that these feelings must be something to do with the hormones, which are just chemicals after all, that your body produces when you are pregnant but I couldn't think of a reason why your body would want you to fantasise about builders.

The throwing up thing I could rationalise. Maybe, your body didn't want to take anything into it that could harm the growing ball of cells that would become a baby until it was developed enough to resist anything nasty that may be (and let's face it, probably was) lurking in your food. The 'baby brain' side of pregnancy I could also rationalise. When you are stressed your body produces cortisol, a hormone that is believed to cause future developmental and behavioural problems when unborn babies are exposed to it. So your body wants you to be stress-free whilst you are cooking that bun in your oven so it makes you forget anything that you might worry about. So, just to be on the safe side, it makes you forget everything. Clever, eh? I'm sure I didn't learn a single new word of Spanish in the nine months I was pregnant. In fact it was longer than that because breastfeeding prevents your hormones from returning to their normal levels. Maybe it is your body's way of ensuring that you remain stress free for a while longer as stress can also affect your milk production. It all kind of makes sense doesn't it?

So, what was the reason for my teenage crush? I had to think long and hard to come up with something that explained it away. Maybe in the old days when we were running around with clubs in our hands we only acted on our instincts so I'm guessing a lot of women got pregnant but the father didn't hang around at all as he was too busy acting on his instinct to keep the human race going and spread his seed as far and wide as his fur-covered feet would carry him. This act of fantasising about men, other than the baby's father, was just a way of finding someone to help support you and your child until you could 'get out there again' club in hand. I'm going to take that a step further and say who better than someone who knew how to build a house for you? So, by my reckoning I just had to avoid him for another year and everything would be back to normal and I just hoped to goodness I wasn't left alone with him, especially not in the jungle!

I was mulling this over as we were getting ready to leave to go to Freddy's parents' house. We, along with my parents, had been invited for lunch at Amado and Flory's.

Freddy had come down on his new motorbike to see if we needed any help exiting the house and wanted to talk to Crispin about something. It was sad to see him give up his horse for modern technology but it was easier and quicker for him and in a way, it was partly our doing. As well as raising money by selling five of his cows, his motorbike had been bought with the money we had given Amado for his land and the bonus we had given Freddy for Christmas. Another son, the only one who knew how to drive, had had a pick-up truck bought for him by his dad.

Freddy's licence had been acquired the way a lot of people acquired licences down here. It was something else that made driving down here hazardous, adding to the state of the roads, under-age children who couldn't see where they were going and now we had people who paid other people to do their driving tests for them. It was all considered perfectly normal but as I kept saying "Just because everybody does it; it doesn't make it right."

Crispin and Freddy were standing outside the house talking and I kept hearing 'El Viejito' being mentioned.

"Who are you calling 'little old man'?" I asked Crispin in Spanish during a break in their conversation. It didn't seem like a very complimentary thing to be calling anybody.

"It's what everybody calls him," said Crispin, "because he is little and old and a man."

"But that's not his name though, surely?" Crispin shrugged, he didn't know.

"It's Eliseo," explained Freddy. He was a Panamanian who thought he was in his late 90s or early 100s (he had lost count of how old he was exactly and the figure changed each time he was asked) and was as deaf as a post, never showered and lived in a little house on Amado's *finca*. He was now working for us in our *finca*.

"Doing what?" I asked Crispin in amazement.

"Chopping with Freddy and Enrique." Chopping was the term used for cutting back the undergrowth with machetes. It was labour intensive and looked bloody exhausting. It was February (one of the hottest months of the year) and absolutely boiling hot.

"We have a very very very old man chopping our undergrowth in this heat?" What had he done that was so bad to make Crispin want to kill him?

"He only works half days," said Crispin.

"Oh, that's okay then!" I said sarcastically.

"No, it is okay actually," Freddy explained to me. "Eliseo lives to work. That is all he wants to do and if he can't work then he'll die." In this heat he just might die anyway, I couldn't help thinking.

It turned out that I wouldn't have to wait very long to meet this character. Somebody I didn't know was sitting in the corner of the rancho at Amado and Flory's when we arrived there, Amado was with him.

191

"That's him," said Crispin nodding towards the skinny little man. Eliseo looked at us, he resembled a scary grumpy old man and his face was a blank; he didn't know who we were. I was surprised, after all Crispin was his boss.

"He doesn't recognise me without my hat on," Crispin whispered in my ear. Crispin took his hat out of his pocket and placed it on his head. Eliseo's face broke into a smile of recognition, transforming him from a scary grumpy old man into a kind (but still a bit scary) one and he waved his skinny arms at us. He was wearing nothing but a pair of grubby trousers held up with a piece of string and his bare feet looked like they could do with a good wash. He stood up to greet us but didn't gain much height as his spine was curved like a bow (he had slept in a hammock all of his life and was now shaped like one).

I soon found out it was pointless shouting at him. It was better to speak slowly so he could lip-read, but he wasn't too good at that either. As Crispin had already demonstrated, his sight was going too.

I had no idea what Eliseo said when he spoke to me, he had lost all of his teeth and it made it impossible for me to understand him but also I wasn't giving him my full attention as I was rather concerned that Estrella was now cowering in my arms, clearly terrified of him. Eliseo took her hands in his and was mumbling at her. Estrella was visibly shaking and was milliseconds away from bursting into tears. Eliseo, thank goodness, was completely ignorant of the effect he was having on her. I really didn't know what to do, I didn't want to appear rude by saying "She thinks you're a scary old man, please leave her alone" – after all, Brits didn't say things like that (even pregnant ones) - but I didn't want to put Estrella through the hell she was going through either. I had never seen her react like this before.

At that moment Flory, (Freddy's mum) appeared and I quickly turned away from Eliseo and greeted her with an enthusiastic peck on the cheek. Flory instantly noticed the state that Estrella was in and intuitively realised why. "Yailin's the same," she said with concern. She gestured us to sit on a bench at the opposite corner of the rancho from Eliseo and then led him off towards the house. As I sat down, Estrella dived into my lap, curled up and refused to watch him walk past.

It was the first time I had met Freddy's mum and she was a lovely friendly round lady. All Tico women seemed to become round when they reached middle age; skinny and large-chested when they were young and very round as they got older.

When she came back she greeted mum and dad and gestured for them to sit in the hammocks in the rancho whilst she got drinks for them. The hammocks were old fishing nets and dad did a pretty good job of getting in one. Mum didn't even try. "I'll never be able to get out again, Jo," she said. She was probably right; there was an art to clambering in and out of hammocks without embarrassing yourself by falling out backwards or turning the hammock 180 degrees and ending up in a heap underneath it. Dad had kept his dignity intact.

We then spent a lovely 'Eliseo-free' afternoon admiring Amado and Flory's garden and everything they had in it. It wasn't easy communicating as they weren't used to speaking to foreigners so spoke incredibly quickly, but with gestures we got by. There was a fantastic breeze in the rancho; that was after all why people built them; to be able to sit outside in the heat of the day and catch the breeze whilst being shaded by the palm frond roof.

"What's this, Jo?" my dad asked pointing to a plant that was used as hedging between the garden and the rest of the *finca*. It was high and cut off the view to the gulf and the peninsula; it was odd how

Tico's didn't see the view as being important. I tried to explain this to Amado and he thought we were funny; getting excited about something he had seen every day for the last 40 years. I didn't recognise the plant.

"What's this?" I asked Freddy. He mimed scrubbing his back.

"I don't understand," I said shaking my head. He ran inside the house and came back moments later with a loofah. "It's a loofah plant," I said in amazement. I had never thought about loofahs growing on plants before. My dad set about taking photos.

A huge pure white fluffy turkey ran across the grass. "Champipe," said Freddy pointing at it.

"Our Christmas Dinner," Crispin said to me with a smile on his face, he was licking his lips. I frowned at him, I wasn't going to eat Amado and Flory's pet! The *champipe* was closely followed by what looked like suspiciously like a peacock.

"I've a peahen too," Amado said. So it <u>was</u> a peacock! "My daughter-in-law works at a zoo just outside of San José," he explained. "I bought them from there."

We were sitting in a Tico's rancho looking at birds that in England were reserved for posh country estates, it was very bizarre.

The afternoon ended all too soon as the sun was starting to go down and we wanted to have a look at how the house was coming along before it got too dark; I had more 'Ruben-avoiding' to do. We stayed until the sun vanished behind the peninsula and then said our goodbyes as the sky turned pink and orange; pecks on the cheek all round.

21 Wood Smuggling

I think the police may be on to us.

It all started a couple of weeks ago when Marco, the guy with the gorgeous eyes who orders our building supplies, came up to the house site with some bad news. "There's a rumour going around that you don't have a licence for your wood," he told Crispin.

"That's ridiculous," I said when Crispin told me later that day. "We must have a licence. We are going to be an eco-friendly establishment that preserves the rainforest. We wouldn't be encouraging the cutting down of hardwood trees from that very same rainforest; trees that take 25 years minimum to grow to a reasonable size, without a licence." I was sure of it. Crispin didn't look so sure. "Would we?" I added in a small voice.

"I'll check with Juan Carlos," said Crispin. "I'm sure he'll confirm that we've got licences."

Unfortunately, he couldn't. When Crispin asked our carpenter if Victor and Evelio, our two main wood suppliers, had licences for the various hardwoods that were piled high by the house site he said that he didn't know and would ask them. "I'm pretty sure you don't need permission for teak though," he said. Okay, so our terrace was safe.

Apparently, if MINAE (the environment ministry) found our wood stash and our permits weren't in order they would confiscate it and fine us. It would be 'bye bye' to our lounge and bedroom floors, 'farewell' to the beams for our roof structure not to mention 'adiós' to all of our furniture. As IKEA hadn't yet found its way to Costa Rica we couldn't let this happen.

The following day MINAE visited our house site. Twice. Toli, our builder, had somehow had prior warning and miraculously our wood piles had become disguised as living quarters for the men. The man deserves a medal.

The news came back from Juan Carlos, who seemed neither surprised nor bothered, that neither Victor nor Evelio had licences to cut down their hardwood trees, if they even were their hardwood trees – maybe they had snuck into someone else's *finca* in the middle of the night and stolen them.

"My goodness, people really do that?" I asked. Juan Carlos nodded. I was shocked.

"Nobody bothers to apply for licences because MINAE never give licences. Unless that is you give them a 'chorizo'," said Juan Carlos.

"Why would MINAE want a spicy sausage?" I asked Crispin.

"It means a bribe," he explained. I gasped. "Or," continued Juan Carlos in rapid Spanish, "the very few people who do have legal licences obtain them legally but then use them over and over again for illegal wood so even wood that appears to be legal, almost definitely isn't."

"Is there someone in MINAE we can phone to find out who they have given licences to?" I asked whoever was listening.

"And ask them whether they gave the licence because they were bribed or because they really felt it was okay to cut the tree down?" asked Crispin just a tad sarcastically. Okay, he had a point; I was going to shut up.

Our 'eco-friendly house' was rapidly becoming 'eco un-friendly'. Plus as the last two guys that had joined Toli's team (Walter and David) were from out of town, we couldn't tick the 'using local labour' box either.

At least I've bought bread and milk from the local *pulpería* a couple of times and we have started using a local fruit and veg man too.

We had finally realised that the various trucks that we passed parked in the road that had locals lining up behind them sold fruit and vegetables. One of the trucks now came to our house on a Sunday so we could tick that box too. Mind you I'd noticed an apple I had bought last week from him had a 'Grown in Canada' sticker on it. I had also lent the veg guy my kitchen scales as his were broken and he couldn't weigh any produce. He avoided me the following week and then arrived at the house the following Sunday saying that my scales had been stolen but he promised that he would replace them. I was a bit upset as they had been a wedding present and I explained that I had brought them over from England. The following week the veg guy handed over some scales that looked like my chrome and black shiny scales but with a rusting blue metal support now holding the bowl in place. It was only after he had left that I realised they <u>were</u> my scales. The veg guy had obviously broken them, lied to me and then tried to mend them. My scales would never weigh anything again and we started buying our weekly supplies from a different truck.

Freddy was standing nearby listening to our wood conversation.

"The police are selling cristobal at 950 a *pulgada*," he said helpfully. Cristobal was the wood our floors would be made from, if it wasn't confiscated first that was. The reference to *pulgada* which comes from the Spanish word for thumb (*pulgar*), was because wood was sold by the inch and there was a complicated formula (well complicated for a pregnant lass) you used to calculate how many *pulgadas* or inches were in a plank. I was confused; maybe I had reached the wrong conclusion.

"Why are the police selling Cristobal?" I asked Freddy

"Because it didn't have a licence so they confiscated it."

"But why are they now selling it?" I asked. Why wasn't it in a police lock-up? Enrique smiled kindly at my naivety.

"They want money," said Freddy, in a 'isn't that perfectly obvious voice'. Okay, so I hadn't reached the wrong conclusion.

"We aren't buying confiscated wood just to line the pocket of the local police," I said adamantly.

"If you don't someone else will," Enrique said.

"No way!" He and Freddy shrugged their shoulders and walked off. I could tell they thought the boss' wife was crazy.

It was stressed to our wood guys that they had to get licences or we wouldn't be buying any more wood from them. They agreed that they would try. Crispin assured me that, come the rainy season, we would plant lots of hardwood trees in our *finca* to redeem ourselves and knowing that made me feel a bit better.

We still needed more teak for the terrace. We had decided to make it much bigger and to stretch it around three sides of the house. Unfortunately it meant one of our mango trees would have to be cut down. We now made any changes to the house design by directly consulting with Toli. Pah, who needed an architect?! Our new one was only contracted to come to check the roof beams before the roof went on. He lived in San José and wanted $500 every time he visited. We would cope without him until roof time.

Juan Carlos sourced some teak from another wood guy, Evaristo. Evaristo wanted to deliver it urgently as he was keeping it in Paso Canoas (the shady border town) and he was worried it would get stolen if he didn't move it quickly. We paid half the total amount in advance and promised him the rest on arrival. He said he would be at the house site with the wood at 7.30pm that same evening.

"But it'll be dark then," I said. The potholed roads were hazardous enough in the day time. It sure seemed a strange time to be delivering anything - in the pitch black. Juan Carlos didn't answer me but looked at me strangely and I got the impression that that was the point.

We left the house site and drove to Paso Canoas. We had shopping to do and needed a new car battery.

By the time we left Canoas it was dark. As we passed one of the little police stations en-route to our house we noticed a truck pulled up outside. It was loaded with wood.

"Bollocks. That's our teak," said Crispin.

"But you don't need a licence for teak though. Do you?" I asked.

"Juan Carlos said you didn't."

We stopped for gas just past the police station and a very large man in a tight black vest and wearing too many gold chains came over to us.

"Where are you going?" he asked in Spanish.

"Cuervito," Crispin replied, hoping it was the wrong answer.

"Can you give me a ride to Conte?" said the man in the vest. We were driving through it so, although he looked a bit unsavoury we agreed and he squeezed his ample bottom onto our rear seat. Estrella had woken up and gave him a Paddington Bear hard stare from her car seat.

After telling him where we lived, he informed us he was one of the local Police *Comandantes* and then burbled on in rapid Spanish for ages. I was too tired to concentrate and he spoke far too quickly for me to understand what he was saying. I caught the odd word occasionally: beans; cows; thieves; wood but that was about it.

"What's he saying?" I asked Crispin whilst our guest drew breath.

"He's going to Conte to help a friend pick beans, someone stole 16 cows using only a car and there's a lot of wood smuggling going on near us apparently."

"Oh," I said in the most innocent voice I could muster.

We both breathed huge sighs of relief when he squeezed himself out of the car again.

"Do you think he knows it's us?" I hissed.

"He said he knew where our house site was when I mentioned it," said Crispin, "but I don't know if that means anything."

Juan Carlos was now living at the house site, with the wood, trying to make it unconfiscatable. Apparently, if wood has been worked on, it can no longer be confiscated. The Ministry thinks it is okay to walk off with someone's wood but not if it is now a table. Crispin drove up to see him to check if Evaristo was still with the police or whether he had managed to deliver his cargo. No one had seen or heard from Evaristo. Crispin explained that we had seen him pulled over the previous night and asked for clarification on the licence issue.

"You don't need a licence for teak though, do you?" Crispin asked him.

"Not a licence exactly," Juan Carlos answered.

"What is that supposed to mean," I asked Crispin later when he told me about the conversation. He admitted that he didn't know.

Our mobile rang at 11.30pm. Crispin stumbled out of bed and got to the phone before its vibration made it jump into the sink, as had happened several times before. Unfortunately the kitchen windowsill directly above the sink was where it got the best reception

"Who was that?" I mumbled as he got back into bed.

"Evaristo. He wanted to know if we would mind if he delivered the wood on Monday instead. He's still with the police."

"Did he mention anything about a licence?"

"He said that he did have a licence for the wood but it was in his house and not on him so things were a bit difficult but would be fine." Okay, so that was good news.

"The *cara de tigre* that Juan Carlos sourced last week," I had just thought of something else - the curved fancy tree trunks we were going to use as columns on the terrace, "where are they coming from?"

"Evelio."

"Does Evelio have a licence for cutting *cara de tigre*?" I asked.

"I don't know, Jo," he said in his tired 'stop nagging me' voice. "I assume Juan Carlos checked to make sure he did."

Maybe by the time we built our next house, an all concrete one of course, IKEA, that Swedish furniture store that made your life easy, will have found their way out here.

22 Lunch at Freddy and Margarita's

It was an exciting day. We had been invited to Freddy and Margarita's for lunch. They had asked us to bring Estrella's paddling pool too plus the water to go in it. It was the height of the dry season, although it wasn't turning out to be a particularly dry dry season, and Freddy said that they didn't have the water to fill it. We filled six huge water bottles and loaded them into the car. Rather bizarrely I thought, ice had also been requested.

Their house wasn't on the road and to access it we entered through a gate in front of Freddy's corral. Freddy was there to meet us, he must have heard the car approaching. I didn't know it at the time but the corral was where, amongst other things, they kept cows who are about to give birth so they can keep an eye on them or assist if necessary. We walked carefully around the corral, empty at this time. The ground was very rutted as, even after the recent rain, the sun had quickly baked the cows' hoof prints and it was now like cement again; it would have been easy to sprain an ankle. Then of course there were the fresh cow pats to avoid.

Yailin was pleased to see us and even more pleased to see the paddling pool. She was standing by the barbed wire fence with Jackie and her mum, both girls were grinning madly. Freddy opened the gate in the barbed wire.

"It keeps the horses and cows out," he explained. It didn't however keep the chickens out and there were several varieties running around the place. One hen had a little brood of chicks chasing along behind her.

There were two beautiful trees in front of the house with an old fishing net strung up between them which served as a hammock. Freddy gestured for Crispin to try it and Crispin stretched out like an expert.

"It's really comfortable," he said to me in surprise. I recognised the trees from Amado's garden. They were aptly called *pluma de angel* (angel feather). These were much bigger and provided brilliant shade for whoever was chilling out in the hammock. The hummingbirds seemed to love them too as there were several bright green ones hovering about filling up on nectar from the fluffy pink flowers.

The paddling pool was set up in the shade of the trees and Freddy started filling it with the water we had brought. Crispin dragged himself out of the hammock to help him. Estrella and Yailin waited patiently next to them. I changed Estrella into her purple swimming costume that said 'little star' on it. Yailin was wearing a little bikini that was too small for Estrella. I'd given it to her the previous week and Yailin looked incredibly cute in it. She was a beautiful child, all smiles and curls.

"Do you want to sit here, Jo?" asked Margarita pointing to a wooden bench near to where the kids were already splashing about excitedly, enjoying the cold water on this hot day. There was some chicken poo on one end of the bench. Margarita noticed that I had spotted it. "The chickens like to sit on it," she said apologetically. I gestured that it wasn't a problem and sat down at the opposite end to the poo. The wood was a bit damp and I tried to pull my maternity shorts down my legs a bit but my bottom had expanded significantly in recent months and there wasn't any spare material to be pulled.

I looked over towards the house. It was a very basic Tico house with no glass windows or bug screens, just square holes with wooden shutters that were pulled shut at night. It was wooden, built on stilts and was probably the size of our new master bedroom. It had a corrugated zinc roof and there were huge containers placed under the eaves so they could catch the rainwater. I could just see in through the main door which led into what I assumed, because of the aluminium pot bubbling away on the open fire, was the kitchen. As I was taking all of this in the mother hen ran in through the door followed by its chicks and I then noticed that the kitchen had a dirt floor. I thought of the house we were building not ten minutes walk away; Freddy and Margarita would be our nearest neighbours and I felt embarrassed.

I was dragged sharply out of my thoughts when I realised that someone was trying to put something in my hair. Freddy had something that looked like a translucent dead cockroach in his hand! I pulled back quickly and looked at him in horror. He tried to hand it to me but I refused to take it. "Follow me," he said laughing and he led me to a tree by the barbed wire fence. It was covered in hundreds of the things. I looked more closely, but still refused to touch them, and saw that they weren't dead cockroaches but the hard outer casing of an insect, presumably one that shed its skin when it grew too big for it. Estrella had tired of the paddling pool and was in Crispin's arms wrapped in a towel, Freddy was putting them in her hair but she didn't like them much and was trying to pull them out again.

"What are they?" I asked Freddy.

"Chicharas." I looked blankly at him. "Chigarra?" he said, using a different name.

"The things that are really noisy at night and in the morning?" I asked him. He nodded and I knew at once what they were: cicadas, the beetles with the huge beautiful wings.

"They wiggle out of the ground," he said in Spanish, demonstrating by holding both of his arms above his head and moving his bottom from side to side, "and shed their skin." He mimed taking off his t-shirt. "Underneath are their wings. When they are dry they fly away." He was now flapping his arms.

"To annoy some poor soul who is trying to get to sleep!" I finished for him. We both laughed.

Freddy had given up trying to put them in Estrella's hair. He started on Jackie's and she soon had them almost the full length of her plait. They did look scarily similar to a hair clip and I was sure if one of the big fashion designers ever found out about them a new trend could be started.

Lunch was pronounced ready and there were shouts of protest coming from Yailin. She was refusing to get out of the paddling pool, although her lips were turning blue and she had goose-bumps (the Spanish equivalent *piel de gallina* translates as 'chicken skin') on her arms and legs. The sun had gone in, the breeze had got up and the skies had started to darken. It looked like we were in for a storm. Margarita was trying to reason with her but, as we would one day learn, reasoning with a two year old doesn't usually work and Yailin was starting to cry.

Margarita stripped Yailin's bikini off and wrapped her in a towel. She paused to study something on Yailin's thigh. With her fingernail she scratched at the skin, brought whatever she had scratched off closer to her eyes and then crushed it between her fingernails.

"What was that?" I asked her.

"Coloradilla," she said showing me her fingernail. I couldn't see anything at all and was none the wiser. "Pica mucho," she said. "Hay muchas aquí." Well, whatever *colaradillas* were they itched a lot and there were lots of them here. I would remember her words the following night.

Freddy motioned us towards the door that the hen and her family had earlier entered by. "Pase adelante," he said as we approached. It was an important custom here and no self-respecting Tico entered your house without firstly asking permission ¿con permiso? and secondly waiting for the *pase adelante* or *pase* indicating you could 'go ahead'. It would be a while before we got the hang of the '¿*con permiso?*' bit; after all when you visit a friend in the UK they tend to hold the door open for you and say 'come in' but you don't stand there asking 'can I come in?'. We hadn't been inside many Tico houses. It was rare for a Gringo to be invited inside; most of our exchanges, or the *fiestas* (parties) we had attended, took place outside, in the garden or on the terrace or in a rancho, so we felt very honoured to be asked to enter Freddy and Margarita's house.

As you entered the kitchen the *leña* (cooking fire) was on the left and next to that the *pila* (washing-up area) which consisted of two shallow rectangular concrete sinks with a deeper one in between them. A tall bucket full of water sat in one of the shallow sinks. There didn't seem to be a tap. Looking at the set-up I had no idea how you were supposed to wash up and seeing as we'd been invited to eat lunch here, I felt we had to at least offer. There also seemed to be something missing but I couldn't for the life of me figure out what it was.

Whatever lunch was it smelled good. "What's in the pot?" Crispin asked Margarita.

"Pollo sudado," (sweaty chicken) came the reply.

"It's one of our own chickens," Freddy added. "Margarita killed it at 4 o'clock this morning."

I was a bit shocked as I was one of those people who liked meat but didn't like to be reminded where it came from and would probably give it up if I was reminded too often. (Crispin was brought up in the true countryside as opposed to in the countryside nine miles outside of Birmingham as I was. The first time Crispin took me to meet his parents I ambled into the kitchen to see what his mum was up to and was met with a cry of "Get Jo out of here!" As Crispin turned me around to shepherd me back into the lounge I caught a glimpse of the blood bath occurring in the sink. There were bits of fur and animal innards everywhere and I was horrified. Someone had hit a hare with their car and had picked it up off the road and brought it to Crispin's mum for her to make our dinner with. We ate road-kill stew for two nights. It was quite nice actually!).

At the time, we had no idea that it was something that was done for special occasions; I'm talking about Ticos killing their own chickens again by the way and not hitting hares with cars; Freddy obviously felt it was a very important occasion having his boss' family over for lunch.

"Do you always get up at 4am?" I asked Margarita. I hoped she didn't just do it for our benefit. Freddy explained for her, he did that sometimes.

"She has to get the water from the well, light the fire and heat the water so Jackie can bathe before school." The school year began in February so Jackie had started six weeks ago. She would be seven next month.

From the kitchen there was a scarily big step up into a small living area with a wooden floor. There was a television in one corner – so they had something we didn't have - and a shelf with a variety of cuddly toys on it including the ones we'd given Jackie and Yailin for Christmas. My eye kept being drawn to the big drop between the living area and the kitchen, it was taller than Estrella. "Has Yailin ever fallen down that?" I asked Margarita.

"Twice," replied Freddy, "but she learnt quickly," he added smiling. Not that quickly if she had to do it a second time I thought. I was beginning to wish we'd brought Estrella's safety gate with us. We had bought a couple in Golfito from the duty-free area when we took mum and dad back to the airport. Estrella was running around all over the place now but we somehow managed to keep her away from the opening. Well, on that visit we did anyway. (In a future visit she would cut her toe on a rusty nail sticking out of the wall on her way down before landing in a heap on the kitchen floor – there would be a lot of tears).

As well as the telly, the shelf and the drop, there was a small hand-made table with a white tablecloth on it pushed up against the window. By the side of the table there was a bench that could seat two people and two hand-made stools. Margarita started bringing bowls out with spoons in them and placing them on the table; sliced tomato; finely sliced green cabbage with lemon juice; black beans; a couple of bowls of rice and a bowl of presumably 'sweaty chicken' which looked like boiled chicken pieces with unrecognisable vegetables which turned out to be *yuca* – cassava, very starchy and not too unlike a potato - and *ayote* – a type of squash.

It was at that moment I remembered I had Estrella's lunch with me – not being too sure as to whether she would eat what was on offer I had grabbed some bolognaise from our freezer. "Have you got a microwave I can heat this up in?" I asked Freddy, during a momentary lapse of reason.

"We don't have electricity," he said, laughing. I could have died. That was what was missing from the kitchen – a fridge! It also made much more sense of the request for ice which incidentally we had stupidly left in a cooler on the side in our kitchen in our rush to get out of the door and not be too late.

"But the television...," I tailed off, pointing at it; now I was really confused.

"I take a car battery up to my dad's every morning to charge it up and that powers the television," explained Freddy.

"But your parents haven't got electricity either," I pointed out.

"They've got solar panels on their roof." I hadn't noticed. I could now see the car battery, something I'd missed when I'd first entered the room.

"How long have you been living here for?"

208

"Eight years," Freddy said. I was speechless and in awe and vowed to never again complain when we had one of our regular power cuts. Needless to say, I forgot about my vow the next time we had a power cut!

Margarita took Estrella's bolognaise off me and heated it up on a piece of flat metal which she put on her cooking fire. It was boiling in seconds – better than any microwave!

"Sit down and eat," she said to me.

"Are you not eating?" I said.

"Later," came her reply. She then took Estrella from me so I could eat in peace. I turned my attention to the food. We hadn't been given plates to put food on or forks to eat with so we weren't too sure what we were supposed to do. Freddy sat on the floor with Jackie and Yailin. He had a bowl of rice with some chicken stew on top and was eating it with a spoon; so I guessed correctly there was a bowl of rice for each of us but we were sharing the other stuff.

"Do you put everything in together?" I asked.

"If you want to," said Freddy shrugging his shoulders. I guess it wasn't completely the right way but not knowing how else to go about it I put a bit of everything on top of the rice then mixed it all up with my spoon. Jackie was grinning at me and then gave her dad a knowing smile.

"What have I done wrong?" I asked Jackie smiling. She looked at her dad, still grinning.

"Nothing," Freddy said. "Margarita mixes it up like that too. Some people do, some don't."

I have to say, I could eat Margarita's beans all day. They cook them with onion and the wild coriander that grows everywhere round here and leave them in their black cooking juices. It was the closest dish I could get to Heinz baked beans over here.

During lunch there were loud bangs on the roof, it sounded like hailstones. "Rain" said Freddy.

The storm had reached us. It didn't last for very long but the noise of the rain on the metal roof was absolutely deafening. We sat in silence for while, just eating, it was pointless talking as no one could hear a word anyone else said.

Suddenly I spotted an intruder. "There's a chicken in the kitchen!" I yelled above the din.

"Shoo it out," Margarita said to Jackie and Jackie dutifully did so but I got the impression it was for my benefit and not because it was a problem.

Estrella turned her nose up at her bolognaise and instead ate most of the cabbage and tomato that had been left on the table. She was a strange eater, no two ways about it. One of her favourite foods was raw onion. I gave her some rice too but most of that ended up on the floor.

After our tasty lunch came the moment that I was dreading: I started walking towards the *pila* to show willing. "Can I wash up?" I asked in a small voice. Then came the answer I was hoping for.

"No, sit down," said Margarita with a frown. Phew. I picked up the broom instead. At least I knew how to sweep. Or, I thought I did. Trying to get sticky rice off a wooden floor with a broom was really difficult. What made it worse was the wooden planks didn't meet properly so there were rice size gaps all over the place. "Just sweep it into the kitchen," said Margarita, "the chickens will eat it." So the chicken shooing <u>had</u> been for my benefit.

I was trying desperately to sweep the rice into the kitchen but eventually I gave up. "It doesn't want to go," I exclaimed to Margarita. Every single grain of rice was now firmly wedged in the cracks between the floorboards. Margarita took the broom off me and with an expert flick the rice was extracted, flew through the air and landed on the dirt floor in the kitchen; the chickens pounced. I smiled sheepishly and she laughed.

After lunch the sun came out again and Crispin went off with Freddy to the *finca*. We five girls were left alone. We sat on the floor (there were no sofas or chairs) in front of the television and the cuddly toys were brought off the shelf for Estrella to inspect. I noticed there were two wasps flying into the bulldog clips that were attached to the car battery. "Wasps!" I said to Margarita, presuming she would grab some bug spray and zap them, squish them with something or at least shoo them outside.

"They are their *hogares*," she said

"Hogares?" I questioned, it was a word I didn't recognise.

"They live there." Okay so *hogares* must mean 'homes'.

"But wasps live in big nests, don't they?" Margarita looked confused. I had used the word *nido* for wasps' nest.

"Birds live in *nidos*," she said in Spanish.

"Pañales?" I said hopefully

"Panales," she corrected me. I had just said that wasps lived in big nappies. We all laughed.

"These live alone," she concluded, shrugging to say she didn't know why, they just did.

We sat and watched them for a while. Coming out, hovering around each other as if dancing then flying back into their circular metal holes.

"Do they sting?" I asked her.

"Not if you leave them alone."

"Do you have any other pets?" I asked smiling. Margarita had a good sense of humour and, in spite of the language barrier, she seemed to understand mine. She also smiled and pointed at the sugar ants running all over the table cloth, particularly interested in the home-made lemonade that I had spilt during lunch - I had been mortified and had apologised at least 20 times. She was to get used to me spilling things on her lovely clean table cloths. Each time I did it, which was a darn sight more often than Estrella did, I had visions of her scrubbing them clean by hand; there was no washing machine here. It made me feel terrible but the harder I tried to not spill anything the more likely it was that I did.

Estrella had finished her inspection of the cuddly toys and was starting to yell so Margarita led us through a door-less doorway into the only other room that led off the living area. It had a large low bed in it with an incredibly soft foam mattress. There was a small window with a wooden shutter and through it the gulf and the Osa Peninsula were perfectly framed. As far as I could make out it was the only window in the house that pointed in the direction of the view and incidentally where the prevailing wind and hence the weather came from. The terrace was tucked around the north side of the house where there was no breeze and no view. It made no sense until you realised the terrace was in the shade for most of the day so was actually the coolest side of the house and it also meant that the torrential rain, blown horizontal by the strong winds, didn't soak you when you were out there. After all, remember, a Tico isn't interested in the view and if he wants a breeze he goes to sit in his hammock. It actually made sense if you put yourself in their shoes, or flip flops, rather.

From the corner of the bedroom Jackie produced the largest ugliest doll I had ever seen. She handed it to Estrella who started pulling out what remained of its hair.

I needed the loo and realised that there didn't seem to be a bathroom. "Can I use the bathroom, please?" I asked Margarita. She gestured to Jackie to show me where to go. I was handed a roll of toilet paper and Jackie walked out through the kitchen door. I had taken my boots off to enter the house and couldn't be bothered to put them back on again. There were various pairs of flip-flops lying in the kitchen. "Can I borrow some of your sandals?" I yelled to Margarita. She shouted her agreement and I put some large blue ones on. There was a steep path that led down through the banana trees and it was muddy from the earlier shower. It had also rained the previous night and as the path was in the shade it hadn't dried out yet. It was slippery and I found it difficult to walk in flip-flops that were too big for me; my centre of balance was off anyway due to my protruding belly. I walked slowly and carefully. I followed Jackie down until we reached a little wooden hut with no door. Inside was a tall wooden step with a hole in the horizontal piece of wood. An old toilet seat with no lid sat above the hole. Jackie left me to it. I weed incredibly quickly, trying not to breathe in or think of spiders and scorpions and instead tried to concentrate on the view, I thought I could just make out our new house between the trees. I struggled back up the path using my hands at the steep bits. I put the toilet paper back on the nail that Jackie had got it from and went to the *pila* to wash my hands.

The dirty dishes from lunch were piled up in the right-hand shallow sink and the deeper central sink. There was no tap and I couldn't see any soap. I looked at the tall bucket full of water on the left-hand shallow sink. Surely I wasn't supposed to put my hands in the bucket to wash them. I made a decision. There was some solid green stuff in a pot, the stuff that Ticos used to wash dishes with. I rubbed one hand in it and then splashed some water from the bucket using my other hand to rinse it off and then repeated it with my other hand. I dried my hands on my shorts.

When I came back Margarita left me with the four girls (I'm including the giant doll) whilst she went to wash up. I was intrigued so stuck my head out of the doorway to watch her. With a sponge she was rubbing the green stuff over each bowl then she took a plastic margarine pot dipped it in the bucket of water and rinsed the green stuff off setting the clean item to one side. I was incredibly relieved that I hadn't washed my hands in the bucket!

The following night I was lying in bed with the most intense itching in the area we were teaching Estrella to call her 'bits'. I smothered my 'bits' in Estrella's nappy rash cream and writhed in agony for three nights. Bizarrely, I wasn't itching during the day. <u>Now</u> I knew what Penny had been talking about the day we moved here. <u>Now</u> I understood the reason for the second shower room and the washing machine in close proximity to the back door.

I was telling a friend about the nightmarish experience a couple of weeks later. "Makes you want to attack yourself with a melon baller doesn't it?" he said. He was right: I would have done anything to get rid of them. I tried painting nail varnish on them and I tried rubbing alcohol and they don't work (maybe I should have tried drinking the alcohol instead!). I tried scrubbing myself with a scouring pad but it was too late. The only thing that would take the itch out was Estrella's nappy rash cream but the relief would only last for a couple of hours and then I would wake up and the terrible agony would start again and continue for half an hour until the fresh application of cream started working. I gleaned more information from various people; 'they are worse where there are animals'; 'especially chickens'; 'they live in animal faeces and in long grass'. The bench that I had been sitting on in my short shorts at Margarita's; the one with the chicken poo on it must have been crawling with them. So <u>this</u> was a chigger, a *coloradilla*, a tiny red mite that attaches itself to you and makes your life hell. I cannot possibly live here I thought miserably.

It was only when Estrella had an attack of them the day after we moved into the new house (we

214

are still a long way off) that we were given advice that suddenly made life here a viable option for me. This advice works. Scrub your elastic line with soap in the shower, sulphur soap works best as the chiggers hate it. If you have missed any and you feel any itching later on (they don't normally start itching until 24 hours later) scrub immediately with a scouring pad and put 'Zepol' (Vicks) on it, the stuff you rub on children's chests when they have a cold. If it's a young child then put a plaster on it too otherwise they may rub it in their eyes and scream all day (yes, we learned that one the hard way). Speaking from experience they tend to lodge in children's ears, armpits and their hair. You can scratch them out, although it doesn't always guarantee that the itch will stop, and most local women can see them and extract them, as Margarita did to Yailin that day. If you want to have a go yourself you can see them better in direct sunlight as they kind of glow orange. I hope I have just made your life in Costa Rica easier.

23 Fiesta at Naranjo

We were going out and I had decided to put trousers on Estrella which maybe seemed like a slightly odd thing to do considering the heat but she was starting to get insect bites, lots of them. The previous day she had finally tired of 'dancing dollies' not to mention dancing cats, balloons, Christmas trees and the 101 other things I could now make from a fan of paper and so we had walked up the small hill behind our house. It was, in my opinion, where Mac and Penny should have built their house instead of building in front of the hill as they had done. Up there was a breeze and a stunning view of the gulf – admittedly also of Lenny Loco's house behind – the house we were renting had the occasional gust and a nice view. I had put Estrella's little pink sandals on her, sun cream and her hat with Velcro under the chin so she couldn't yank it off and we had walked up the hill very, very slowly.

Estrella had bent down to grab every blade of grass and pick up every fallen leaf so it had taken us 15 minutes to walk what would have taken me 30 seconds had I been by myself. The hill had two adjacent building sites cut into the top of it so it was easy flat walking once we were up there. The far end of the sites afforded one of the best jungle views around here. I'm sure it's primary rainforest as the trees are enormous. In the middle of this magnificent *vista* stands a huge majestic ceiba tree. It is one of the most beautiful trees I have ever seen and I love standing and staring at it. It is so tall and graceful; I hope nobody ever cuts it down. This was where we had walked to. I picked Estrella up and pointed the tree out to her. "Arból grande," (big tree) I said to her in Spanish.

"Bol ginde," she repeated. I hugged her, marvelled at her blatant natural ability to speak Spanish and hoped that one day she would remember this moment and realise how lucky she was to have seen primary rainforest; there isn't much left.

That night, when I got Estrella ready for bed, I'd noticed she had five bites on one leg, seven on the other, two on her stomach and even one on her little finger. She had scratched two of the ones on her leg and they were bleeding. I was horrified and dotted cream and stuck plasters all over her little body. These were the reason for the trousers for our trip out today.

All I knew was that we were going to what was being called a *fiesta* in the nearby village of Naranjo and there would be bulls. We were taking Freddy and his family and were going to meet Enrique and his pregnant wife Grace there. I'd met Grace once before and under rather embarrassing circumstances. During one of our trips away Enrique had been asked to be our *cuidador* at night. In a scene scarily similar to that when Juan Carlos was looking after our house, we had arrived back late one night found Enrique and Grace fast asleep and had been unable to rouse them. Not much of a deterrent to any passing thieves!

On the way to Naranjo we discovered that Jackie was 'car sick'. She was moved to the front seat which seemed to help. The first thing I saw when we arrived was a sign for *churros*. I remembered them from a school trip to Spain. They are long sugar-coated doughnuts. Jackie and I shared a bag. "Perfect for vomiting children and pregnant women with cravings, eh Jackie?" Jackie nodded, wholeheartedly agreeing with me.

Whilst we stuffed *churros* into our mouths like they were going out of fashion; I surveyed the scene. The fiesta was kind of like a fairground with a few food stalls, a stall that sold kids' toys and cheap hats, a kids' trampoline and a very rickety looking big wheel that had cages that also spun round. There was a covered bar area that was playing really really loud music and had a karaoke machine. It was full of girls wearing tiny tight tops and tight jeans and guys in smart short-sleeved shirts, jeans, cowboy hats and leather belts with large shiny buckles. Enrique was 'salsa'ing with a slim young girl who definitely wasn't Grace. He spotted us and smiled. "It's my niece!" he yelled at us in English. He was laughing and was obviously having a great time. He only ever plucked up the courage to speak English to us after a couple of beers, excellent English at that.

The *churros* bag was now empty and Jackie was licking her fingers and dipping them in the sugar that had been left in the bottom of the bag. I hoped they stayed firmly in her tummy on the way home.

We were the only foreigners and were being stared at but we were used to it by now. A few people came over to greet us: the man from a nearby garage where we had been towed to when the car had broken down last week, the man with the fantastic voice who had sung at Bilkez's sister's birthday party, other people who looked vaguely familiar and treated Crispin like a long-lost brother but I couldn't place. After they had gone I would find out that Crispin couldn't either!

We wandered about a bit, waiting for the bulls to start. I was surprised to see food stalls selling candy floss just like any fairground in England. From the toy stall we bought an inflatable *Bob Esponja* (Sponge Bob) hammer for Estrella and an inflatable *Hombre Araña* (Spiderman) for Yailin. Returning to the bar tent, we saw that Enrique was still strutting his stuff. Salsa is a very sexy dance and I hope I never see Crispin doing it with anybody's niece, never mind his own. Grace appeared by my side and we greeted each other with pecks on the cheek. "How did you get here?" I asked her, knowing that Enrique had been here a while.

"With friends in their car," she said and indicated her huge belly. I understood. It must be difficult to ride pillion on their motorbike when you are heavily pregnant. I couldn't think of anything else to say to her in Spanish so reverted to watching Enrique. Grace did the same.

"It's his niece isn't it?" I said to her to make conversation. She raised her eyebrows in a 'is that what he told you?' look. Ah, maybe she wasn't his niece.

Grace wore the tightest jeans I had ever seen. I guess being eight and a half months pregnant didn't exempt you from the 'tiny top and tight jeans' fashion statement; muffin tops are the norm here, embarrassment hasn't yet found its way to Costa Rica. I decided it was a good thing and that it wouldn't hurt for others to take a leaf out of their book.

"Can we find somewhere to sit down, hon?" I said to Crispin. "The music is too loud for Estrella and my back and pelvis are killing me. Grace must be in agony too as she's three months ahead of me."

"How about over there?" he said indicating a concrete step near the trampoline. "You go and sit down and I'll go and get some food and cold drinks for us all." Cold drinks were a great idea and I knew exactly what food I wanted.

"Could you get another bag of *churros* please?" I asked him. Jackie's eyes lit up.

There was no breeze at all and sweat was running down between my shoulder blades. Although there was lots of room on the step, Grace still didn't sit down. "How's your back?" I asked her.

"Fine," she said. Maybe it was because I was a good ten years older than her. Or, hey, maybe I should try skin-tight jeans.

219

It was starting to get dark by the time we entered the seating area of the bull ring. Small dark spots were appearing on the earth floor where the bulls would shortly appear; it was starting to rain.

"They don't kill them do they?" I asked Freddy, meaning the bulls. That was something I couldn't watch.

"No, they just ride them," he assured me.

"Ride them?!" I queried. He nodded smiling. Now that sounded like a really crazy thing to do!

There were four levels of wooden benches and the ones near the entrance were already full of people so we continued shuffling past people's legs to the far side of the ring. The entire structure looked very old and rickety, there were no emergency exits and I had no idea what we would do if there was a fire. There was a nice atmosphere though and men were walking round with boxes or coolers on their shoulders selling beer, *churros* or brightly coloured plastic sticks that glowed in the dark.

"The bulls will come out of there," said Freddy pointing to a wooden gate to the right of us. Before too long the gate opened and a bull charged into the ring with a man hanging on its back. One arm he held high in the air making him look like he had done this before. The bull was not happy and did his best to throw the rider off. He snorted and bucked and shook his huge horned head and careered around the bull ring. It did the trick and, to high pitched squeals from the crowd, the rider narrowly missed being speared in the groin by one of the bull's horns and landed on his backside. He quickly scrambled to his feet, as if his life depended on it (which it probably did) and made a dash for the exit gate. The bull gave chase. It could run much faster than the rider and was gaining on him. I held my breath willing the rider to run faster. Suddenly, an odd-looking woman with 'big' hair, bright red lipstick and wearing a long skirt appeared in the ring and ran straight at the bull.

"What's she doing?" I asked Freddy.

"Trying to distract the bull," he replied.   It worked and the unseated rider made it to safety whilst the confused bull stood still, trying to make his mind up as to who he should chase; now that he had another option. He decided on the woman but it was too late, she leapt high onto the wooden railings out of the bull's reach. The crowd went mad. The high-pitched squealing got louder and louder – it was a really bizarre sound. She was very entertaining and dodged the bulls like the expert she obviously was. There were guys who tried to distract the bulls too, even some spectators jumped in the ring after one too many beers, but the lass in the skirt was our favourite.

Suddenly, the power went out and the ring was thrown into darkness momentarily.   As the low voltage emergency lights came on the lass in the skirt clambered up into the crowd and ran round the spectator's area between the benches.   The crowd went wild cheering her on.   She drew level with us then grabbed Crispin and kissed him on the lips.   She then threw herself back over the wooden railing in front of us and back into the ring again.   The crowd roared.

"It's a man isn't it?" said Crispin trying to wipe the lipstick off his mouth with the back of his hand. Freddy and Enrique nodded.   They couldn't speak. They were laughing so hard I thought they were going to fall off the bench. Crispin laughed too.

Unfortunately, when it was obvious that the lights weren't coming back on again anytime soon we said we should leave.   Estrella and Yailin were exhausted and keeping them amused was getting harder and harder; the inflatables had been fought over and were now discarded.

Estrella and Yailin were fast asleep.

"How are you feeling, Jackie?" I asked her, wondering if she was suffering from car sickness again. She didn't reply. I looked over Margarita's shoulder to where Jackie was sitting on her knee in the front. She held a bag of *churros* in her hand and would be keeping the ones she had eaten firmly in her tummy; she had joined Estrella and Yailin in the 'Land of Nod'.

25 The Moths of May

May brought lots of butterflies and lots of Dannys into the country. It started off with just a few; butterflies I'm talking about now. We were sitting on the terrace one morning eating our usual pineapple and watermelon breakfast when a neon green and black butterfly fluttered past. "That's unusual," I commented to Crispin. He looked in the direction I was pointing but the butterfly was already out of sight, hidden by the lemon tree.

"I see that bird all the time," he said, thinking I was pointing to the large blue water bird that often strutted its stuff in the garden.

"No, not that, the butterfly. Look, here comes another one."

Now there are probably hundreds of different varieties of butterflies and moths in Costa Rica and they are every colour of the rainbow. There are so many of them that you can get complacent about them and forget they are there. Except for the *Morpho Azul* that is; the queen of butterflies. It is an iridescent blue and can grow to be the size of a dinner plate. They tend to flap rather than flutter, their movements somewhat jerkier than you would expect. Les, a friend of ours, says that if he sees one he knows he is going to have a lucky day and I understand why he thinks that because there is something special about them and you will know what he means too if you ever see one.

The reason this neon green and black one caught my eye was its shape. It seemed to have a tail; two tails in fact and they were long and pointed. Also you couldn't really help notice them because after a day or so they were everywhere. Over the next few weeks they would continue to grow in number until one day I stood on the terrace with Estrella watching the sky in disbelief. It was almost black with them, there were thousands of butterflies flying past the house. They were all heading in the same direction; from north to south. Estrella lifted her hands to the heavens trying to catch them. Unfortunately, we no longer had the video camera and Crispin was in Neily that day so missed the show.

Gradually the performance drew to a close and their numbers started reducing daily until by August there would just be the stragglers left dotted around small puddles in the road, unable to summon the energy to continue on their way.

In September there was an article in 'The Tico Times' that explained it wasn't a butterfly but a rather unusual day-flying moth called *Urania fulgens* aka Green Page Moth or Sunset Moth (the difference between a butterfly and a moth by the way is in the straightness, or 'wonkyness', of their antennae). Every few years their food source, a woody liana (vine), in an act of self-preservation becomes toxic to them so they migrate 'en masse' south , right past our house, where I guess they find more woody lianas to eat. Further research on the internet suggested that there was a small migration most years and a mass moth migration on average every eight years[1].

There isn't an adjective to explain how amazing it was but I know I feel really honoured to have witnessed such an incredible event. I can't believe that David Attenborough missed it, he must have been a very busy man not to have been here and I hope he has the next one pencilled in his diary.

So, Danny was in town. THE Danny of 'it's Danny's land' fame. He was out of jail and he had come back because he had, once upon a time, owned 85% of the beach front in the Pavones area and now he wanted his land back and he had an expensive team of lawyers who were supposedly going to do just that.

He had brought his son, Danny, with him, and his grandson, also imaginatively called Danny. They were staying with Lenny Loco and Karin although I'm not really sure why. I guess Lenny wanted to be in on the action, if there was any.

One day I did the neighbourly thing, or maybe I also wanted to be in on any action, and took a pineapple cheesecake up to their house. Medium Danny and Little Danny were there and we all made small-talk whilst we ate cheesecake. The 'Original Danny' was out at the time so I didn't get to meet him.

He was all anybody was talking about. Whenever you met anybody at all, even Freddy and Enrique, the first thing they would say was "Have you seen Danny?" At least I could say "No, but his son likes my cheesecake."

Danny caused a huge stir and I'm sure there were some people who didn't even notice the millions of wonky-antennae moths because he was around. The papers were full of stories about him, new ones and old ones, and one didn't know what to believe. One of his lawyers was quoted as saying that the locals loved him and that years ago he had thrown gold coins out of an aeroplane whilst flying over the area[2]. After his departure there were more stories saying it was alleged that he had threatened some locals and Immigration were looking into it and maybe they wouldn't let him back into the country again. Whether the stories were true or not, one thing was for sure; Pavones was the most talked about place in the country for almost as long as the moths lasted.

26 Money Worries

We were sitting outside on the terrace still marvelling at the ever increasing number of neon green and black butterflies (we didn't yet know they were moths) fluttering by and debating money, or more specifically our lack of it. We had just finished doing our finances. It was pay day for everyone on Friday: Toli the builder; Freddy; Enrique; and Bilkez.

"By Friday evening we will have $500 left in the bank," announced Crispin sombrely. He put the calculator on the floor and lay back in the hammock. Estrella instantly grabbed the calculator and started chewing it.

"What about the $30k your parents lent us?" I asked.

"Gone."

"We've still got £10k in the UK for emergencies, I guess we'll have to transfer that over," I sighed.

"Done. And gone," admitted Crispin. Things, once again, weren't looking too good.

"But where's it all gone?" I asked him. "We were supposed to build the family house, a guest house, a couple of *cabinas* and a pool with that money. We've not even finished the guest house yet."

"Urbano's *finca*, the other little bits of land, the road is now officially the most expensive road in Costa Rica..."

"But Lenny said it would cost three thousand dollars," I interrupted.

"It's more like thirty thousand," he said. "Then there's the house. We're three times over budget with that. It's fast becoming the most expensive house in Costa Rica."

"Why is it costing so much more that we thought?" I asked perplexed. "I know I wanted the thickest concrete block but Ernesto said they weren't that much more expensive than the narrower ones."

"I guess it's not just the blocks though is it? It's more cement and more wood for the windows. It all adds up. Plus we now want a bigger terrace."

"But three times more? That's crazy," I said. "And it's not even finished yet."

It was now June, the month that Toli said our house would be ready and, although it now had a roof and the outside was about to be painted a fantastic bright yellow colour, it was far from ready. We had been way off in our calculations, both those of time and money.

"We've never been so skint," I said to Crispin.

"I have," he replied.

"Really, when?" I was surprised; he'd never mentioned it before.

"Oh, for years."

"Skint?" I repeated. He had been a partner in a law firm and I found it very hard to believe.

"Oh, I thought you said skinny!"

We laughed. Sometimes we don't seem to be on the same planet, never mind the same wavelength.

"I bet you wish you hadn't lent that money to Toli now don't you?" I slipped the dig in referring to something that had happened the previous week. He hadn't consulted me about it and I was annoyed. Crispin looked a bit sheepish. I didn't bother to mention the money he'd lent to Juan Carlos to buy a new car (his old one had fallen apart driving over here every week before he decided to live on site) or the fact that Freddy and Enrique had asked for a pay rise and we'd argued that one for an hour or more the previous night; him trying to convince me we could afford it and me sure that we couldn't.

We owed the guy with all the heavy duty machinery who had been putting lots of material on our really expensive road to fix it, fifteen thousand dollars. Now that is a lot of rock. He had been to see us the previous night and told us in the nicest possible way (through a mouthful of home-made

227

mango cheesecake that, after hearing what he had to say, I regretted giving him) that he wouldn't be dumping any more material on the road until we had some money and could pay for it. It was fair enough. At least he had put sufficient on that we could get up to the house site now without sliding over a cliff edge – something we couldn't guarantee anyone wanting to see the lots we were selling. He hadn't yet put rock on the road inside the *finca* and although the road had been perfectly passable in the dry season it was now quickly vanishing with the rains. The rainy season was fast approaching.

Two nights ago we'd had the loudest, brightest and scariest thunderstorm I have ever witnessed. The rain poured down for hours and the width of our internal road reduced dramatically, washing away down the hillside. Driving up there was getting scary. This morning I'd taken Estrella up to see Yailin. I had parked the car on one of the lots just off the road. When we returned to it, it was raining again. I tried to turn the car around but the wheels couldn't get a grip in the mud and the car started to slide towards a really steep drop. Luckily the car stopped just short of the edge. Crispin was nearby in the *finca* and he finished the turn whilst I watched crying my eyes out. Anyway, we needed to get the roads sorted out before the rainy season really started otherwise clients wouldn't be able to see our lots and if they couldn't see them then they couldn't buy them.

It's crazy that we are so skint because in April, Lenny Loco had finally come through for us and had sold our biggest and best piece of land, the beautiful 'El Señor'. It was so gorgeous that putting a high price on it so that we could keep it for as long as possible hadn't worked as Lenny had brought some Hawaiians up to see the lots and they had instantly fallen in love with it. With our financial situation heading the way the car was this morning we had no other option but to agree to the sale.

The problem had occurred when we tried to complete the deal; we found out that our chubby surveyor, recommended to us by Lenny Loco, who got some much needed exercise and probably lost an awful lot of weight walking up and down our hills following the boundaries of the lots, hadn't got around to registering our lots at the land registry. Our clients wouldn't buy 'El Señor' until it was registered.

Our lawyer, whose real name I found out after calling him Artoodle for about a year isn't actually Artoodle but Arturo (I had seen an advertisement for the movie 'El Rey Arturo' [King Arthur] and the penny dropped. We now like the name so much that since finding out that we are having a boy it is what we have been calling my bump) is doing some complicated double mortgage thingy to enable us to get some money until the sale of 'El Señor' can be finalised. But the contract is taking an age to draw up as the buyers' lawyer keeps adding clauses into the contract without consulting anyone. Luckily the buyers have met us and liked us instantly. They sent us $10k in 'good faith money' to help us out (there are some good people in the world) a grand of which Crispin instantly lent to Toli (and there are some very daft people in the world).

"If I went into labour now we couldn't pay the hospital bill," I said to Crispin.

"Then you'd have to go to Golfito," said Crispin.

"We couldn't afford the gas to get us there," I said. "You would have to deliver him here."

"You've still got five weeks to go," Crispin said cheerfully, "something will come up."

"Y'know, I feel it will too." I joined him in the hammock. Estrella clambered on too.

"Marco wants more money off us for building materials," said Crispin shifting uncomfortably. "I've

229

checked the receipts and I'm sure he's still got three grand of ours. Budge over 'gordita'."

"Is this the Marco who turned up yesterday on a brand new motorbike?" I asked, elbowing him for the 'little fatty' comment.

"He asked me if we'd lend him five grand to set up his own *ferretería*."

"What did you say?" I said trying not to get mad.

"I said I would talk to you about it."

"Great, so I'm going to be the bad guy who says 'no'? Why can't you just make the decision and say 'no'?"

"I made the decision for Toli and you told me off for not consulting you about it!" He was right, I had.

"But you said 'yes' to him, you should have said 'no'."

"Are we saying 'no' to Marco?" he asked.

"Have you been participating in the conversation we just had?" I asked in amazement. "We don't have five grand!"

"But we will have when we get the money for 'El Señor'."

"We need it!" What planet was my husband on? I needed to try another tack. "Okay hon, if a guy in the UK that you had just met asked you for five grand to set up a business and you hadn't seen a business plan and you knew that he was going to have fierce competition from two very large and established businesses, would you give it to him?" I was sure he couldn't possibly say yes.

"But it's Marco," he said.

I had already heard "But it's Juan Carlos" when he needed a new car and then a motorbike when he didn't want to damage his new car travelling on these roads. Next it was a new roof for his house as it was leaking. One day we turned up at his house to discuss the windows and got the shock of our lives. He had had his entire house remodelled, presumably

230

with our money. He proudly showed us the huge kitchen and bedroom complete with en-suite bathroom. "It's so you can shower when you come and visit on your way back from Neily," he said, rather bizarrely.

Next came "But it's Toli." Crispin never even bothered to ask why Toli needed the cash. Then of course "But it's Freddy and Enrique" when they asked for a pay rise. That was always his argument to justify giving more of our money away, as if they were all life-long friends of ours.

I won the Marco argument; or maybe, as he seems to still have three thousand dollars of ours, I didn't.

27 Grace

"Congratulations!" I said to Grace giving her a big hug and handing over our very thoughtful present: a bag full of chocolate. I had become a bit of a chocoholic after Estrella's arrival so thought I would also help her on her way to becoming one. Crispin gave Enrique some beers and shook his hand. Crispin had had his fair share of those after Estrella's arrival too.

We were on the same terrace where we'd eaten fried pig skin at Christmas. Enrique and Grace and now their new baby, Yeudin, were living at his parents' house and had been since their shotgun wedding in December. Enrique's parents were present and so was another man. I smiled at the man. He was wearing shorts and I couldn't help noticing that his right leg was red and incredibly swollen. Then I saw that part of his thigh was missing, it was as if someone had poured acid down his leg. Oh my goodness, I knew who he was. I vaguely recalled Enrique telling us that his brother had been bitten by a deadly snake; what the locals call a *terciopelo* but we know it by its French name, fer-de-lance.

"How's the leg?" Crispin asked him in Spanish.

"Más ó menos," he replied (literally 'more or less' but translates better as 'not too bad') holding his hand out, palm down and wavering it slightly in the gesture that often accompanied the expression *más ó menos.*

I felt it was a reasonable answer for somebody who had been through what he had been through.

"Where were you when it happened?" Crispin asked him.

"Up in the mountains. I had to ride for an hour and a half before I found someone to help me."

"You managed to get onto your horse?" Crispin asked in disbelief.

"I had to, I would have died otherwise," Enrique's brother said. "It then took three hours to get to Neily hospital to get the anti-venom."

"How long were you in hospital for?" I asked.

"Three weeks," he said. "I came out a couple of days ago." Wow, three weeks and his leg still looked like that!

"You're lucky to be alive," Crispin and I said in unison.

"Gracías á Díos," (Thanks to God) he said.

Grace was rushing around her in-laws' house like a mad thing; stirring pots and carrying plates and, unbelievably, taking Estrella off me so I could eat in peace. Enrique played the doting daddy and had this little bundle with a full head of thick black hair snuggled in his arms. He didn't stop smiling. With Grace's energy you would not have believed that she had given birth only four days earlier.

The day before Yeudin arrived she had sensibly caught the bus to Golfito to stay with some friends that lived near the hospital. We were going to give Enrique a lift there. We had to go and see a wood carver about the designs we wanted carving on our doors and also needed to collect Enrique's monthly 'caja' slip from the office in Golfito which dealt with 'caja' contributions. The slip of paper would prove to the hospital that we, as Enrique's employers, had paid his 'caja' contributions (equivalent to National Insurance contributions) which meant Grace, being Enrique's wife, would get free medical care.

After ensuring our carver had the wood he needed, Crispin collected Enrique's 'caja' slip and drove him to the bus stop in Golfito where he was supposed to be meeting Grace. We arrived just a couple minutes after the bus had been due, hoping it would be late but of course it had been early.

Grace was nowhere in sight so we drove up the incredibly steep hill to their friend's house. There she was sitting outside the house on a bench sweating profusely with a glass of water in her hand. She had walked the whole way! It was no surprise to me she went into labour the following morning.

She had felt the need to go to the loo at 5am but despite several attempts hadn't been able to do anything. At 8.45am she 'felt a bit weird' and decided to walk the 15 minutes to the hospital. When they examined her on arrival they said she was already six centimetres dilated. They sent her to the bathroom with a sample bottle as they wanted to test her urine. On the way to the bathroom the first contraction hit and Grace grabbed a strategically placed metal pole (I guessed it was supporting the roof) to hold on to and, when the need arose, to bite. When she made it back to her bed Yeudin was well and truly on the way and two deep breaths later, half an hour after arriving at the hospital Yeudin met his mother and it was at that point that Grace started to cry; they were tears of joy. He was to have to wait a couple of hours before meeting his daddy as Enrique had been at work when we had received the call that his presence was required. He had arrived at the hospital way after the event, which may have been a blessing as he had been unsure as to whether he wanted to see that bit anyway.

Grace became pregnant after they had been dating for just two weeks. They had however been childhood sweethearts years ago but then she had left the area and gone to San José. She experienced life in the city for a while, working in factories and for a family cleaning their house and looking after their children. Whether it was doing this that had given it to her or having it that made her leave her village I didn't know but she certainly had a bit more 'oomph' about her than a lot of the local women. Grace knew that living with her in-laws wasn't working; I don't think having two women in the same house ever does (except maybe if it's your own mother) and certainly not when one of them is a new mum. She wanted a house of her own and she wanted it desperately. What was Enrique going to do about it?

"Enrique needs some money to build his house," said Crispin. I turned on him instantly as I knew what was coming. "I know! I know we can't afford to lend it to him. He wants to sell some land that his father gave him to raise the money."

"I hope he finds a buyer soon," I said genuinely.

"Why don't we spend the day on the beach down at Punta Banco this weekend?" Crispin asked me. I was instantly suspicious.

"Where's Enrique's lot?" I asked him. Did he think I was daft?

He laughed. "Okay, maybe I'll just go and have a really really quick look at it."

Punta Banco was the other side of Pavones. It's the last village before the road ends. Except for his parents and a brother, most of Enrique's family still lived there. His father owned a *finca* there and was one of only a few landowners who hadn't sold out to the famous Danny Fowlie. His dad had given Enrique a small piece of that *finca* and now he wanted to sell it to raise the money to build a house on another piece of land that his parents had also given him. This land was sandwiched between their house and that of an older brother. It was far enough away from his parents' house; a few hundred metres maybe, for Grace's much needed space.

"I want to help them more than anybody but we don't have the money," I said. "You are just going to get their hopes up!"

"Let's just look at it?" Crispin pleaded with me. He had discovered a habit that maybe wasn't quite as harmful to the body as smoking or drinking or drugs but was just as addictive and even more harmful to the bank account; buying land. We had never found that perfect beach lot that Lenny Loco had been searching for; Crispin was hoping that this was it.

So, in the guise of all of us spending the day at the beach in Punta Banco, Crispin arranged with Enrique to go and see this perfect beach lot that we couldn't afford to buy. Freddy's family came too and after eating *ceviche,* a local delicacy which is raw fish soaked in lemon juice and coriander (something I avoided being seven months pregnant), and walking Enrique's lot (something else I avoided for the same reason but also not wanting to fall in love with it and figured, as I had with Ruben, avoidance was the best policy) we all settled on the beach.

We built sandcastles with the kids; buried Jackie and Yailin in the sand, ate the picnic lunch that I had packed and watched the guys boogie-boarding, all the while with three week old Yeudin snoozing away in his sensible car chair – you see, Grace WAS different to other Ticas.

As the sun started to drop we bought snacks from a nearby *pulpería,* owned by Enrique's extended family and washed the salt and sand off our bodies in a fresh water plunge pool. It had been a wonderful day but it didn't change the fact that we didn't have the eight thousand dollars that Enrique needed. To be fair his lot was probably worth four times that amount.

"We could swap it for one of our lots," said Crispin in bed that night, just as I was dozing off. He was clutching at straws.

"He still needs money to build a house," I replied sleepily, "that's the whole point."

"Maybe I can speak to dad." He was determined, I would give him that.

"They can't lend us any more money." They had already bought one of our lots off us and then lent us the same amount again. They weren't a bottomless pit.

The following day his straw was in a little pile on the floor; Enrique had sold his lot to his brother for six thousand dollars.

28 Once more into the breech

The following week we drove to San José for my 36 week scan, my last appointment before giving birth. We were approaching the city when Crispin cursed. "What's the matter?" I asked.

"Look at the traffic." I looked at the road ahead and the traffic was stationary. "I'll turn off here," he said, taking an exit that wasn't signposted to anywhere. I'd given up using maps so couldn't help. We were suddenly on a dual-carriageway.

"You've found the ring-road!" I squealed in amazement. I had been looking for it for almost a year now. In fact, I had given up looking for it, sure that it only existed on our map and hadn't yet been constructed. Driving around San José suddenly got a whole lot more enjoyable and a million times quicker.

Our first stop was to see our lawyer Arturo at his home. His wife Alita had offered to look after Estrella whilst I was giving birth. "It would be nice if Alita and Estrella can spend a bit of time together wouldn't it?" I had just had a brainwave. "So, why don't we ask Alita if she can babysit Estrella tonight and we can go to the cinema?"

"Good idea. Do you know what's on?" he asked. I'd noticed the cinema listings in the back of 'The Tico Times' and spotted something that I wanted to see and was sure that Crispin would too.

"Star Wars III." In our previous life we had been to Leicester Square in the springtime to see I and II. They were lovely romantic memories: drinking Strongbow in the floating Tattershall Castle, strolling along the Thames holding hands, gazing into each other's eyes over margaritas in a nearby Mexican restaurant. A romantic evening would be lovely before our life went mad again. Madder, I mean.

"I don't think I've seen I and II," he said.

"You git!" I said, glaring at him.

"What?" he said, looking surprised. "What did I do wrong?"

"I've got some documents you need to sign," Arturo said to Crispin as he opened the door, "I've worked out a way I can get you some money for 'El Señor'." Oh happy days! He had knocked the double mortgage thingy on the head and was now concentrating on something to do with share certificates. We entered the lounge and I cringed when I saw the multitude of candles. They were in glass candle holders and were lined up neatly on the glass coffee table in the middle of the room. Pre-requisites for couples without young children, all at a convenient child-grabbing level.

While Crispin signed the 'El Señor' share certificates over to the Hawaiians, Estrella didn't disappoint. She grabbed a candle and hurled it at the coffee table – holder and all.

"No," I said to her firmly, retrieving it and the hundred others and putting them on a shelf out of her reach. "Sorry," I said to Arturo.

"No, it's fine," he said.

"Where's Alita by the way?" I asked casually, wanting to ask her about babysitting.

"She's met someone at a climbing club and has gone to live with him in Limon." He had tears in his eyes as he spoke.

WHAT! Who was going to look after Estrella whilst I was in labour? was my first thought closely followed by there goes our trip to the cinema. "But that's awful," came out of my mouth. It <u>was</u> awful. 18 years they'd been married! They met when she was 16, she was now 40. She still looked 16 mind you – she was gorgeous and there was no way we could say "You're better off without her".

"I'm okay about it," he said, forcing a smile. I didn't believe him. We joined him in a conciliatory glass of wine and some olives which Estrella kept insisting she liked even though she kept spitting them out and putting them back in the bowl. Arturo, kindly, pretended not to notice. Or maybe he just had other things on his mind.

The following day we went to the hospital for the scan that would tell us how big Arturo was going to be. As we waited to be seen I flipped through a Spanish pregnancy magazine and managed to muddle my way through an article about labour. It suddenly hit me that there was a possibility it was something that I might have to go through soon! My mother-in-law had tried to describe it to me when I was pregnant with Estrella.

"What is the hardest thing you have ever done?" she'd asked. There was no contest - The Great South Run. My auntie had died of cancer and a very good friend of mine hadn't. I was doing it for them to raise money for Cancer Research. My brother had agreed to do it with me and we'd said we were going to try to stay together. I had been determined to run the whole way.

"I can't run any more sis, you're going to have to carry on without me," my brother panted in my ear. We had just reached the nine mile mark.

"No. You can do this, come on you big wuss." But no amount of persuasion would make him run another step. "I'm sorry," I said to him, "but I have to do this for Auntie Doreen, my friend that had survived, and for me. I promised myself that I would run all the way."

"Go for it," he said as he slowed to a walk.

The finish line was in sight when an out-of-breath voice said "Hiya sis" in my ear; my brother had somehow found the energy to keep going. If I hadn't already sweated every drop of moisture out of my body, I would've cried with joy. We held hands and crossed the finish line together and then hugged for all we were worth, partially to stop ourselves collapsing in a heap.

"The Great South Run," I said to Crispin's mum with tears in my eyes.

"Well it's going to be harder than that. That's why it was named 'labour'. It will be the hardest day's work that you will ever do". Remembering that conversation, I suddenly wasn't sure it was something I wanted to go through.

The ultrasound doctor started above my belly button. "That's a head," he exclaimed. "He's in the breech position."

"I knew it," I said. "A week ago he did a huge wiggle and I said to Crispin that I thought he had just turned around."

"You don't seem very surprised," said the doctor.

"Estrella did exactly the same thing at exactly the same time," I said. "Bang goes my water-birth," I said to Crispin. I had been consulting with another doctor at a private clinic about the possibility of having a water birth; he was the only doctor in the country who would do them as it was considered a dangerous practice over here. That was now out of the question. "Caesarean number two here we come. No labour for me then!"

"His head is of the size you would need a caesarean anyway. It's almost abnormal." That was worrying. "It isn't abnormal though," he added when he saw our alarmed looks. "So don't worry."

We sat in the waiting room mulling over the results when my doctor appeared.

"Have you heard?" I asked him. "He's breech."

Dr Smile rolled his eyes and motioned for us to enter his office.

He wanted to see us again for another ultrasound on 29th June and if Arturo was still breech he would perform the caesarean the next day, a Thursday.

"We've lost our babysitter," I said to him without going into details.

"Well, if you can't think of anyone, there may be nurses around who could look after Estrella whilst you are in surgery. So that Crispin can be with you."

"I couldn't go through it without you being there," I said to Crispin. It was an awful thought and I felt quite tearful about it.

"Don't worry, I'll be there," he assured me. Mind you, the thought of me coming out of recovery to 16 month old Estrella was pretty awful too. I could picture her trying to pull my catheter out, using the nurses' buzzer because she liked the sound and poking my boobs when I was trying to get Arturo to latch on, not to mention screaming whenever I had my BP taken because the cuff reminded her of the tourniquet they'd used when they'd taken blood from her a couple of months ago to check her iron levels. It was something that was standard practice over here. We had gone to a private laboratory an hour from the house to have it done and Estrella had screamed the place down and fought like an alley cat, even kicking the needle out of the nurse's hand. Crispin had tried to hold her still whilst I'd sobbed outside in the waiting room feeling like the worst mother in the world. "Is that her blood?" I'd asked when they'd finally appeared, startled to see the large patch of red on her shorts. Crispin had nodded, looking rather pale himself. "They didn't get enough the first time so had to use her other arm too".

Well, all things considered, it was just too much and wouldn't have been fair on any of us but especially not Estrella. We needed another solution.

We phoned our parents with the news. "Maybe you've got a malformed uterus," said Crispin's mum referring to the fact that our second baby was also breech. Thanks for that, I thought.

"My doctor seemed to think it's the size and shape of their heads," I said defiantly, defending my uterus.

I explained to Crispin's mum that we had lost our babysitter and she kindly offered to fly out and do the job herself. Crispin and I discussed our options. We didn't have very many. There was Jack, wonderful as he was I wouldn't trust him with my cat if I had one, and I don't even like cats. There was Sofia, Jack's still on/off girlfriend who worked full-time and also had two kids of her own to look after. They all loved Estrella but we didn't feel we could ask her as it would mean her taking time off work and it was a lot to expect. Finally there was the teenage daughter of some friends who lived the other side of the mountains, they had said we could leave Estrella with them but it would mean we wouldn't see Estrella for several days and this distressed me.

"Let's ask your mum to just look at flights," I said. "In the meantime, maybe something else will come up." I was sure there wouldn't be any flights at such short notice, or they would be too expensive, plus it would mean her missing Crispin's dad's 70th birthday which we didn't feel it was a fair thing to ask her to do. (We were building him a rancho, complete with hammocks, on their lot as a surprise birthday present).

That night we met up with Jack and Sofia for dinner. "Have you got anywhere to stay yet?" Jack asked.

"No, we need to sort that out tomorrow really," I said. I intended going through the 'Lonely Planet' to see if there were any, what they called, 'aparthotels' near the hospital so we would be able to cook for ourselves.

"I'm off to the UK for a couple of weeks so why don't you stay at my place?"

"Really?" I said. "Are you sure?"

"Absolutely sure," said Jack. "I'm not going to be there." Our luck seemed to be in so I asked Sofia if she would mind looking after Estrella for us whilst we were in surgery.

"Of course I would, I would love to. If you want I can take Friday and Saturday off work too." Hurrah, we had our solution! Crispin left a message for his mum first thing and then had a rather annoyed phone call back from his dad saying that his mum had already booked her flights. Oops.

I called Jack to let Sofia know that she wouldn't be able to look after Estrella for us and to thank her for offering. Before I could say anything Jack said that Sofia was now going to go to the UK with him so wouldn't be able to look after Estrella for us! Wow. At least that problem was sorted out.

Our other problem wasn't so easily solved. We couldn't leave the hotel as we didn't have the money to pay our bill. The paperwork that Crispin had signed at Arturo's had been sent to the Hawaiians on Monday, it should have arrived with them on Wednesday, which was today, and then they could send us the money. By Thursday we would definitely have it. Thursday arrived and Crispin checked our account using the hotel's computer. Balance $69. Fiddle. One of the Hawaiians called us before we had a chance to call them. The certificates had been sent to her office address and not her home as requested. She hadn't been in the office for a couple of days so she had only just received them. She was going to wire the money that instant. We bought bread and cheese for dinner.

Friday morning and Crispin checked our account at 8.30am and 11am.

"It's in?" I asked him hopefully

"Balance $69," he said to me on both occasions.

The phone rang. It was Marco for the umpteenth time. "Is it in?" he asked.

"No, not yet," said Crispin.

"I've got three suppliers phoning me constantly wanting payment. I said we would pay them today. What do I tell them?" We had accounts with several *ferreterías* and they were due to be paid.

"Can you keep putting them off?" Crispin asked him. "The money has definitely been sent. I'll phone the bank and find out when wires come in."

"I'll see what I can do," said Marco but he wasn't very happy about it. I felt sorry for him but this was his job, what we paid him to do. (Crispin, by the way, had been through all of the accounts with Marco and eventually if we included the 8% commission that he wasn't supposed to be getting until the house was finished, Crispin felt all of our money was accounted for. We had been lucky and I hoped it was a lesson learnt).

Crispin phoned the bank, "What time do wires normally come in?"

"When was the money wired?"

"Yesterday."

"They arrive at 2pm but if it was only sent yesterday it probably won't be in until Tuesday." TUESDAY!! It was only Friday. Crispin phoned Marco back with the news.

I was getting fed up with clock watching. "Let's go down to the pool," I suggested. "It will take our minds off it."

I watched Estrella zoom off around the pool in her armbands, champion swimmer one day no doubt. Crispin looked deep in thought and hardly paid her any attention. It wasn't taking his mind off it at all.

"Lunch is ready," I called to them. It hadn't taken very long to make. I'd used up yesterday's leftovers as we couldn't afford to buy anything else.

"Mmmmm, cheese sandwiches again," Crispin said as he stood dripping over them.

"At least Estrella's getting her calcium this week," I said.

We both joined Estrella for her afternoon snooze. When I awoke it was 2pm and I debated prodding Crispin. At 2.01pm his phone rang and saved me the prod. It was Marco again.

"I'll go and check now," I heard Crispin say. "I'm just going to go and use the computer in the lobby again," he said to me. I crossed my fingers on both hands and held them up to him.

He returned with a smile on his face.

"It's in!" he said.

"Hurrah! We can go home," I said to Estrella.

I tried not to think that almost half of the $70k sitting in our account was already spoken for and the final $40k payment for 'El Señor' wouldn't be coming for another four and a half months.

29 BoBo Arrives

The next few days were pretty miserable. It rained non-stop which was highly unusual for June. Crispin went to the *pulpería* to get some milk and a bar of chocolate. They were the only two things I had asked him to get.

"Do you need me to write them down?" I'd asked him seriously.

"Don't be ridiculous," he'd answered, "my memory isn't that bad!" He returned half an hour later with some milk and a tomato. How Margarita laughed when I told her about it. At the time I didn't see anything amusing about it at all.

"Well I remembered the milk," he was trying to explain himself, "and I knew there was something else but couldn't quite remember what it was..."

"So you got me a tomato. Where's the logic?! Why not a packet of biscuits or an ice cream?"

"I thought 'tomato' was a pretty good guess!"

"I can't get a chocolate fix from a tomato! I'm pregnant, I need a chocolate fix!!"

Later that day, rather deservedly I felt, Crispin suffered a bout of diarrhoea.

Even later that day Freddy arrived and handed me a plastic bag of something. "What are they?" I asked him looking in the bag at the small white things.

"Frijoles tiernos," (young beans) he said. He and his family had been harvesting some of their bean crop early. It would be several months before we would see thousands of them spread out on huge tarpaulins outside all the locals' houses drying in the sun.

"Thank you, Freddy," I said. "I know exactly what I'm going to do with them." My 'Food for Thought' recipe book had a recipe in it that had caught my eye. I had waited a long time for this moment. I put the beans on to simmer and started chopping tomatoes (including the one that fate had brought me; Crispin's).

A little while later Estrella and I were eating beans in tomato sauce on hot buttered toast topped with grated cheese. Mine had a swizz of freshly ground black pepper. It tasted fantastic. The best 'beans on toast' I had ever eaten, even better than Heinz!

Crispin's tummy troubles were to last several days and by the end of the second day he was getting 'cabin fever'. He wasn't stuck to the toilet any more so we decided to go up to the house to see what was happening. I was disappointed to see that Ruben wasn't around and I casually asked Toli as to his whereabouts.

"His wife isn't very well," Toli told me. WIFE!? Could *esposa* mean something else? 'Sister' maybe? "She's pregnant and has got her first scan today," Toli continued, completely unaware of my internal voice yelling at him. I didn't hear any more. PREGNANT!? How could he do this to me?! He had a wife and was now having a baby with her!! I had known him for six months (and had avoided him for at least five of those). How did I not know that he had a wife? I knew about everyone else's wife.

"Did you know that Ruben was married?" I blurted out to Crispin

"Yeah, I think so."

"And you didn't think to mention it to me?!" I was angry with him and with a confused look on his face he watched his crazy wife walk off towards the small bathroom where Cristian, our 'electrician who wasn't', had almost finished tiling. Before my shock I had been looking forward to seeing it. We had word poetry fridge magnets on the fridge in the house and they were always being arranged into different sentences by whoever was visiting us. Lenny Loco spent most of his time when he popped in making up unprintable sentences. Kathryn and Kevin had also brought us the Spanish word poetry set when they had come to visit after Christmas. Lizzie one day, in a mixture of Spanish and English had written 'Estrella, the little angel with the blue eyes and the beautiful smile.' It had made me cry.

One day a new sentence had appeared 'A friend laughs and it feels like home'.

"That's true," I said pointing it out to Crispin when I spotted it. "I wonder who did that."

"Me," he said, looking very pleased with himself.

"Really?" I was impressed and when we spotted the blue and white letter tiles in one of the tile shops in San José I knew I wanted it in our new house as a border. We'd bought the relevant letters and Cristian was putting them in the little bathroom at shoulder height. I'd laid the letters out in the right order for him a few of days earlier. He was just finishing off when we arrived. I rounded the corner from the entrance hall and then stopped. I stared at the walls of the little bathroom in horror, and all thoughts of Ruben's pregnant wife were swept from my mind. Cristian saw my face and looked really worried. 'A RIEND LAUGHS AND IT FEELS LIKE H' it read. An 'O', 'M', 'E' and an 'F' were lying on the floor by his feet. Cristian looked at the words and then at my face and back at the words again and tried to fathom out what he had done wrong. "CRISPIN!" I yelled.

"It can be fixed," Toli and Cristian assured me when I explained; Cristian would just take them all off, except the first 'A' and start again.

The next day, June 9th, Freddy arrived at ours just after 9am with some fantastic news.

"Gilly has had her foal," he said excitedly with an even bigger smile on his face than usual. We were equally excited and Crispin and I rushed around getting the change bag ready, grabbing snacks for Estrella, looking for the camera, digging out the umbrella - it was still raining - and finally made it out of the door half and hour later – record time.

They were near what we called the rancho site; just above the pool site where we hoped we would one day build a large rancho that may house a coffee shop or even a restaurant. It was a stone's throw from where Gilly would die ten weeks later. The foal was a browny grey colour, he would fade to grey as he got older, and sat on the floor with his spindly legs tucked under him. He was 40 minutes old and completely adorable. Gilly was soaking wet and I wasn't sure whether it was just the rain or whether it was sweat from her labour, she still had the afterbirth hanging down from under her tail. Freddy warned us to keep our distance as Gilly would be feeling nervous and agitated with us around her, so near to her newborn foal. Crispin took photos whilst I held Estrella in one arm and the umbrella in the other hand.

"What are we going to call him?" I asked Estrella.

"BoBo," she said. It was her word for horse, her attempt to say *caballo*, the Spanish for 'horse'.

"Sounds like a good name to me," I said. BoBo had sufficiently recovered from his birth experience to try to master standing up. It took several attempts before he managed to stagger to his feet. It's amazing that it takes a child a year to learn to walk and it takes a horse an hour.

BoBo was getting hungry and staggered over to his mum and tried to latch on to her teat. Gilly didn't like the nip (boy, did I know how that felt!) and moved away. Freddy lassoed her around the neck and held her still whilst BoBo tried again. He got there eventually and we watched him take his first meal.

It was an amazing thing to witness. I had never liked horses that much; my last two experiences with them hadn't been very pleasant. Before we left the barn we had asked a nearby farmer's wife if she could give us a few horsey tips knowing that our horses were in Costa Rica waiting for us and she happily agreed. We turned up at their farm pushing Estrella in a buggy with a brightly coloured parasol. The farmer's wife took one look at the parasol adorned buggy and said it was going to scare her horses silly and one look at my Teva-sandaled feet and said that my toes were going to get broken. I spent the entire lesson emitting 'I am petrified of you' signals to 'my' horse and, as I was attempting to put the bridle on it, I tried to stay as far away from his shod hooves as possible. The last horse I had ridden, 11 years earlier, had trodden on my foot so you would have thought I had learned my lesson.

In spite of my previous bad experiences I had grown quite fond of our horses and really connected with Gilly that day. When we were with her I felt this calming sensation that was wonderful. She had just had her second foal and I was about to have my second child. It was a bond that would be broken by a careless builder and a bullet in just a few short weeks.

30 Arturo Arrives

"Do I have to take my contact lenses out?" I asked a very young nurse with braces on her teeth. I was speaking Spanish.

"Yes," she replied

"That's okay, I've got my glasses," I said amiably

"You can't wear those either," she said. "You can put them on briefly to see the baby but that's all."

"Really?" I was surprised as I'd worn them when I'd had Estrella.

The anaesthetist arrived to tell me what he was going to do to me. I decided to get a second opinion on my glasses. "It's fine, you leave your glasses on," he said and then left. The nurse with the braces had been listening.

"He's wrong," she said. "The machine they use to cut you open heats up metal and you'll burn your face," she added abruptly.

How bizarre, I thought.

She left and the anaesthetist returned. I told him again what the nurse had said. "Rubbish," he said. "I'm going to be wearing my glasses." That was good news. I put my glasses on. The nurse came to wheel me down to theatre and told me to take my glasses off. This was getting ridiculous, we hadn't even made it to the lift yet! Once I was in theatre and she'd gone I put them back on again.

Arturo John Freeman was pulled into the world at 1.19pm on Thursday 30th June. It should have been an hour earlier but Dr Smile left me lying in the freezing cold operating theatre for an hour. He stank of cigarettes when he eventually arrived. "I've never seen you in glasses before," he said when he saw me. "I almost didn't recognise you."

"I normally wear contact lenses but the nurse said I had to take them out."

"Rubbish," he said, "you would have been fine with them in. I'm wearing mine." More good news.

I thought I would never be warm again. I was in the recovery room, shivering from the spinal block wearing off when Crispin came in empty-handed. "Where's Arturo?" I said, panicking.

"He was cold so they've put him in an incubator for a little while to warm him up."

"What's wrong with him? Tell me." I was sure Crispin was keeping something from me.

"Nothing, he was just a bit cold that's all. It's only for a couple of hours. Don't worry," he said with the same dopey look on his face he'd had after Estrella was born. "He's fine. Perfect in fact." He took hold of my hand. "You did it," he said really, really sweetly. I looked into his eyes, he had tears in them.

Whilst we were waiting for Arturo to be brought to us, the hospital started shaking. I looked at Crispin in alarm.

"Earthquake," he said. We had little ones at home quite often but this one was more violent and seemed to go on for ages. Above the bathroom door a sign said 'Earthquake Secure Zone'.

"Do you think that means the whole room or just the bathroom?" I asked him indicating the sign.

"I'm not sure. It's not obvious is it?"

"Do I have to walk to the bathroom with my shaky legs and carrying my bag of wee do you think?"

"It's a dilemma," he agreed. "I could carry your bag of wee."

"You are so thoughtful at times," I said.

At that moment Arturo was wheeled into our room in one of those see-through plastic cots and the earthquake was forgotten about. I wanted to hold him

253

so badly I thought I was going to burst. A nice nurse took him out and placed him in my arms. I could see that there was nothing wrong with him at all. He was perfect and gorgeous and.......“Oh, look,” I said softly pointing to the top of his right ear, he had a tiny hole with a little tuft of hair growing out of it just like Estrella had. “It's so cute” I said to Crispin, kissing it. I had a daft smile on my face.

"It's freakish," he said. I frowned at him.

After a cuddle with his son, Crispin left to fetch Estrella and his mum. It was a difficult journey to make in rush hour, even with the ring road. Jack's house, where they were staying, was the other side of San José. Whilst Crispin was gone I tried to get some sleep.

Estrella's face was a picture when she saw her new baby brother and she was even more excited when we produced a present from him, a little doll. We decided to call her 'Adriana' after the only nice nurse on the ward. That evening we also had a surprise visit from 'big' Arturo and Alita. No comment was made about how the weather had been during her 'trip to Limon' and it was so nice to see them together again.

The first 24 hours were tough. I was starving but wasn't allowed to eat anything. I had to sit and watch Crispin tuck into three course meals and, being in a private hospital, the food was pretty amazing. I was told that my doctor had said I would be able to eat breakfast the following morning. I wiped the saliva from my chin and drank my luke-warm chamomile tea.

I had a hellish night. My pain wasn't under control at all, they don't give you morphine for the first 24 hours the way they do in the UK. I kept begging the nurses for more painkillers but they wouldn't give me any. Crispin's snoring kept me awake and no amount of yelling at him could wake him up to get him to put Arturo back in his cot after I'd finished feeding him. I had nothing left to throw at Crispin; the one pillow I could spare had gone wide, so Arturo slept with me for the rest of the night as I'd long since dropped the nurse's buzzer. I slept in an upright position as I had dropped the bed controller too. I was knackered and if anybody else tried to grab my cracked nipple and put it into Arturo's mouth I was going to scream. At least I had breakfast to look forward to.

Crispin's pancakes, bacon, scrambled eggs, orange juice and coffee arrived. My mouth was watering; I hadn't eaten for 36 hours. Maybe I could have the same? Just the scrambled eggs and a piece of toast would be heaven to my poor empty stomach. Eventually a tray was put in front of me. On it was more luke-warm chamomile tea, apple juice, an unidentifiable bright green liquid (washing up liquid perhaps?) and an unidentifiable white liquid.

"But I'm eating today," I told the orderly with tears in my eyes.

"That's not what I've been told," he said. Seeing my tears, he added he would go and check.

"What are those two?" asked Crispin, his mouth full of pancakes.

"The green stuff is liquid jello and the white stuff looks like rice water," said the orderly.

The nurse with the braces on her teeth arrived and I rolled my eyes at Crispin, she was all I needed. "How long has the baby been asleep?" she asked me.

"Not long," I lied.

"You can't leave him longer than three hours without feeding him," she said. Bollocks, I thought and almost growled at her.

The paediatrician, yet another Arturo, came in next and I told him what the nurse had said.

255

"Rubbish," he said, "if he's got wet and pooey diapers and is feeding well, Arturito can sleep for five hours if he likes, it's fine. I'll come back and check him later when he's awake. Get some sleep," he said to me. 'Arturito' (little Arturo) I liked the sound of that. I dozed off, my tummy rumbling.

I awoke to find Dr Smile in the room.
"How are you feeling today, Joanne?"
"Hungry," I said. "You said I could eat breakfast but the orderly said I couldn't."
"You can eat tonight." TONIGHT! I'd been lied to.
"What is my body supposed to produce milk with?" I asked him, tears welling up in my eyes again.
"Maybe you can have some toast at lunch-time. It's to prevent gas forming in your bowel," he explained. I resisted telling him I had had chicken and mashed potato shortly after giving birth to Estrella and hadn't had a problem with gas; I doubted it was going to make him change his mind.
"How's the wound?" he asked next.
"Reeeeeally painful." I must have been his worst nightmare.
"Ask the nursing staff for more painkillers," he said as he turned to walk out of the door.
"I did," I said, fully aware that I was whining but I didn't care, "I was begging them all night but they said they couldn't give me any more."
"Tell them I said it was okay," he said from the doorway.
"You tell them it's okay," I pleaded, "they won't listen to me." I guess he did as the nice nurse came in with more tablets and I was reasonably comfortable for the next two days.

We stayed in San José for another week, initially at Jack's house whilst he was in England and then, when he returned we had to find somewhere else to stay. It wasn't easy. I was still finding it difficult to walk, there was the constant breastfeeding, the sleepless nights, a tiredness you can never imagine if you haven't been through it, catching naps whenever Arturo slept, a toddler to amuse during the day, having to pack...

Crispin's mum had brought a little Harley Davidson motorbike over with her. It was a slightly strange 21st birthday present of mine from an ex-boyfriend who knew I hated motorbikes because my cousin had broken his leg on one (years later his sister would tell me he'd been drunk at the time). It had been collecting dust in my parents' loft for 14 years and I was so pleased that it was now going to get some use and Estrella absolutely adored it and had been riding it around Jack's garden pushing herself along with her feet. Luckily Crispin spotted it out of the corner of his eye in Jack's garden as we were about to drive off, it had almost been forgotten.

The aparthotel we eventually found was lovely and had a swimming pool. This meant Estrella was in her element and Crispin's mum finally had a bit of relaxation before going home. It had been tiring for her looking after a toddler, cooking for us and doing our washing by hand or taking it up the hill to the launderette (there was no washing machine at Jack's). One of the motel cleaners came to do our washing every day and I had a bit more energy so started to cook again.

Rather bizarrely, I kept getting electric shocks from the oven. A maintenance man came to have a look at it and then pointed at my bare feet. "It's because you haven't got shoes on," he said and then promptly left. Silly me.

We even had a television, something we still didn't have at home, and it was great to hear about London winning the Olympic bid. However we also got full coverage of the terrible bombings of the

London transport system.   There were some evil people in the world.

We had more bad news that day.   The hotel phone rang at 7.30am. Crispin answered it. "It was the receptionist. I've got to go to the front desk," he said, "they want to talk to me about something."

"That's odd," I said, "did she say why?"

"No but I bet somebody's complained about the noise we're making. She didn't sound very happy."

"But it's difficult to be quiet when you've got a new baby and a toddler," I said, "surely they'll understand that.   Can you take Estrella with you then I can go back to sleep?"   Arturo was still sleeping as he'd been awake most of the night.

Half an hour later Crispin wasn't back.   I wanted to go to reception to find out what was happening but Arturo was asleep on our bed and as Crispin's mum had flown back to the UK the day before I didn't dare leave him by himself. Her help was already being missed.

Suddenly, I had a horrible feeling it was something to do with the car. The car park was next to the road and there were signs up saying 'do not leave anything in your car'.   There was a security guard and a locked chain to secure the cars in and as Crispin was unpacking the car on our arrival I noticed that he had left some stuff in the boot which he'd covered with a black tarpaulin. I registered what he was doing but didn't comment on it. We were tired, the car was black too, so maybe I thought we would get away with it but I had known at the time it was a silly thing to do. How did we get so careless?

We'd had our laptop and video camera stolen from the house on April Fool's Day (wasn't that apt?). We could only assume that someone had been watching us one evening as we had no curtains in the living area. My credit cards had been taken out of my wallet and Crispin's wallet had had the cash taken from it. Nothing else had been touched so they knew exactly where to look for what they wanted. The insurance company said we weren't insured for theft because we didn't have metal bars on our windows.

Although it was a shame losing the video of Estrella's first steps, one of the worst things about being without the laptop was the absence of music in the house now. I'd spent half of my life dancing around the room with Estrella to keep her amused. She knew the actions to 'The Timewarp' at a very young age and now we had nothing to play our CDs on and the only music I could get out of the radio was Spanish stuff. Maybe we would get it back.

We had received a lead a couple of weeks later, a response to the 'stolen' posters we had put up between our house and Laurel, where the bank was. Dee had kindly done them for us adding photos of our camera and computer that she had got off the internet. A neighbour of a friend had been offered our camera by a man who lived nearby. We passed the information on to OIJ (the CIA equivalent) but the man was a known drug smuggler and OIJ had already raided his house looking for drugs since our robbery had occurred and nothing resembling our stuff had been found in the raid. OIJ felt like they couldn't go bothering him by raiding him again. I was ready to go round there, bother him with a baseball bat, and smash his face in but Crispin persuaded me that he was a very, very bad man and messing with him probably wasn't a very good idea. Although Crispin clearly felt the same way as he admitted to driving down the man's driveway once. He had been persuaded by the friend who had shown him where the house was and was sitting in the car with him at the time, to turn around again. I know where the git lives and I glare at his house every time we drive through Naranjo.

Maybe now we were getting careless because we'd had some good luck the week before. It was immediately after we had picked Crispin's mum up from the airport. As we'd stopped at the supermarket for supplies, Crispin had dropped his wallet in the car park. It was dark and raining, full of cash and he hadn't noticed until he was trying to pay for gas at the nearby gas station. As he was phoning the banks to cancel his cards, *Banco Nacional* amazed him by saying that his wallet had been found and they gave him the name and number of the guy who had it. He was a doctor at one of the local hospitals. Crispin's wallet was returned to him intact and the doctor hadn't wanted a reward (there are nice people here too). Unfortunately the hospital he worked at burned down a few days later (whilst I was giving birth).

We weren't to be so lucky today. Crispin eventually came back from reception carrying Estrella. "The car's been broken into," he said.

"No." I'd been right. "What's gone?" I asked him.

"Everything. Thieves put a gun to the security guard's head at 3am and told him to go for a walk, so he did."

"Did he not call the police?"

"No, they told him not to, said they'd kill him if he did. He was terrified. He called the receptionist at home at 5am and she called the police when she got into work this morning."

It read like a list from 'The Generation Game'. Kid's paddling pool, a bread-maker that we had bought the day before, ditto the hall light, a hair-dryer which was going to be a surprise for my birthday, my Helly Hansen waterproof I had bought during a trip to Brittany, Estrella's cuddly toys, a double blow-up bed that belonged to Mac and Penny and the little Harley Davidson motorbike which upset me more than anything.

"I'm amazed they didn't take Estrella's car seat," I said to Crispin as he was running through the list of things for the police. A policeman was writing everything down in a notebook.

"Oh, bugger," he said and vanished. "They did," he said when he reappeared.

The OIJ were useless, as usual. For some reason they phoned us a few days later to assure us they were doing something and were planning on coming to the hotel to interview the guard – don't rush yourselves boys! They also mentioned an identity parade but we knew that nothing would come of it and weren't surprised when we didn't hear from them again.

The hotel manager was very unsympathetic. The girl from reception brought him to see me when Crispin was out getting quotes for repairing the damage to the car. "You never leave anything in your car," he said to me sternly. For some reason I was expecting to hear "I'm sorry the guard in my employment fell asleep and then didn't bother to call the police." I'm speculating.

"I know," I said good-naturedly, "it was a really silly thing to do. I know it's our own fault."

"You never ever leave ANYTHING in your car," he repeated.

"She's just given birth," the receptionist said to her boss, trying to make him go easy on me but it didn't make any difference. I kept expecting him to say "I'm sorry it happened" but of course he was a Tico so I was to wait in vain. He didn't even bat an eyelid when I told him about Estrella's Harley Davidson motorbike. They had a notice in reception saying that they were the home of the only official Harley Davidson tours in Costa Rica so I thought that might soften his ice-cold heart but I was wrong.

The receptionist knocked the cost of a night off our bill without the boss' knowledge. They also paid the insurance excess for the repairs but only after

Crispin had signed a document stating the hotel weren't to blame. Our insurance agent had informed us over the phone that our really expensive car insurance only covered theft of the car radio and not the other stuff. The car radio was the only thing the thieves hadn't taken as, presumably, they hadn't been able to find it.

We drove the long drive home with black plastic flapping over where the window should have been. We stopped overnight at the 'Mirador Valle del General', a restaurant and *cabinas* just the other side of the mountains at km 119. There were great views of Chirripó, the highest mountain in Costa Rica and wonderful views of the General Valley below. Their bird feeders regularly attracted groups of bird-watchers.

It was run by a wonderful Tico family that we had first met on our 'recce' trip two years earlier. The eldest daughter had been our 'plan D' for looking after Estrella.

The mother had given me a crucifix when I had told her I needed to have another caesarean. She had had three caesareans herself and she had hugged me and slipped it into my hand (we both had tears in our eyes) when Crispin, Estrella and I had left to drive up to San José for the birth. They were all overjoyed to see us this time but spotted the flapping black plastic and knew instantly there was something wrong. I cried my eyes out when I recounted our tale. "We are so sorry that this could happen to you in our country," they said.

We felt slightly happier as we waved goodbye to our friends the following morning to complete the journey home but the feeling didn't last long. Things were to get a lot worse.

31 Local Advice

Once home I tried to shake the cloud I was under caused by the hospital stay, the robbery, the long drive, the pain my wound caused, the tiredness that came with having a new baby and the realisation that we weren't going to be moving into our house in the immediate future. The four of us were now sleeping in the same bedroom in our little box. We had no daily visits from midwives or health visitors to tell me we were doing okay, no close family members to amuse Estrella whilst I napped with Arturo; I couldn't nap. The sun wouldn't come out for a while. But at least I wasn't going through this difficult patch alone; I had Crispin.

Our first morning back Crispin was clearly getting ready to leave the house.

"Where are you going?" I asked him.

"To the *finca*," he said as he walked out of the door to get some peace and quiet leaving me to look after ten day old Arturo and 16 month old Estrella who I wasn't supposed to be picking up for a couple more weeks at least and who seemed to be coming down with a bad cold. I bet he had a hammock up there strung between two coconut palms. I really hoped the coconuts were loose.

Estrella cried all day; when she is ill she just wants her dad. Not knowing what else to do, I phoned my sister and I cried down the phone to her. She cried too.

We had been warned that going from one child to two was more difficult than going from none to one and adding to that their closeness in age and the fact we were living in a shoe box, well we were struggling to say the least. We were getting no sleep as Estrella was suddenly waking up five times a night, I have never seen so much mucous come out of a child's nose, and Arturo thought night was day. We were knackered and our nerves were frayed. I was doing things that I shouldn't have been doing like risking a hernia by lifting Estrella in and out of her cot and her high chair and carrying her around when she needed cuddles but because Crispin wasn't around I had to.

One day Estrella kicked me in my wound when I was changing her nappy and I smacked her for the first time ever. I cried and cried and cried. I resented Crispin for having the freedom to be able to walk out of the door whenever he wanted to, I felt like I was a prisoner and so desperately wanted to go back to England, thinking that that would make everything right again. Then Arturo caught Estrella's cold and I didn't think I would make it through another day.

Crispin and I stopped communicating with each other and just snapped at each other. We would converse via Estrella. When I was sitting breastfeeding I would say "do you want to help daddy fold the washing Estrella?" knowing that it was something that I would be doing if I wasn't breastfeeding so figured he could do it instead. How could he not notice that there was washing that needed folding? He hated me 'ordering him around' as he called it.

One memorable exchange was during breakfast after a particularly difficult night. Arturo needed feeding so I moved to the sofa to be comfortable whilst I fed him. I thought Estrella would still be hungry after her fruit. "Do you want a bagel and blueberry jam Estrella?" We'd stocked up on such goodies in San José. It was my way of asking Crispin to make it for her without having to speak to him directly. It was something I would be doing if I wasn't already feeding Arturo. She nodded.

"Do you want peas and poo Estrella?" retorted a very knackered Crispin who looked like he'd aged ten years. Estrella nodded. My eyes met Crispin's and we both laughed. Maybe we would get through this.

Luckily we did have a few friends, even though we didn't speak the same language. Our second day at home, Grace and Enrique brought lunch over for us.

"It's bad for your tummy walking around like that," Grace told me after we had hugged and pecked.

"Like what?" I queried, maybe I still had a slightly hunched appearance, not wanting to stretch my wound too much.

"Barefooted," she said, looking at my bare feet.

"Why?" I asked. And I had thought, because Grace didn't tie a daft tea towel around her neck when she had a cold like other Ticos did that she was different. Silly me!

"It's cold," came the reply.

Bilkez agreed with her. Cold!? It must have been close on 30 degrees centigrade inside the house. Walking round on the slate floor in the barn in winter, now that was cold. I couldn't see how having cold feet would be bad for my wound anyway.

"Peter says you aren't supposed to see rain or sun for 40 days either," said Crispin. He'd bumped into him at the bank that morning.

"What's that supposed to mean?" I asked.

"You're not allowed out," he said with a grin. Nothing new there then, I couldn't help thinking.

Being a second-time mum I suppose I should have been used to strange comments from people, I had certainly been given my fair share by friends, family or complete strangers after Estrella was born. "Give her a chicken bone to chew on." "Put breast milk in her eyes." "Rub a sugar cube on her gums like sand-paper to help her teeth come through." "Don't let her sleep in your bedroom, she'll only disturb you." You know, the kind of stuff that you try to meet with a polite nod and a smile. I know that you do because I hear examples from friends who are new mothers all the time. Just recently I had a letter from one that read 'Florrie can't sit up yet but for

265

some reason my mother says she is ready for a rocking horse!' I was now experiencing the 'Tico version' of what happens in the UK. It might interest you to know that it's the norm over here for kids to share their parents' <u>bed</u>, never mind their bedroom. Grace's sister was eventually booted out of her parents' bed at the not so tender age of 14 (and I'm not talking months either!). Locals were horrified when they found out that Arturo slept on his own in a Moses basket instead of in bed with us and under a fan too! "Puracito," (poor little thing) they would say. As for the fact we went outside without a woolly hat covering Arturo's ears...! It was 30 degrees centigrade for goodness sake! Nod, smile, nod, smile; there is an art to it.

A few days following Grace's visit, Crispin had a meeting in Amado's rancho with the owners of the neighbouring *fincas* to get the title process rolling for our *finca*. He was waiting in the house for the judge to arrive when I heard voices outside. Freddy had brought Margarita, Jackie and Yailin down to see us on his motorbike (yes, all of them together!). Maybe I wasn't as alone as I had originally thought.
"You looked at a solar eclipse didn't you?" said Freddy pointing to red marks on the back of Arturo's head and the top of his nose.
"No, they're stork bites," I said to him. "The marks that the stork made when they brought him." He looked at me for a moment trying to judge whether I was serious or not, then he started laughing. I laughed too.
Margarita was holding Arturo and he had the hiccups. Fiddle, I was going to have to breastfeed him again to get rid of them. "Have you got a piece of paper?" Margarita asked me, instead of handing him over. I presumed he'd puked on her so handed her a piece of kitchen roll. "That's too big," she laughed,

tore off a corner, licked it and stuck it in the middle of Arturo's head.

"Why have you stuck some paper in the middle of his forehead?" I asked bemused

"To stop Arturito's hiccups," she said. WHAT?

"You can use a piece of material too," added Bilkez.

I happened to mention the story to the doctor's receptionist at the private clinic in Neily when we took Arturo there for a check-up. I expected her to laugh but she said very seriously, "Just saliva or a piece of cotton works too".

"Really?" I said politely, nodding and smiling.

"Did it work?" she asked.

"No," I replied honestly.

The judge eventually arrived and Crispin gave me a hasty kiss before jumping into the car and heading up to the *finca*. He was a bit nervous. Getting title was a lengthy process. We had title for Urbano's *finca* so that wasn't a problem; the two extra bits of land we had bought from Amado and German via Amado were being tagged onto that *finca*. We had been told by our surveyor and lawyer that it was the easiest route to take and was an option because it was increasing the size of the *finca* by less than 10%.

It was the original *finca* that we bought from Lorenzo that we needed title for. The surveyor had already visited us and produced a drawing of our land showing its boundaries and its size i.e. a *plano* of the *finca*. It was somewhat confusing that the *finca* straddled a public road ('public' although we had paid to put it in and were maintaining it) so we had two *planos* for the *finca* and each had a different number, one for either side of the road. The judge's job was to interview our neighbours and make sure they all agreed with the boundaries and that everybody was talking about the same piece of land.

Lenny Loco had said that it was easy and Crispin wouldn't have to do any preparation with the neighbours and that he shouldn't worry. "They probably won't even be asked any questions," he had said. Crispin was told he was allowed to sit in on the meeting but wouldn't be allowed to say anything. Although Lenny Loco had said "don't worry", Crispin couldn't help it. I wished him luck as they drove off.

Crispin returned a couple of hours later a defeated man. He settled himself in to the hammock with a cold beer and told me the story.

"Is the terrain of the finca in question mountainous or flat?" The judge posed the question to Amado, Mario and Peter in turn.

"Flat," said Amado, who has a *finca* higher up in the mountains.

"Mountainous," said Mario, who doesn't.

Peter, who likes to talk, gave a lengthy explanation that didn't really answer the question at all.

"What water sources are there?" the judge asked next.

"There's a spring," said Amado.

"Maybe a stream or two," said Mario who hadn't been up there in 20 years.

Peter once again, 'went off on one'.

"Is it pasture or forest?"

"Forest," said Amado, whose *finca* was all pasture.

"Pasture," said Mario, and to be fair it probably had been the last time he had seen it.

Peter excelled himself this time; the judge almost ran out of paper frantically scribbling notes.

"Who is the neighbour to the east?" he asked Amado. Amado wasn't sure where east was.

"What about the second *finca* now," said the judge as he prepared to ask them all about the second half of the *finca*; the bit on the opposite side of the road. Everyone in the room, except for Crispin (and the judge) who knew we had two *planos* for our original *finca,* thought the judge was now talking about Urbano's *finca,* the second one that we had bought. Crispin was almost bursting with the effort of keeping quiet. He had already been told to 'shhh' twice. When the witnesses started answering the judge's questions all over again, and it was clear they were all referring to our other *finca* and not the other half of this *finca,* Crispin couldn't hold back any longer and explained the confusion to the judge who then had to cross out what he had written and start again. Crispin wouldn't be taking Lenny Loco's advice again for a long time!

We waited whilst the judge wrote his report. It would then get passed through various departments of the local government, the *muni.* Because a forest was mentioned MINAE (the environment ministry) would send someone along to check to see if there were any ancient trees that might mean they would have to take it off us and make it into a National Park. It was raining so the MINAE guy didn't bother getting out of the car. Then Christmas would arrive and nothing would happen for a month and then another month or two whilst the backlog was cleared and workers talked about what they did in the holidays.

The water-board (AYA), during their review of the report, would then notice that one of the witnesses had mentioned a spring and they would need to make sure there wasn't sufficient water to supply the local village. There wouldn't be. Then someone would write a list of questions that our lawyer would consult us about and would then reply to, some of which would already have been replied to a year earlier but staff would have changed and documents would have been misfiled blah blah blah. During the final report reconciliation somebody, maybe the new guy in the office wanting to impress the judge with a cool comment, would say they wanted 'Forest' written on the *plano* where the forest was so the *plano* would have to be re-done.

It would be three and a half years before we would legally own the bit of land we had built our house on.

32 Losing Friends

I was slowly changing my mind about going back to England and it was a good thing too because, once again, we were running out of money. We didn't even have the money for the air-fares. We were down to our last $10k. I found this out at the same time I found out that Crispin had agreed a pay rise with Freddy and Enrique three weeks earlier and purposefully hadn't told me about it. In a matter of weeks we weren't going to be able to pay them their original wages never mind anything extra!

One evening I was sitting trying to catch up with my letters to friends and family. I always tried to put a personal letter and photos in their birthday cards and I spent hours writing them and now with a new baby and a toddler, I began to wish I didn't have quite so many friends! Crispin sat on the sofa opposite me. Receipts that Marco had brought round earlier in the day, on his shiny new motorbike, were spread all over the coffee table. He had the calculator on his knee, a pen in his hand and was deep in concentration. After a couple of hours my hand was starting to ache so I put my pen down and massaged it. Crispin was still lost in the pile of receipts.

"Everything okay?" I asked him. The pause told me that it wasn't. We did seem to be spending an awful lot of money on building materials.

"When did Marco start working for us?" he asked.

"End of January I think. Why?"

"Some of the latest receipts date back to early January and I'm sure he was still at Pachicha then."

"There's something else isn't there?" I could read him like a book. He picked two receipts up off the coffee table and handed then to me. They were hand-written and I couldn't read the scrawl. I looked up at him expectantly. For neither the first or last time in my life I was missing the point.

He used the patient voice he normally saved for explaining film plots to me. "This here," he said pointing to the spidery writing on one of the receipts, "says 'six giant culverts' and is from a *ferreteria* in Neily." I knew what he meant, I'd seen them lying next to the road inside the *finca*. "This here," he continued, this time pointing to some spidery scrawl on the other receipt, "also says 'six giant culverts' and is from Marco's new *ferreteria* in Golfito." The dates on the two receipts were the same and along with the other items on the receipts each receipt totalled six thousand dollars.

I suddenly knew what Crispin was getting at. "We've only got six on the *finca* haven't we?" he nodded.

Wow, Marco had been unlucky. If it was concrete blocks or bags of cement he could have got away with it, we had no idea how many of those we had used on the house, but giant culverts – they were kind of noticeable!

"There are lots more examples. He's even changed dates on some receipts to make it look like stuff was bought on different days; some of them are really obvious. He's been charging us for the same materials twice. It's not just that either. It's the commission too; he's been charging us up to 40%!"

"Now what?" I asked him. He didn't answer straightaway. He was upset. My darling husband is the most trusting guy in the world (odd for a lawyer I am sure you'll agree) and he couldn't believe anyone, especially someone he considered a friend, would do this to him.

"I'll get the delivery notes from Toli. Anything delivered to the house, Toli will have a delivery note for and the original price will be on them. They are more reliable than the hand-written receipts that Marco's given me from his new business."

"We refused to lend him the money so he's taken it hasn't he?" I said.

272

"It looks like it," Crispin said. "That business was started with our money."

Crispin went one step further and contacted all of the *ferreterías* (either by phone or in person) and asked them to provide him with duplicate receipts of everything that had ever been bought in Crispin's name. For the *ferreterías* with computerised systems it was easy, others had to trawl through hand-written records and produce a hand-written list. Collecting the evidence was going to be incredibly time-consuming but Crispin was determined to do it. He contacted our lawyer Arturo and discussed our options. Arturo said he would help Crispin to write a *denuncia* (an official statement) that could be handed to OIJ, the Costa Rican FBI-equivalent, and he would fly down to meet with Marco if that was what we decided to do.

Crispin asked Toli to come down to the house and explained the situation to him.

"I've never trusted him," said Toli.

"Really?" He'd never said anything before. In fact, I was sure I remembered him saying that it was a good idea getting Marco to order our building materials for us.

"No, I always thought there was something funny about him." It was a shame he hadn't voiced his opinions a tad earlier. "I'll help you any way I can. If you need me to be a character witness in court for you, Crispin, then you just have to ask. You're very good people and I love working for you and you don't deserve this," he had tears in his eyes when he spoke. It was a speech we heard frequently but it was nice to hear.

"And we love working with you Toli," Crispin and I both said together. We did the 'mutual appreciation' thing at least once a month. It was a terrible shame we were going to have to tell him what we were about to tell him. The time had come; I

273

looked at Crispin willing him to start. He looked back at me. I raised my eyebrows in a silent 'go on then'. He frowned slightly in a 'you do it, you're much better at this than I am'. I rolled my eyes at him and took a deep breath.

"Toli, we are almost out of money. We thought we would have sold some more lots by now but we haven't. We are going to have to put the team on half pay for the next four weeks and hope that we have sold something by then. If not then we'll have to review the situation." That would leave us with $3k in the bank. "I'm sorry, Toli." He had tears in his eyes again.

"I love working for you, you're wonderful people, my men love working for you, we work very hard for you, I pay them fairly. Do you not like the house?" He thought we were letting him down gently because we didn't like the work he had done.

"We think you're wonderful too and we love the house. It's the most beautiful house around here. It's just we really really have no money."

"It is a beautiful house isn't it? I'm so glad you like it because you are lovely people..." The mutual appreciation conversation went on for another half an hour.

"That was horrible," I said to Crispin after an upset Toli had left. "You are such a wuss."

"I'm no good at that sort of thing."

"You need to practice!" I said to him. "You can break the news to him in four weeks time when we have to let him and the team go."

"Something will come up," he said. "We won't have to let them go."

"How do you know that this time?" I didn't feel sure at all.

He shrugged his shoulders. "I just do," he said.

We asked the bank for a loan but were told that we would have to put the house up as collateral but as we didn't have title for the *finca* that the house stood on, the bank wouldn't accept the house. We weren't going to get a bank loan. Crispin's mum kindly offered to send us her £5k emergency savings.

Once again we were about to be stuffed. We needed to sell some lots desperately.

It was at that point in time that we received a surprise visit from our newspaper. Whilst we had been away Lenny, Karin and Coral had moved into their new house in Pavones. We hadn't seen them since we'd got back home from San José with Arturo. It was good to see Lenny and it reminded us that we did miss having him just up the hill.

"Why the long faces?" he asked.

"We've just had to tell Toli that he's down to half pay for the next month. If we don't get some money in by then we'll have to let the team go," I said miserably.

"I can lend you some money if you like," Lenny said chirpily. "I paid the bank off when I sold my house and with the commission I made from selling land last month it means I don't need to make any more for ages." He had a huge smile on his face and was completely unable to sense the atmosphere in the room. Then came the final nail in his coffin. "I've got so much that I've not bothered to do any work for the last three weeks!"

I jumped on him. "Did you just say that you aren't making any effort to sell our lots?!" I couldn't believe it. "We are down to almost nothing, our hopes have been resting on you to sell our land and you've just said <u>that</u> to us! We're your clients, Lenny!"

He tried to back-peddle. "That wasn't what I meant exactly. I meant there aren't any clients around so I've been trying to find more..." It was too late, the damage was done.

I asked my dad to do our web-site. He had offered enough times.

"How does www.southerncostaricaland.com sound, Jo?" he said the same day.

"Brilliant," I said.

We were also going to advertise with the real estate agents in Golfito. Lenny Loco was no longer going to have sole rights to sell our land. It was something we should have put more effort into ages ago. I set about painting a sign to put at the bottom of our road 'Finca Estrella – Lots' with an arrow. We waited for the crowds to descend.

They didn't, not yet anyway, and our salvation wouldn't arrive until September, in the shape of Crispin's parents.

33 Gilly

We were once again car-less so decided to go for a walk up to the house site one Saturday. We stopped off to see Les and Carolina on the way. We'd spent the previous Sunday there watching a movie, well watching as much of it as we could whilst trying to prevent Estrella from breaking their photos and throwing their collection of DVDs on the floor. Les had found her a plastic bulldog to play with to distract her. Ticos loved stuff like that; little nik-naks littered their homes, and some Tico neighbours had given it to Les and Carolina as an anniversary present.

"Don't worry Jo, she won't be able to break it," Les said to me as he handed it over to Estrella. "It's indestructible." It did look pretty sturdy. Five minutes later Estrella held the dog in one hand and one of its legs in the other.

"I think it's time we left, hon," I said to Crispin after apologising profusely.

In our hurry to get out of the door and leave the rest of Les and Carolina's possessions intact we had left one of Arturo's toys there and intended to get it now.

"Looks like they're out," I said to Crispin when I saw their car wasn't there. I shouted for Carolina in case Les had gone surfing and Carolina was in by herself but there was no answer. "Okay, what's plan B?"

There was no one else around to visit now that Lenny Loco had gone. The new owner of the duplex lived in the States for much of the year so he wasn't an option.

"Feel up to walking up to the house?" Crispin asked me.

I did. My wound was healing nicely and rarely 'pulled' any more. "Do you feel up to pushing the kids up to the house?" I asked him. I didn't need any midwife's scales to tell me that, at six weeks old, Arturo was rapidly becoming a big fat lump. He was an incredibly good-natured baby who (once he was over his cold) had slept for three hours, fed for five minutes, slept for three hours, fed for five minutes almost ad infinitum. He was just starting to break this sleep/feed routine now and usually had a long period of activity in the mid-morning and another one mid-afternoon. He also never ever cried when he woke up but just lay in his moses basket gurgling happily. His only problem was he constantly fed and cried for hours and hours in the evening (usually starting at about 5pm and sometimes continuing until midnight!). He would alternate between the two; feeding, crying, feeding, crying and that was utterly exhausting and was proving impossible for me to cook dinner. The only way to stop him crying was to put him over my left shoulder. Nobody else's shoulder would do and the right one wasn't good enough. My back was really starting to suffer.

"Doesn't look like it's going to rain," Crispin said, checking the skies for signs of approaching thunderstorms. The clouds were white and fluffy so we turned right into 'our' road and started up the hill.

It took us less than 30 minutes to reach the house which surprised me as we had walked slowly. When we arrived there we found that Juan, Toli's brother, had been left to look after the site, making sure no-one walked off with our expensive toilets and light fittings. His wife had also joined him to keep him company. The rest of the team had left for the weekend. Juan's wife took Arturo off me straightaway, marvelling at the size of him, whilst Juan walked around the house with us pointing out what had recently been done. The wooden and tile floors were in the middle of being laid and the house looked lovely but any optimism I had felt at being able to live in it soon had been well and truly beaten out of me. I only knew we would be in by Christmas. We had some friends coming just after Christmas so it would be perfect. I wasn't going to panic any more. Toli's team had five months and it was plenty of time. They had missed the deadline of Arturo's birth but couldn't possibly miss the new Christmas deadline that I had firmly planted in my brain.

Juan Carlos, our carpenter, was still living on-site. He had come for two weeks and was still here six months later. His wife wasn't happy but at least he had almost finished the floors. After the floors were finished he would return to his own workshop and his wife (if she would have him) and make a start on our windows and doors.

"They'll be ready before the end of October," he said. "Isn't it Crispin's birthday at the beginning of November?" he added. I knew where the conversation was going to head. He worshipped Crispin and because of this seemed to spend half his life making 'presents' for us: a wooden *pilon* that was used for crushing rice in the olden days with Crispin's name next to it ('Krispin' it read), a cannon for my parents, a beautiful bed for Estrella's birthday (which was an amazing piece of craftsmanship and would soon be put to good use so I wasn't complaining about that one), a rocking bird for Estrella, and a bizarre square carved flower that he wanted to put on our ceiling. I insisted it was only going to go on our ceiling over my dead body.

"I'm going to make you a huge desk, suitable for a man of your standing." I almost choked on my coffee. "I'm going to put your name in big letters above it in a big arch." Juan-Carlos swept his arm in a rainbow shape demonstrating how huge the letters were going to be.

"Mmmm, nice," I said to Crispin sarcastically.

"We just want our windows and doors," I said to Juan Carlos. I was always saying this to Juan Carlos but he never listened to me; the inferior woman. "The best present we could possibly have is for our house to be finished." I felt I would be saying this to him for the next five years, I wasn't far out.

The other thing that was lovely about him initially but then became problematic was that he insisted on cooking for us. He was forever inviting us up to the workshop next to the house site, where he was living, to fry us stuff. He was spending time that would have been better spent working, and money that we were paying him, to buy food for us! It was a crazy situation.

Juan Carlos also had the bizarre habit (because I was a woman so couldn't think for myself) of asking Crispin if I would like more rice or chicken or whatever else was being fried that day. 'HELLO, I AM SITTING RIGHT HERE!' I felt like yelling at him. I played along with it for a while, so as not to hurt his feelings, but eventually even Crispin got fed up with being the go-between. "Would Jo like some milk in her coffee?" Juan Carlos asked Crispin one day.

"Why don't you ask her, Juan Carlos?" Crispin said kindly. "She's sitting right there." Then he was always buying Estrella cartons of milk or packets of biscuits, once again spending his wages (or, worse, the money we had lent him!) on us. One day he asked me what we were going to do about choosing godparents for Arturo. Was he putting himself forward as a candidate?! He seemed desperate to please us in any way possible. He was a lovely man but somehow refused to take on board that what would please us most was for him to do what we were paying him to do, i.e. work.

"Someone left the gate open between Juan Carlos' workshop and the house site," Juan told us as we walked out onto the terrace, balancing carefully on the beams as it hadn't yet been laid. They were going to make a start on it on Monday. A fence had been put up around the house site specifically to keep the horses out, somebody had been careless. "The horses got in and one of them trod on a rusty nail," he said.

"Are they okay?" I asked.

"I think so," Juan said, "but best ask Freddy." For some reason I assumed it was BoBo but we passed Freddy on the way back down the road and he said that it was BoBo's mum, Gilly.

"It's nothing," Freddy said. "It will heal by itself. We don't need to do anything," he assured us.

Unfortunately Freddy was wrong and, a few days later, Crispin said that he'd seen Gilly and she was limping badly. As we had the car back again he drove to the vet's in Neily to get some antibiotics for her.

The next day we were sitting on the newly-laid terrace at the house site. I noticed Crispin staring down towards the mango tree in front of the house, it was making an impressive comeback after its mauling by the bulldozer. "What's up?" I asked him as I followed his gaze to where the horses were grazing. Crispin made to stand up.

"Nothing," he said relaxing again, "I thought there was something wrong with Gilly but she looks okay now." I replayed the scene in my mind and noticed something that I had missed first time around. Gilly hadn't looked quite right, she'd been standing in a way I can only describe as 'too still'. I looked at her again and Crispin was right, she seemed okay now.

The following day we went to check on her and found the oddest thing. She was standing on the rancho site absolutely rigid, every muscle in her body tense. BoBo was trying to feed off her but kept pulling away as if he wasn't getting anything.

"I've never seen anything like it before," Freddy admitted.

"Have you got the vet's number on you, hon?" I asked Crispin.

"Yes, it's in my phone." We walked up the hill a bit until Crispin had a decent signal on his phone. He dialled the number of the vet in Neily then handed the phone over to Freddy. Whilst Freddy was explaining her symptoms in rapid Spanish to the vet something was ringing vague bells in my mind. What was that injection you have to have, the one for the bacteria that is present in soil? Why didn't I go to more microbiology lectures?! It came to me in a flash. "It's tetanus," I said to Crispin. "Lock-jaw."

"Tetano," Freddy said into the phone, the vet had reached the same conclusion.

"The vet said that the only thing we can do is put her in the shade," Freddy said after he had hung up. "She'll be fine," he assured us.

"She has to be," I said to Crispin. She'd given birth three weeks before I had. We'd seen her shortly afterwards, seen her foal stand, take his first steps, feed from her for the first time. I didn't want BoBo to lose his mum at the tender age of 10 weeks. She was me; BoBo was Arturo, that was how I felt.

I looked up 'tetanus' in my 'Merck Manual'. It didn't sound good. It talked of 'immediate wound debridement', literally giving it a really good scrub, but that hadn't been done. Also we needed to neutralize the toxin produced by the bacteria that had infected her wound. It talked of an antitoxin for humans so surely there was an antitoxin available for horses.

I lay awake all night worrying about her. There must be something we could do. Two of my best friends were what I considered to be 'horsey people'. I could call one of them I thought. Then I remembered that Crispin's cousin was married to a vet.

First thing in the morning Crispin called his sister to get their number. His aunt answered. I tried not to stand over him impatiently while he caught up with her. He left a polite amount of time before coming to the reason for his call. Then he spoke to his sister for what seemed like days. I eventually snapped. "Hurry up!" I hissed. I was glared at and the conversation continued. The minutes ticked by.

Eventually he hung up and phoned his cousin. Her husband was still at his vet's practice and we were to call back in an hour. It was a very long hour.

Eventually Crispin spoke to him. He confirmed that we should try the antitoxin but said that it was probably too late but she may pull through anyway. We were to clean the wound then dress it with sugar, honey or maggots. Not having any of the latter and our organic honey seeming inappropriate we decided on sugar. "Shade and water" he had also said. There was a vaccine so we could get the other horses vaccinated and he was going to send us a book on horses. She wouldn't be producing any milk but the toxin wouldn't have got into her milk supply anyway so BoBo was going to be okay, one bit of good news.

Crispin called the vet in Neily again and the vet said he had the antitoxin in stock. Why the bloody hell hadn't he mentioned it when Freddy had spoken to him yesterday? We had been told it was $200 a shot in the UK. It was $3 over here. It didn't sound right.

"Are you sure?" I asked him. "Fiddle," said Crispin, "maybe he thought I said 'antibiotic' and not 'antitoxin'". He called him back to check but the vet had heard correctly. We grabbed the supplies and the kids and dashed out on our rescue mission. We were headed for the vet's in Neily but went to see Gilly first to give her some water and make sure she was in the shade. We couldn't see her standing with the other horses on the rancho site so we drove past towards the gate which served as the entrance to the workshop. Juan Carlos was standing there waiting for us.

"Casi muerta," (she's almost dead) he said. No, no, no we were going to save her; we knew what to do now. "She's been like it for ten hours," he added.

We had been mistaken. Gilly <u>was</u> with the other horses but was lying down which was why we hadn't been able to see her. She was still rigid and obviously in agony. BoBo was standing over her licking the salt off her body, occasionally trying to feed and getting kicked whenever Gilly had muscle spasms. It was an awful sight to witness.

As soon as I saw her I knew what we had to do. "We have to put her down," I said to Crispin. I was distraught. Tears kept pouring down my cheeks.

We didn't know how; we needed Freddy and Enrique. Freddy arrived at that instant on his motorbike, Ruben had been sent to fetch the guys. We stood and waited for Enrique.

"They know," someone said pointing to the vultures circling overhead. My tears fell faster.

"Can we bury her?" I managed to say to Crispin.

"Better that she's food for the vultures," he said and I couldn't speak for crying.

Enrique arrived with his family's gun shortly after. I was sent back up to the house with Estrella and Arturo. I didn't want BoBo to watch what was going to happen but I couldn't get the words out. Crispin understood and nodded at me. I said my silent goodbyes to Gilly and left.

Walking back up the hill towards the house pushing the pushchair I heard two shots and felt sick to the stomach. I didn't look back. I reached the house and walked onto the terrace where the builders were gathered and heard a third. It was then I looked over; I couldn't help myself. The other horses, BoBo, George and Lucero had been led away and were standing near the gate. Gilly was lying still and alone on the site where our rancho was to be built. Crispin, Freddy and Enrique were walking back down towards the other horses, I didn't notice which of them held the gun but presumed it was Enrique. BoBo started walking back up the site towards his mum. I thought I would never stop crying. Seeing him sniffing and licking her lifeless body was one of the saddest sights I have ever seen.

I cried all day. Cried because BoBo at three weeks older than Arturo had lost his mum; cried because maybe, if we had done something sooner, it wouldn't have happened.

34 Saving BoBo

Crispin turned the car around at the top of the hill and drove back down towards the house. "Oh shit," he said.

"Shit." came a little voice from the backseat, I barely noticed. I saw what was concerning Crispin. Coming towards us were Negro, Freddy's brother, with his two oxen. They were dragging something behind them. Crispin hadn't told me about this as he hadn't wanted me to see her. Gilly had a chain around her neck. I turned away; I didn't want to see it either. 'It's just her body, it's just her body' I told myself this over and over again.

"Where are they taking her?" I asked Crispin tearfully.

"Mario's *finca,*" he said. The entrance to Mario's *finca* was at the very top of the road. He didn't live there, instead he had a house on the main road into Pavones. If you have ever been here you will immediately know the house I am talking about. You will have stopped just past it to take a photo. That first amazing view that you see of Zancudo (when the land just opens up all of a sudden and there it is in all of its glory?), well, his house is the little Tico house right there. He wants a lot of money for that piece of land. But, Mario is a very ill man. He has had three heart attacks and prefers to sit under a tree in his garden; he certainly never comes up here to his *finca* any more. He, foolishly one might say, sold the best piece of his *finca* to one of Enrique's brothers for $5k who sold it to Lenny Loco for $20k who sold it to his own dad the following day for $50k. It was land that bordered our *finca.* What remained of Mario's *finca* didn't have great views and the price he wanted for it, well, it was a lot of money. Occasionally Mario jumped in front of our car as we drove past his house offering us various deals if we found a buyer for his land. Lenny Loco said Mario frequently jumped in front of his car to get his attention. The price of the land doubled with each jump. I guess Mario still had a bit of energy left in him, in spite of the heart attacks. Anyway, Mario never came up to his *finca* any more; he didn't have that much energy. Gilly could lie there in peace.

The following day was Sunday and coincidentally one of my horsey friends, phoned me. I sobbed her the full Gilly story. She was very matter of fact, as teachers tend to be, and told me that we had done the right thing shooting her and leaving her for the vultures (burning her was her other suggestion). It was also the right thing not letting BoBo watch but then letting him go back to his mother's body so that he would know that she wouldn't be around for him any more. "You guys did everything right, Jo," she assured me. Then she worried me. "What are you going to do about the foal, Jo?"

"I don't know," I admitted, "we hadn't thought that far ahead."

"You are going to need to bottle-feed him or he's going to die."

I hung up and went inside to tell Crispin the news. He was sitting on the sofa staring into space. He had been listening to me talking to my friend and knew he had to tell me something. "Are you okay?" I asked him.

"It was me," he said, his head now in his hands.

"What was you?" I had absolutely no idea what he was talking about.

"I shot her," he said. He couldn't look at me. "It was expected of me; she was my horse. Enrique just handed the gun to me. I didn't have a choice." When he did finally look at me, he was pale.

I felt sick. The man I married, the one I shared a bed with every night. He had killed a horse. Even

287

though it was a horse that I knew needed killing; that I had said needed killing. How could my husband do that? I went back out onto the terrace, phoned my parents and sobbed some more.

I don't think my parents could take much more bad news arriving by telephone. My brother's heart problem had worryingly just advanced and my sister (she had left Sydney and was now living in Yellowknife in northern Canada) had scared the life out of us all the previous week. After a hellish 24 hour labour (though producing a healthy little baby boy whom they had named Alex) and a disastrous start to breastfeeding they had been discharged from hospital but in all the chaos that having a new baby causes my sister had somehow forgotten to eat. After talking nonsense for 48 hours and scaring her husband silly her health visitor arrived to check on the new family and immediately sent them all back to hospital where her and her husband were both diagnosed with exhaustion and Alex with jaundice. They would all be fine but I wasn't sure how much more my parents' nerves could take. At some point during the phone conversation with my parents, I pulled myself together and although it was a while before I felt I could understand why Crispin had done 'the deed', I set about concentrating on the more important matter to hand: saving BoBo. I was not going to let him die too. I moved into my 'sensible phase' the same one I used for organising Crispin's funeral when he was home late.

"Dad, could you look on the internet for me and try and find something out about orphaned ten week old foals?"

"Sure," he said and hung up.

The following morning Crispin left the house early for yet another mammoth drive and was on his way to Panama to buy parts for our, once again, lamed car. He would then return to a garage in Neily to get the parts fitted and visit the vet's to get some milk for BoBo.

"Make sure it's horse milk and not cow's milk!" I yelled after him

That night I had to cope with both Estrella and Arturo on my own as Crispin didn't make it home. The car wasn't ready and he had to stay in Neily overnight. It was now probably five or six days since BoBo had had any milk from his mum.

Crispin eventually returned with a giant baby's bottle with a huge rubber teat on the end of it and a bag of white powder. It said *ternero* on it. The word meant nothing to either of us.

"Okay, how much milk powder do we use for each feed?" I asked him.

"The vet said 5 spoons per something or other."

"Teaspoons, tablespoons, shovel loads?"

"Don't know," he admitted sheepishly.

"Crispin!" I said, exasperated. I could see him casting his mind back to the conversation with the vet. "How long will he need it for?" I asked.

"Don't know"

"How often do we give it to him?"

"Don't know."

I phoned my dad to see if he had found out anything useful. Luckily, he had. He had found a site on the internet that said that foals usually weaned themselves at 12 weeks so BoBo was close. He also read that if we couldn't find horse's milk, or a nursing mare, then we could use semi-skimmed cow's milk and add dextrose to it; horse's milk being less fatty and sweeter than cow's milk. He would need feeding every four to six hours, less often was okay but more often could give him diarrhoea. I looked *ternero* up in the dictionary. It said 'calf'. Fiddle! Crispin phoned the vet back.

When he got off the phone he turned to me. "The vet assures me that the milk is okay for foals too. He said five *cuchas* per litre of water, twice a day". Crispin looked pleased with himself. He had remembered to ask everything. There was one problem: *cuchas* wasn't a word.

"Cucharas? Cucharaditas? Cucharadas?" (Dessertspoons? Teaspoons? Tablespoons?) I asked him.

"Bugger," he said and picked up his phone to redial and check.

"Bugger," came his little echo from her high chair. I rolled my eyes at him.

"Cucharada," he said as he hung up. "I thought he had said that," he added.

Okay, tablespoons it was.

We took a bottle of water, the milk powder, teat and bottle and drove like the wind to the *finca*. I was determined to give BoBo his first feed, I felt I owed it to Gilly but how the hell was I going to make him drink from a large bottle with a rubber teat on the end of it?

I tried waving it at him. He ran off. Crispin was laughing at me. I started laughing too; it was a bizarre situation to find ourselves in. Estrella and Arturo sat in the double pushchair watching us. They were transfixed.

"Can you catch him do you think?" I said to Crispin.

"There might be some rope in the car, hang on." He came back a minute later carrying a rope. He made a loop in one end and the other end he coiled up in his hand.

"You look like you know what you're doing," I said to him, impressed.

"I've seen Freddy do it before," he said as he threw the loop in the general direction of BoBo. It missed by a mile.

"You don't now," I said laughing as BoBo ran off. He tried again a couple of times. The last time he got it caught around a tree. I had tears rolling down my cheeks at this point.

"We need Freddy," he said. I indicated for him to turn around. I'd seen Freddy appear behind him, like the shop-keeper in Mr Ben, a couple of minutes earlier. He had been enjoying the show. He'd seen Crispin catch the tree and was laughing more than I was.

Freddy took the rope off Crispin. After several failed lassoing attempts and one semi-failed one (the rope had ended up around BoBo's nose but had then slid off), Freddy grabbed BoBo's friend George and led him up to his corral. The other horses followed, including BoBo.

BoBo refused to open his mouth. I surprised myself by remembering something that the farmer's wife had told us during that 'horse lesson'; about the gap a horse had at the back of his mouth, there are no teeth there and it is safe to put your finger in and prise the mouth open. This is what I did. BoBo took the teat and started sucking but didn't seem to be getting much. Freddy made the hole bigger and then BoBo drank half of the bottle. The other half Freddy suggested we put in a bucket for him.

"I'll try later on," Freddy promised us. (It was the only day BoBo drank the milk. The next day he weaned himself and refused to drink any more. He just wanted to hang out with his friend George and his half sister Lucero in the *finca* and eat grass, and the occasional bucket of horse feed. He didn't need us to save him; he was going to be just fine with them).

As we drove back home we had to pull over sharply, a car was approaching. It was Lenny Loco and he had someone in the passenger seat. "I'm just going to take Mario up to his *finca* to have a look

291

around so I can finally persuade him to put a sensible price on it and sell it whilst he can still enjoy the money," Lenny said. I waved at Mario.

"You just might find a dead horse up there," Crispin said. "I'll explain another time." We drove off quickly leaving Lenny looking very confused.

I tried to write a long email to friends and family about our Costa Rican adventures every couple of months. The next one had Gilly's story in it. We got lots of replies back. One was from the friend who had suggested we named Gilly after her. It said simply 'Crispin, you shot me?!' Even I managed a tiny smile.

35 Toilet Training

We had decided we couldn't do double nappy duty any longer. It was a pain in the backside. Estrella had grown out of the L plastic pants that pull up over her terry nappies but the XL ones were still far too big for her and the weight of the wet terry towel dragged them down around her knees. She was 18 months old and it seemed as good a time as any, after all, I had read somewhere that African women toilet train their babies at six months.

We bought a kiddie toilet seat for Estrella from the supermarket in Neily. She chose one with bunny rabbits on and loved it. She kept kissing it and putting it on her head.

We sat her on her bunny seat on the toilet the following morning. She loved sitting there cross-legged and could even chew her big toe whilst sitting there. She demanded sheet after sheet of toilet paper to shove down between her legs and then she would watch whilst the white paper vanished into almost nothing as the water soaked into it. She was fascinated. She sat there for about half an hour. Crispin, Arturo and I sat there with her, in admiration and with the torch for better viewing of the pan. We waited to hear a 'tinkle' or a 'plop' and once we thought we did so clapped furiously.

"Clever girl," we both said. After a while Arturo was hungry so I went off to the sofa to feed him. Crispin continued to sit with Estrella. Eventually, I guess her bum was going numb and she agreed it was okay to lift her off and have her hands washed.

"I'm going to leave her nappy off," Crispin yelled "just going to go to the loo myself then I'll stick her in the shower."

"Okay," I mumbled. I was still feeding Arturo and was deeply engrossed in a new magazine that a friend had sent over and we had picked up from our PO box in Neily. I was reading about what a naughty boy Jude Law had been; his kid's nanny was spilling the beans on their relationship and it was riveting stuff. I loved getting magazines so I could catch up with all of the gossip in what I called the 'real world'. Crispin loved them too although I doubt he would admit it to anyone else.

I was vaguely aware that Estrella had come in and sat herself down on Arturo's play-mat. She claimed it as her own. If she couldn't be on it (for example, if she was in her high chair) then he wasn't allowed on it either. "No, no, no!" she would yell whilst wagging her finger at him; the finger wagging was something she had learnt from Karin. If he was put on his play-mat and she saw, she would immediately pile as many toys, books and cushions as she could fit onto it – sometimes narrowly missing him and sometimes not - and then do a running dive on there herself, throwing in some James Bond-style rolls for good measure. Again, sometimes missing him and sometimes not.

I think she probably loved him, even though she'd whacked him on the head with a maraca the day before. I think she was just doing it to see what kind of noise he would make if he was whacked on the head. An experiment really. We were trying to discipline her a bit now and then. If she was really horrible to him then we would take her favourite toy off her and put it in the cupboard over the fridge; we had a cupboard now. The following day we did it again and she handed us all of her toys, one by one, so they could be put up there. She had discovered a great new game and she loved it! We quickly gave up the 'toy confiscation' tactic and tried the 'praising good behaviour' tactic instead.

Suddenly I heard her gagging. I tore myself away from my magazine and surveyed the scene: the pile of poo on the floor with the footprint in it, the pooey footprint on the play-mat, the pooey foot waving in the air along with the pooey finger and finally the look of complete distaste on Estrella's face. It didn't take a genius to work out what had happened.

"Crispin," I yelled. I figured it was his fault so he could clean it up. "Are you going to be long?"

"I'm on the loo," he yelled back.

"I know. Are you going to be long?"

"Why?"

"She's done a poo, stepped in it and now she's eating it," I said.

Silence.

Day two of toilet training. Estrella did three wees and a little poo in the toilet. We clapped her and she then clapped herself. Our little genius, toilet-trained at only 18 months of age. We left her nappy off and I phoned mum and told her the fantastic news. Whilst I was talking to mum Estrella walked into the kitchen squatted and then pooed on the floor.

Day three and Estrella did her first big poo in the toilet. She clapped herself immediately and beamed. Her nappy went back on instantly. We aren't that daft.

36 Accidents

In the early hours of the morning, Crispin caught the bus up to San José to meet his parents. He was also taking my cell phone back to where we'd bought it from to get it fixed; Estrella had thrown it on the floor once too often. He was going to drive back down with his parents as they were renting a car in San José.

It meant I was on my own for two days and nights which wasn't much fun. Trying to get Estrella fed, washed and ready for bed when Arturo was having his 'colic-time' i.e. refusing to be away from my left shoulder without screaming the house down, was a nightmare but then Crispin had to sit next to a smelly woman for ten hours in a bus that didn't have air conditioning so I'm not sure who had it tougher; the smelly woman I'm guessing as Crispin's snoring is pretty horrendous.

Now Crispin's parents have always been incredibly supportive of our mad idea to start a new life out here and also to help us out financially, they had bought a piece of land from us 'unseen' at the very beginning. They were now to see it for the first time and, once they had walked round the *finca* and seen all of our lots, they declared it the one that they would have chosen for themselves - if they had had a choice in the matter (which was a relief as we had already built his dad's 70th birthday present rancho on there!). It was great for Crispin to have people here that took an interest in the *finca*. Whereas my parents, I can honestly say, couldn't give two hoots about it; Crispin's parents, particularly his dad, were immensely proud of what Crispin had achieved so far and told him so. They had travelled over together when Estrella was five weeks old so his dad had seen the *finca* before anything had been done to it, in fact he and Crispin had been lost in it for several hours

296

before the breeze got up. They had been starting to get worried so it was very welcome. By following the direction that the breeze came from had they had eventually made it out alive!

It was nice to have a pep talk as the events of recent months had left us both feeling pretty miserable and empty: the two robberies, huge problems with the car, losing Gilly to tetanus, spending all of our money and now Crispin was also doing battle with Marco.

In the six months Marco had been sourcing our building materials he had proven himself to be the unluckiest man in the world. Every meeting he was supposed to have with us he was late for, sometimes days late. When he did eventually turn up, or phone us, he had the most incredible stories to tell: the ferry had got stuck on a sand bank and he was stuck out in the river for five hours in the relentless sun with no water (a friend of ours could vouch for him as they had seen him stuck there), a tree had fallen across the road and the bus couldn't get past so he had to go home again (we saw the remains of the tree by the side of the road the following week), during a trip to San José to source materials for us he had almost frozen to death on *Cerro de la Muerte* when his motorbike got a puncture and it had started hailing on him (Freddy had told us that the freak weather conditions had made headline news). Also, the only other things to get stolen from our house on the day of the break-in on April Fool's Day were his expensive sunglasses that he had left on the windowsill! His luck wasn't about to change.

After collecting as much evidence as he was able to; Crispin, bravely for a man who was crap at this kind of thing (he was just too nice and he cared an awful lot about what people thought of him), went to confront Marco with our lawyer Arturo. Marco had been very upset by Crispin's insinuation that he still had an awful lot of money of ours and had come up with plausible excuses for everything. Crispin came away from the meeting feeling terrible; he felt he had completely misjudged Marco. It was only when Crispin and Arturo were discussing the meeting in the car on the way home that the two of them found huge holes in what Marco had said. The holes got bigger when even more original receipts turned up from the various *ferreterías* that Crispin had requested them from; the holes were now so big you could almost climb through them!

Just before their second meeting Marco phoned Crispin to say that his *ferretería* had been broken into and some stock had been stolen, I was sure he was only after sympathy and he wasn't going to get any from me although my nice husband did seem to be wavering again.

During the second meeting Marco showed his true colours and had turned nasty. At that moment Crispin said that he knew without a doubt that he was right and that Marco had stolen somewhere between 18 and 30 thousand dollars from us.

"Well that goes some way towards explaining why the house is costing us so much," I said to Crispin, "and his shiny new motorbike. What can we do about him? Do we file the *denuncia*, that Arturo's writing, with the police?" The official statement for the OIJ would be ready in a couple of days.

"I just don't know," said Crispin. "Can we really win in a corrupt legal system?" We were both aware that judges could be bribed. "I'm considered a Gringo, he's a Tico, and my Spanish is far from perfect. I just don't know."

"We don't have the money for a court battle either do we?" I added

"No, we don't," Crispin sighed. "Plus, Arturo said that Marco got us a really good price for the roof tiles too, probably saved us thousands."

"But that was what he was supposed to be doing, that was why we hired him in the first place," I argued.

"No, you're right. It was just something Arturo said, that it wouldn't look good in court."

"But then we can't just let him get away with it can we?"

We went around in circles with it for a very long time before deciding absolutely nothing. The 'head in the sand' approach always worked best.

We would be sitting in a restaurant in Golfito many months later; the dilemma still hanging over us like a black cloud, it was still on the back burner because Crispin understandably hadn't wanted to deal with it, and the man in question would cycle past the restaurant window. I would do a double-take. He would look really odd and I would realise it was because I had only ever seen him on a motorbike. Crispin would go outside to get something that we had left in the car and Marco would spot him and ride over, rather jerkily. After a while Crispin would then join us again at the table and would say to me, "You are not going to believe what Marco has just told me." He was right, I wouldn't.

A couple of months after the second meeting, Marco had been knocked off his motorbike by a car. It had been a horrific accident and, whilst having a metal plate inserted into his head, he had actually died for a while but had then been resuscitated. He was then in a coma for three weeks. He'd bowed his head and showed Crispin the scar that was still very visible though his dark hair that was growing back. He had been left with a limp and both his long and short term memories had been affected. He was never going to ride a motorbike again and had bought a bicycle.

I would suddenly feel sick remembering a conversation with Del that Crispin had told me about. "This isn't anything to do with us is it? Del didn't..." I tailed off, unable to bring myself to say what I was thinking. Crispin would pause for a few seconds mulling over my comment.

"No way," he'd said finally. "There is no way." Okay, I believed him.

Our dilemma had resolved itself, we were sure there was no way we could win a case against him now. What judge would rule against a man as unlucky as Marco? If there was any justice in the world we felt he would get his comeuppance some other way; maybe he had just had it.

Now when Crispin's parents heard about the financial hole we were in, his dad set about trying to find a solution. He had been an accountant before he became the local vicar. He was in his element and we valued his advice. The immediate problem was that we were about to lose Toli and his team. We hadn't paid their wages for a month and there was no way they could continue working for nothing for much longer. They would have to leave, find somebody else's house to build, and we would probably never see them again.

Whilst the cogs in Crispin's folk's brains turned we had a pleasant few days with them; we spent time at the beach and finally made the huge steep trek up to Bilkez's gran's *finca*. It was about time too, the visit was long overdue. We took ice and a banoffee pie that I had made and Emilse had killed a chicken and made *arroz con pollo* (chicken and rice) for the occasion. We spent a lovely afternoon, playing with her piglets and baby chicks, taking cuttings from the beautiful flowers in her garden and marvelling that she lived so far away from the rest of the world with no electricity. At least she had her husband, son and daughter-in-law for company. Bilkez and her family were probably a 45 minute walk away and, although it wasn't an easy walk, Emilse did it almost daily.

She was a lovely old lady and she would also come to visit us from time to time on her sprightly little legs and flashing her gold teeth. We would sit across from each other not being able to communicate too well; I find that the older generation seem to speak much faster than people our age. At times she would bring her young grand-daughters or neighbours' children and I would try not to stare in horror at the scars on their legs from insect bites that have been scratched at relentlessly or at the state of their teeth. A dentist checking Yeudin's teeth told Grace that it is unusual for a two year old here to not need fillings. There is actually an advert on the radio that says, 'eat sugar every day, it is good for you'. When I mentioned the advert to Freddy he told me that his dad used to take half a *tapa de dulce* (about half a kilo of raw cane sugar) to eat for his lunch whilst he was out working on the *finca*. EVERY DAY!

"Gave him lots of energy," Freddy said.

"But how are his teeth?" I asked.

"Yeah, pretty bad," Freddy would admit.

Crispin's parents were staying at Greg and Heidi's but drove over to see us most days and we had days out showing them the local sights (in fact it was more a case of them showing us the local sights as I really didn't go anywhere other than the house site any more and we had given up our game of 'guess the tide' – we were really bad at it – and consequently hadn't been to the beach for months!). It was nice having someone to watch the kids whilst Crispin and I went off for a swim together but it was a brief swim as I wasn't accustomed to or comfortable with anybody else looking after them (even though Arturo was asleep). I barely trusted Crispin with them! There were a few minor mishaps: Estrella wandered off to sit under a coconut palm with

301

coconuts on it and then was left alone on the beach whilst a camera was retrieved from a bag but luckily she was so engrossed in digging her way to Thailand that she didn't notice her new-found freedom so didn't do her usual ten metre dash towards the sea (it was something she excelled at and she always scared the life out of us when she attempted it but we had always been close enough to her to grab her before she so much as got her toes wet) and I inadvertently caught a glimpse of my father-in-law's bottom whilst he was showering starkers in our outdoor shower – I could now see where Crispin got his best asset from! (Crispin and I always wore our swimming costumes when showering out there ever since the day Toli arrived unexpectedly and Crispin barely had time to cover his bits and hence his embarrassment).

In the middle of their stay we found we had the day to ourselves and so decided to do something different and have a picnic at Catkin's waterfall. It was a sunny day and Freddy, Enrique and Crispin had recently cleared the path down to the river bed. Margarita had never been and wanted to see it and there was no doubt it was a beautiful place to spend a Sunday.

It wasn't an easy walk down, Freddy carried Arturo in his car chair, Crispin had Estrella in the back carrier, Margarita carried Yailin and I helped Jackie. From the road, if you didn't know the entrance was there, you would never find it. It was next to a huge bamboo but was very narrow and dropped down sharply so was almost invisible. Unfortunately, not invisible enough as someone else had found it; there were several old bags of rubbish near the entrance and some of them were full of used disposable nappies. How anyone could dump their rubbish in such a beautiful spot was beyond me but until the *muni* (local government) get a garbage collection sorted out it will sadly continue to happen.

When he was clearing the path Enrique had had the unpleasant experience of finding one of the bags with his weed-eater. It was hidden in the long undergrowth and he had torn it open; showering himself with the contents. He didn't smell too great that day. Crispin had also been there with his machete, helping out and working up a sweat. Lenny Loco was driving past and stopped to watch.

"You know, I have never ever done that," he said to Crispin with a look that was a mixture of surprise, slight admiration and a lot of 'isn't that what you pay your workers for?!'

The path made a 'z' shape down to the river bed and then we made our way along the river, sometimes in it, or when it got too deep, along the side of it. There was one steep, slippery bit that if you lost your footing you would end up in a pool up to your waist but the only casualty was Estrella's dummy that had slipped out of her mouth (or maybe was thrown). We all made it past okay, in spite of Freddy's cumbersome load (Arturo was no lightweight) and then had an easy walk along the river bed to the waterfall itself.

The last time we had visited in the dry season it was a mere trickle but now the rainy season was reaching its peak and there was much more water. It was no Niagara but it was practically thundering down the 15m high cliff and into the pool below. With the sunlight reflecting off the water droplets and the lush greenery surrounding the pool and scaling the cliff wall, it looked amazing. We were all very impressed. It was full of wildlife too and turn over a leaf and you may find a blue jeans frog, the size of a fingernail and aptly named because of its blue legs. I guess the 'frog naming committee' felt that 'red t-shirt frog' didn't quite have the same ring to it although the name would also fit the appearance. It is a member of the poison-dart frog family so very very cute but deadly. Best not to touch them as a cut on your finger, or an absent-minded lick of the finger afterwards may spoil the rest of your day, not to mention your life. (We had several gorgeous 'green and black poison-dart frogs' [I'll let you work out for yourselves what colour they are] living around our terrace and they often hopped into the house!).

"Where do you want him, Jo," asked Freddy. I pointed to a bit of grass that was in the shade and Freddy gently placed Arturo and his car chair on it. I pulled the bug screen over him. At ten weeks old the beauty of his surroundings was lost on him, he was fast asleep. Crispin got Estrella into her swimming costume. With her armbands and inflatable vest she looked a lot like the Michelin man but at least we knew she would float safely. I changed into my favourite red bikini and was quite impressed that I could get into it so soon after giving birth. In fact I filled out my bikini top like never before, I almost had a cleavage! It's amazing what breastfeeding does for you. The NHS don't mention that on their advertising poster 'reasons to breastfeed your baby'.

Lenny and Margarita didn't get changed out of their shorts and t-shirts. "We don't wear swimming costumes," Margarita said to me. In fact she hadn't the day we went to the beach in Punta Banco, neither had Grace, and I got the feeling that 'we' meant 'local adult Ticos' as opposed to just 'their family' or 'all Ticos' as Jackie was wearing one and I had certainly seen Ticos on holiday from San José wearing bikinis on the beach. Some that really shouldn't have been wearing bikinis mind you, so large that the little strings were hidden amongst the rolls of flab.

The water was cool and refreshing as I waded in with Estrella. If you walked too quickly you stirred up the dead leaves on the bottom. Estrella was out of her depth quite quickly and started paddling but even in the deepest part it didn't get above my ample chest. Jackie and Margarita climbed the rocks to

304

shower under the waterfall. The water was cold and powerful so they didn't linger for long.

"Ow!" I jumped suddenly. Something had just pinched my bottom. "Ow!" and again. Freddy laughed and then jumped himself. Then everyone was doing it.

"Fresh-water shrimp," Freddy explained. "They are really good to eat." He put his hand under a rock and brought out a small grey shrimp. Jackie took it from him, squealed and threw it back in the water.

"It nipped me," she said giggling. We all laughed.

The fresh air and cool water were making me hungry so I got out and dug out crackers, bread, cheese and tomatoes from our day-pack and set about making lunch for us all. Estrella was jumping off a log and into Crispin's arms. It was the 47th time and Crispin was tiring of it, Estrella wasn't.

After lunch we lay about relaxing with our toes in the water, Estrella scratching about with a stick and filling her bath toys with the sandy mud. Arturo was still dreaming. We could hear little squeaks indicating monkeys were nearby, parrots were squawking in the distance and there were lots of other jungle sounds (animals and birds that I couldn't name) but that was all. It was bliss.

Suddenly, I heard something else. Voices. We all sat up and waited. I looked back up the riverbed waiting to see who the voices belonged to. The shadowy figures filled in as they got closer, it was Karin and Coral with Ronen's family from the vegetarian restaurant in Pavones. They were carrying a large watermelon. We were all kind of a bit embarrassed. You really don't expect to meet anyone else down there.

"I've been trying to persuade them to come down here for ages and they finally turned up today and said 'let's go'," Karin said sounding a bit apologetic. But it was Karin who had shown us the

305

waterfall in the first place. We had come through the *finca* on the far side of the river, a much longer and steeper walk down and it was that trip that led us to persuade Crispin's dad to buy the other side as we didn't have the money. He said it would be for Crispin's sister Catkin as he thought it would be nice for her to have a piece of paradise and I bet it made for good after-dinner conversation. Anyhow, because of the Costa Rican law that stated that rivers and the land 10m either side of a river was public property, they had every right to be there.

"Hasn't Arturo grown," she cooed. Then went back over to join Ronen and Adina on the other side of the pool.

"I feel silly," Margarita whispered to me.

"Why?" I whispered back to her.

"Sitting here in wet t-shirt and shorts in front of complete strangers."

Karin had a stunning bikini on and Adina wore one that looked very like mine. I made a mental note to dig one of my old swimming costumes out of a drawer when I got home and give it to Margarita.

"Don't worry about it," I said. "They won't mind." We carried on chatting amongst ourselves, playing with the kids and scanning nearby trees for the monkeys but the light carefree mood had vanished a bit.

"Shall we go?" said Margarita.

"We can't go straightaway as they'll know we are leaving because of them," I said.

"Let's give it half an hour and then go," said Crispin.

Ronen and Adina had two girls. Miri was four, the same age as Coral, and an older girl whose name I didn't know. They ran into the water to play with Coral splashing and jumping and having a whale of a time. Ronen clambered up the rocks to shower under the waterfall and Karin and Adina were perched on a rock deep in conversation. Nobody was watching the girls.

The three girls were now under the waterfall, laughing and yelling as the water hit their faces and the powerful spray splashed them. They may never appreciate how lucky they are to be able to experience something like this, I thought. Miri's face suddenly changed. She was trying to stand up but couldn't. "I think she's in trouble," I said to Crispin. I was sure she wasn't out of her depth but the force of the cold water hitting her was making her panic. She started to struggle, unable to catch her breath.

"No, I think they are just playing," Crispin was saying but his voice tailed off towards the end of the sentence.

I was already rising and screaming, "Ronen grab her" at the top of my voice trying to make myself heard over the sound of the water. Ronen had his eyes shut enjoying the water thumping down on his body, unaware what it was also doing to his four year old daughter. Karin and Adina had started to turn their heads. As my brain registered that I had to start running I realised that Crispin's was way ahead of mine and he was already tearing though the water towards Miri. Seconds later he had grabbed her, lifted her out of the water and held her while she coughed and choked up the water she had gulped down in her struggles. Ronen had finally realised what was happening and had also reached the girls. He took Miri off her rescuer and held her tightly. Nothing was said. Crispin walked back towards us looking shaken. I felt a mixture of shock, relief and an awful lot of pride. My husband was a hero.

The incident was soon forgotten and after lots of cuddles from her parents Miri was back in the water but was watched closely and stayed away from the waterfall. Ronen came over to talk to us, bringing a piece of watermelon for Estrella. He gave me a hug and admired the still sleeping Arturo who he was yet to meet and we chatted as if nothing had happened. Sometimes words aren't necessary.

37 Salvation

We were having a meeting with Crispin's dad on the terrace. He had found a solution; a way to stop us from losing our builders to somebody else. "We have decided to use Toli and his team to build a holiday house on our lot. I've always wanted a holiday house," his dad said excitedly. So, Crispin hadn't just inherited his backside from his dad, now I knew where his impulsive streak had come from too!

The plan would give us a bit of breathing space until we sold a lot, or got the final payment from the Hawaiians for 'El Señor', which was due in two months' time in November, and then we could pay the boys to finish our house and we should still be in by Christmas.

It was an idea and the only one we had.

Crispin spent the next two weeks running round with his parents, visiting architects, having meetings with Toli, choosing tiles and sinks and taps and paint and everything you need when you are building a house. Even though Crispin's dad's Spanish was pretty good, he was a bit shy about using it so it was decided that Crispin had to accompany them everywhere they went. Even though I probably should have been a bit more understanding, knowing how long it had taken me to become comfortable speaking Spanish (and I still wasn't when it came to speaking on the telephone), I couldn't help think that when they gained their translator I lost my extra pair of hands, ad hoc though they were.

One day Crispin said they were going out to choose more stuff and would be back about lunch-time. I had at least been left the car so I drove the 45 minutes to Heidi's (when the roads are at their worst the 10km journey can take an hour, in September they tend to be bad but not <u>too</u> bad) so Estrella could play with Jackson but I didn't stay long as I needed to get back home so I could get lunch ready for us all. When Crispin and his parents eventually turned up at 7pm I absolutely hit the roof.

"What's taken you so long?!" I said glaring at Crispin.

"It's our fault my love...," his mother started to say.

I ignored her. "What on earth could have taken you so long?!" I snarled at Crispin again.

"It's not his fault...,"she said again.

I turned on her, "I'm not talking to you!"

"Yes I know love but it really isn't his fault..."

I cut her off. "No, actually it <u>is</u> his fault. He does this to me all the time. He tells me he is going to come back at a certain time and he doesn't and he never phones and I'm left on my own with the kids at bedtime which is the worst possible time when you are trying to breastfeed one continually, feed the other, change two nappies, wash them both, heat up milk, read a story, get them both in their pyjamas..." I was yelling at her now.

"I know what it's like, I brought up four children and my husband was <u>never</u> around," she had raised her voice too.

"You didn't bring them up in Costa Rica. You haven't got a clue what my life is really like here!" I continued yelling. Yelling because of Gilly and Marco and the gits who had stolen our stuff, yelling because I felt the reason we had no money was because her son was a fool and kept handing it out to any old Tomas, Ricardo or Gerrardo, yelling because the police were useless, yelling because I was an exhausted mum and yelling because she had dared to say she could imagine how I felt because she had brought up two more children than I had under entirely different circumstances.

310

They left and I instantly knew that, no matter what had been said, I had just been incredibly rude and out of order. Unlike most people out here I knew how to say sorry and I would phone her at Heidi's and apologise as soon as they got back. Heidi, bless her, was already explaining to her how difficult life was out here especially with young children and that she struggled with just Jackson, she couldn't possibly imagine how I was coping with two, particularly two so close in age.

Crispin, still not used to the way I can boil up and then calm down instantly when his way of dealing with any conflict is to sulk for days, started yelling at me. He told me how busy they had been all day, choosing stuff for the house, that they had rushed as quickly as they could and that he didn't think to phone me from a public phone (my cell phone was still in San José getting fixed so he had left me his phone) and that anyway his parents were doing all this to help us out so our builder wouldn't leave and go and work for somebody else.

"There's something I should tell you, Jo," Crispin said to me sheepishly. It was much later that evening and we were snuggled up in bed. "It was something I left out earlier on when I was telling you why we were late."

"Go on," I said to him, wondering what on earth he was going to say.

"We stopped off on the way back at the internet café so I could check the cricket scores." I hit him with a pillow.

The following day Crispin's dad sat us down and said he had come up with another idea. "I am going to buy three more of your lots off you," he announced. Crispin was speechless and my eyes welled up with tears. We were saved, hurrah!! "But," he added, "you do realise you are going to have to sell

311

the house don't you?" Our beautiful perfect house!?
Crispin and I nodded but I saw the look in his eyes
and I knew that he didn't want to either.

So, we had the money, all we needed were our
builders back!

38 Mud

It had been raining heavily all night and showed no signs of stopping. I couldn't face the thought of a day in the shoebox with the kids but lacking a playgroup, coffee morning, kids swimming lesson, jingle jangle music class, baby sign language class, toddler gym club, neighbours I could walk to, baby massage class, indoor soft play area, 'bumps and babes' group, teach your baby algebra by whistling at it class (okay, I made that one up), relatives to descend on or a 'Toys R Us' to go and hang out in, my options were kind of limited. It was a crazy idea but I grabbed rice cakes and bananas, the change bag, two umbrellas, threw the kids in the car and drove off. Obviously it wasn't quite as simple as that as Arturo had done a poo and I had to change him and then Estrella had done a poo and I had to change her and then Arturo vomited all down his t-shirt and me so I changed us both. I then had to put them in their car seats one at a time as I had to hold the umbrella in one hand so I took Arturo out first and Estrella stood at the doorway and screamed because she thought I was leaving her behind.

"I'm not leaving you behind I just don't have enough arms," I yelled at her. It made no difference, she still screamed. I strapped Arturo in and went back for her. The instant I left him, Arturo started screaming. "I'll be back in a minute, I've got to get your sister," I yelled at him. I strapped Estrella in, shoved a book in her hands, and then jumped into the front seat.

"Bugger, what did I do with the car keys?" Arturo was still screaming. I ran back into the house and ransacked it, if Crispin turned up whilst I was out he would think we'd been robbed again. I couldn't find them anywhere. "They must be in the car," I mumbled to myself.

I could still hear Arturo screaming. Then I had a thought. I unclipped him and took him out and there they were, in his car seat.

"No wonder you were screaming, little fellow," I said to him as I strapped him back in again. His crying had stopped. I started the engine. "Fiddle, did I lock the front door again?" I really couldn't remember. I ran back to the house to check to screams from both Estrella and Arturo. I was a bag of nerves by the time I drove off. I slid some calming music into the CD player.

Crispin had gone with his parents to San José to pick up my phone which was finally ready and he would be back on the bus in a couple of days. Since his late arrival the night of 'the row' we had started to niggle each other, I recognised the beginning of the familiar cycle. He was tired so would help with the kids less so I would ask him to do more which he saw as nagging so he would react by getting angry and doing even less so I would get angry and start nagging more until eventually we would end up having an almighty row. I knew the break would do us good. His parents wouldn't be back until the following September as they knew for sure that their house would be ready by then and we would have electricity. (Of course it wouldn't be and we wouldn't have).

That was where I drove to; their house-site. Toli's boys were there sheltering out of the rain as best they could. They all looked thoroughly miserable and I felt sorry for them and vowed to have them around for dinner as soon as we had moved in to the house for a bit of 'team-building'. They would get much soggier before the sun came out again.

I explained my plight to Toli. "Can I borrow somebody, please?" I asked. 'Please not Ruben, please not Ruben, please not Ruben' I willed Toli to read my mind. Toli gestured for Einar, his eldest son to come over. 'Fiddle,' I thought.

I wanted to go and see Margarita but I knew that the path to their house would be treacherous with all the rain and that I couldn't carry both Estrella and Arturo at the same time, it was too muddy for Estrella to walk by herself, there was no way the pushchair would make it and I couldn't leave one of them in the car and then go back for them. I needed an extra pair of hands.

I got back in the car and parked it as close to Freddy's corral as I could. I opened Estrella's door and, with the umbrella propped up above the door to shelter her from the worst of the rain, I took her out of her car seat and handed her and the umbrella to Einar. I put the change bag on my back and grabbed the other umbrella from the boot and propped it up in the same manner on Arturo's side of the car whilst I got him out of his car seat. I shut the doors, locked the car and we were ready to go. The mud around the corral was thick and gunky and refused to let go of my boots. Every step was an effort. I suddenly found myself with only one boot one, I'd left the other one stuck a step behind me. Carefully balancing on one leg, so as not to muddy my sock, I located my boot again with my foot and managed to pull it out without dropping Arturo. Poor Einar's trainers weren't looking their best any more. After we had gone through the worst of it it was still difficult walking as my wellingtons weighed twice as much as they had done previously because of all of the mud and cow pats that were now stuck to them. There was an eerie low cloud all around us, the view had vanished completely and I couldn't see Margarita's house until we were almost there. Somehow we all made it without falling.

Margarita couldn't believe her eyes when she saw me. "You're mad" she declared! She was on her own with Yailin as Freddy had taken Jackie to the

'Hospital de Los Ninos' the Children's Hospital in San José to see a specialist about her 'lunar'. If her birthmark was considered to be dangerous they would remove it for free. They had gone on the bus a couple of days ago and I had given her a supply of travel sickness tablets, knowing how horrendous her journey would be without them.

"Have you heard from Freddy yet," I asked her.

"Yes, he called Amado and Flory."

"Are they going to take it out?

"The specialist said it could become cancerous in the future so she will remove it. She'll do it in three sections over two years then when she's 12 they will cut the scar out and she'll have plastic surgery."

"Wow, how does Jackie feel about it all."

"Tearful," Margarita said. It must have been a lot for a seven year old to take in. Crispin and I had already talked about paying for Jackie to see someone at CIMA, the private hospital where we had had Arturo if the state refused her the operation but it looked like it wasn't going to be necessary.

Margarita's ever-present pans of rice and beans were raided for lunch and she collected some eggs from her chickens and scrambled those for us too. Dessert was a can of condensed milk spread onto crackers. After lunch the rain had stopped so whilst Arturo and Yailin slept on Margarita's bed Estrella ran around outside like a mad thing jumping in all of the puddles in her wellington boots. Margarita and I sat on the terrace watching Estrella. We couldn't help laughing at her; I had never seen a child so wet and muddy in my entire life.

"You'll have to bathe her before you go," she said. "I'll find some clothes of Yailin's for her."

"Don't worry, she'll be fine until we get home," I said.

"Those holes that she's jumping in," Margarita said, "are where the dogs urinate." Yuck, suddenly it wasn't quite so funny any more.

I stripped her and Margarita hoisted her up so she was standing in the washing up area. Margarita then handed me a bar of soap. As I had been clueless about the washing up, I was equally clueless about the 'Tico bath'. I shrugged my shoulders. "I have no idea what I'm supposed to do?" I admitted.

Margarita laughed, took the soap off me, soaped Estrella all over, dipped the margarine pot into the bucket of water and rinsed her off. Estrella loved it and from then on demanded a 'Tico bath' from Margarita every time we visited.

All too soon, my taxi appeared. Einar arrived, this time bringing David with him, and we said our goodbyes and thank yous and left; Estrella wearing some of Yailin's clothes. It was starting to drizzle again but not so much that I needed to put the umbrella up. We made our way back along the slippery ridge and then down towards the corral and its sticky mud. The rain got heavier and was bouncing down again when I pulled away waving to the guys and thanking them for their help. It would then rain for eight long weeks.

As I pulled into the garage I reached down to take the CD out of the CD player and accidentally pressed the wrong button. The radio came on and I was surprised to hear 'Raindrops keep falling on my head'. The display said 99.5. Could it be Radio Dos? It is the station we listen to in the car when we are in San José but I had no idea that we could get reception down here. As we are driving away from San José we lose reception in the mountains and always turn the radio off and put 'The Streets – A Grand Don't Come for Free' on; it's our 'mountains' CD and listening to it makes the journey seem shorter.

The following morning I found 99.5 on our tiny little radio that was too small for the thieves to notice.

I broke into a smile as I heard Evan Luck's voice. It was like discovering a long lost friend. I just caught the tail-end of him telling me about the office block that was still for sale in Zapote. I couldn't believe that nobody had bought it yet. Then 'The Timewarp' came on and I grabbed Arturo and Estrella and we danced crazily around the room laughing, Estrella with her hands on her hips and wiggling her bottom. Arturo fell asleep on my left shoulder. The eight weeks of rain would have been much worse without Evan Luck.

Crispin returned from San José and we were like newly-weds again, all arguments forgotten. We spent a wonderful cool, wet and windy October day on the beach. It was lovely wandering along with Estrella collecting driftwood, old coconuts that had washed up on the beach and smooth brown seeds. We paddled in the tide pools, dipping Arturo's feet in the cold water and making him giggle; it was nice not having to worry about me or the kids burning. Back at the car, I slipped my hand into my shorts pocket to search for a tissue. I was starting with a cold. My hand closed on something cool and hard. I pulled it out and smiled. It was a beautiful heart-shaped seed; Crispin must have slipped it into my pocket when I wasn't looking. He was strapping Estrella in, I was doing Arturo; he looked up at me and smiled.

As we drove home, my hand on top of Crispin's on the gear-stick, I said to him, "You know, I could murder fish and chips tonight. It would be the perfect end to a perfect day."

"Aww, me too," agreed Crispin, our mouths watering at the thought of a takeaway from a Great British Institution; 'The Chippy'. Unfortunately there wasn't one so I mentally checked off what we had in the fridge to see if there was anything in there that I could magic a meal out of. When we got home there was a message from Les on Crispin's phone. He listened to it, grinned then dialled into his mailbox again and held the phone to my ear.

"You aren't going to believe this," he said. I could hear Les' voice. "We were going to fry some fish tonight and do some fried potatoes and wondered if you guys wanted to come on over. Give us a call, it would be great to see you."

Wow, we were going to get our fish and chips after all.

39 The Treasure Map

Although life got soggier it also seemed to get easier for a while and this change coincided with the arrival of Del; the man who knew people. In fact he knew everybody. He also seemed to know how to get things done.

Crispin had already been making enquiries about getting electricity put in along 'our' road. He had not long ago had a meeting with the head of the phone and electricity company, ICE in Neily, we had given a lift to his daughter (Karin's niece) when we had raced Lenny Loco to the hospital and hoped he could return the favour, but it was out of his area so he couldn't help us.

Crispin then got a quote from a private contractor who ICE used to do their installations at times but at twenty five thousand dollars it seemed ridiculously expensive. He also looked into solar power and just to generate enough electricity for our house would cost us a whopping forty one thousand dollars! Then he heard that a man had arranged to have electricity installed up the road where a friend lived on the other side of Pavones. He had done a good job. This friend gave Crispin the man's contact details and Crispin came back from their first meeting fit to burst. "Not only did Del say that he could arrange for the electricity to be put in for half the price of our cheapest quote but he also said he could get the *muni* to fix our road for us for free!"

"Free? What's the catch?" I asked

"No catch."

"We aren't bribing <u>anybody</u>," I said assertively.

"I know. All I have to do is go to the *muni* with Del and give a donation."

"Ah, you see, we are bribing somebody." I knew it.

"No, the money will be used to fix one of their bulldozers that's broken. I'll be given a receipt and, outside normal working hours, the *muni* team will come and fix our road."

"You mean bring us lots of rock and spread it out?"

"Exactly."

"Why?"

"I don't know but it's a public road and they should be maintaining it anyway."

"True, but they haven't bothered to up to now."

"Just accept it's a good thing," said Crispin tired of his suspicious wife.

"Okay," I said, still highly suspicious.

"I told Del about Marco stealing all that money off us too," Crispin said. "I explained all about the receipts and his excuses."

"What did Del say?" I asked him.

"He said he had heard Marco wasn't very pleasant and that, if I wanted, he knew people that could sort him out," Crispin said laughing.

"I hope you said 'no'!" I was shocked and wasn't laughing at all.

"Of course I said 'no'!" Crispin said indignantly. "He said they would just scare him a bit, nothing serious, but I said 'no way' and I reminded him that I was a lawyer!" I couldn't help thinking about this conversation after hearing about Marco's accident months later.

"So what's the story with the electricity?" I asked, pushing the vision of Marco's scarred head from my mind.

"A good friend of Del's owes him a favour. He's worked for ICE for 20 years so is very experienced. If we pay for the posts, cable and all the other materials then Freddy and Enrique can help him do the actual work."

"What happens when we have a power cut? A tree falls down on the line. Who fixes it?" It happened, so I felt it needing asking. I didn't want

Crispin up there sorting it out and getting blasted to smithereens, not usually anyway.

"That's one of the great things, as long as the line is installed to ICE standards then, once it's checked by an ICE engineer, ICE will then take over the maintenance of it because it'll be a line that runs along a public road."

But the road had to get fixed first as the rainy season was giving it a real hammering. Every time it rained Crispin would don his bright yellow raincoat, grab a spade and drive off to rescue the road. Water always follows a downhill course and if one of the drainage ditches that ran along the entire length of the road became blocked either by a landslide or a fallen branch, the water would instantly rise up and cut right across the road, scouring its course deeper and deeper. Crispin spent half of his life digging out the drainage ditches. The other problem was the heavily laden *ferreteria* delivery trucks that were constantly bringing building materials up for Crispin's parents' house. They were churning up the road surface and often got themselves stuck making a delivery too soon after a heavy downpour. Pulling the trucks out made the road even worse, not to mention what the strain was doing to the engine of our car, as there was inevitably a lot of wheel-spinning involved which left deep ruts in the road. It was going to be impossible to drive on it soon. We were planning on moving into the house really soon, Juan Carlos was saying that the windows would be ready by the end of October; we needed to be able to drive on the road.

Rather worryingly Del's story was already changing. The material for the road was no longer going to be free but would cost us $20 for every truckload. "It's still much less than we've paid in the past," Crispin assured me.

I have to say they brought their first load up just two weeks after they promised they would which is quite impressive for Costa Rica, but the price was now $60 a load. At times they would vanish for weeks with no warning. Crispin was constantly putting his hand in his pocket to buy them gasoline so they would return the following day and I lost count of the number of times he paid for them to get their machines fixed when they broke down. It was now $70 a load the driver informed him.

"Don't give them any money," Del said to Crispin every time he visited. "I will pay them. Even if they are on their knees begging, don't pay them." But he wasn't there when the *muni* guys were standing in front of Crispin refusing to do any more work or even return again if he didn't hand over some cash. With his hands tied he paid up. It was costing us a small fortune, the same amount as if we had used our previous guy, but at least we could drive up to the house.

Now Del liked Crispin; everybody liked Crispin even I did most of the time, and one day Del turned up at the house with a map. The two of them had a secret meeting in the corner of the terrace with the map, pouring over it as if it led the way to pirates' treasure; which in a way I suppose it may do one day.

"What was all that about?" I asked after Del had left.

"He wants me to become Danny's real estate agent," he said.

"What?" I was completely blown away. "Why doesn't he ask one of the local real estate agents?" After all, there were enough of them cashing in on the rocketing land prices.

"Danny's upset because they've been selling his land illegally so won't use them," explained Crispin.

Del had been one of Danny's right hand men and had remained loyal, unlike some of his other right-hand men who had allegedly faked title documents and bribed lawyers and judges to sell on the land they were supposed to be looking after for him. Del's reward was a fabulous piece of land right on the beach. Anyway, once Danny and his huge team of lawyers had served their 300 writs and won their court battles and got his land back he was going to need someone who he could trust to sell it for him. Somebody was going to make a hell of a lot of money and Del wanted Crispin and now Danny, who trusted Del's choice, also wanted it to be Crispin.

Crispin was terribly flattered and was not only thinking of the commission he could earn but was also thinking how he could feed his habit - we could have the pick of the best bits of land and most of Danny's bits of land were pretty amazing. The 'treasure map' had been one of the local area and all of Danny's land was highlighted. It seemed the rumours were true, he did once own 85% of the beach-front in the Pavones area.

I brought Crispin back down to earth with a bump. "You told me last week that you hated selling land." We had had several clients come to look at our lots and he had spent almost the entire week either driving or riding around the *finca* on horseback with various people. They had all left saying the lots were wonderful and the prices were reasonable but nobody had actually bought anything. If they had said "I hate the view" or "I'm allergic to monkeys" he could have understood why they had left empty-handed but they hadn't. "You took it really personally and were really miserable all week," I reminded him. He had only just come out of his slump.

"You're right," he said to me "I would hate it. But think of the land," he said with his eyes shining.

"Everyone hates real estate agents," I added. "More than they hate lawyers!" I finished, grinning at him.

40 The Party

We were approaching the house. I was under strict instructions to have him up there by 11am. He didn't suspect a thing which was good because if he had then I knew he wouldn't be here now; he hated being the centre of attention. A tarpaulin had been put up on this side of the terrace to act as a screen and it caught my eye, along with a stray balloon. It caught Crispin's eye too. He looked at me. "No!" he said. "You _are_ joking?"

"Nothing to do with me," I said and it was true. It had been Toli's idea; he had arranged the whole thing.

"Please try and act grateful and happy?" I said to him.

"I'll try," he said.

Wow, I was impressed. There must have been 30 people crowded onto our terrace! There were streamers and balloons and a huge _'Feliz Cumpleaños'_ (Happy Birthday) banner. Everybody was there and Toli's team brush up well when they have showered and aren't in their work clothes. This time, habit was broken and there were kisses and hugs all round. I didn't breathe in when it came to Ruben's turn, I did not want to know what he smelt like and I made sure that I let go before he did; I was still breastfeeding so still felt a bit 'silly' around him but the feeling had lessened thank goodness.

I have never seen so much food. Laid out on a makeshift table in the middle of the terrace were huge bowls of rice and _chicharrones_ and salad and in the centre of it all there was a massive cake, made by Toli himself, with a surf board and a '39' iced on the top. As Crispin had been surfing three times since our arrival I supposed he could almost call himself a surfer so it was sort of apt. Toli really did worship the ground that Crispin walked on, but then he did have Lenny Loco for a boss beforehand so maybe it wasn't too surprising.

I admired Angie and Gustavo's new baby for a while whilst they marvelled at how huge Arturo was, and then went over to talk to Walter and David.

It was the first time I had seen Walter in something other than his 'Beckham' shirt. Unfortunately David's romance with Bilkez turned out to not be a romance but was just a young lad having his fun, I hoped Bilkez wasn't too upset about it. Alfredo was also at the party and he was treating David the same as he was everybody else so he obviously didn't have a problem with him. "We're just friends," said David when I tried to coax some information out of him.

We somehow got onto the subject of my name and how to pronounce it properly; I was still called 'Joy' by half of the team. "Jo is short for Joanne," I explained and that seemed to make more sense to them.

"Why don't you like 'Joanne'?" asked Walter.

"I don't know really. I always tend to shorten people's names. It took me a long time to get used to having to call my husband Crispin when lots of other people get away with calling him Chris. What do you call Juan Carlos?" I asked Walter, I had noticed that he wasn't present, presumably working on our windows. Walter was currently on loan to him and was working with him at the workshop in his house. "That's a mouthful to be yelling all of the time."

"Wanker," said Walter. I was shocked.

"You call him that to his face?" I asked. He nodded.

I felt the same way about him at the moment it had to be said. Our windows were very very late, he had said October and it was now November and it was the main thing we were waiting for. I gestured for Crispin to join us. "They call Juan Carlos 'Wanker' for short!" As I said it, it hit me; why Walter

326

and David looked very confused at the fuss I was making. "It's not 'Wanker' it's 'Juan Ca'!" Crispin and I laughed. Walter and David looked even more confused and then Crispin set about trying to explain to them what 'wanker' meant in English, using hand gestures.

It was nice to see Alfredo, Bilkez's dad again. He had stopped working on Toli's team a week ago but had still come to the party. Emilse, his mother, had sold her *finca* up in the hills, the one with the piglets that we had walked to with Crispin's parents and had bought a palm oil plantation near the Naranjo bull ring. She had also bought Alfredo one and Alfredo's family finally had some money. He would probably be able to earn a thousand dollars a month. They would be moving out of their little house on the corner of our road after Christmas and we would lose Bilkez's help. I think she was quite glad about it really as she wasn't looking forward to walking up the hill once we moved into the new house.

We had recently heard quite a few locals and Gringos were buying into palm plantations. There was good money to be made and the whole world wants palm oil; it's considered to be not quite as bad for you as butter or lard but that is about it. Consumers are fooled because it is a vegetable oil and therefore assumed to be low in saturated fat and therefore healthy. Well, it isn't[3]. Start reading labels in your cupboards now and you will see that it is in everything; biscuits, soap, crisps, crackers, cakes, breakfast cereals, microwaveable popcorn to name just a few, sometimes it is disguised as merely 'vegetable oil'. In Costa Rica alone thousands of hectares of rainforest have been cut down and are still being cut down to plant palms that grow the fruit that palm oil is extracted from. The area is intensively sprayed with herbicide. After the trees become too tall to harvest the fruit they will have poison injected into their trunks to kill them and then they will be burnt, new palms would already have been planted next to them to take their place. The fruits get taken to the processing plant an hour away from us where a thick black smoke rises from the chimney. The prevailing wind carries it into Panama.

Not long ago, I read a list of ten things everyone can do to save the rainforest. It may have been in 'National Geographic' but I wouldn't swear to it. One of them read 'Stop buying products that contain palm oil'. If I had been reading that list in England it would have meant little to me. Here, in Costa Rica I could see the damage first-hand but I could also see that it was Alfredo's lifeline, his way out of poverty, and I wasn't about to start preaching to him.

In spite of Alfredo's recent good fortunes I noticed that his bright smile wasn't burning quite as brightly as usual. Then I remembered Bilkez saying that Emilse was ill and had been up to San José for tests at a private hospital, it was great that they now had the money to be able to pay for that.

"It's cancer" he said with tears in his eyes when I asked if the results had revealed a diagnosis yet. I gave him a hug not knowing what else to do. She didn't have long.

Then came the announcement that it was cake cutting time. Harmless little black bees had been nibbling away at it and their cousins, the yellow honey bees had also now arrived. If anyone wanted any icing at all we were going to have to be quick. Poor Crispin had to stand there, centre-stage, whilst 30 people sang 'Happy Birthday' to him in Spanish. He squirmed but managed to smile a bit, the three beers he had consumed had lessened his embarrassment. He picked up the knife to start slicing but everyone started yelling at him. They wanted him to try it first by putting his face in it! It was tradition everyone insisted. So, he did. And then Estrella did. They had blue icing from their chins to their noses. "It tastes good enough to eat," Crispin said and started serving.

After the cake Toli led us into our bedroom and showed us two patches of orange paint, slightly different shades, which he had put on the wall so we could choose which we preferred. They were both gorgeous. "Use them both," I said eventually, unable to decide. "Paint three walls with the darker one and this wall with the lighter one". It should have been the last room to be painted. All of the lights and fans were up although the expensive fans that we had had imported from the States were covered in plastic at my request as they were starting to attract wasps and the nests were difficult to remove.

We moved to the other side of the house. The kids' room was a fantastic dark purple which we all loved. Their multi-coloured fan that we had seen working a few weeks earlier, powered by the generator, was also now covered up; I would never be able to scrub two of the wasps' nests off it. The guest room opposite was a lilac colour, I didn't like it. Both rooms still needed another coat of paint.

"Can you paint this room the same colour as the kids' please, Toli? I don't like this lighter shade at all. I'm sorry about giving you all more work."

"It's my job," he said, waving away my apology. He pulled the colour swatch out of his pocket.

"This one?" he asked me. The sun was going down; the light was fading and the five different purple shades on the swatch all looked pretty similar.

"I think so," I said as he made a note of the paint code. I looked up and noticed that the light fittings were starting to rust. "I'm sorry Toli, can you take the lights down again until the windows are in. Look, they are going all rusty." It had been a very very wet rainy season and some days the rain had blown horizontally into the house, wetting the unprotected wooden floors and making everything damp.

"We'll sand and repaint them, don't worry," he said. I think he was desperate to show us that the delay wasn't his fault, that it was Juan Carlos', and he wanted to finish everything that was his responsibility even if it meant rusting the lights and ruining the fans. Our beautiful wooden floors also had toad poo stains on them; it had seeped into the bare wood and would never completely come out. Toli's guys weren't great at covering floors before painting above them, no matter how many times you asked them to. I would be scratching paint spots off the wood and tiles for months. Things were starting to slip a bit; maybe they were just getting as fed up as we were. They had been living on-site in little wooden shacks for almost a year now and we were just coming out of the wettest rainy season in local memory. It was amazing when you thought about it. I complained about our tiny place and the four of us sharing a bedroom but at least we had running water, electricity and a roof that didn't leak.

We said our goodbyes and our thank yous and left. This time there was no avoiding Ruben's smell. He stank of beer!

"I wish we didn't have to leave," I said sadly to Crispin as we got in the car, I was looking back towards our beautiful yellow house. "I wish we could live here now. Everything is getting ruined."

"We'll be in soon," he assured me. He then surprised me, "It was a nice party. I enjoyed it," he added.

41 The Countdown

It is six weeks to go to Christmas and then our friends arrive shortly after, on the 28th. I have recently found out that one of them is pregnant. We are missing doors, electricity, windows, furniture, and granite in the kitchen. Once the granite is down; the kitchen sink, stove-top and oven can be fitted.

We order a sofa from a furniture shop in Paso Canoas, we are told it will be here before Christmas. Tick that box.

Crispin arrives back from the house a very unhappy man. "Estrella's room and the guest room have been painted that lilac colour that you didn't like. And the wooden columns on the terrace have woodworm and so does the hardwood floor in the lounge."

"I thought Juan Carlos said that the wood for the floor is too hard to get woodworm."

"He did, but it's got it. I've injected the holes with something that'll kill them. Oh, Toli also said he needed to add another concrete block on the garage walls to make them higher. I told him to go ahead."

"Is it going to disturb the view?" I ask him.

"I stood on the terrace and checked. It's fine," he assures me.

"What about from the guest bedroom and the lounge?"

"It's fine in the lounge too." I know he is purposefully ignoring the guest bedroom part of the question.

"Standing up or as if you were sitting down on a sofa?"

"Standing up," he admits.

"And the guest room?"

"I didn't check but it will be fine." I knew better than to believe him.

It was getting dark as I rushed up to the house to look at the paint and check our view. In Estrella's

331

room I could still see the beautiful dark purple paint underneath, a millimetre of it still visible above the floorboards. Instead of painting the guest room the same colour as Estrella's room they had painted both rooms the insipid lilac colour that I didn't like. I was really annoyed but thought that it may have been my fault. "After all, I agreed the colour code with Toli," I said to Crispin when I returned.

"There is no way this is your fault," insisted Crispin. "I saw two of the guys open the tin and I told them it was the wrong colour but they insisted it would go darker once it was on the walls and it had dried. I should have told them not to use it but I gave them the benefit of the doubt." Rather than wasting money buying more paint we decided to wait until the floors had been sanded because Toli felt they would need another coat to cover up the scratches caused by the sander. We could change the colour then.

As for the view, Toli had put a piece of wood upright on the garage to show where the highest point of the roof would be. In the lounge, as I lowered myself pretending to be sitting on a sofa, the view vanished. I did the same in the guest bedroom but pretended to be sitting up in bed with my morning cup of tea. The view of the Osa Pensinsula would vanish to be replaced by our green garage roof. Crispin left a message on Toli's phone telling him not to put another layer of concrete block on the garage walls.

We turned up early the following morning; but not early enough, the guys were half-finished. Toli hadn't received the message, sometimes they can take four or five days to reach you for some bizarre reason. They started taking the concrete blocks off again. The roof pitch was then lowered to save the view. Crispin and I knew nothing about roof pitches. "Will it be okay like that?" Crispin asked him.

"Yes, fine," said Toli. The next rainy season we would find out that 'fine' actually meant 'fine if you want it to leak like crazy' but that is another story, for another book maybe.

We go and see the guy who is carving pictures on our doors. We have received a message via Juan Carlos saying that Luis has finished and needs paying.

"It was very difficult," Luis said, "the wood is as hard as concrete. I was continually sharpening my tools." That wonderful smoky woody smell fills my nostrils and I breathe deeply.

The panels are lined up on the floor of his workshop in the back of his house. There is a frog clinging to a branch for our room, two dolphins for the bathroom, a coral reef scene for the small bathroom with fish darting about, hummingbirds and delicate orchids for the guest bedroom and monkeys (what else?) for the kids' room. "They are absolutely beautiful," I said to Luis in awe.

"Amazing," agreed Crispin. He is an incredibly talented man. Luis looks bashful but very pleased.

"Where's the front door?" I ask, realising there is a panel missing. This is the first thing that people will see when they arrive at our house. It is supposed to be a condensed version of our view. Matapalo, the tip of the Osa Peninsula, at one end and the bay of Zancudo at the other. Luis walks towards a large wooden panel at the far end of the workshop. It is facing away from us so that we can't see it. Luis turns to face us and suddenly looks apprehensive.

"I couldn't remember what your view looked like," he said nervously, "so I found this picture in a book." He held out a book of bible stories. There was a picture of a woman on a brick terrace overlooking the sea. There were mountains in the background. Luis then turned the huge piece of wood around. I winced, I couldn't help it.

333

To be fair to him, the carving did look like the picture in the book but the picture in the book looked absolutely nothing like our view. The brick terrace covered almost half of the carving; we didn't even have a brick terrace! The one saving grace was that he hadn't put the woman in it.

"I hate it," I said to Crispin in a cheery voice so that Luis wouldn't be able to work out what I was saying from my tone.

"Me too," said Crispin, unable to hide his disappointment.

I broke the news gently and Luis took it reasonably well. "Why didn't you call us to discuss the design or even come over to look at the view again?"

"I tried calling you using my neighbour's phone, we can't afford ours any more, but there was a voice that I didn't understand so I didn't want to leave a message."

"Our voice-mail messages are in English aren't they?" I said to Crispin. Luis could still have left a message though!

"I asked Juan Carlos to tell you that I wanted to discuss the front door," continued Luis," but I guess you didn't get the message."

"I remember Juan Carlos calling us about the front door but I thought he'd said that it was almost ready. I guess I didn't understand properly," I said to Crispin in English.

"I couldn't come and see you as I can't afford the bus fare," Luis said, he was rather embarrassed about the fact.

Crispin gave him some extra money for his trouble, it sounded like it hadn't entirely been his fault. He then showed us some more of his work, short thick wooden clubs with bird's claws carved into them; he was hoping that we would buy them. They weren't very nice and I found it strange that someone who was obviously an amazing craftsman

334

could use his talent to make something so revolting. We politely declined them, made our excuses and left. After the carvings were finished the panels would go to Juan Carlos so that he could assemble the doors. The Christmas deadline seemed a possibility.

Next on the list: electricity. Crispin goes to the *finca* to meet an engineer from ICE. He arrives back three hours later. The engineer hadn't turned up.

Crispin goes to see Luis' front door carving and declares it much much better. The brick terrace is gone and has been replaced by more sea and a tree with a toucan sitting in it.

Sofa man calls to say the price has just gone up by $400. I cancel the sofa. Untick that box.

Four days later, the ICE engineer comes to the *finca* to work out what equipment is needed. How many posts? How many transformers? How much cable? Del will then order the materials from San José. "It'll be two weeks from when they start to when you'll be switched on," Del tells me. So, once again, Christmas sounded like a possibility.

We eat Thanksgiving dinner at 'La Manta' (a great restaurant when it has someone to run it. It had re-opened earlier in the year). We sit with Greg, Heidi and Jackson and thoroughly enjoy our platefuls of turkey, mashed potato, sweet potato with marshmallows, vegetables and gravy. I can't decide on a desert so have pecan pie, apple pie and pumpkin pie all in the same bowl. It's wonderful.

Juan Carlos says he will bring windows at the weekend "Si Dios quiere" (God willing). He wasn't.

The following weekend He (or She) was and some window frames are delivered to the house. They are absolutely beautiful but there is a problem: there are only four of them.

The sun finally comes out. Evan Luck at 99.5 Radio Dos stops playing 'Where's the Sunshine?' and 'Raindrops keep Falling on my Head' and plays 'Here comes the Sun' constantly.

It is three weeks to Christmas. We need to buy our electrical appliances. We are getting them from the duty-free port in Golfito, known locally as the *deposito*. Not only does it sell every electrical appliance imaginable but it also has a reasonable toy shop and sells wine and beer too. Every year, anybody who has a passport or a *cedula* (like our National Insurance cards) can go to the office in the *deposito* and be given a ticket that has a $500 limit. The catch is that you can't spend it for 24 hours. It was the government's idea and maybe not a bad one. After the banana company moved out of the area in 1985 and the area fell into ruin the government decided to do something about it. It was a kind and sensible thing to do although the idea maybe needs fine tuning and would be a few years down the line.

It is a beautiful location for a town and, in my opinion is one of the most beautiful places in the country. It is a gulf within a gulf, the name Golfito means 'Little Gulf', so the water is perfectly calm and protected. The rainforest-covered mountains rise up behind the scruffy town; also rather sensibly the government has made those into a National Reserve to protect the town's water supply which originates in springs up there. There are some beautiful wooden buildings left over from the banana company days which are now used as offices and university buildings. There is also talk of a massive marina being planned for 2008 which is what the town needs maybe. But at the moment, to regenerate the area, all Golfito has is its *deposito*.

The '24hr' rule was put into place so that people would stay overnight in local hotels, eat in the local restaurants, drink in the local bars and put money back into the locals' pockets. It was a good idea. But what actually happens is that people, local and otherwise, take out their $500 tickets with no intention of spending them. Instead they 'sell' their allowance for about $20 to shoppers who don't want to wait 24 hours to use their own tickets and want to buy today. There are always lots of people milling around the entrance or coming up to you in the shops asking you if you want to use their ticket. If the first shopper they find doesn't use up the whole $500 allowance then that shopper has to sit and wait until another shopper is found and then another until the $500 has been spent. It wasn't unusual for the person with the ticket to have five or six shoppers waiting for them at the exit. Guards at the exit then check all receipts against items purchased and ensure they are all in the ticket holder's name. It was in this manner we had bought Estrella's safety gates and we had had to wait ages whilst the ticket holder rounded up all of his other shoppers before we could leave.

This time we needed all of our electrical appliances and Crispin's parents had asked us to get all of their's too. We also wanted to get Christmas presents for our kids and the local kids. We calculated we would need 13 tickets, including ours. We decided to get Freddy and Enrique to ask some of the locals if they would sell us their tickets. After all it was coming up to Christmas and if they weren't going to use this year's allowance then let us buy it off them, as it was Christmas the price of a ticket had gone up to $30. We were also warned it was going to be really busy; think Oxford Street on the run up to Christmas.

On 8th December we drove to the *deposito* with Bilkez, so she could help us out with the kids whilst we chose everything we needed, whilst half of Cuervito, (our 'helpers') got the morning bus into Golfito to have their tickets issued. They then caught the lunch-time bus home again.

The following day we all returned and met up at 9am. Crispin's pockets were bulging with cash and he handed half of it over to me. We had remembered our list and Crispin's parents' list; as well as electrical appliances they also needed crockery and pans. I was incredibly excited at the thought of all that shopping; Crispin was dreading it.

If you were immediate family you could have your tickets 'attached' together making them worth $1000, handy if you needed to buy an expensive washing machine and fridge/freezer like we did. There was another catch. There were some appliances, for example washing machines and fridge/freezers, which you could only buy once every three years and it was printed out on your ticket if you had done so. Some of our 'helpers' had.

It took an awful lot of concentration and organisation to work out who was going to buy what. A couple of times I messed up and was stuck at a till with a helper only to find that they couldn't buy the appliance I wanted them to because they had already bought one two years ago. I would then have to run off and try to find another helper who hadn't previously bought the appliance in question and also still had enough allowance left on their ticket after buying Crispin's parents' toaster and blender for example, to buy the appliance. I also had to be careful that I didn't use one half of the 'attached' family members tickets items costing less than $500 as we needed to save those for the more expensive items. Just to complicate matters further, Crispin's parents had chosen their stuff during their visit two months before so a lot of what they wanted was out of stock and replacements had to be chosen on the spot. It wasn't easy when you had 40 shops to choose from all selling slightly different stuff at slightly different prices. I was getting brain-ache. Thank goodness Bilkez was with us to help us out with Estrella and Arturo.

It was the hottest day imaginable and no breeze whatsoever reached inside the high concrete walls of the *deposito*. Some women had brought their children with them and several times I went off and bought bottles of coke and water and handed them out to keep everyone hydrated. The very last thing I did was grab Margarita, Vilma (her sister-in-law) and Chila (Bilkez's mum) and go and choose Christmas presents for their kids and ours from the only toy shop. It was as close to a girlie shopping trip as I was going to get and I loved every minute of it. There was a mad panic at the end when we realised that the last bus was leaving in 20 minutes time, the place was closing and we had to try and get 15 people through the guard checkpoint with the right appliances and matching receipts. Somehow we did it and it was over. It had been Crispin's worst nightmare. The heat and all the waiting around and there hadn't been a single complaint from anybody.

"Bugger," said Crispin as we stood outside waiting for Enrique to arrive with a friend's van so everything could be piled into it. He was checking through the lists. "We forgot mum and dad's washing machine."

We arrive home at 8.30pm to a house full of termites. There were little trails of them everywhere; they were heading up to the roof structure to munch on the wood there.

The granite men arrive from San José with my beautiful blue and black sparkly granite for the kitchen. Arturo has a temperature. I push him and Estrella in the pushchair to Les and Carolina's whilst Crispin's fumigates the house to get rid of the termites. Arturo projectile vomits. With everything that's going on Crispin forgets to collect the granite men from the house-site to bring them down to what was Dee's house to sleep; we had rented it off the new owner for them. He finally remembers at 9pm and zooms up to the house to find them lying down on the hard slate floor in our dining room trying to sleep.

Two weeks to go to Christmas and we do the two day drive to San José. Once again we manage to find the ring road by accident. We also discover Escazú Shopping Mall (I am in heaven) and its fantastic indoor playground (Estrella is in heaven). We eat fresh fruit tarts in a French café; I have a lemon one too. Mmmmmmmm.

We buy lots of household stuff like sheets and mattress covers and soap dishes, towel rails and wire shelving to go up in the bathroom. We buy door handles and window locks, in the hope we will soon have windows to fit them onto, and the few light switches and plug sockets that we are still missing. We even go and talk to a swimming pool company about starting on our swimming pool. A pool, how exciting is that?!

We head up to Grecia and Sarchí, an area to the north-east of San José that is famous for its furniture. We are specifically looking for sofas. We search all day and find none that we like; they all have too much material and not enough wood showing. We end up buying six rocking chairs, including two children's ones. After looking in 30 different furniture shops it is getting dark and we call it a day and start heading back along the main highway. After five minutes we pass a huge furniture place.

"I think I saw 'it'," I said, "in the window on the top floor. I think there was a sofa with wooden arms."

"I think I saw it too. Do you want me to turn around?" I don't know, did I? We had been looking for hours and had agreed no more shops.

"It's up to you. You decide."

He does a U turn and it turns out he has made the right decision. The sofa is beige, has wooden arms and is declared perfect. "Do you have another one please as we need two?" I ask. A friend of mine had two three-seater sofas and I thought it was the best idea ever that you can both lie down whilst watching telly without fighting over who gets the sofa and who is left with the armchair. We had bought a telly at the *deposito*; now all we needed were the sofas.

"We've got a pink one but we can change the material on it easily enough so that they match; it's a quick job."

I've just spotted mattresses out of the corner of my eye. It's our lucky 'box-ticking' day. "We need some of those too, don't we?" I ask Crispin.

"And some for my parents," he replied nodding. It is the shop-keeper's lucky day. Crispin asks if we can unload the rocking chairs from the car roof and leave those with him too. He says he will get everything delivered as soon as he can but probably only as far as Neily. Juan Carlos lives just outside of Neily and he would be bringing windows and doors over so if the sofa, mattresses and rocking chairs were delivered to him he could bring them too. Before Christmas is a possibility he says. Unlike Juan Carlos, he makes no promises.

Now, I don't like the word stupid. We use 'silly' with the kids and tell them that 'stupid' is not a nice word to use. The following day I deserved the word. I was stupid. Crispin takes the car to get new shock absorbers and to find out why the car's back end zig-zags across the road in a dangerous manner whenever it is driven above 60km/h. He is gone most

341

of the day. I am sitting on the bed with Estrella and Arturo watching a movie on the laptop and a man walks into our room. He sees us, apologises and leaves again. Our room is on the ground floor and our door opens on to the swimming pool. There are always tour guides or car rental company representatives hanging around the hotel reception. We have also met some wonderful people in the hotel. The staff are really friendly, there is a security guard and a barrier before you can enter the car park and it feels a safe place to be. I presumed the guy had simply got the wrong room.

A bit later on it is getting hot and I open the door to let the breeze in. Our computer is hidden away again. I notice the same man standing outside our door talking on his cell phone. He has black curly hair, is smartly dressed and carries a briefcase. I don't acknowledge his presence and continue sitting on the bed with Estrella and Arturo, singing nursery rhymes and reading books. He knocks on the open door and looks at Arturo.

"He's lovely," he says in Spanish,"I have a five month old baby."

"Same age as Arturo," I say, surprised by the coincidence.

He then says, "Con permiso?" but starts to enter the room without waiting for an answer. He sits down on the bed and looks at Estrella. "What beautiful eyes she has." Estrella is eating a banana and gives him her Paddington Bear hard stare. "I'm a tour guide and I'm waiting for a woman who is supposed to be doing a tour with me," he tells me.

I am not incredibly comfortable by his presence but am not yet sure what to do about it.

"Are you the hotel owner's wife?" he asks.

"No," I say but feel I need to add that I am married. "My husband has just popped out to fix the car; he'll be back at any moment." I hope that it's true.

Estrella starts coughing; she's got some banana stuck in her throat. I whack her on the back.

"She needs some water," the man says. There is no way I am going into the bathroom to get any.

"She's fine," I say as I whack her harder. She continues to cough and I know that he is right and I am going to have to get her some. I purposefully glance at my phone that is behind the man on the bedside table. I want him to know that I know it is there. I don't notice my handbag by his feet. I move as fast as I can and am gone for less than five seconds, I can see the kids through the crack in the door but can't see him.

As I enter the room again I see my cell phone is still where I left it, Estrella has stopped coughing and the man is on his cell phone. "No, I'm still waiting for the woman," he says into it, "but I've found someone to talk to; a lovely woman with two beautiful children." The pauses are all wrong and I know he is pretending.

I pick up my phone and call Crispin. He doesn't answer. "Please, please, please be nearby. There's a man in our room and he's starting to freak me out." I leave a short description of him and hang up. I hope that message doesn't take four or five days to reach him. My visitor has also finished his phone call. "My husband is on his way back," I lie.

He reaches over and feels Arturo's hair and declares it soft, he does the same to Estrella's then he takes me by surprise and touches my hair. I am horrified and back away. "I'll go and wait outside," he says standing up. "Give me a shout if you need anything." He leaves and I shut and lock the door behind him. I am shaking. I notice my handbag on the floor and see that all five zips are open. I reach inside and my wallet is gone. All of the effort he went to and he had an American dollar that a friend had given me which said 'Happy Birthday Jo' on it. There was no other money in my wallet. My credit cards, which I had only just got around to replacing from the last time they were stolen, were easily cancellable. I hoped the bastard enjoys looking at our wedding photo.

I grab the kids, one in each arm and run to reception. I am blabbering and suddenly can't remember any Spanish. It has finally hit me that the situation could have turned out much worse for us. I just about manage to hold it together for the kids' sake. The Italian manager is nearby, hears me and without wasting a second jumps in his car and chases after the man. He doesn't catch him. On his return, one cleaning girl tells him that the man had entered a bedroom she was cleaning and had left when he saw her. The other one says that she had seen him hanging around the lobby and had asked him twice what he was doing there and he had said he was waiting for a woman. She had assumed it was me he was waiting for.

"Why didn't you tell me?" the manager said, he was Italian and he was angry.

"I tried to but you were on the phone and shooed me away," she replied hotly.

As well as being stupid I had been lucky.

In complete contrast to our last robbery the manager was incredibly apologetic and wouldn't accept any money for our five night stay.

Driving home we stopped at a huge supermarket and bought a turkey and other Christmas goodies. It took us longer than we thought so we didn't leave San José until very late and ended up driving through the mountains in the dark. At least we knew the kids would sleep. Our luck was holding as it was a rare clear night and there was a full moon. Every now and then I would catch a glimpse of it through the trees. As we reached the top of the mountains it appeared right in front of us. It was huge and beautiful and we were almost level with it; I felt we could drive right to it. I put my hand on top of Crispin's on the gear stick and squeezed it; he squeezed the tips of my fingers in response. Then the moon vanished behind the trees again and was gone.

It is one week to Christmas. After more broken promises and deadlines from Juan Carlos he phones us on the 23rd. "The rocking chairs, sofas and mattresses have arrived," he says. "I'll bring them along with the windows on the 26th. Si Díos quiere," he adds.

"No, Juan Carlos, not if God wants; if YOU want," Crispin replies.

"Maybe I'll be able to bring a bed too." He thinks Crispin is annoyed with him and is now trying to please him.

"Don't worry about the bed," Crispin says.

"No, I'll be able to get a bed made by then; definitely," Juan Carlos promises.

"Well, if you can make the bed in time brilliant but please don't delay the other items if the bed isn't ready in time. We need the windows. We can cope without the bed as long as we have the mattresses. Remember, our friends are arriving on the 28th." He has been told our friends are coming on the 28th about six zillion times. The date was carved in his brain. I had also told him six zillion times that he needed to manage our expectations better. "If it's going to take you a month, tell us two months and then, if it's delivered earlier, we'll be really happy with you," I said again and again. 'Under-promise and over-deliver' was a concept he was never going to understand, preferring instead to over-promise, under-deliver and have us constantly annoyed with him. Instead of admiring his work when it arrived our reaction was always "About bloody time too". At least the presents had stopped. The day before Crispin's parents left he had presented them with a huge beautiful wooden boat but there had been nothing since. Thank goodness Crispin's desk had never materialised.

"We're going to be spending Christmas here aren't we?" I said to Crispin when he'd hung up the phone.

"It looks that way," Crispin sighed. We were sitting on the tiny terrace at Mac and Penny's place. It had been home for 15 months and it was somewhere we really didn't want to be any more. I was throwing in the towel and admitting defeat.

"We'd better put the Christmas tree up then," I said. Fed up with clearing away pine needles, we had decided on a plastic one this year. Crispin put it together, Estrella and I decorated it, Arturo then zipped up to it in his walker and pulled it over. We had no oven in which to cook our Christmas turkey and were thoroughly miserable.

At least Christmas Eve put a smile on our glum faces. We were invited to Amado and Flory's and spent the afternoon with their family in the rancho. By 'family' I mean most of their ten children and 25 grand-children. Christmas Eve to Ticos is like Christmas Day to us so we handed out the presents we had bought for the kids at the *deposito* and forgot about things for a few hours. I had made a photo calendar for Amado and Flory. It had taken me hours to scroll through all the photos we had of them and their family and choose the best ones. It was worth the effort to see the tears in Flory's eyes; they rarely saw photos of themselves. Everybody laughed at the photo I had put in for 'March'; one of Amado with a serious look on his usually smiley-face. I took a photo of Amado laughing at it for next year's calendar.

It's Christmas Day. Crispin phones Juan Carlos to wish him 'Merry Christmas'. When the

346

conversation is over Crispin walks over to me and puts his arms around me. He hugs me tightly.

"I'm not going to like this am I?" I ask.

"The rollers that he needs for our sliding windows were delivered to Paso Canoas instead of Neily by mistake. He won't be able to bring everything until the 28th."

"But that's the day our friends are coming." I want to cry but can't. "I suppose if he gets here early it will be okay," I say, but I have completely forgotten that the windows won't have glass in them.

"We'd better go, Freddy and Margarita will be waiting for us," Crispin says.

I grab the banana cake that I had managed to make in the replacement bread-maker, we grab a child each and we leave.

We drive to the river with Freddy, Margarita, Jackie and Yailin. We spread an old green throw from IKEA on the floor to keep the ants at bay. As Margarita unties the tea towels that are wrapped around the pans and bowls that hold our Christmas dinner; I take the lids off one at a time: rice, beans, spaghetti with tomato sauce and salad. Sitting cross-legged, we eat our way through the feast. It's followed by banana cake and washed down with Margarita's home-made lemonade. I can't help thinking how different it is to our previous Christmas.

We all swim (except Arturo who just paddles) and Jackie spends hours catching fish inside her swimming costume using banana cake as bait. Freddy somehow manages to carry the pushchair down to the river bed. How he doesn't slip and break a leg I don't know. Arturo sleeps in it for two whole hours. Everything is perfect.

I didn't look for snakes once.

Postscript - April 2008

On Christmas Day at the river when I sat and watched the fish darting about, the sun glinting on the water, laughing as Jackie used her swimming costume as both a net and a bowl, I realised that <u>this</u> was what our adventure was about.

Understandably maybe and partially down to the fact I was pregnant almost as soon as we had arrived here and was then the exhausted mother of two little ones - I had been missing the point. Our adventure wasn't about a fancy house with its granite countertops, jacuzzi bathtub, sliding windows and jungle door-carvings but instead it was about the wonderful people and the wonder of nature; waterfalls, rivers and the wildlife that surrounds us daily.

As I sit here - in the third house that cute Ruben finished last year - typing away, I can hear little squeaks outside the door and I know that the squirrel monkeys have arrived to eat the white blossoms from the tree I am ashamed to say I still don't know the name of. I am going to make the effort, pause in my writing and watch them because they are an endangered species and we are incredibly lucky to have them living on Finca Estrella, plus they are just amazing to watch. Come and see for yourself.

That Christmas Day I thought about how much our Spanish had improved and that our best friends here were probably the ones we were sitting side by side on the rocks with, ones who couldn't speak a word of English, had left school at the age of 12, and who lived in a wooden shack smaller than our lounge. It suddenly struck me that, at some point over the last 16 months, we had left the world of Gringos and had been welcomed into that of the Ticos and we hadn't even noticed the shift.

We had two beautiful children, a marriage that probably needed a bit of work (but didn't everybody's?), BoBo was healthy, lots of friends and family were visiting in the coming year, we had the best view in the world and monkeys and toucans in the garden, we had sold a lot (and not just to Crispin's parents), electricity may be going in soon, possibly even the pool and a *cabina* too and we were talking about getting a dog and chickens, oh and Crispin a vasectomy. Plus, he still hadn't said "No" to Del's crazy 'Danny's Real Estate Agent' idea so Crispin was possibly going to have a job.

In the stress of the days that followed, when the focus once again would switch to the fancy house, I would forget again, I often would. But in the odd moment of calm, when I walk around the *finca* by myself and spy a hummingbird's nest the size of an eggcup, a tiny baby peaking out, I would once again be reminded and life would be wonderful for a short while.

The day our friends were due to arrive Crispin would phone Juan Carlos at lunch-time. After taking 16 months of crap off people and being polite to them Crispin would finally lose his temper and yell at him to send whatever he had ready.

"But you said you wanted me to wait until I had made the bed," Juan Carlos would say.

"ONLY BECAUSE YOU SAID YOU WOULD MAKE IT IN TIME!" Crispin would yell in reply and then hang up the phone.

Crispin would then go chasing around in Toli's truck trying to find an inverter which would mean we could run the house off batteries rather than having to have the noisy generator running the whole time. It would be Lizzie's Steve who would tell us we needed an inverter. I would phone him after Toli had told us that our three really big expensive batteries wouldn't power our house but only a 12 volt light bulb. What's more Toli didn't know what we needed to buy so that the batteries <u>would</u> power our house. Why he had told us this the day before we were moving into the house and not three months ago when we told him of our plan I would never know. I needed to speak to an electrical engineer, preferably one who had been here and knew the crap we had to deal with.

"Where the hell are we going to get an inverter from?" I would ask Steve.

"They sell them round the corner in Halfords," he would say and I wouldn't even be able to raise a smile.

Bilkez and I would be running backwards and forwards between the rental house and our house all day. Packing and cleaning and cleaning and unpacking and, between his wonderful two hour naps, also amusing Arturo. Estrella would spend the day with Margarita and Freddy up at the new house. In the chaos, I would forget to leave any lunch with her and during one trip up to the house I would notice the pushchair parked at Freddy's corral. My brain wouldn't compute the information, I wouldn't realise that they had taken her back to their house to feed her. We wouldn't have hot water that night so I wouldn't bath or shower her. Her screams from the chiggers, and other bites, still haunt me but her scars would heal (two days later a doctor would diagnose her with an allergy to insect bites and it would take a lot of acupuncture, homeopathic treatment, Chinese herbal medicine, Vitamin B1 tablets and antihistamines to get it under control).

At 4 o'clock I would ask Toli's guys to nail bug screens up over the holes where our windows and doors weren't going to be, not today anyway. The truck with the sofas, mattresses, rocking chairs and windows would arrive at 5 o'clock. Crispin would arrive back at 5.30pm and would then instantly leave again to go and buy more bug screen as the guys had run out. Our friends would arrive in the dark at 6pm. My pregnant friend would collapse in a tearful heap on a mattress, the journey and the potholes had been too much for her. I would feel knackered and stressed and guilty; knowing I should have told her to cancel her trip the minute I found out she was pregnant. I wanted to join her on the mattress but I had two kids to put to bed and dinner to make.

That night, I would lie on a mattress in a house that I owned for the first time in my life. I would feel the resident bats swooping low over my face as they darted in and out of the room and feel no sense of achievement whatsoever. Moving into the house would be a complete anti-climax.

Our friends would find a scorpion in their bedroom that night and we would move them down to our old house that we were paying rent on until the end of January for just such emergencies. The snake under the play-mat would be killed by one of Toli's guys and later be declared harmless by Freddy (in spite of my fears I have never seen a living deadly snake here).

The windows would go in, the glass men would put the glass in, our friends would leave (early I have to say and probably never to return) and then my best friend in the whole world would arrive with her husband and five month old Alex.

Their first morning, John would appear on the terrace holding one of our plastic mugs. "Look what I found trying to climb into Kirsty's jeans," he would say in a voice that made me think it was probably going to be a fluffy lamb. It wasn't. I would look in the mug and reel backwards; he had caught our resident scorpion that had terrorised our last visitors. "I'll go and relocate it," he would say calmly walking towards the front door. A rather surprised Kirsty now understood our 'never leave anything on the floor' rule.

I would suddenly realise that I was sure I had had an uninterrupted night's sleep. I hadn't been woken up by our kamikaze resident bats. Not even once. "Did the bats bother you last night, Kirsty?" I would ask.

"John opened the bathroom window, let them out then shut it again," Kirsty would reply. Crispin and I would look at each other in disbelief. That was all it had taken?! A window?! Every single stupid night for a month!! (The bats would retaliate by pooing down the walls outside 'their' window for years).

Juan Carlos would arrive with some shelves, wait for it, two days EARLY. They also had drawers in them. I had said to him, "Don't worry about the drawers as the shelves will take longer to make if you put them in." He had under-promised and over-delivered for the first time.

"Thank you," Crispin and I would say a hundred times. Juan Carlos would smile; pleased he had finally made his boss happy.

After I had got over the shock, I would resume my conversation with Kirsty about my brand new fan oven that wouldn't work properly. John would over-hear and open the oven door.

"It's 220," John would say, closing it again. I had read that sticker too.

"But I said that to the builders and I was told that it couldn't be 220 because the cable was too thick, and it's just that the generator won't power it," I argued.

"Jo, it's 220, it's wired up as 110 volts," John would say calmly. He said everything calmly. When the world ends, he should read the announcement. I assure you, nobody will panic.

The following day the builders would be informed and the day after that I would turn the temperature knob on the oven and the fan would whirl into life. I would stand in front of it for ten minutes, watching the needle creep higher and higher. "Hurrah, we can cook the turkey!" I would announce as the oven thermometer hit the right temperature for the first time ever. Kirsty and I would start planning Christmas dinner. My first task would be a phone call to Les and Carolina. "Fancy coming to a typical British Christmas dinner in mid-February?"

"Is the pope catholic?" would come the enthusiastic reply.

John and Crispin would go to Paso Canoas to get supplies for Christmas dinner, taking Estrella with them. Alex and Arturo would be lying on the jungle play-mat facing each other. They would be dressed in identical vest tops and disposable nappies. The vest tops were bought in Paso Canoas and would say 'Welcome to the Toys Store' in grammatically incorrect English. They would both be fast asleep. Little squeaks would reach my ears and I would scan our incredible view, as if seeing it for the first time, and would finally spot the squirrel monkeys in the trees to the side of our unfinished garage. Once again I would think how appropriate the jungle-themed play-mat was.

"Let's paint our toenails!" Kirsty would say. We would sit across from each other, as we had done many times when we were teenagers and we would paint each other's toenails. For reasons I'm not too sure about, maybe the bizarreness of us sitting on a terrace in the jungle, both of us now mothers, meeting our nephews and niece for the first time, a world away from England when we had last spent time together, we would start giggling. My sister is the only person I know that I can have uncontrollable laughing fits with and our giggling would rapidly turn into one.

Our little bathroom is right I would think; it did feel like home.

References

1. SMITH, N. G. 1972. Migrations of the day-flying moth *Urania* in Central and South America. Carib. J. Sci. 12(1-2):45-48

2. THE TICO TIMES, June 2005, Ex-Convict Returns to Claim Property.

3. BROWN E., JACOBSON M. F., May 2005. Cruel Oil, How Palm Oil harms Health, Rainforest and Wildlife. Center for Science in the Public Interest.

Photo Credits

Inside photos by Ken Tomlinson (mum and me, barn, angel feather, Canoas, starting to build, veg man, Estrella's bed, house takes shape, Great South Run), Rodney Freeman (ferry, beach lot, Freddy's house, quad, our terrace, approaching storm, waterfall, workshop), Michael and Rebecca Sneath (ice-cream beans, Crispin surfing), Tracey Mason (1st photo), Lizzie and Steve Ascham (last night together) and Catkin Seel (wedding). Others by Jo and Crispin Freeman

Cover   Casa Amarilla (our yellow house) by Michael Sneath
Fridge magnets

Back   BoBo, Lucero and Enrique on Pilon Beach by Rebecca Sneath
Jackie, taken after her first operation
Green and black poison dart frog by Ken Tomlinson
Squirrel monkey
Green page moth by Steve Ascham
Eliseo
Jo and Crispin at Crispin's 39th
Margarita cooking at her house

Lightning Source UK Ltd.
Milton Keynes UK
12 October 2009

144830UK00002B/52/P